FALLEN LEGACY

A Dark High School Romance

HAWK BAY DUET
BOOK II

CARA E HOLT

njoy
reading book two
Many thanks
Cara E. Holt x

Published by Cara E. Holt

Cover Design: Haelah Rice Covers.
Formatting: Haelah Rice Covers.
Editing: Runyard Editorial Services.

NOTE TO THE READER

This book is meant for those age eighteen and above. It contains swearing, sex, and scenes that some may find triggering, including, death, kidnap, threats, intimidation, violence, and use of knives.

If you are sensitive to any of the above triggers, please think twice before continuing.

CHAPTER ONE

ELIZA

It's been four days since I packed my things and up and left the Alderman mansion. Silver hasn't pushed me for information. He's just let me be. I've spent these last two days wallowing. Drowning in pain. Angry at myself for being such a fool, and angry at the people that have used and betrayed me. Truth is, I was never really one of them. How could I be? I didn't grow up with them; they have a loyalty to each other that I will never be granted. Whilst I have been sitting here drowning in my feelings, I have wondered how different my life might have been had I grown up here. Would I have just gone along with the engagement like it was nothing?

I miss my brother, Kit. Him not standing by me has been the hardest part to process. For the last four years it's been just the two of us. We have relied on each other and no one else. As much as I am angry at him, I understand. Kit has yearned for a family and somewhere to belong and he's so desperate for it he can't see the manipulation and lies. I'm not sure what my next steps are. I've contemplated ringing Hayley, my old social worker, and telling her everything. I mean, there are laws against this kind of thing; but then would she believe me? Wilbur is a well-respected man. Why would anyone believe a washed-up teenager like me over someone like him?

There's a knock on the bedroom door and Silver appears in the doorway. He tilts his head and observes me sitting in bed, twisting a piece of tissue round and round in my hands. He shakes his head and comes into the room, standing at the foot of the bed.

"Okay, I've let you do the whole self-pity party for four days now, princess. Enough is enough. Time to shake it off, pull up those big-girl pants and face the world." He grabs the duvet and yanks it off me. "Come on, up. You need a shower."

"Can't you just leave me be?" I whine, trying to reach for the duvet, which he throws on the floor. "Can I at least have one more day of wallowing and then I promise I'll sort myself out?"

"No," he says with a firm shake of his head. "This isn't the fiery girl I met just a couple of months ago. Whatever has gone on, princess, you are a fighter. Don't let them dampen that spirit."

I chew on my lip and nod my head. I know he is right. This isn't me. "I feel broken," I admit to him, keeping my eyes on the shredded tissue in my hands. Silver comes round and sits on the side of the bed. He places a finger under my chin and raises my face, forcing me to look at him.

"You're not broken Eliza. You've taken a knock and now you get back up and you come back stronger than ever." He pats my leg. "Come on, up. I'm taking you out."

"Ugh, where?" I groan. I'm not in the mood to face the outside world.

"Just get dressed and meet me downstairs. I'm not taking no for an answer." He strides out the room, and the fucker takes the duvet with him, making sure I can't bunker back down underneath it and continue my pity-party. With all the energy I can muster, I swing my legs out of bed and head for the en-suite. Time to look like a human being again.

WE'VE BEEN DRIVING FOR ABOUT TWENTY MINUTES, AND I still have no clue where we are going, and Silver is keeping stum about it. I turn the radio on because the silence makes all the noise going on in my head feel ten times louder. Silver grumbles at the song on the radio and changes the station. He grins and turns up the volume and starts singing at the top of his voice.

"Come on, princess. I know you know this one. Sing it with me," he says with an infectious grin that has me fighting a smile. "Sing it with me."

I roll my eyes but join in with him; I think I even break a genuine smile for the first time in the last four days Silver takes one hand off the steering wheel and starts dancing in his seat as he drives. He nudges me when I'm not joining in, and I do a shoulder roll and sing louder.

"There's that beautiful smile," Silver says, throwing a soft wink my way. You can say what you like about this guy. On the outside, he looks like a rough diamond with his tattoos and ear and eyebrow piercings but look past that and he's genuinely a great guy. If only I'd have been more attracted to him from the start, maybe I wouldn't be feeling the hurt I do now. "What's going on in that mind of yours?" he asks me as he turns the radio down now that we have finished our karaoke session.

"Why couldn't I have chosen you?" I ask him with a weary smile.

Sighing, he shrugs his shoulders. "We don't always do what's best for us, princess." He looks over at me and winks. "Although I'm glad you're regretting not sampling the Silver goods."

I lift my foot from the floor and jab him in his thigh with it. "Drop the smugness."

Laughing, he pushes my foot off his leg and grins. "Are you going to tell me what happened?"

I avert my eyes to the scenery outside and shake my head. "Not yet. I'm still processing."

I see him nod his head from the corner of my eye. "In your own time, princess."

I sit up in my seat when he turns off the road onto a dirt road that leads up to a farmhouse. The driveway is full of cars, and he parks up next to a large grey range rover. Silver kills the engine and climbs out of the car, so I do the same and meet him at the front of the car.

"I hope you're hungry," is all he says as he strides towards the house. The place looks like it has stood here for centuries, with its thatched roof and weathered stone front. When he opens the front door, the warmth hits me, followed quickly by the most delicious smell of home cooking.

"Hey Grandma," Silver shouts as we enter. A voice hollers from further into the house that they are in the kitchen. Intrigued by why Silver has brought me to his grandma's house, I follow him through the place until we come out into a large country kitchen, complete with an aga. The kitchen is filled with people, and I falter in my steps.

A lady in her late sixties with grey hair pulled back into a messy bun looks up from the stove. She wipes her hands on the tea towel in her hand and she opens her arms to him.

"Get here, boy, and give your grandma a hug."

Grinning, Silver strides around to her and lifts her in a big bear hug, spinning her round. "Missed you, gran" Silver tells her as he puts her back down on her feet and drops a kiss on her head.

She pats his cheek with her hand and looks up at him with such love and affection that it makes my heart ache. It's been a long time since anyone looked at me that way. I'm so lost in my thoughts that I don't notice her attention has fallen on me.

"You brought a girl to lunch?" She shakes her head in disbelief. "Hey Frank, get over here. Damon bought a girl with him."

I smile as I pick up on the teasing tone in her voice and Silver rolls his eyes and laughs. "Don't get too excited. She's just a friend." Silver gestures me over. "Eliza, come and meet my gran."

I make my way over to where they are, and his gran smiles warmly at me. "Well, aren't you a gorgeous little thing?" She surprises me when she pulls me in for a hug. "Welcome to our home, Eliza."

"Did someone say Day bought a girl?" a female voice asks from the open door that leads to outside. A young woman in her early twenties comes into the room. She's slim and has blonde shoulder length hair and a blunt fringe. "Wow, it's a real girl." She grins and bumps her hip into Silver playfully.

"I'm Emma, this one's big sister," she tells me as she leans in and drops a kiss on my cheek. "Eliza, is it?"

I nod. "Yeah, it's Eliza, and it's lovely to meet you. I hope you all don't mind me turning up like this?" I ask, feeling uncomfortable that I have clearly gate crashed a family get together.

"The more the merrier," his gran assures me as she lifts the lids off a pan on the stove and gives the contents a stir.

"Gran cooks the best Sunday lunch, princess," Silver tells me as he leans over her and takes a spoonful of what looks like gravy from the smaller pan. "Hands off, you," she tells him softly, slapping his hand with her tea towel. "Take Eliza out to meet everyone and get out from under my feet."

Chuckling, Silver beckons me to follow him outside. There are about ten more people outside. "Grandad, come and meet Eliza," Silver says, shouting over to an older man. He's a formidable figure. He has a large belly and a sleeve of tattoos up both arms.

"Pleased to meet you, Eliza. I'm Frank, the head of this rabble of a family," he tells me as he takes my hand and shakes it in his firm grip.

"Nice to meet you," I reply, just as an arm appears over my shoulder and I look up to find Silver's brother, Luca, smiling down at me. "He finally got you out of bed, huh?"

Frank coughs up his drink and I look in wide-eyed horror at Frank and then at silver. Damon laughs and jabs his brother in his side. "Ignore my brother. We all do. Eliza has had a bit of family drama going down, so she's been staying at ours the last couple of days," he explains, and I feel the fire in my cheeks lessen.

"Damon's been a great friend and let me stay with him," I explain to his granddad.

Frank shakes his head, smiling and gives Luca a look that says don't tease the girl. "I don't think I've ever seen your brother with a female friend."

"That's because Day only befriends girls for one thing." Emma chuckles as she comes up beside her brother and ruffles his hair.

"Okay, can we quit the Damon bullying?" Silver says, placing an arm around his sister and dropping a kiss on her cheek. "Where are the brats?"

Emma grins and points with her bottle out to the fields. "Playing manhunt over on the back field. Hopefully, they'll wear themselves out and I'll get them in bed early tonight."

"Emma has twin boys, aged five," he tells me. "Oliver and Noah."

"Twins wow," I exclaim. "I bet they keep you busy."

She laughs, nodding her head. "Not a minute of peace, I tell you. Take my advice and don't have kids." Laughing, she shakes her head. "I'm kidding. I wouldn't be without the two little devils." She points her bottle at me. "Anyway, enough about my devil spawn. Tell us how you know my brother?"

"Oh, we go to the same college," I explain, and see her brow arch in surprise.

"You go to the posh school like Day. No offence, but you don't strike me as the type of girl that goes to that school."

I hold my hands up. "None taken. I only moved here a couple of months ago. I didn't grow up like those girls, trust me."

Emma nods her head. "Never understood why Dad felt the need to send him there. Luca and I had our education at the state school, and it did us no harm."

"I'd much rather be at the state school as well," I reply. "The girls at the Hawk are something else."

Emma laughs. "In other words, they are a bunch of pretentious bitches." She reaches behind her and offers me a bottle of fruit cider. "So long as my brother never brings one of them to a family lunch, we won't have any issues."

Silver snorts in reply, as if the idea he'd bring a girl from school to lunch is ridiculous.

"Come on, Eliza. Let's escape the men, and I'll introduce you to the real boss in the family."

Smiling, I allow her to guide me away from Damon and his brother. She leads me over to a small group of women who are sitting under a gazebo, all laughing and enjoying each other's company.

"Everyone, this is Eliza. She's Day's friend from school and no, before anyone asks, she's not one of the posh ones." Emma points to a lady in her mid-forties with long dark hair and a friendly smile. "Eliza, this is my auntie, Ruth. Next to her is my little sister, Milly. The two at the end are my cousins, Megan and Eve."

"Nice to meet you all," I say with a little wave. "I didn't know Damon had so many siblings."

Emma laughs. "There are six of us. Our older brother, Christian, hasn't arrived yet. He'll be here with his rabble soon. Our other sister, Faye, lives in Spain, so we only get to see her on the holidays."

Silver's gran shouts for everyone to get seated before she plates up. Emma guides us over to a large table that is big enough to comfortably seat thirty people. Silver gestures for me to sit beside him, and Emma takes the seat next to me. She introduces me to her husband, Nick, when he comes and takes a seat opposite her. He's carrying a lively twin under each arm. The twins are adorable. They both have curly blonde hair and blue eyes. They have flushed cheeks from running around in the fields playing. The family dinner is heart-warming to observe. They all are so warm and comfortable in each other's company; I enjoy sitting and watching the family interact as we eat. It stirs that longing in me to feel the love and warmth of a family unit. I feel more alone than I have ever felt sitting here at this table.

After lunch, the guys take the twins to play football on the field, with Frank groaning that he's too old for this, but joins them despite his protestations. I help Emma take the pots through to the kitchen and Emma orders her grandma to sit outside with a beer whilst she washes up. I offer to help and despite her insisting I am a guest; she agrees to let me dry. From the kitchen window above the sink, we can see the boys playing football.

"So, Eliza, tell me more about yourself. Because even though you are just friends with my brother, you are exactly the type of girl we'd want him to bring home one day."

"There isn't much to tell," I reply, taking a plate from her hands and trying to steer the subject away from me and my fucked-up life.

"Did you move here with your parents?"

Okay, so we are starting with this conversation. "No. I moved here to live with my grandfather. My parents both died when I was thirteen."

Sympathy crosses her face as she hands me another plate. "Oh, I'm so sorry to hear that. That must have been so hard for you, especially at that age. What about brothers or sisters?"

"Just the one. My little brother, Kit. He's fourteen and getting taller by the day."

Emma laughs. "Tell me about it. I remember the days when Day was smaller than me. I hate how he towers over me now."

I nod my head in agreement. "Yeah, Kit's not far off being taller than me, which he takes great joy in reminding me about at every opportunity." My eyes glisten with emotion from talking about my brother as the events from four days ago run through my mind.

I'm pulled from my thoughts when Emma places a soapy hand on my arm. "Hey, I'm sorry. Did I touch on a difficult subject? If I did, I'm sorry. I'm glad that you felt you could come to my brother when you needed help. He's a pain in the arse most of the time, but he has a big heart."

"Ah, it's fine. It's just been a rough few days. Damon has been a good friend to me when I've needed one the most."

Emma smiles as she hands me a glass to dry. "Well, you're welcome here for our family lunches anytime, Eliza. And well, if you ever need a female to talk to, I live just up the road from my brothers. Get Day to bring you over next week. In fact, he can bring you for tea one Thursday. There's usually a game on, so my brothers usually come round and eat with us and watch the match with Nick."

"I'd like that," I reply. Being around Silver's family today has been bittersweet. In some ways, it has lifted my spirits and distracted me from my thoughts. In other ways, it has been a stark reminder of what I am missing in my life.

SILVER FORCING ME TO ATTEND HIS FAMILY LUNCH DOES THE trick and pulls me out of my depression. Now I need to decide what I'm going to do next. I can't just hide away here forever. Damon has been kind enough to let me stay, but I can't imagine it's an open invite.

"Where are your parents?" I ask him over breakfast the next morning. Silver is in his uniform, ready for another day at Hawk Grammar.

"My dad is away on business right now. He should be back by Friday."

I nod my head as I play with the cereal in the bowl. "Does he know I've been staying here?"

Silver clears his throat and shakes his head. "Not yet, no."

"I'll make sure I'm gone before he comes home Friday," I blurt out. "I don't want to cause any trouble."

Silver looks at me from over the table. "It won't be any trouble. Besides, my dad hates your grandfather and the other three families, so I'm sure he'll be delighted to get one over on Wilbur by letting you stay here." He pauses. "Plus, where else are you going to go, princess?"

"I'm sure I could sort something out."

"Look at me princess," he orders me. "You're staying here for as long as you need to. Okay?"

My heart clenches in my chest. "Thank you. I don't know what I'd have done if I didn't have you as my friend."

Damon sighs as he offers me a half-smile. "I need to be clear here, Eliza. I don't want to be your friend. I want you to look at me the way you look at Savage." He holds his hand up to silence me when I open my mouth to speak. "I know you're hurting right now and not in a place to even consider looking at me that way, but I'm a patient guy. I'll be the friend you need for now."

I chew on my lip. "I'm not sure I can ever give you what you're asking for."

He shrugs his shoulders at me. "Never say never, princess. Anyway, I have some errands to run. Will you be okay here on your own?"

"Sure," I reply. "I could come keep you company?"

He shakes his head as he stands to his feet. "I'm going someplace a girl like you is too good for. Just enjoy the quiet time. I'll be back in an hour, tops."

"No worries," I tell him with a nod of my head. It feels too vulnerable to tell him I don't want to be alone with my thoughts. That I need him to distract me. My nightmares are back. They are plaguing my nights, but it's not just the nightmares, it's also the dreams I'm having about Archer fucking Savage. He consumes my sleep. I dream of him touching me and holding me and whispering his sweet lies into my ear.

CHAPTER TWO

ELIZA

"You ready for today, princess?" Silver asks me. He grabs his car keys, and we make our way outside to his car.

I nod my head confidently and hitch my bag up over my shoulder. "I'm ready. Fuck all of them."

Silver grins in approval as he slides into his seat. "There's the girl I know."

"Are you ready?" I ask him as I fasten my seat belt. "This could bring trouble your way, you know?"

Silver chuckles as we head down the road towards school. "You mean Savage is going to likely knock ten tonnes of shit out of me?" He shrugs. "Not like we haven't fought before. At least now we have something worth fighting over."

My smile falters at his words. "He'd only cause a fight over me because he sees me as his possession."

Silver bobs his head from side to side. "Maybe. I think maybe you made a bigger impression on Savage than you might want to believe. I've seen the way he looks at you when you walk into a room."

"Yeah, like something he thinks he owns," I say with a snort. "I'm just a means to an end. To get revenge on my dad and to ensure he gets his inheritance."

Silver doesn't reply at first, then he says, "I wouldn't be so sure."

When we step out of Silver's car at school, everyone notices. I take a deep breath and pull my shoulders back, but falter when

I spot Archer, the boys, and Vee standing over by their cars. My heart thunders in my chest when our eyes meet across the car park. It hurts seeing him. It hurts seeing all of them.

I see Archer clench his fists at his side. He takes a step forward, but Seb and Rafe hold him back and I can see Seb trying to reason with him.

I turn to Silver in a panic. "I can't do this. I'm not ready."

"Come on, you can, and you will, because you have to, Eliza," Silver urges me, placing a hand at my elbow. With one last look at the four people who are partly responsible for my pain, I turn my head forward and head into school.

Everyone we pass stops what they are doing to stare. Me showing up with Silver was always going to be big news. So much for me just slipping quietly back into school with no one noticing.

"I wish they'd quit staring," I hiss as we near the main doors.

"And just when we'd hoped that they had removed the trash from our school."

I look up to find Georgie in our path. Arms folded. She bitch-smiles at me. "Have you finally realised that trash should stick with trash, Eliza?"

Silver goes to speak, but I put a hand on his arm to stop him. I'll deal with this. "No, George. I realised the real people from the fakes. Now move or I'll move you."

She scowls at me but does as I ask and moves to one side. "Bitch finally got her comeuppance," I hear her gloat to her friends. If only she knew the truth. That I have refused the one thing she has always wanted. The urge to throw it in her face is tempting, but I don't want everyone at this school to know my business, so I keep my lips sealed and keep walking.

"She is a piece of work," Silver snickers as we head inside.

"You haven't been there, then?" I ask him out of curiosity. I mean, Georgie is a poisonous bitch, but even I can't deny that she's attractive.

Silver looks at me like I've told him the moon is made of

cheese. "Have I fuck! I keep to the girls on my side of the bay. The girls at this school only want a guy like me for two reasons." He holds up a finger. "One, they want to rebel and slum it with a boy from the other side of the bay so that they can say they've lived dangerously, and two," he says, holding up a second finger, "they want to piss off daddy and get his attention. I don't need that drama in my life."

❧

VEE IS IN MY FIRST CLASS OF THE DAY, AND I FEEL HER EYES follow me as I take my seat at the other side of the classroom. I chance a glance her way and she latches onto it and smiles at me. I immediately look away; I can feel her disappointment from across the room. She was the one girlfriend I had at this school. I thought she was my friend, but friends don't keep the kind of secrets that she did.

My second class is going to be the hardest, as all four of them are in there. Luckily for me, Silver is also in this class and, knowing I have to face the four of them, he walks with me into the classroom. I don't dare look towards the back as I rush to a seat two rows from the front. Silver kicks the boy out of the seat next to me and sits beside me, 'thank you' I mouth to him, and he winks in reply.

I don't hear a word the teacher says for the entire class. I'm distracted throughout the lesson. His eyes are burning in the back of my head. I keep shuffling in my seat and I'm itching for the bell to ring so that I can get out of here. I hope Silver has some weed because I'm in dire need of something to relax me. The bell goes and I jump to my feet and shove all my things in my bag. I urge Silver to hurry. I don't make it out of the room. An arm crosses over the door barring my exit.

"Scarlet. We need to talk," he says, his voice quiet and steady.

I breathe in his scent, struggling with my emotions. I keep

my eyes trained on the hallway outside. "I have nothing to say to you. Now please move out of my way."

"Five minutes," he growls. "Just give me five minutes, Scar."

I twitch. He's never called me Scar before, and it pulls at my heartstrings. "My name's Eliza, not fucking Scarlet," I hiss, ducking under his arm.

"Come on Savage," I hear Damon scoff and I turn to see Archer is still blocking the doorway. He's refusing to let Damon pass.

"I warned you to stay away," Archer snarls. His jaw is tight with tension as he eyeballs my friend. Sighing, I stalk back over, and I get in-between him and Silver.

"Leave him alone Archer. He's my friend. Damon's been there for me when I needed someone I could trust." He flinches at my words. "If you want to do something for me, then leave Damon alone. After what you all did, don't I deserve a proper friend?"

Archer seethes, trying to hold in his frustration, and Vee puts a hand on his arm. "Come on Arch. Let them go. She's right. She deserves to have someone in her corner."

"I'm in her fucking corner," he snaps. "I will not let you go, Scarlet. Never," he vows, and my stomach sinks because I know he's going to be relentless.

"You had your fun. I'm sure you all had a great laugh at my expense. The silly little orphan girl."

"No, Eliza," Vee protests, but when I send a frosty glare her way, she takes a step back. Rafe rubs her shoulder in comfort.

I wait for him to remove his hand from across the door and, grabbing a hold of the sleeve of Silver's blazer, I drag him away and head outside for some much-needed air.

"Please tell me you have some weed, because I need to ease some tension?"

"Of course," he says grinning, and gestures for me to follow him round the back of the school gymnasium. He lights the spliff and hands it to me, and I take a deep inhale. I close my eyes and I lean my head against the cold brick wall.

"I'm not sure I can do this. Come here every day and see the four of them."

"Oh, you will, princess, and you'll do it with your head held high," Silver insists.

I SHOULD HAVE KNOWN WHAT WOULD HAPPEN NEXT. OF course, he'd ring Wilbur and tell him I'm back at school. I'm in my last class before lunch when I'm called to the headmaster's office. I head over there thinking the headteacher is going to read me the riot act for missing school these last few days. When I walk into the headmaster's office; I stop still in my steps when I find Wilbur waiting for me.

"Close the door, Eliza, and take a seat," he tells me with a calm composure, gesturing to the seat nearest to me.

With a deep roll of my eyes and a huff, I throw myself into the seat and fold my arms across my chest. I sit there and glare at him. "Make it quick. I'm missing German for this."

His shrewd eyes study me. "Have I not given you and your brother a roof over your heads? A brilliant education at one of the best private schools in England?"

"And your point is?"

"I know you are angry that I didn't come for you both sooner."

I snort in disbelief. "There are many things I'm angry about. That is just one on a long list, Wilbur."

Wilbur gets to his feet and holds out a file. "This file has photographic evidence of some of the cars you stole and the places you broke into during your time in care. I think you and I both know that if I handed it over to the police, you'd be spending the next six months in a young offender's unit."

I snatch the file from him and look inside. Fuck. He has done his homework. There is photo after photo of me breaking into and driving stolen cars with the group of guys I used to hang around with when we lived in Farnlea.

"Eliza, you will be engaged to Archer. You will marry him, and you will bear a child to him before your twenty-first birthday. You will do for this family what your father failed to do, and you will do it with a smile on your face. Because if you don't, not only will this file find its way into the hands of the police, but your brother will also find himself back in foster care."

My eyes snap up to his as an icy chill runs through me. "You wouldn't?"

His gaze doesn't falter. "Oh, I would. I'll call that social worker up and say I can't manage you both and that I want to relinquish you back to the care of the local authority. You know what that means, don't you, Eliza? Your poor brother would have to move again. Another foster family. Only this time without you, as you'll be away in juvie."

"You heartless bastard. We are just pawns in your game, aren't we? No wonder my dad left this place and did everything in his power to cut all ties with this bay and its poison."

My words have no effect on him. The man is cold and calculating and I don't think he loves anything or anyone but himself.

"You have until the end of the month to return home, or I will follow through on my threat." He picks up the file and walks out of the office without a backward glance. I dig my nails into the palm of my hand as pure anger and rage burns through me. When I unclench my fists, I see I have dug my nails in so deep that I'm bleeding. Fuck. He has me over a barrel. There is no way of getting out of this. If I don't do as he orders, my brother will go back into care. I don't give a shit about him threatening juvie for me. What is six months of my life compared with a life I didn't choose for myself? But Kit. It would destroy him. He can't go back into care, he just can't.

THE DOOR TO THE BAR OPENS AND I LOOK UP FROM MY DRINK to see Silver walking into the room. Shaking his head and sighing, he heads my way.

"Thanks for letting me know she was here, Jim."

"Anytime, son," Jim replies, looking over at me with a smile that says 'sorry, but it's for your own good.'

Silver sits beside me at the bar and, leaning his hands on the counter, he looks at me and waits.

"Are you going to tell me what has led to this little drunken party for one?"

Knocking back the vodka and coke, I wince. I hate vodka, but right now I need the alcohol. "I'm screwed, Damon. I am well and truly fucking screwed."

I reach for the next glass of vodka in front of me, but he stops me, taking my hand in his. "Talk to me. Maybe I can help."

I chortle at his suggestion. "No one can help me. My dear grandfather paid me a visit in school today. If I don't go home and play the dutiful little granddaughter and let Savage put a ring on my finger, then he'll hand a file over to the police that will see me locked up for the next six months. He also threatened to put Kit back into foster care."

"Fuck," Damon exclaims, shaking his head in shock. "He said this to you?"

I smile and nod my head. "Oh, he did, and he meant every word. He wasn't bluffing. I have until the end of the month to drag my sorry arse back to the Alderman mansion or he'll make good on his threats."

Damon runs a hand through his hair and blows out a big breath. Good to know I'm not the only one who didn't see this coming. "My dad is home tonight. Let me talk to him. Maybe he can help."

"No." I shake my head. "It will only bring trouble for your dad. Wilbur holds all the power in this town. I won't bring your family into this mess."

My stomach roils and I cover my mouth, feeling nauseous.

"How many have you had?" Silver asks me, sending a dirty look Jim's way.

"Only two. Ugh, I need the bathroom. I'm going to be sick." I jump from my seat and run to the ladies. I only just make it on time before I barf up the two vodkas.

When I feel a hand on my neck, I realise he has followed me in here. He leans down beside me and holds my hair away from my face whilst I empty more of the contents of my stomach into the toilet bowl. When I'm done, he offers me some tissue so I can wipe my mouth.

"Sorry, you didn't need to see that."

He chuckles as he helps me stand to my feet. "I've done it many a time for my sisters. How are you feeling?"

"Okay, I think. I shouldn't have drunk on an empty stomach."

Damon nods his head, leaning against the sink beside me whilst I wash my hands. "No, not the smartest idea. Come on, I'll take you home."

"What about school?"

He wraps an arm around my shoulder as he guides me towards the exit, waving at Jim as we pass. "Fuck school. It'll still be there tomorrow."

CHAPTER THREE

ARCHER

I stare at the door to the cafeteria waiting for her to come through. But she never shows, and neither does that opportunist prick, Silver.

"Do you think she's fucking him?" I ask out loud to no one in particular.

"No," Vee says firmly from where she sits opposite me. "Trust me when I tell you, Silver is well and truly in the friend zone."

"He wants her, though."

Seb snorts, and I glare at him. He shrugs his shoulders. "Of course he wants her. Look at her. Your fiancée is fucking hot."

Vee elbows him in his side and scowls at him. "Not helping dickhead." Vee turns her attention back to me. "Silver knows she doesn't see him that way. Anyway, enough of him. What are you going to do to get her back with us where she belongs?"

"Who said he wants her back?" Rafe sniggers, looking across at his future wife.

She shakes her head in exasperation at him. "He wants her back. Look at him!" She gestures with her hand to me. "He's sitting there staring at the door, willing her to walk in here. He needs her like he needs air to breathe."

"Don't talk bullshit, Vee," Rafe says dismissively.

"She's right," I say, still staring at the door. "Fuck," I exclaim. I don't know how, but Scarlet has me in knots. I fucking miss her. I miss her smell. I miss her snarkiness and her body, and I miss waking up with her in my bed.

"You mean to say..."

"Yep, my docile twin. Archer has caught the feels for the lovely Eliza," Vee says delightedly, grinning at her brother. She arches a brow and looks at me, daring me to tell her she's wrong.

"How do I win her back?" I ask her. I don't miss the open-mouthed stares of both my brothers as they realise that I'm serious.

Vee beams at me. "Now we're talking." She leans forward, placing her hands on the table like she means business. "You woo her."

"Come again," I say with a frown.

"You woo her. You be everywhere. Pull her chair out for her in class, you open doors for her. You offer to carry her bag even if she tells you to go to hell. Send her flowers. You take every chance you can get to be in her space."

Seb scrunches his forehead up and shakes his head. "I don't know, sis. I think little red will probably punch him in the dick if he's up in her space all the time."

"Am I not her best friend?" she asks us all.

"No. Not anymore," Seb says matter-of-factly. "She hates you just as much as she hates the rest of us."

Vee scowls at her brother. "Thank you for reminding me, Seb. What I mean is that I know her. Underneath all that hard demeanour and sass, she's just a girl who wants to feel cherished and protected."

"Look out for her brother. That will win you brownie points," Rafe suggests, as he tucks into his sandwich.

"If you really want to win her back. I know how you could do it."

We all look up at the unwelcome intruder. "Did we ask for your opinion, Chester?" I glower at him. I don't like this fucker. He's like an unpleasant smell that lingers.

Chester grins, taking a seat at our table.

"What the fuck?" Seb hisses, clenching his fist. "Remove yourself from this table before I do it for you."

Chester ignores Seb completely, leaning back in his seat, studying me.

"What do you know?" I ask him, and a smirk covers his mouth.

"I knew you were the astute one of the trio. I know more than you think. I was with your girl when she found that file in Wilbur's office and I know what she was in there looking for." He stops and waits.

"What's your price?" I ask him. Cutting straight to the point. This fucker does nothing to help anyone if it doesn't serve himself.

"I knew you'd understand," he says with a smug smile. "I want in. I want to be an Ace."

I smirk. Who does he think he is?

"No."

He doesn't seem perturbed. "A Jack then."

Rafe tilts his head, studying Chester before his eyes meet mine. How does this sly shit know so much about the society? There were only four Jacks. They held higher status than our Clubs. They were our right-hand guys, the ones we trusted above all the Clubs.

"You seem to know a lot about our world, considering you've only been here a few weeks," Rafe comments.

Chester's lips peel up at the sides. "It's amazing what Georgie will spill when she's riding your dick."

Georgie. I should have known. She can't keep her mouth shut for shit. I knew something was going on between the two of them after I saw them together a while back.

"You do know what being a Jack entails, don't you? It means you take whatever orders we give you. We say jump. You say how high."

He nods his head. "But it also gives me authority over the Clubs and who is selected as a potential and running their challenges."

"Wow, Georgie really has run her little mouth off," Seb growls angrily. "How do we know what you have is worth it?"

His cocky grin widens. "Oh, it's worth it. It's what she broke into Wilbur's office for. Sadly, she doesn't know he keeps some of his files in the safe in his bedroom, but I do. I guess I could have shared that knowledge with her, but where's the fun in that, right?" He leans across the table and holds out his hand. "Do we have a deal?"

It goes against everything in me, but with a swift nod of my head, I reach over and grip his hand in mine. "You try to fuck us over and I will kill you, Chester, and it will be a slow and painful death."

"I wouldn't expect anything less."

I cock a brow and wait.

Smirking, he tells us what he knows. "She wants to find out if her mum had any living relatives. That's what she was searching for in Wilbur's office. Instead, she found the folder on her and Kit."

Vee shakes her head. "I still can't get over him leaving them in foster care for years."

"So, what do you know? Is there a living relative?" I ask Chester, keen to stay on point and utilise anything I can to convince Scarlet she belongs by my side.

His lips curl up at the side into a smug smile. He loves holding this power over us. Knowing that he knows something that we don't and using it to his benefit. "There is." He reaches into his pocket and slides a piece of paper across the table to me. "You should know, Wilbur paid her off to keep quiet and not make a guardianship claim for Eliza."

"Wow," Vee exclaims, looking speechless. "Are there no ends to the depths of his deception?"

Chester yawns and stretches before standing. "Well, this has been a pleasure. I shall look forward to my swearing in ceremony."

We all watch him saunter through the cafeteria. He takes a

seat at the football table. Sitting beside Kit, he ruffles his hair and smiles at him.

"I don't trust him," Seb states, his stony face watching Chester.

"He can't be trusted," I agree. "We need to keep a close eye on him. Where he goes, who he's seen with."

"I'll call Greg," Rafe announces, pulling out his phone. He strides out of the cafeteria to make the call away from prying ears.

CHAPTER FOUR

ELIZA

I still don't feel too good. Damon brought me home and made us both some spaghetti bolognaise. Damon had errands to run for his dad, so I'm alone in the house again. I'm curled up on the sofa with my kindle, snuggled under a blanket, when the front door opens and a deep male voice shouts into the house.

"We're back." I hear footsteps and banging. I jump to my feet and walk through to the hallway.

"Who the hell are you?" asks a tall, tattooed man with a beard.

"I'm Eliza," I reply. Shit, is this Silver's dad? He isn't supposed to be home until Friday. "I'm a friend of Damon's."

The man studies me as he takes off his jacket and passes it to a red-haired woman in her early thirties who is standing beside him. "Are you now, and where is that son of mine?"

"He's out," I explain. "He should be back soon."

The door opens again and a young girl about fifteen, with long blonde wavy hair in a leather jacket and ripped jeans, walks in behind them. "I am so ready to sleep in my own bed tonight." She comes to a stop when she sees me. "Oh, hi. It's Eliza, right? You came to grans for Sunday lunch last week?" I recognise her. She's Damon's little sister.

"How many times have I told your brother about keeping his conquests out of the house?" his dad says with a deep frown on his face.

I blush profusely. “Oh no, Damon and I, we’re just friends. I’m not...one of his conquests.” I clear my throat, feeling all kinds of awkward. “We go to school together.”

“You attend the academy?” He asks me, his brows arching in surprise.

I understand his surprise. I’m not exactly dressed like an academy girl. I’m in my old blue leggings and a weathered old Nike T-shirt. “I do.”

“You don’t know who she is, do you?” Milly grins at her dad then points a finger my way. “Eliza’s the new girl everyone’s talking about. The long-lost Aces heir.”

The man’s gaze sharpens at the mention of the Aces. “You’re the Alderman heiress?”

I push my hands behind my back, holding them together, conscious that I am fidgeting under their scrutiny. “I guess I am.”

“Well, well, this is an interesting turn of events.” He takes out his phone and puts it to his ear. “I’m home and there’s a stranger in the house who your sister says is an ace.” He continues to study me as he listens to the other caller. “We’ll speak further when you get home. Did you collect today?” He nods his head as he listens. “See you shortly.”

“Will you be staying for tea?” Milly asks me enthusiastically.

If it felt awkward before, it now feels extremely uncomfortable. “Actually, Damon has been letting me stay here. I kind of moved out because of a family disagreement.”

His dad arches a brow. “Did you now.”

“I can go find somewhere else if it’s a problem,” I offer, pointing towards the door behind them.

“Nonsense,” his father says, suddenly smiling at me. “If you’re Damon’s friend, then you are more than welcome here. I have some calls to make. I look forward to hearing more about you, Eliza, and why you upset dear old Wilbur.”

I WAKE UP AT SIX IN THE MORNING AND MY STOMACH churning again. I think I must have picked up a stomach bug. My stomach lurches when I sit up in bed. "Shit." I race for the en-suite, barely making it in time before my stomach empties. I stay there for a couple of minutes, hugging the toilet to make sure there's no more. I stand and I rinse my mouth under the tap. Stripping out of my bed shorts and vest, I step into the shower, letting the warm water spill over me. As I close my eyes, my mind drifts to the last time I shared a shower with Archer. His hands soaping my body before things became heated, and he nudged my legs apart and entered me from behind. I shake my head, trying to rid myself of my memories of him. I miss him. I miss his body and the feel of his lips and his hands on my skin. I miss the way he moans my name as he comes inside me. I rest my head on the tiles and close my eyes and give in to the need that the memories of him have created. When I come, it's his hands I imagine on me.

I head downstairs in my uniform, and I falter in my strides when I find all the Silver family seated at the dining table.

"You're up. Come join us," Milly urges me with a welcoming smile.

"You heard her, princess. Come sit your butt down. My dad doesn't bite," Damon tells me with a cheeky grin, gesturing to the seat next to him.

The elder two men of the house stay silent, but I can feel their eyes on me as I sit down. The woman, Elle, who I met yesterday is busy in the kitchen. My stomach lurches when I smell bacon. Please, not now.

"Are you okay?" Damon asks me, with concern etched across his face as he looks at me.

I nod my head and rub at my stomach. "I think I've eaten something that doesn't agree with me."

Damon reaches for a jug of water and pours me a glass. "Here, maybe just try some water first. See if you can keep it down. You could have picked up a bug."

"Yeah, probably," I agree, taking small sips of my water.

"Are you sure you're not fucking her?" his dad asks, making me spray the mouthful of water out of my mouth all over the occupant of the seat opposite me.

"Jesus!" Luca says, jumping to his feet and looking down at his t-shirt that is splattered with water from my mouth.

"Oh shit. I'm sorry," I mumble. I grab a napkin and rush around to the other side of the table. I pat at the wet patches on his t-shirt. "If you take it off. I'll go stick it in the dryer for you."

"Take it off, huh?" I look up into Luca's mischievous eyes to find him grinning at me. He lifts at the hem of his t-shirt from the back and pulls it over his head. Leaving me standing there with the napkin in my hand gawping at his naked chest. It's covered in tattoos, and I can't help but study them for a minute. "Enjoying the view?" he asks me, pulling me from my staring.

"Quit flirting with princess, brother." Damon says from behind me, and I can hear the humour in his voice. "And no, dad, we're not fucking."

"But you'd like to be," his sister chuckles, earning her a clip around the ear from her dad.

"Wash your mouth out, young lady," he tells her with a frown.

She scowls at her dad. "So, you lot can all talk about fucking and make jokes, but the female in the house isn't allowed."

Her dad rolls his eyes. "It's got nothing to do with you being female. It's the fact that you're fifteen and a girl your age shouldn't be talking about sex."

Luca places his bunched-up T-shirt in my hands. "Dryers that way," he says, pointing over to the utility room. His eyes dance with humour.

"Go put it in the dryer yourself," his dad tells him. "Eliza's our guest, not your skivvy."

"I don't mind," I protest, but Elle comes and retrieves the shirt from my hands, glaring at Luca. "I'll do it. You two sit down and eat. Adam, you have a zoom call at eight thirty."

Luca takes his seat again, and I walk back round to mine and sit down.

"I have swim practice tonight after school," Damon tells me. "You okay waiting until I'm done?"

"I can walk back," I suggest, and he scoffs at me. "It's not that far. I can get the bus."

This brings a snicker from them all, and I look at them in confusion. Damon sighs and puts me out of my misery. "There are no buses from the school to this side of the bay, princess."

"I can pick her up," Luca offers, and I'm not the only one who looks up in surprise. "She can come and help me at the club."

"No," Damon says firmly. "Not a chance."

His brother waggles his eyebrows. "Are you scared I will corrupt your little princess?"

"I don't mind helping," I say, wanting to feel like I am not a liability whilst I am here.

"See, she's happy to help." Luca stands to his feet and winks at me. "I'll wait for you at the front of school, princess. Don't be late."

❧

WE PARK UP AT SCHOOL AND I BREATHE A SIGH OF RELIEF when I see the Aces aren't over by their cars. I jump when my car door opens and the very person I've been hoping to avoid stands there.

"Morning, Scarlet."

"Go to hell," I say with a scowl. "What are you doing?"

He smiles at me, and it's not a sarcastic smile. It's genuine and warm and it disarms me immediately. "I'm opening the car door for you." He gestures with his hand for me to exit.

"I'm perfectly capable of opening the door myself," I hiss, sliding my bag onto my shoulder. I glare at him as I leave the car.

Damon leans on the roof of his car, watching us both, and I eyeball him. "Well, are we going inside?"

"Yup," he says with a quirk of his brow.

I still when Archer closes his hand over mine. "Can we talk, please? Just five minutes of your time. That's all I'm asking for, Scar."

"We have nothing to say to each other," I tell him. My stupid heart twinges in my chest at the feel of his hand on mine. I look down at our joined hands and the electricity that I feel whenever he touches me rushes through me. This hand has explored every inch of my body. I jolt myself out of my head and snatch my hand away, rubbing it on my skirt. "Leave me alone Archer. Just please let me be." I turn my back on him and fall into step beside Damon.

"I can't leave you alone, Scarlet. I'm not giving up on us."

I whirl back around and storm back over to him. He stands there with his hands in his pockets, looking delicious. I jab my finger in his chest. "There is no us. There never was because we built everything we had on secrets and lies."

He closes his hand over mine and holds it on his chest over his heart. "Do you feel that, Scarlet?" he asks me, referring to his galloping heartbeat. "That's what you do to me. We both know what we have is real. We both feel it. I'm not letting you go. Not now, never."

His words pierce through the bubble wrap around my heart. I close my eyes and pull myself together. "We were nothing," I tell him, my voice void of emotion.

I pull my hand from his chest and walk back over to Damon. I push at his elbow for him to walk. I'm eager to put distance between me and Archer.

"I know you love me, Scarlet. You can try to deny it, but I know it," he shouts after me and I freeze at his words, my heart stuttering in my chest.

"You, okay?" Silver asks me, noticing how pale I've gone. He places a hand on my lower back.

"Please, just get me inside," I whisper. I'm terrified I'm going to breakdown right here in the carpark for everyone to see.

Damon wraps an arm over my shoulder and with me tucked into his side, he hurries us into school. As we pass through the main doors, my eyes lock with Vee's, and she looks at me with so much sadness and regret.

Once we're inside, I make a beeline for the girl's toilet. I throw my bag on the floor and drop down beside the toilet, feeling like I might vomit again.

"You feeling sick again?" Damon asks me, having followed me in here.

"I don't know. Maybe." I sigh and take a deep breath. "I just need a minute."

He's silent for a second and I almost forget he is there as I attempt to pull myself together.

"Do you love him?"

I stand up and turn to face him and I shrug my shoulders. "Maybe. Maybe I was starting to, before he shattered my trust, and I learned it was all a lie."

Damon offers me a sad smile as he tugs me into his arms and envelopes me in a hug that I didn't realise I needed. "I'm sorry, princess. I'm sorry you let him in, only to have him hurt you."

The toilet door bangs open, and Georgie takes in the sight of Silver holding me in his arms.

"Well, isn't this cosy? At least you've finally learned that you belong with the trash on the other side of the Bay. Be careful you don't catch something from him. Boys like him carry all kinds of nasty diseases."

Damon drops his arms from around me and glares at Georgie. I take his hand in mine and pull him with me, shoulder-checking the bitch as we pass her. "Go to hell, George."

"It's Georgie!!" she screams after me. I chuckle out loud. It's childish I know, but she brings out the worst in me.

At lunchtime, I feel his eyes on me. I risk a glance his way and find him staring at me. Seb is talking to him, but he doesn't answer. He holds my eyes prisoner. I thought I could cope with seeing him every day, but now, I'm not so sure.

"You, okay?" Damon asks me, pulling my attention back to him.

I plaster a smile on my face. "I'm fine. So, tell me about this club. You didn't seem happy about your brother taking me there later."

Damon chews on his lip. "It's a strip club, princess. That's the kind of business my family runs."

"Oh," I reply, ripping a piece of bread off and dipping it into my soup. "That's okay. It's nothing to be embarrassed about."

"I'm not embarrassed. I just don't think it's the kind of place you should step foot in," he explains, then blinks at me when I laugh.

"Oh, Damon. I'm not some innocent little rich girl. I've never stepped foot in a strip club before, but I'm not that green. I didn't grow up as a little rich girl in this Bay. I've seen things in my time. Don't make me out like I'm someone who needs protecting from the harsh realities of this world."

I look up when he doesn't reply and my heart lurches in my stomach when I see my brother hovering at our table.

"Hey, sis," he says sheepishly, messing with the strap of his bag as he assesses my reaction.

"Hi, Kit," I reply. My voice croaks as I fight the emotions warring inside of me.

"How have you been?" he asks me. Kit glances over at Damon, who averts his eyes and pulls out his phone, trying to give us some semblance of privacy.

"I'm okay."

"When are you coming home?" he rushes out the words like he's desperate to say them.

I sigh and shake my head. "That house isn't my home, Kit.

Not with a man that just wants to use me as a tool to further his success."

Kit winces at my words. "He's not that bad when you get to know him. He cares about us. If you'd just come home, the two of you could patch things up and we could be a family again."

There it is. My brother is so desperate for the family unit he's been missing for all these years that he can't accept what's in front of him. It breaks my heart that he's so desperate to feel like he belongs, that he's trying to deny the glaring truth.

"I love you. You know that right, but you need to open your eyes Kit, and see Wilbur for what he really is. Why do you think our dad ran away and never came back? Christ, he even changed his name to break ties with that man."

"You're wrong about him," Kit's voice rises in protest and a few people from the neighbouring tables glance our way. "He's just trying to do what's best for the family."

I look over at Damon and he grimaces and bobs his shoulders as if telling me it's useless to try to get Kit to see sense. "How about we have tea together tomorrow? Just the two of us," I suggest, eager to spend some time with my brother.

He chews on his lip. "Oh, I can't. Wilbur's got us tickets for United's away game tomorrow night."

His rejection pierces my delicate heart, but I keep my poker face, and I force a smile. "Oh wow, that's great, Kit. Maybe some other time."

He nods his head enthusiastically. "Definitely. Maybe Thursday?" he suggests.

"Maybe," I reply. The rejection I feel is making me defensive. "I'll let you know."

His face drops, and he looks down at the floor, swallowing. "Sure. I guess I'll see you later."

He walks away with his shoulders slumped, head down. It takes everything in me not to chase after him and grab him by the shoulders and try to shake some sense into him. Why can't he see Wilbur for what he is? How can he be okay with any of this?

"He'll come around," Damon assures me, softly gripping my shoulder. "Just give it time."

I clear my throat, battling with my emotions. What is happening to me? It's like since I cried that night at the dinner party, I can't stop. Every little thing has me tearing up. I need to shut this shit down and become a wall of steel again.

"I should tell him that Wilbur has threatened that if I don't return that he said he'll send him back to foster care. That would make him see sense." I sigh. "But I can't do it. I can't devastate Kit like that. Look at him. He's beaming from Wilbur's attention."

Damon frowns as he watches Kit take his seat beside his friends. "I don't think he'd believe you if you told him, princess. He's well and truly under Wilbur's influence. One day he'll realise, and you'll just have to be there for him when he does."

Damon's right. Kit thinks the sun shines out of Wilbur's arse right now. Nothing I say will change that. I just have to keep faith that Karma will makes it way to Wilbur at some point and that Kit will see for himself who his grandfather really is.

I'M MAKING MY WAY OUT TO THE FRONT OF SCHOOL TO MEET up with Luca when I'm grabbed from behind. A hand covers my mouth to stop me from making a scene.

"I'm sorry Scar, but if this is the only way to get you alone, I'm taking it," says a voice in my ear that haunts my dreams every night. I kick out and try to fight my way out of his hold, but it's no good he has me in his iron grip.

"Do it now," he orders, and I feel a sharp pain in my arm.

Out of the corner of my eye, I see Seb holding a syringe in his hand. "Just a little something to make you sleepy, Little Red."

The fuckers have drugged me. Again! I will kill them both just as soon as I can open my fucking eyes. I fight the drowsiness with everything in me, but it's no use. As my eyes close, the last thing I see is Archer's face.

CHAPTER FIVE

ELIZA

I snuggle into the soft, warm pillows. Why do they smell so good? I inhale again and recognise whose scent it is. I sit up sharply, groaning, when the room spins. I'm in a bedroom I don't recognise. I remember then. The bastard kidnapped me from school. Jumping out of the bed, I rush to the window. Where the hell am I? As far as the eye can see, there are trees and hills. He's brought me to the middle of fucking nowhere. I look down and my anger ramps up a notch when I see I'm not in my school uniform anymore. I'm dressed in one of his long-sleeved plain T-shirts. His smell surrounds me and, like the pathetic creature I have become, I press my nose into my shoulder and inhale his scent.

I stomp over to the door and blink in surprise when it swings open with the force of my rage. I come out onto a large landing. There are doors to my left and right, and an oak staircase leads to the ground floor. I make my way downstairs and pause at the bottom when it opens out to a large open-plan living space. Even in my anger, I can't help but appreciate the view. Where the two corners of the room meet, there are floor to ceiling windows that make the most of the beautiful scenery. It's almost so perfect that it looks like a painting.

"Ah, good. You're awake."

My head snaps toward the sound of his voice. Archer is standing in the kitchen. He's shirtless, with his perfect chest on display. He hasn't shaved for a couple of days, and he has that five o'clock shadow that always sets my libido on high alert.

"Where the hell are we?" I growl. I stomp across the room to stand in front of him on the opposite side of the large kitchen island.

"You're just in time. The food's almost ready," he tells me with a smile, completely ignoring my question.

"I'm not hungry," I lie. "You can't just kidnap me, Archer!"

His lip quirks up at the corner. If he smirks at me, I will take that knife beside him and stab him with it. "You wouldn't talk to me, so I did what I had to."

Sighing, I run my hands over my face. "Only you would resort to kidnapping. Take me home, Archer."

He puts the pan back over the boiling food and cocks his head at me. "Your home is with me, Scarlet."

I snicker, and this earns me a glare from him.

"How many times do I have to tell you? This. Me and you. We. Are. Done," I say it slowly and clearly, hoping he will get the message.

He scoffs and shakes his head. "We are far from done. We're just getting started, Scar. You're mine, and not because our families decided. Because I decided you are everything I need."

"And what about what I need?" I hiss, folding my arms across my chest to protect myself from the effect his words are having on me.

He leans on the worktop and studies me silently before he walks around the island and stops behind me. He places both hands on either side of the worktop, caging me in.

"You need me. You need my darkness to balance out your own. You need me to calm the demons that haunt your sleep," he says. He steals my breath from my lungs and makes me feel things I don't want to feel. His eyes focus on my neck, and he reaches in and twirls the necklace he gave me between his fingers, smiling. Damn, why didn't I take it off and throw it away? "We need each other. You're my sunlight in this dark, fucked up world and I'm never letting you go, scar."

"We're toxic," I protest. "What we had, it was built on lies and revenge. It's unhealthy."

He smirks as he moves his fingers to my hair and curls a piece around his finger. Being this near to him is messing with my rational brain. The part that is screaming at me to push him away and tell him I'll never be his.

"We're perfect for each other and if I have to kidnap you to make you realise it, then so be it."

He leans in so his lips are a breath away from my own. He focuses his dark eyes on my mouth and he half-smiles, before he pulls away and he walks back around to the hob. I suck in the breath that I had been holding and scold myself because I know had he pressed his lips against mine, I would have kissed him back.

"I'm leaving," I announce, stepping away from the island and heading towards the door.

"Good luck with that. We're in the middle of nowhere. We flew here by private jet and the nearest town is hours away," he informs me in a matter-of-fact tone.

I open the front door and step outside. It's cold, and I'm only in a T-shirt and knickers, with nothing on my feet. I don't doubt he's telling me the truth. If there's one thing I know about Archer, it is that he will have planned every detail with precision.

I step back inside and close the door behind me. He's leaning against the worktop, with one ankle crossed over the other, watching me. "Now that we have established that you can't escape me, shall we sit down and eat?" He gestures towards the table. He has set it for an intimate dinner, complete with candles and rose petals scattered along the tabletop.

Rolling my eyes, I cross the room and I pull out a chair and sit down, all the while scowling at him like my life depends on it. Satisfied that I'm doing as he asked, he turns his back on me and scoops out the contents of the dish onto two plates. I've never seen him cook before. If I'm honest, I presumed, he didn't know how, given he's grown up with a nanny and a housekeeper, to attend to his every whim. Watching him doing ordinary domestic tasks has my heart flipping in my chest. He opens a bottle of red wine and pours a glass, and he brings it over to me, placing it on the table. Scowling at his back, I pick up the glass and take a large drink.

When he brings the food over, I can't help but salivate. He's made carbonara, my favourite pasta dish, and it smells amazing.

"So, you cook. Something else to add to your CV, alongside lying, scheming and kidnap."

He smiles as he takes his seat opposite me. He picks up a remote and Sheeran comes through the speakers singing soulful lyrics about making sure you want them before you dive in.

"Well, this is cosy," I comment with a roll of my eyes. Archer is doing romance, and it scares the shit out of me. I can cope with a moody, demanding Archer, but this, this is undoing me.

"Eat before it gets cold," he suggests, picking up his own fork and tackling the food on his plate.

There's a defiant part of me that wants to pick up the food and throw it over his head and tell him he can go to hell, but then my stomach grumbles at me reminding me I'm starving. With some reluctance, I pick up my knife and fork. I groan when I take my first mouthful, and his lips quirk up at the corner in reaction.

"If I'd have known food would bring moans like that from you, I'd have cooked for you every day."

I put my fork down and glare at him from across the table. "Maybe you should have recorded it because food is the only way you'll get a moan from me again." I offer him a snarky smile and pick my fork back up.

He scoffs in response, his lip lifting at the corner. "We both know that isn't true, Scarlet."

We eat in silence for the next few minutes. I refuse to engage in polite conversation with him. Just because he has me trapped here in the woods somewhere, it doesn't mean I have to interact with him or acknowledge him.

"Have you heard from Wilbur?"

My eyes snap up to meet his. I'm surprised he has dared to mention Wilbur. "Are you trying to tell me you don't know about his visit to school and his ultimatum?" I ask him, with a brow arched in question.

"He came to see you at school?" he asks me, his brows furrowed.

"Don't pretend you don't know," I reply. "Let's agree not to play games anymore, Archer."

He leans his elbows on the table and looks me straight in the eye. "I promise you here and now, Scar; I will be nothing but truthful with you. I didn't know Wilbur visited you at school. I haven't spoke to him since the evening of the dinner party."

He doesn't look like he's bluffing, but then again, this is the guy who played me before, so I can't make a judgement based on the way he looks at me.

"Yes, dear old granddad came to see me at school and told me what would happen if I don't return home and agree to our engagement. He has me over a barrel. He has a file full of incriminating photos of me engaged in illegal activities that he says he will hand over to the police." I take a sip of my wine and lean back in my chair, studying his face for a reaction. "Oh, but that isn't the best bit. If I don't return and put your ring on my finger, he's going to call social services and relinquish my brother back into care."

"Fuck," Archer says, shaking his head. "I had no idea, Scarlet. What are you going to do?"

I snort in response. "I'll do whatever I need to do to ensure Kit remains at HBA and gets the education that will give him the best opportunities in life. It means I'm going to let you put an obnoxious rock on my finger and I'll smile and pose for the photographs and look like the doting fiancée."

He's silent, watching me as I watch him. I'm wondering what is going through that lying, scheming head of his. He stands to his feet and collects both our empty plates, and he comes back over with the bottle of wine. Taking my glass from my hand, he tops it up.

"I'm not going to lie and say I'm sorry," he admits as he takes his seat again and rubs his fingers up and down the stem of his glass. "I want you, Scar. I want to own your body and soul."

I shake my head and snicker at him. "Oh, yes, that's right, so that you can break me and get revenge for your mum."

"That was my plan. I've admitted that. Now, I'm re-thinking things."

I knock back my drink and the cool wine slides down my throat, helping to drown out the torrent of feelings he elicits from me when he's nearby. "Don't re-think it. Do it. Give me your worst, because I am going to make you regret ever agreeing to this farce of a marriage. You'll rue the day you ever put a ring on my finger, Archer. I'll make sure of that."

He smiles in response. "We'll see." He looks at his watch and, yawning, gets to his feet and stretches, showing off that muscled physique.

"Come on, let's watch a movie."

I chuckle at his ludicrous suggestion. "You honestly think I'm going to play nice? That I am going to sit here with you and watch a movie! Like you haven't betrayed my trust, used me, and lied to me?" I stand up and glare over the top of my glass as I neck back the last bit of wine. "I'm going to bed."

"Suit yourself," he replies with an eye roll and a shrug of his shoulders, strolling over to the sofa. Archer throws himself down and picks up the remote turning his attention to the television.

I expected him to insist, to manhandle me and pin me down on the sofa and make me watch a movie with him. I did not expect him to shrug his shoulders and stroll away. Scowling at the back of his head, I stomp past him and up the stairs. I am seething. I pace up and down the room. There's no tv up here so I can't watch anything, nor are there any books and the fucker has taken my phone off me too. Realising there really is nothing for me to do but go to bed, I pull back the covers and angrily climb under the covers and close my eyes. One problem. I'm not tired. I'm wide awake and I'm hopping mad at him.

I lie staring at the ceiling for around twenty minutes. I pull back the covers and stomp to the bathroom. A bath will help me calm down. I run myself a bath and step into the tub. The warm soapy water feels like heaven. I rest my head against the lip of the tub and close my eyes and try to think calm, happy thoughts. When the water cools and my hands shrivel, I climb out. I glance at the clock; it's still only eight in the evening. What the hell am I supposed to do for the next couple of hours? I can't lie here and do nothing!

Fifteen minutes later, I cave and begrudgingly head downstairs. Archer doesn't react when I enter the room. I take a seat at the opposite end of the sofa from him. He keeps his eyes trained on the television the whole time. He's watching one of the marvel movies. I love the marvel films. They're my favourite. We sit in silence for the rest of the movie and when it ends, Archer turns the power off with the remote. Ignoring me, he strolls through to the kitchen and pours himself a glass of water and then walks past me and up the stairs. He doesn't look my way or speak to me. It's as if I'm not in the room. I curse under my breath when I realise he has taken the tv remote with him so I can't even sit down here and watch more tv. I climb the stairs after him, ready to call him out, but I falter in my steps when I see him undressing in the bedroom.

"We're not sleeping in the same room," I tell him, folding my arms across my chest and popping my hip out.

Archer side-glances at me as he pulls back the duvet, and he climbs into bed. "This is the only room with a bed in it."

I glower at him. He has to be lying. Pivoting on my heels, I stride across the hallway and open the door opposite. No bed. Every room I go in is the same. They all have wardrobes and drawers, but there is not one bed in any of them. Scowling, I storm back into the bedroom.

"Did you seriously have all the beds removed before we got here?"

He's sitting up in the bed, leaning against the headboard with his hands cupped behind his head. He fights a smirk. "I did. You know me, Scar. I plan every detail in advance."

"I'll sleep on the sofa," I tell him defiantly.

"Good luck with that." He shrugs. "There are no blankets for you to use. This is the only bedding in the house."

I bite at the inside of my mouth, silently fuming. I stalk over to the bed and grab at the duvet, intending to pull it off him, but he grabs at it and stops me from taking it.

"Give it to me, Savage," I hiss as I yank with all my strength on the duvet.

"No," he insists, keeping a firm grip on the bedding. "Just get in the fucking bed, Scarlet. We both know your nightmares are back."

I freeze and stop tugging on the duvet. "How do you know that?"

He sighs and offers me a sad smile. "Because I know you. I know that every night I held you in my arms, the nightmares never came. That in your sleep, your body and mind knew it could trust me to keep you safe."

"I hate you," I seethe, and I tug on the duvet, determined to get it off him. He tugs back, yanking sharply, and before I know it, I'm pinned under him on the bed. My chest rises and falls fast as I try to control my anger and thrill I feel at being in such proximity to him.

"Are you done?" he asks me. He's not laughing or being smug for a change.

"Get off me," I demand, pushing up at his chest.

"Just stop, scar. Just let go and give yourself what we both know you need," he whispers. His beautiful brown eyes burning into mine.

I gulp as I feel a wave of nausea wash over me. "You need to get up, Arch. Now!" I tell him, pushing on his chest again.

"How many times do I have to-"

"Move. Now!" I shout, covering my mouth with one hand as the other continues to press up against his chest.

He must realise I'm not okay, because he rolls away from me in a flash, and I dart to my feet and run to the ensuite as quick as I can.

I make it just in time before I throw the contents of the lovely food he cooked us up into the toilet bowl. I can't help but smile inside briefly at the thought that all his hard work slaving over the stove for me was for nothing.

I flinch when I feel his hand rubbing my back. "Are you okay? Are you unwell?"

I nudge my shoulder to move his hand away, but the persistent bastard continues to move his hand up and down my back. "Yes, I'm ill. Which I would have told you if you'd asked me before you kidnapped me. I have a bug, okay?"

I hear him stand to his feet and I arch a brow when he comes back over and offers me a glass of water. I want to tell him to stick the water where the sun doesn't shine, but my mouth tastes like death, so I begrudgingly take it from him.

He leans against the sink. His legs crossed at the ankles in nothing but his black Armani boxers and damn if it doesn't make my heart beat faster. I dab my mouth with some toilet roll then flush the toilet and get to my feet.

"Just let me go home," I beg him.

I'm not quick enough to react when he snakes out a hand and pulls me into his space, pulling my body flush with his. "You are home. Your home is with me, Scarlet."

"You're deluded," I snarl, glaring up at him, trying to deny that my heart isn't going at the speed of ten galloping horses right now.

"Can I kiss you?" he asks me gruffly, looking down at my lips as he holds my body against his.

For a second, I want to say yes. I want to forget everything that has gone on between us and just give in to my desires. To close my eyes and lose myself in the feel of him. His touch. His kisses.

"No," I reply weakly as I push on his chest to make some space between us. "You think you can just romance me with wine and dinner, and I'll forgive you. Well, I won't."

"What will?"

I blink in surprise at his question. "What do you mean, what will?"

He runs the back of his thumb over my bottom lip. "What do I need to do to get you to forgive me?"

"I'll never forgive you," I vow firmly, my stony eyes glaring up into his.

"That's okay." He sighs. "I have forever to prove my loyalty is with you now. I'll spend my life earning your forgiveness."

I gulp, warring with my own emotions. When he looks at me like this and makes me such promises, I can feel my resolve weakening. I shake my head, trying to shake some sense into my befuddled brain.

"Can we just get in bed now and save the fighting for tomorrow? I was out on a job for the Elders last night and I'm beat."

I can hear the weariness in his voice.

"What did they have you doing? Torturing an enemy, or maybe burying a body?" I snipe.

He looks down at me, without a drop of humour on his face. "Something along those lines. It's better you don't know, Scar." He drops a kiss on my forehead and walks away from me.

Admitting defeat, I walk back into the bedroom in just his T-shirt and my knickers. I can feel his hungry gaze on my body as I walk around to the other side of the bed and join him. He turns the light out and we both lie on our backs in silence. So much remains unsaid between us. I can hear every breath he takes, and my body is aware of every time he shifts or sighs. It's a whole new form of torture for me. Being so close to him and yet so far away at the same time.

CHAPTER SIX

ELIZA

When I wake in the morning, my cheek is resting on a warm body. I open my eyes and the first thing I see is his naked chest. It's not a bad way to wake up, if I didn't hate him like I do. I tense when I realise he is stroking his fingers up and down my right thigh, causing goosebumps as he goes. For a second, I just enjoy the feeling. I pretend that nothing bad has happened between us. But it has. He lied to me and manipulated me for his own gain. He wanted to use me in some twisted revenge plot, and I am a means to him getting his fortune and his legacy when he turns eighteen. Just like Wilbur, he is out for what he can get from me.

"Can we go home today?" I ask him. My voice is dry from the night's sleep.

"We're here until Monday morning, Scar. So, you can fight me every minute of this weekend and have yourself a thoroughly miserable time, or you can just accept that you're here with me and just live in the moment."

Taking a deep sigh, I lift myself up off his chest and sit up, looking down at him. "I'll take fighting with you every time."

He closes his eyes and releases a throaty chuckle that sends a shiver all the way down to my sex. I can't deny how truly magnificent he looks right now. This is the Archer I like. The one who is relaxed and undone, with morning bed hair and all that skin on show that just begs to be touched.

"What are you thinking?" he asks me, his eyes finding mine and pulling all my attention.

"I'm thinking that it's a shame you fucked up, because it's moments like this that I remember why we were good together," I admit to him, my heart clenching in my chest.

He sits up, and it brings him up into my personal space. He runs his thumb and forefinger under my chin. "We can be good together again, Scarlet. Me and you against the world." He leans in and gently but barely runs his lips over mine and when I don't pull away, he cups the back of my neck and places his lips firmly on mine. I don't push him away. I wrap my arms around his neck and climb into his lap and I kiss him back like he is the oxygen I need to breathe. Why does this have to feel so bloody good? Why does it have to be his kisses that set me on fire and make me forget who I am? Before the kiss deepens, I climb off his knee. I can't go here again. I've felt bone-deep heartache before, and I can't survive it a third time. It will destroy me once and for all.

"You can fight this, but we both know we're inevitable," he whispers into my ear before he climbs out of the bed and leaves me in a mess of jumbled thoughts and conflicting emotions.

❦

ARCHER COOKS AGAIN. HE MAKES US A FULL ENGLISH breakfast, complete with mushrooms and hash browns, and I eat the lot. I am ravenously hungry this morning, but then it's hardly surprising given I threw up my food last night. I let myself pretend for a minute that this is what married life between us would be like. Just the two of us, tucked away from the world, enjoying each other's company. If only that were true. The reality is a lot different, though.

"Go get dressed. We're going out today," he tells me as he takes my plate and walks over to the dishwasher.

"We are?"

"Yes. I've brought you some sturdy boots, as we'll be doing a lot of walking today."

"You can go walking. I'm staying here. You might be able to force me away with you, but you can't force me to do things with you, Savage," I tell him, leaning back in my seat and waiting for his reaction.

He stops what he is doing, and for a second he doesn't react.

"If you want to play this game, then we can, Scar. You can get dressed or I'll just throw you over my shoulder and take you hill walking in nothing but that t-shirt of mine you're wearing."

"You wouldn't," I reply, my voice uncertain.

He turns and faces me, and I can tell from the look on his face that he means every word. Scraping my chair back abruptly, I stand to my feet and glower at him for a second before I turn and head upstairs. As I climb to the first floor, I can hear the fucker chuckling away to himself. Bastard!

I huff and puff as I get dressed, getting more and more angry at this situation. Being in his company twenty-four-seven is too hard. I can't do this, and I'm pissed off that he has forced this on me. Typical, pretentious rich boy, just thinking he can force me to spend time with him.

❧

ARCHER LEADS THE WAY UP INTO THE HILLS AND EVEN THOUGH I am a reluctant walking partner, I must admit it is beautiful out here. The sun is shining and whilst it's a little nippy; the scenery is breath-taking.

"Are you going to tell me where we are?" I ask him as we stop to have a drink.

"Scotland."

"Wow. I've never been to Scotland before."

He looks out at the rolling hills around us. "Me and the boys and Vee come up here every Christmas break and have some time away from the parents. We finish the week by seeing in the New Year in Edinburgh. Hogmanay in Edinburgh is special."

"Your parents don't all mind you leaving the family celebrations to come up here?" I ask, surprised. There is no way my parents would have let me miss out on all our Christmas and new year family traditions.

Archer shrugs his shoulders. "Rafe's parents rarely stay home beyond boxing day and my dad is usually away on business or holidaying in Monaco with his buddies."

I nod as I study him. I don't think Archer has any idea what it is like to grow up in a normal, loving family. His father may be alive and well, but he may as well have been an orphan. "What about your grandad?"

He bobs his head. "Yeah, he's usually around, but he's never really been into Christmas that much after grandma died." He screws the cap back on his water bottle. "When I have kids, I'm going to make sure I'm with them throughout the holidays. I'll bring them up here and we'll go sledging and build snowmen." He clears his throat and offers me a tight smile.

"You want kids?"

He gives me a lopsided grin, hearing the shock in my voice. "What? You think I'm too cold and unfeeling to be a dad?" He looks from me then back out at the view. "I want kids, Scar. At least three. I want a little girl who looks just like her mummy and two older brothers who will protect her and love her."

"Three, huh?" I repeat. "The contract says I only have to give you one, so it looks like you are out of luck. Unless, of course, you can find yourself a mistress to give you the other two," I tell him, laughing. He doesn't laugh along with me. When I look up at him, I find him looking at me with an expression I can't fathom.

"When I take you as my wife, Scar, that will be it. I would never disrespect you by being unfaithful."

His response surprises me. "Once I've given you an heir,

there will be no further sexual relationship between us, Savage. I'll do my duty in order to keep Kit safe, but no more."

He sighs and smiles at me. "Keep telling yourself that, Scar. Out of everything between us, the sex was always amazing. You miss it just as much as I do."

"It's only been a week," I snort, playing off his comment with nonchalance.

"A week too long. I miss those little sounds you make when you're about to come and the way you look at me when I'm inside you. Like the world could burn down and we would be oblivious, lost in each other."

I swallow, my pulse quickening at his words. God help me. How am I supposed to keep this up when he says things like that to me? Fuck! I stand up, grabbing my rucksack. "We should keep going. We're not far off the top now."

He doesn't answer for a second and I can feel his eyes boring into my back, but I dared not turn around, too terrified that if I do, he'll see the warring emotions etched across my face.

"This way," he announces, breaking the silence, and as I put my poker face back on, I turn and follow him.

❧

"THIS IS AMAZING," I GASP AS WE REACH THE TOP. ALL YOU can see in every direction is rolling green hills and countryside. It is beautiful, and the views of the Loch are breath-taking. I could stay up here forever and hide away from the harsh realities of the world we both live in.

"Beautiful, isn't it?" he asks, looking out at the picturesque view.

"I hate Wilbur," I tell Archer. "I plan to destroy him. I don't know when and I don't know how, but I'm going to take him down."

He's quiet for a few seconds before he surprises me with his reply. "If that's what you want, Scar, then I'll help you."

I stare at him, open-mouthed. He walks over and with a finger under my chin; he closes my mouth. "What part of me telling you, you are my priority, did you not get?"

I swallow, and steel my expression. "I guess I just presumed it was another lie. I mean, that's what you're good at, right, lying and scheming?"

He releases a big sigh before he grabs the back of my neck and smashes his mouth against mine. I'm not prepared, and I kiss him back. Why does it feel so right being in his arms? I come to my senses and wrench myself away from him.

"You can't kiss me like that anymore," I hiss, wiping my mouth with the back of my hand, when all I really want to do is grab him by his jacket and pull him close.

"Why deny what we both want?" He pulls his bag off his back, and digs inside, pulling out a blanket. "Let's eat." I watch him as he places the blanket down and gestures for me to sit down. I want to fight him and tell him I don't want to sit with him, but I'm starving despite that big breakfast this morning. As I sit down, he pulls out two sandwich boxes and hands me one.

"Turkey salad, no mayo. Just salad cream," he tells me and my heart twinges that he remembered I hate mayo.

"Thanks," I say reluctantly as I pick up the sandwich and take a bite.

"I don't know the ins and outs, but Wilbur needs this marriage more than my grandfather does."

I pause mid bite at his words and wait for him to continue.

"There have been some rumours that he's struggling financially. That he may have made some poor investment and expansion decisions lately."

"So, he needs this marriage to save his legacy?"

Archer shrugs his shoulders. "Possibly. Like I said, it's just a rumour I heard."

"But you could find out if there's any truth behind it?" I push.

Archer sits down opposite me and opens his sandwich box. "I could. For you."

"Then this is your chance to prove to me you mean what you say. That is, if you mean it when you say I'm your priority now?"

He frowns at me. "I told you from now on you'll get nothing but honesty and the truth from me. I meant every word. You want info on Wilbur. I'll get it for you, Scar."

❧

BY THE TIME WE MAKE OUR DESCENT AND ARRIVE BACK AT THE cabin, it's almost four pm. I want to tell him I've had a miserable time, but I can't. I enjoyed it, and I hate myself for it. I'm exhausted though. I don't know why I'm so tired. Yes, we did a lot of walking, but I'm fit and healthy.

I throw myself down on the sofa when Archer announces he'll take the first shower so that he can make a start on dinner. I cuddle up in amongst the pillows and rest my head. I could stay here forever and hide away from life and the harsh reality that waits for me back home. I'm fighting an internal war with myself over Archer. I hate him, but there is a part of me that misses him and wants his company. I can't let him in again. Look where that got me last time.

❧

"SCAR," A VOICE WHISPERS SOFTLY AND I OPEN MY EYES TO find Archer leaning over me. "Hey," he says softly, smiling at me like I'm his entire world. "I ran you a bubble bath."

"You did?" I say surprised, rubbing my eyes and sitting up, which places me far too close to him. I scoot my bum back on the sofa to put some distance between us. He doesn't miss it, and he quirks a brow.

"Go on up. I've put some clothes out on the bed for you. I'll make a start on dinner. Are you okay with steak and chips?"

My belly rumbles in response. "Sounds good." He walks away and I sit there for a second and stare after his retreating figure as I war with the feelings inside. Annoyed with myself, I head upstairs to find a welcoming warm bath, complete with bubbles. Vanilla and coconut fill the room, and he has put candles around the bath to complete the cosy ambience. Smooth fucker.

The bath is just what I need. I feel relaxed and reinvigorated. Maybe I am over the bug as I haven't been sick at all today. When I return downstairs, I falter in my steps on the bottom step when I take in the room. He's turned the lights down. and sultry, slow music plays on the sound system. He has set the table with candles and rose petals.

"Anyone would think this was a date instead of a kidnapping. You can't romance someone you have forced here against their will you know?" I comment as I walk further into the room and lean my arms on the kitchen island.

"Like I said, if you hadn't been so insistent on ignoring me, I wouldn't have had to resort to such drastic measures." He pours a glass of wine and holds it out to me.

"I'm not your possession, Archer."

He cocks his head, fighting a smile, and that just gets my back up even more. "I don't see you as my possession, Scar. I see you as my woman. My fiancée. The person I want at my side. I will always treat you with respect."

I snicker. "Like you did when you lied to me all these months. Laughing at me because you knew a big secret that I didn't."

He stalks towards me, and I gulp. There's nowhere to run. He has me cornered. I can cope with him when there is some space between us, but when he's this close, it does things to my stupid heart and my libido.

"I'll apologise every day if I need to. Now take the wine, go sit and relax. The food won't be much longer." He holds out the glass of wine again and I take it off him and begrudgingly take a seat on the sofa. I watch silently as he moves around the kitchen. He looks at ease in a kitchen and it makes me wonder who taught him to cook. I can't see it being Edward or his dad, Phil. It must have been Jenny. Thank God he had that woman in his life to show him some love and affection. Is it sad that I find watching him cook is sexy? I mean, when he licks the sauce off the spoon and moans, I almost come right there. Why does he have to be so infuriatingly gorgeous? The guy oozes sex appeal.

"Scar, did you hear me? I said the food's ready."

I shake my head, pulling myself from my daydreaming, and he looks at me with a knowing smirk. Did I mention I hate him?

I silently drop into my seat at the table, and he brings my plate over. It looks delicious.

"It's shepherd's pie. I remember you told me your mum used to cook it for you every Sunday. It's probably nowhere near as good as your mums."

I swallow, saying nothing, as he takes his seat opposite me. He remembered when I told him about my mum's cooking and my favourite meals that she used to make. It makes my stupid heart squeeze at how thoughtful he's being. Sneaky fucker is bringing his A-game.

We eat in silence. It should be awkward, but it isn't. In fact, it's a comfortable silence. When we're done, he takes my plate, and he clears the table. He offers me another glass of wine, but I don't feel like another, so I ask for a coke, and he pours me one into a glass.

"Come on," he says, holding out his hand. "I have something I want to show you?"

I stare at his open, waiting hand. I get to my feet and ignore his hand, tucking my hands behind my back. The fucker laughs. He heads upstairs and my eyes narrow in suspicion. If he heads for the bedroom, I'm going to knee him in the balls. Does he think he can just cook me food and I'll roll over and open my legs for him? Think again.

He surprises me though, when he passes our bedroom and goes

into one of the other bedrooms and out through some patio doors. I follow him out and we walk around the balcony that wraps itself the whole way around the first floor. Here, there is a set of steps up to the roof. Intrigued by where he's taking me, I silently follow him. We come out onto the rooftop, and I stop in my steps. Wow, it is pretty up here. The night stars are so clear in the sky. I look over to an area that has cushions and a rug laid out on the floor. He doesn't turn to see what my reaction is. He just sits down on to the rug and, looking up, he pats the space beside him.

"Come, take a seat. If you're brave enough?" He smirks, knowing damn well that if he challenges me, I'll rise to it. I take a seat beside him, ensuring I leave a decent space between us. He reaches for a telescope on a tripod in front of him. "I read you can see Jupiter and one of its moons tonight." He leans up on his knees and put his eye to the scope, turning the focus. "Here, look." He beckons me over. I can't resist a look, so I shuffle up beside him and I place my eye to the lens. I'm amazed at the detail. You can actually see the different colours that give Jupiter its marble like appearance.

"That's so amazing," I gush, forgetting I hate him, and I give him a genuine smile. He smiles back at me, and my heart pounds in my chest.

We stay out there for over an hour, looking at different stars and Archer amazes me with his knowledge of our solar system. Who knew he was such an astronomy geek? He frowns when he tells me his mum bought him his first telescope and they would star gaze together in the back garden at their house. I feel somehow privileged he wanted to do something that he did with his mum with me.

I yawn. I'm exhausted. It's been a full-on day and I'm ready for sleep.

"Come on, let's head inside," he suggests, standing up and offering me his hand. This time I take it, letting him pull me up and for a second we both just stand and stare at each other. I clear my throat and pull my hand from his. "You head to bed. I'll tidy up out here and bring you a hot chocolate up."

It's on the tip of my tongue to tell him that all this sweet attentive behaviour won't work on me, but the words stick in my throat. It really feels like he's trying to make amends and change. Feeling unnerved by him. I almost run to the bedroom, and I quickly change into the leggings and T-shirt he has left out on the bed for me. He comes into the bedroom some ten minutes later and places the hot chocolate on the bedside table next to me. I don't miss that he has put whipped cream and marshmallows on it for me.

I try not to ogle him as he strips down to his boxers and climbs into the bed beside me. "Shall we watch Peaky?" he asks me, pulling out his I-pad and opening the Netflix app

I nod my head. We both love the show. Archer reminds me a lot of Tommy, the main character. He's cocky and self-assured, but he'll do anything to protect his family.

❧

ON SUNDAY, WE SPEND ANOTHER DAY HIKING. ARCHER PACKS us another picnic and we sit and eat our food surrounded by the Scottish countryside. It's so peaceful and serene that you really can forget that there's an entire world out there. We're in a little bubble, just the two of us. I can't even lie and say I've hated every minute, because I have enjoyed myself. We stayed up late last night and binge-watched our favourite show. I've enjoyed his company, and that's what is making this so hard. I hate him for lying to me, and I feel like he conspired against me with Wilbur. Can I ever move past that and forgive him and trust him again? He swears I'm his priority now, but how can I believe him? After losing my parents, I haven't been good at letting people get close, but I let him in and look where it got me. I was left humiliated, hurt, and exposed. It made me feel weak.

We return to the lodge at three in the afternoon and I head

straight upstairs for a bath to soothe my aching feet. I return downstairs, finding a very relaxed Archer sitting in a comfy-looking armchair by the large floor to ceiling windows. He's reading a book. I don't know why, but I didn't expect him to be a reader, and it makes me realise there is still so much that I don't know about him. Our relationship, if that's what you could even call it, has been fast-paced and very physical.

"You can read," I state as I enter the room and take a seat on the large sofa to his left.

"I can do many things, Scar, and I do them well," he replies, briefly lifting his head from his book and sending that signature panty-melting smirk my way.

"What are you reading?" I ask him, being nosey. I'm curious what kind of books he likes to occupy his mind with.

"It's a book about a guy who travels back in time."

"Wow, I didn't have you down as a sci-fi kind of guy? Isn't that a little geeky for you, the big, bad, leader of the Aces?"

He places his book down on his knee and he arches a brow. "Are you mocking me, Scar?"

"What if I am?" I retort back, feeling brave.

I yelp when he rises quickly from his seat and stalks my way. "Archer," I protest, holding out my hands to keep him at arms-length. "What are you doing?"

He waggles his brows playfully at me. "Time to put you in your place, little miss sarcasm." He dives for me, and although I try to get away, his arm wraps round my waist and he lands on the sofa with me on top of him. My back is to his chest. With his other hand, he reaches under my armpit and tickles me.

"I'm not ticklish there," I tell him with satisfaction.

"Looks like I'm going to have to tickle you everywhere then. Everyone has a ticklish spot." I protest and squirm as he explores my body and I screech when he touches my left foot.

"No, no please, not my feet," I beg him. My feet are ridiculously ticklish, so much so that I've never been able to get a foot massage or have my toenails professionally painted. "Archer, stop, please. I'll do anything," I beg him in between laughing. "I'll wee."

"You wee on me, Scar, and I'll spank you so hard you won't be able to sit down for a week."

"Hah! We both know I'd enjoy that, so that's not really a punishment. Argh, stop," I say between chuckles, squirming to get his hand away from my foot.

He rolls us so that I end up under him on the sofa. Our bodies are pressed tightly against each other. "You'll give me anything, huh?"

"Well, I may have overstretched that statement slightly."

"A kiss," he tells me. "I want a kiss. And I don't mean a peck, I mean I want tongues and everything."

"I hate you," I snap, pouting at him. The more I kiss him, the more my stupid heart tells me to forgive him, and my head starts arguing that what he did wasn't all that terrible. "One stupid kiss," I tell him.

He nods his head, grinning at me. "One amazing, toe-curling kiss. I promise."

I sigh, shaking my head at him. So cocky!

With my heart pounding in my chest, I raise my head up and press my lips against his. He immediately cups the back of my head and brings me closer, his tongue slipping inside my mouth. I forget all reason and I kiss him back like my life depends on it. Why does he have to be so good at this? He surprises me when he ends the kiss. I expected him to take things further, but he holds my gaze for a second before climbing off me and stalking off the to the kitchen without saying a word. I sit up and stare after him, my stupid libido begging me to call him back here to continue what he started. Thank goodness we're going home tomorrow because too much more time holed up in this cosy lodge with him and I might lose all reason and just give in to my desires. Monday can't come quick enough.

CHAPTER SEVEN

ELIZA

It's seven in the morning on Monday when Archer drops me back at the Silver mansion. I didn't tell him I was staying here; he, of course, knew where I was staying. The car journey has left me feeling a little offside. This stomach bug is still hanging over me a little bit.

As we pull up, the front door opens and Damon leans against the doorframe, watching as we both climb out of the car. Archer hands me my school bag and my phone. He nods his head briefly at Silver as he climbs back in his car and peels off down the drive.

"How was it?" he asks me as he steps aside and holds the door open for me.

"How do you think? He kidnapped me, you know?" I tell him, pointing down the drive. "That arsehole drugged me and put me on a plane."

"I know, princess."

I blink in surprise and do a one-eighty, turning round to face him. "You knew!"

"Not beforehand," he says, holding up his hands in defence. "He texted me to say you were safe, that he'd used gentle persuasion to whisk you away somewhere remote where the two of you could talk."

Hands on my hips, I blow out my cheeks. "Gentle persuasion. He drugged me and took me by force to a cabin in the middle of nowhere. Sixty-four hours! I had to put up with him parading around with those perfect abs on display, having him cook for me and run me baths."

Silver chuckles. "Sounds like hell. I'm sure most of the girls at school would see that as a horrific way to spend the weekend."

I'm about to tell him to shut it when my stomach rolls and I cover my mouth with my hand. "I'm going to vomit." It comes with no warning, and I lean over a bowl on the console table beside the front door and I empty the contents of my stomach into it. "Ugh, that came from nowhere. Damn, I haven't been sick for a whole forty-eight hours, too."

Damon grimaces, looking from me to the bowl. "My car keys are in that bowl."

"Oops. My bad." I wince, wiping my mouth with the back of my hand. "I think this bug is still lingering in my system," I offer in explanation as I pick up the bowl and head through the house to the downstairs loo. Holding the bowl over the toilet, I stick my hand in and pull out his car keys that are dripping with the contents of my breakfast and I throw them into the sink. I soap up my hands and wash the vomit away. If I wet his keys, will they still work?

"Are you pregnant?"

I almost drop the bowl as I catch his eyes in the mirror's reflection. "Pregnant. Don't be ridiculous."

Damon pops his shoulder. "You sure? Because I've watched my sister go through terrible morning sickness and this 'bug,'" he says using air quotes, "looks a lot like morning sickness to me."

I shake my head, ready to tell him his theory is ridiculous, but then I stop and think. When was I due on? I pull out my phone and open my period tracker app, and I inhale a sharp breath. No. It isn't possible.

"You're late," he states rather than asks.

I stand there frozen to the spot. This can't be happening.

"I think you should sit down. You've gone awfully pale," Damon suggests. He flushes the toilet and closes the lid. He guides me to sit down on the toilet.

"I don't understand. How can this have happened?"

Damon cocks a brow at me. "I think you know how babies are made, princess."

I frown at him and shake my head. "Humour is not helping, Damon. I'm on the pill. I take it religiously every day. I'm just late. I can't be pregnant." I'm not sure who I am trying to convince, him or me.

"How late are we talking?"

Running a hand through my hair and chewing on my bottom lip, I look up at him. "Two fucking weeks. I'm never this late."

"Well, come on," he says, offering me his hand. "There's only one way to find out."

I look up at his open palm. "I can't just stroll into a chemist in the bay and buy a test, Damon. It'll get back to Wilbur in minutes."

Damon nods his head. "You're right. I'll go. You stay here."

"Damon," I shout out, causing him to pause at the door. "Buy like five or six."

When he's gone, I freak the fuck out. I pace up and down the living room. "Fuck. Fuck. Fuck!!" I shout out, cupping the back of my neck in my hands and praying to God that this is a false alarm. I cannot be pregnant with Archer's baby.

❧

"OPEN THE NEXT ONE," I TELL DAMON, WITH THE PITCH OF my voice bordering on hysterical.

Cursing under his breath, he crouches down in front of me and takes my hands in his. "Princess. You've done four positive tests," he says gently, like he's scared I might shatter into pieces. "You are well and truly pregnant."

A tear escapes, and it falls down my cheek, and he wipes it away with his thumb. "I can't be pregnant. I can't. He broke me, Damon. He lied to me."

"I know he did," he agrees, rubbing his hands over mine in a comforting gesture. "It doesn't change the fact that you are preggers. It isn't the end of the world, though."

"Isn't it," I scoff. "Because I can't see anything positive about this situation."

He pauses, chewing at the corner of his mouth. "Just because you're pregnant, it doesn't mean you have to stay that way. There are options."

He's right. I could have an abortion. "I can't think straight. I need time to process."

"Of course you do. I'm just saying this situation isn't as desolate as you think. You have a choice whether you have this baby."

I grasp onto Damon's hands tightly. "He can't find out, Damon. He'll be furious."

Damon tilts his head. "You think? Savage is many things, but he's not one to shirk his responsibilities."

"Technically, if I have an abortion, then he doesn't need to know."

Damon sighs and he looks at me like he doesn't agree. "Do you think that's fair? I know he hasn't exactly been honest with you, but don't you think he should know? Whatever you decide to do."

"No," I hiss. "He lost all rights to have any say when he lied to me and plotted with his family and mine."

"Okay," he says, holding his hands out in front of him. "Whatever you decide, I'll support you."

I lean forward and drop a kiss on his cheek. "Thank you. For being here with me." I rest my head on his shoulder and he strokes my back. "Promise me, you'll help me keep this quiet whilst I decide what I want to do."

"Of course. You know I have your back." Damon leans up and checks his watch. "We've missed first class. Do you want to bunk off today?"

I would love nothing more than to bunk off, but I've missed quite a bit of school these last couple of weeks and, baby or no baby, I need my education. "I've already missed enough. I'll go and change quickly."

Damon nods his head, and I follow him out of the toilet. "I'll make you some toast. You need to eat and keep your strength up."

I want to protest, worried I'll just throw it straight back up, but he's right, I can't run on empty. I head upstairs, and in a daze, I pull my uniform out of my wardrobe. I strip down to my underwear and pause in front of the mirror, staring at my stomach. Fuck. There is a baby growing inside of me. I place a hand on my belly and stare at my reflection. Seventeen and pregnant. This is not how I saw my life going.

❧

We get to school in time for second class. Damon checks I'm okay before he leaves me outside my history class. I take my seat and stare out of the window, lost in my own little world. It's strange how your entire world can tip on its axis in just one hour. Everything is different now. I'm different. Whatever I decide to do about this pregnancy, I'll never be the same again. Vee walks in and she smiles longingly at me before she takes her seat. Vee would know what to say right now. She'd arrange a girl's night, and she'd talk me through my situation and help me see things calmly and with a clear head. I could really do with a female friend to lean on right now.

I head to the cafeteria at lunchtime in a trance. I'm queuing for my food when the smell of bacon hits me, and my stomach turns over. Oh no. Not now. If I keep rushing off to vomit, people will put two and two together. I take deep breaths and, grabbing a cheese sandwich, I rush away from the smells assaulting me. I take a seat at the table I now share with Damon. I see who I assume to be Damon taking the seat opposite me and I look up to smile at him, only my smile drops when I see Archer sitting there.

"What are you doing here?" I don't have the mental capacity to be around him right now. Staring into his face, my mind drifts to wondering if the baby we've made together will have his nose or mine. Fuck. I can't think like this. I can't allow myself to think of this baby.

"Are you sick?"

"What?" I squeal. My eyes widen in fear. What does he know?

He frowns at me, looking concerned. "You went really pale for a moment. Are you still not over that bug?"

"I'm fine," I hiss. "Not that it's any of your concern." I frown as I watch him put his plate down and start eating. "You can't sit here."

"Make me move then," he challenges, waggling a brow at me.

I fold my arms across my chest. "Well, I'll move to another table."

He shrugs his shoulders, smiling at me. "Then I'll just follow you. I told you Scar; I'm not giving up."

I'm about to tell him where to shove his smiling face when Seb drops into the seat beside me, closely followed by Rafe. Vee loiters at the bottom of the table, watching my reaction before she pushes back her shoulders and sits beside Archer.

"This table's crowded today," Damon comments as he takes the remaining seat to my left. He looks sideways at me. "You, okay?"

I nod my head, knowing what he's asking me. When I look up, I find Archer coldly observing the interaction between Damon and me.

"What?" I snap at him. "You got something to say?"

He shakes his head and returns to eating his food. Laughing and hollering coming from the table my brother sits on snags my attention. Chester is there again. His arm hung over my brother's shoulder as he says something to him, and they both laugh.

"I don't like his interest in Kit. He's up to something," I say, watching the two of them laughing together like old friends.

"I'll sort it," Archer announces. He stands up and strides across the cafeteria to my brother's table. He smiles down at Kit and the two of them exchange words. I watch as Archer gestures with his head over to where I am. Kit gets to his feet and picking up his tray, he lets Archer guide him over to our table.

"Hey, sis," he says as he takes a seat opposite me. Rafe and Vee shuffle along to make room for him and, a second later, Archer takes a seat beside him.

"Hi, Kit," my voice clogs up with emotion. I miss my little brother so much. He's been the centre of my life for so long now that it's hard not having him around. "How are you? How's football?"

He grins at me as he tells me he's made the first team for the home game this weekend.

"That's amazing, Kit. Though they'd have to be stupid not to want you playing."

He nods his head and scratches his nose, a sure sign that he wants to say something, but he's unsure.

"Spit it out," I tell him with a reassuring smile.

"You could come to my game and cheer me on," he suggests. His eyes are full of apprehension as he waits for my reply.

"I have no plans this weekend. You free Damon?"

Damon pulls his attention from his phone and looks at me. "Sorry, I'm working for my dad this weekend."

"We're free, right Archer?" Vee chips in, her eyes focused on Archer.

"Oh, yeah, we can bring Scar to the game and cheer you on, Kit," Archer suggests.

"Yeah, that'd be great," Kit tells him, smiling from ear-to-ear. Archer Savage, the sneaky fucker, has wound his way into my plans again.

CHAPTER EIGHT

ELIZA

It's early Saturday morning. We pull up into the car park and Damon kills the engine and waits silently. I blow out the breath I have been holding as I eye the private clinic.

"I'm scared," I admit to him.

Damon wraps his hand over mine. "I'm here with you. You're not on your own, Eliza."

I clear my throat and I say what has been on my mind all morning. "Can I ask a favour?" He nods his head. "Can you pretend to be the father? Just for the scan." I look down at my stomach. "I just don't want them to judge me as some washed up girl who's single and pregnant."

"Eliza, look at me," he says softly, and I lift my face to meet his eyes. "I told you I'm here for you. If you need me to be the dad, then that's what I'll be."

I lean over the car and kiss him on the cheek. "Thank you. I don't deserve you."

He smiles, swallowing. "Yes, you do. You deserve people in your corner. I wish you'd stop all this talk that you don't deserve to have people who care." He picks his phone up out of its holder. "Come on. We don't want to be late."

We enter the clinic hand in hand and head over to a reception desk. I give my name, the one on my birth certificate, and we take a seat in the waiting area. I gulp when we take a seat across from a heavily pregnant woman. She looks to be early thirties, and she's sitting reading a book as she waits for her appointment. She rubs her swollen belly, and my eyes fixate on her stomach. What will I look like heavily pregnant? Would I be one of those women who is all bump, or would I put on weight everywhere? The harsh reality of my situation hits me. I have a baby growing inside of me. A real life, human being. A little person who is half of me and half of Archer.

"Miss Holton," a female voice announces, pulling me from my thoughts. Damon squeezes my hand as we stand and walk over to where the friendly-looking doctor waits for us. "Come through and take a seat."

We enter a small office that has a desk and two comfy chairs on one side, and an office chair on the other. On the wall are various posters about pregnancy and birth. She places her arms on the table and looks at me.

"So, Eliza, you have come for a scan today. How far do you think you are?"

I grip Damon's hand tightly. "About nine weeks, give or take a week."

She nods her head and gestures over to a hospital bed. "If you can pop yourself behind the curtain and take off your jeans and underwear and place the blue cover over you. As you are quite early on, we'll need to do an internal scan so we can get a good look."

Clearing my throat, I let go of Damon's hand and make my way over to the bed, drawing the curtains around me. On shaky legs, I undress my bottom half and lie down on the bed. I announce that I'm ready, and she pulls back the curtain and gestures for Damon to take a seat beside me. Damon comes and takes the empty chair, and he reaches for my hand and holds it in his, rubbing his thumb back and forth in comfort.

"Okay, if you can open your legs for me lovely, that's it," she tells me. She types on a keyboard in front of her before she pulls a contraption from the side, and she covers it with a condom and lots of gels. "Now this may feel cold. Just try to relax," she tells me as her hands disappear under the cover between my legs.

I shift slightly when the cold device enters me and she asks me if I'm okay. Nodding, I watch as she moves the device around inside me, busy looking at the screen in front of her. "Well, you're definitely pregnant, Eliza," she announces, smiling over at me. "Would you like to see?"

I nod my head, turning my attention to the screen as she turns it towards us. The screen is black, but in amongst the darkness is a small circle with what looks like a peanut and a small white light flickering in and out.

"This is baby," she tells us, pointing at the peanut shape blob on the screen. "And that light you can see flickering in and out is the baby's heart beating."

"Woah," Damon states, leaning in closer to get a better look. "It has a heartbeat already?"

"Yes," she replies, smiling at him. "You look to be about eight weeks pregnant. Was the pregnancy unplanned?"

I tear my eyes away from the screen, and I nod my head. "Yes, it's unplanned. I'm on the pill, or I was until I did the tests."

The doctor nods her head. "Well, how about we print you a scan photo and then you can pop your bottoms back on and we can have a chat?"

I take one last look at the tiny heartbeat before she turns the screen away and types away on the keyboard.

Five minutes later, I'm dressed, and we're seated back at her desk. "So, Eliza, you have told me the pregnancy is unplanned. Have you decided if you want to progress with the pregnancy?"

I shake my head. "No. To be honest, I think I've been in denial up until now. I mean, I know I'm pregnant. I've been having the morning sickness and the tiredness but it's only now, seeing it on the screen, that it's sinking in that this is real."

The doctor nods her head and offers me a sympathetic smile before her gaze turns to Damon. "I take it you are dad?"

Damon nods his head, squeezing my hand. "Yes, I'm the father."

"Well, you do, of course, have options, Eliza. If you decide you do not want to go ahead with the pregnancy, we can book you in for a termination. We can give you medication that will cause the pregnancy to end."

"So, I wouldn't need an operation?" I ask her, surprised.

"No. The tablets would cause the pregnancy to end, and it would cause you to bleed. It would feel like a heavy period. We'd keep you in for the day to be sure that the pregnancy has come away. Then we'd invite you back for a scan and a pregnancy test to ensure that everything has come away naturally."

"I'm not sure what I want to do. Do I have some time to think things through?"

"You do," she says, smiling. I wonder how many young girls who have ended up in my situation walk into her clinic every day. "We can perform a non-surgical termination until twenty-four weeks, but the earlier you decide, the easier this will be."

She holds out an envelope. "Here are your scan pictures. Just get in touch and book an appointment when you're ready to decide what you want to do. We are here to support whatever decision you make."

I'M LOST IN MY OWN THOUGHTS ON THE DRIVE BACK FROM THE clinic. I have a scan photo of the baby in my bag, but I can't bring myself to look at it. It all feels so real now. I saw its little heart beating on the screen, a little light flickering on and off. I can't wrap my head around the fact that Archer and I have made a life. That tiny bean on the screen has the potential to grow up and be a living person who will have hopes and dreams. I shake my head to rid myself of thoughts of this baby as a person. After all, I'm likely going to terminate.

"Are you okay?" Damon asks me, glancing my way with a look of concern.

I nod my head. "It's real Damon. This is really happening."

"It is princess. But what you do about it is completely your choice."

I swallow, my emotions making me tear up. "I know you think I should tell him, but if I decide to have an abortion, then he can't know. He would try to stop me. You know how controlling he is."

Damon doesn't answer me straight away. "You're right, he would. I guess, coming at it from a guy's point of view, I would want to know."

I sigh. I know he's right, but Archer can't know about this baby. Not yet anyway. I wish I could talk to Vee about this, but her loyalty is with Archer, not me. I can't trust her and that hurts my heart.

"Right now, I could really do with a girlfriend to talk this through with."

Damon looks over at me and he slows the car and does a U-turn in the road. "Er, home is that way."

"We're making a detour. I think I know just what you need."

FIVE MINUTES LATER, WE PULL UP OUTSIDE A LARGE, DETACHED house. I arch a brow in question at him.

"Emma's house. My sister."

I realise he has brought me to have some girl talk with Emma. We both climb out of the car, and he waits for me to reach him. I step up on my tiptoes and throw my arms around his neck.

"Thank you. For everything. For giving me a place to stay, for being there for me, especially today."

He relaxes, and he places his arms around my waist, returning my embrace. "You going soft on me, princess?" he asks in a teasing tone.

"Maybe a little but tell anyone and I'll have to kill you."

We pull away from each other, chuckling, and Damon clears his throat and scratches at his head. "Come on, let's head inside."

The house is a hive of activity when we enter. Noah comes charging into the hallway from the right. He's wearing a knight's outfit and wields a sword in his hands.

"Uncle Day!" he exclaims, his face lights up with excitement. Damon swings him up into his arms and spins him around. "Uncle Day, you'll make me dizzy," Noah says, giggling. Oliver must hear the commotion as two seconds later, he comes charging through. He is also dressed in a knight's outfit.

"Mummy, Uncy Day's here!" Oliver stops in his tracks when he sees me, and he suddenly goes all shy and unsure.

I crouch down to his level and smile at him. "Hi, Oliver. Do you remember me? I came to your great grandmas for dinner the other week."

He scrunches his face as he studies me, trying to place me, and he shakes his head and holds out his sword.

"Is this yours?" I ask, and he nods his head. "That's a cool sword. How many dragons have you killed with it?"

He scrunches his nose up and giggles. "We're killing bad knights, not dragons. Dragons aren't real."

I giggle along with him. "Silly me. You're right."

"Well, well, this is a pleasant surprise." Emma comes through from the back of the house. She has a cup in one hand and a tea towel in the other. "Eliza! It's great to see you again. Come through." She gestures with her hand towards the kitchen, and I follow behind Damon.

"Nick, look who's here, and he brought a girl, again," Emma teases, turning around and winking at her brother.

"Hey Day. Eliza, nice to see you again," Nick says from where he sits in front of the television; the football is on.

"I was thinking, me and Nick could take these two to play some footy on the field. It'll give you a break and a chance to get to know princess."

"Are you a real princess?" Noah asks me from over his uncle's shoulder.

"No. I'm not and your uncle needs to stop calling me one," I reply, giving Damon the eye, to which he just grins at me.

"Come on, get your trainers on and grab your footballs," Damon tells them and yelling in excitement, they both take off to find their shoes.

"Tea or coffee?" Emma offers.

"Er, neither. I'm kind of off both at the moment. Do you have coke or lemonade?"

"Sure," she nods. "Diet coke, okay?" she asks me, heading over to the fridge.

"Perfect thanks." I take a seat at the island, and she brings my drink over and she sits down beside me. Two seconds later, the boys come charging through the kitchen with Damon and Nick hot on their heels.

"Enjoy the peace," Damon says, and he winks at me and gestures with his head towards his sister. I know what he is trying to say. He's telling me to talk through my situation with her.

We watch them head out through the back gate to the field. "Let's hope they wear them both out, and then they'll just want to chill when they get back."

"They're full of energy, that's for sure," I say, smiling, cupping my drink with my hands.

"It's exhausting," she agrees, "but I wouldn't be without them."

I nod my head. "They are adorable."

Emma places her cup down and she studies me. "So, still just friends?"

I realise she's asking about me and Damon. "Yep, just friends. My life is complicated right now. Damon doesn't need my kind of complicated."

"Complicated as in a guy?" she asks, and I sigh in response.

"Ah, it's a long story, but let's just say I don't let many people close and, well, recently I did and they betrayed me. They lied and used me."

Emma tucks her blonde hair behind her ear and bobs her head. "He broke your heart."

I shrug my shoulders. "He gained my trust, and I don't trust easily, and now, well now, everything is just spiralling." I pause and take a drink. "You know about the Aces, right?"

She scoffs. "Everyone knows of the Aces. The four families, the society."

"Well, they brought me here to marry one of them. They had it all arranged, and I'm supposed to just fall in line with their plans like a good little girl."

"Wow," she exclaims, shaking her head in disbelief. "And which one are you supposed to marry?"

I laugh. "Archer Savage. The worst one of them all."

Emma chews on her lip as she processes. "I had heard rumours of arranged marriages between the families, but it's the thing you see in films, not in real life. Is he the one who hurt you?"

I bob my head in reply. "And to make things worse, my grandfather has me over a barrel because if I don't go back and marry Savage, he'll put my little brother back in foster care and provide the folder of evidence of my teenage stupidity to the police."

"Shit."

"Yep. Welcome to my fucked-up life. But that's not all. It gets better," I tell her. "I'm pregnant."

Emma arches a brow. "And the father is?"

I laugh, seeing where her thoughts are leading. "It's not Damon's. Trust me, it would be so much easier if it were. Archer Savage is the father."

"Ah," she replies, grimacing. "You are in a pickle. How do you feel about the pregnancy?"

I sigh and shake my head, looking out towards the garden. "Honestly. I feel lost. I'm not ready to be a mum. Babies were not part of my life plan until way down the line. But then I have to marry Archer anyway if I want to keep my brother safe and part of the deal is a child before I'm twenty-one. I guess this way I play my part a little earlier than planned."

Emma reaches out and puts her hand over mine. "It's your life, Eliza. No one else's. If you're not ready, then that is okay."

I smile at her, and she squeezes my hand. "Did you feel ready when you found out you were pregnant with the boys?"

She scoffs and shakes her head. "Absolutely not. I was only nineteen and Nick and I had only been together a year. Honestly, I don't think you ever feel ready."

"I feel so trapped. Like my life isn't my own anymore. I wanted to have an abortion, but then I had the scan this morning and I saw its little heartbeat and now, now I just don't' have a fucking clue."

"I take it Archer doesn't know?"

I nod my head.

"And how do you think he'd react?"

I snicker and rest my head in my hands. "I've thought about this a lot. He's a lot of things. He's arrogant, a bully, and he thinks he's in charge, but he is loyal to his family." I shake my head. "It's more complicated than that though, and it's too long-winded to explain."

Emma gets up and heads over to a cupboard. I smile when she comes back to the table, waving a large chocolate bar in her hands. "Seeing as we can't drink, chocolate is the next best thing to help us think through this dilemma."

I laugh and accept the sizeable chunk she offers me. "Honestly, as much as I hate him right now. I think he'd make a good dad."

"And you're marrying him anyway, right?"

"I am." I double blink on hearing myself admit this. Fuck. I really am going to marry him.

"Look, I'm no expert. I can only speak from experience." She pops a piece of chocolate in her mouth. "I was terrified when I found out I was expecting, but when I held those boys in my arms, it felt like the rightest thing in the world. Being a mum is exhausting and emotional, but they are my life."

"So, you think I should keep it?"

Emma smiles at me and offers me another chunk of chocolate. "That's your decision to make. But if you go ahead with the pregnancy, look at it this way. You'll have a roof over your head and money, and you'll hold the power then. You'll be giving both families an heir. And as much as this Archer sounds like a conceited arse, he would protect your child. And look, don't shoot me, but he may have hurt you, but you love him, don't you?"

I release a long sigh. "Truthfully, I don't know how I feel. I just know when I was with him, everything else went away. He and I. We're so alike. It was like finding the other broken half of me when I met him. He just knew what I needed and what made me tick. Does that sound stupid?"

Emma chuckles. "No, it doesn't. Look. You don't have to decide right now. Give yourself some time to think it through."

She's right. I don't have to decide today, but the clock is ticking and the longer I leave this decision, the harder it will be.

Emma grabs her phone from off the worktop. "What's your number? Let's catch up next week for coffee. I know a great little place just outside of the bay, away from prying eyes."

I give her my number and I honestly feel so much better having talked it through with her. Damon has been great, but having another female to talk to, especially one who got pregnant in her teens, has been really helpful.

CHAPTER NINE

ELIZA

There's a sizeable crowd at the football match tonight. Hawk Bay is playing local rivals Beaumont Hill, and according to Kit, it's always neck and neck when the two teams play each other. We pay our entry and take our seats in the stands. Archer text me to say he'd pick me up, but like I am going to let that happen. He thinks he can just barge back into my life, and I'll just accept it. Well, he's got another thing coming. Calvin dropped me off. I'm more than capable of going to watch a match on my own. I'm scrolling on my phone, waiting for the match to start, when someone sits down in the seat next to me.

"Scar."

Sighing, I look up at Archer. Vee plops herself down next to him and Seb comes over and takes the seat to my right, Rafe taking the one beside him. Vee has gone all out for the match. She's wearing blue and yellow face paint stripes on her cheeks, and she has blue and yellow scrunchies in her hair. Vee's even done a banner that says 'Team Kit'. She gives me an uncertain smile and I bob my head slightly in acknowledgement to her. It's a chilly night so I'm wrapped up and wearing a hat and gloves. Vee leans over Archer and offers me a flask.

"Tea, one sugar. To keep you warm," she informs me. She chews on her lip, waiting to see how I'll respond.

"Thanks," I mumble, taking the flask from her. I'm touched

that she brought me tea. She rummages in her bag and passes another flask to Rafe and Seb.

"Ooh, look," Vee says excitedly, hitting Archer on the arm. "Kit's coming out." She jumps to her feet and cupping her hands around her mouth, she hollers his name as loudly as she can.

Kit is chatting away with a friend, but he looks up at hearing his name and I jump to my feet and wave along with Vee. Kit reddens in the cheeks but smiles at us both and waves back before going off to warm up for the game.

"Is she always like this?" I ask Seb as I sit back down in my seat.

Seb snickers and nods his head. "You should see her when she watches me and the lads play rugby. It seriously cringe."

"I heard that!" Vee pipes up, leaning over Archer and pointing at her twin. "You love it really."

Seb cocks a brow at me and winks. "She brought a megaphone once and got escorted off the grounds."

I laugh along with him. I can just see her doing something like that, too. Vee catches my eye and smiles sheepishly at me. I swallow and look away. I can't just forget about what she did. What they all did.

Seb nudges me in the arm to get my attention. "Dear old Wilbur's even shown up." He gestures with his head to our right a few rows down, and I grimace when I see Wilbur and Alexis sitting in the stands. Wilbur catches my eye and nods his head in greeting. A satisfied smile crosses his face when he sees' Archer sitting beside me. I hate the man. I hate everything he stands for.

"You look like you want to hurt him something bad, Little Red," Seb comments, watching me as I glare at Wilbur.

"I want to hurt everyone who has hurt and betrayed me. Even you," I tell him, and he pouts at me.

"Look at this gorgeous, cute face. You can't want to hurt this face?" When I continue to glare at him, he laughs, but his face drops into a serious frown. "I'm truly sorry, you know. I always wanted you to be a part of our inner circle. I see how good you are for Archer, and I want you to stick around."

"I have no choice but to stick around, Seb. Dear old Wilbur's making sure of that, but how can I truly trust any of you again?"

Seb sighs and gently nudges my arm with his. "You can trust us. I promise you. You're one of us now."

"The games starting," Archer growls, and I pull my attention from Seb. I realise the other three have all been listening to our conversation. Vee sighs and looks away, looking like someone stole her sunshine. Archer just mutters something under his breath and turns his full attention to the game. It's too hard being around them all again. I feel like I fit in with them, even if I shouldn't. Worse than that, I enjoy their company and try as I might, I can't find it in me to keep up the hate. Does that make me weak? Maybe it does.

Fifteen minutes into the game, Kit makes a pass that sets up a shot for their striker and he scores. He and Kit celebrate together, patting each other on the back. Vee and I are on our feet shouting his name and cheering him on. One player from the opposing team walks past Kit and shoulder checks him. Kit says something to him and the player doubles back and snarling says something back to Kit. Kit explodes, charging at the other player and taking him to the ground. He raises his fist, but he doesn't get a hit in as two of his teammates pull him up off the guy. The ref blows his whistle and produces a red card, resulting in a series of 'Boo's from across the stadium.

"What's going on?" I ask no one in particular, standing to my feet and watching as my brother glares at the other player as he strides off the pitch. I don't miss the fact that his fists are clenched at his sides. My brother is brimming with anger.

"That fucker said something to wind him up," Archer concludes. A deep frown is on his face as he studies the smug opposition player who is laughing with his teammates at Kit getting sent off.

"He'll be gutted he got carded," I say, biting my lower lip. I watch the coach say something to my brother before he heads off into the changing rooms. "I need to check he's okay."

Archer tugs on my sleeve. "They won't let you through to him until the match has finished, so you may as well sit back down."

Begrudgingly, I retake my seat. Vee and I make sure we 'boo' loudly every time the player who got Kit sent off touches the ball. He looks up at the sound of our boo's and he winks at us both and blows us a kiss. Cocky fucker. Is it bad of me to hope that someone tackles him and does it badly?

When the final whistle blows, it's to a loss of four to one. Beaumont Hill ran the game after Hawk Bay went down to ten men. We had no chance. They all celebrate, patting each other on the back and grinning whilst our team walks off, heads down and looking beaten.

I'm straight on my feet. Eager to get down and check if Kit's okay. When we turn to exit the stands, I notice that Wilbur and Alexis are no longer in their seats. Did they leave after he got sent off?

I don't invite them to follow me, but they all do anyway. Archer puts his hand on my lower back, and I pull away and glare at him. He doesn't get to touch me anymore. We reach the tunnel down to the changing rooms and a security guy stops us, but one word from Archer and he lets us through. We wait for the players to change and start filing out. Kit comes out with one of his buddies, his head down, looking totally pissed off.

"Kit," I say, trying to get his attention. He looks up frowning but gives me a half-smile when he realises it's me.

"Hey guys," he greets flatly, as he walks over to us.

"What happened? What did that guy say to you?" I ask him.

Kit chews on the side of his mouth and looks from me to Archer and back again. "It was nothing you need worry yourself about, sis."

I place a hand on my hip and stare at him, brow arched. He

should know me better than that. "I know you, and it takes a lot to rile up that temper of yours."

"Was it something about Scar?" Archer asks him, folding his arms across his chest and studying my brother's cagey posture.

Kit sighs and looks at me from under those long eyelashes of his. "He said stuff about the leaked tape and said some disgusting things about you, sis."

"What kind of disgusting things?" I ask, my gaze narrowing. I'll deal with that fucker.

"I'm not repeating what he said, but I would not stand by and let him speak about you like that. The boys should have let me hit him. At least that would have been worth being sent off for," he growls, kicking at the floor with the heel of his trainer.

"Well, I'm glad they stopped you. Otherwise, you'd have been looking at a ban and your team needs you. Don't worry about that fucker, Kit. It's just name calling. Sticks and stones and all that jazz." I attempt to reassure him it doesn't matter what the other guy said, but he still looks unconvinced.

We all walk out to the car park together and Kit looks around as if looking for someone. "Granddad said he'd take me home. He must've had to leave," he says, the disappointment clear in his voice.

"You know Wilbur," I say, shrugging my shoulders. "Probably some business emergency."

Archer and I share a look, and we both know what the other was thinking. Wilbur likely left when Kit got sent off. No doubt unhappy that Kit has shown up the Alderman name.

"Calvin's picking me up," I tell him, wrapping my arm around his shoulder, which is getting increasingly hard as he keeps growing and getting taller.

"Actually, he isn't," Archer pipes in, clearing his throat. "I texted him and told him I'd drop you off."

I glare at him. Who does he think he is? "Looks like we need to call an Uber, then."

Archer sighs and he shakes his head at me. "Just let me drop you both off. You can give me the silent treatment all the way there and pretend I don't exist."

This brings a chuckle from Seb, and I turn my frosty glare on him. He holds up his hands and backs off, but something snags his attention. "That the fucker talking shit about your sister?"

We all follow his line of sight and see that tall, cocky Beaumont player who caused my brother's red card.

"That's him alright," Kit snarls as he watches the guy swagger into the car park, laughing and joking with his teammates.

"Take Scar home, Vee," Archer orders. He's suddenly no longer interested in being up in my space at every opportunity.

"What are you going to do?" I ask him, knowing he's up to something.

"Just do as you're told for once, Scar. Go with Vee and Kit and I'll see you at school tomorrow."

A part of me wants to tell him I'm not his to order about, but I know him well enough now to know he'll just throw me over his shoulder and chuck me in Vee's car if I don't do as he asks. Scowling at him, I turn on my heels and stomp over to Vee's car. Yes, I know I'm being dramatic, but he somehow knows how to push all my buttons. Vee unlocks the car and we all pile in. As we exit the car park, it's just in time to see Archer, Seb and Rafe circle around said player.

"What will they do to him?" I ask Vee as I look behind as we pull away.

"They'll make sure he knows he doesn't get to talk shit about one of our own without paying the consequences. Like it or not, Eliza, you are one of us and we protect our own."

I don't argue with her. She is wrong, but I don't have the energy to protest. I'll never truly be one of them. I'll always be an outsider.

CHAPTER TEN

ELIZA

I'm lounging on my bed; it's a Tuesday evening and I'm binge-watching my favourite Netflix show with Damon. We're both half-watching the television and half scrolling on our phones. Damon sits up and nudges me, fixated on his phone.

"Look at this," he says, and I lean over to look at his phone screen, curious what has him so focused. It's an online news article by the local gazette paper. The headline reads 'Promising local footballers' career in tatters after a terrible accident.' My eyes widen when I see the photo of the player. It's the guy who got Kit sent off. The guy that when I left the car park that night after the match, Archer had insisted they would deal with him. I immediately bring up his number and hit call. He answers on the second ring.

"Scar," he greets. "Everything okay?"

"Did you do it?" I ask him. I don't know why I'm asking him when deep-down I already know the answer.

"Do what?"

"The player who got Kit sent off. Did you purposefully drive over his foot and cause him an injury that may mean he'll never play professionally again?"

There's a silence from the other end of the line for a second. "No one talks about you that way and gets away with it, Scar. He's lucky I only broke his foot and left his pretty face untouched."

"He'll have you prosecuted," I exclaim. What was he thinking?

This brings a loud laugh from him. "You think he's going to tattle and tell anyone how it really happened? You seriously think that if my brothers and I tell him he keeps his mouth shut that he'd do anything but what he's told. Haven't you learned yet, Scar? We make the rules around here and everyone obeys them."

I roll my eyes at his cocky confidence. "You didn't need to do that for me."

"Yes, I did. No one disrespects you like that. I told you, Scar, I protect what is mine, and you're mine."

"How many times are we going to have this conversation, you big buffoon? I am not yours." I end the call and throw my phone down beside me. I look Damon's way when I notice he's unusually quiet, and he's looking at me with a grin on his face.

"Did you really just call him a buffoon?"

I break out into a grin and we both start laughing. My phone rings again and I groan expecting it to be Archer, but it's a number I don't recognise. Intrigued, I answer it.

"Hello."

"Eliza Alderman. The Elders have requested your attendance at a meeting this evening. Please come to the lodge at nine and come alone."

"Wait, I..."

The line goes dead, and I swear in frustration at my phone. "Fucking Elders."

"Fuck them. Don't go," Damon says, handing me the bowl of popcorn.

I snicker. "If there is one thing Archer made clear. You come when summoned. I can't ignore them; the consequences aren't worth it."

He laughs. "What are they going to do?"

I don't laugh along with him. "You've heard the rumours, right? Well, they're all true. You obey a call, or they'll make you pay. This society has the power to make people disappear, Damon."

"I don't like it," he says, frowning. "At least let me drive you up there and wait for you?"

I shake my head firmly. "No, not a chance. Besides, no one is supposed to know where the lodge is. I'll order a taxi."

"If they knew you were pregnant, I bet they wouldn't summon you like this," he growls, looking really unsettled.

"Well, they don't and besides, what's the worst they could want me for?"

An hour later, I take the key they gave me on the night of my swearing in ceremony and unlock the door. A masked man takes my coat, and silently gestures for me to follow him. We don't go towards the room where they held my ceremony, instead he heads in the opposite direction and up a small flight of stairs. The place is eerily quiet.

We come to a stop before two double doors, and he raps loudly twice. A firm voice calls for us to enter. The man opens the door and stands to the side, holding it open for me. He never once makes eye contact with me. It's like I don't exist.

I walk into the dimly lit room and falter when I see who else is here.

"Eliza. Take a seat please," I recognise his voice as the one who conducted my ceremony. They're all wearing stupid masks again to conceal their identity.

Composing myself, I walk towards where the three Aces are sitting and take the empty seat beside Archer.

"We have a job for you all," the elder announces, and he places a file on the table that sits between us and the four Elders.

Archer reaches forwards and grabs the file. "We'll do the job. Eliza doesn't need to help."

"Eliza will join you on this job," an Elder states firmly before looking over at me. "It's time for her to show her loyalty to her Elders."

Archer frowns as he looks at the contents in the folder and I'd be lying if I said I wasn't curious.

"You'll go straight from here to the private jet that will fly you out there. Everything you need will be waiting for you."

"Wait. Tonight?" I say in surprise, and one of the other elder's glowers at me.

"Do you have somewhere more important to be?"

"No," I reply with more confidence than I feel. "I just didn't think it would be tonight. What time will we be back tomorrow?" I have an appointment at the clinic tomorrow at nine. Damn.

The elder who addressed me scowls deeply. "What time you are back is irrelevant. We will inform the school of your absence, and you'll be back when you have completed your mission."

"You may leave," the one sitting to the left tells us, and I get to my feet when the boys do. "Oh, and Archer, you need to teach your mentee better manners."

Archer simply nods his head and places his hand on my lower back as he ushers me out of the room.

"You need to teach her better manners," I mimic as we walk down the stairs towards the exit. "Who does he think he is?" I snipe.

Archer grabs my wrist and pulls me to a stop, placing his hand over my lips. "Not here, Scar. The walls have ears in this place."

I'm about to tell him to get his hand the fuck off me when the front door opens, and I see a car waiting out front for us. It's Archer's.

Seb slings an arm over my shoulder. "Looks like you're coming to play tonight, Little Red. I hope you're a talented actress, because for this job you will need to be."

"What's that supposed to mean?" I growl, eyeing him with suspicion.

He simply winks. "You'll find out in good time." He removes his arm, following Rafe into the back of the vehicle, leaving me to sit up front with Archer. Tutting, I climb inside and close the door.

"Aw, it's like old times. The four of us are together again," Seb says from the back. "Admit it, you've missed this, Little Red."

"Like a hole in the head," I grumble as I pull on my seat belt. My phone pings just before Archer starts the engine. I pull out my phone and look at my screen. It's Damon checking to see if I'm okay. I look up to find Archer watching me, a frown marring his perfect face.

"Let me guess...Silver. Is he worried about you?" The sarcasm drips from his voice.

"Jealous?" I ask, arching a brow.

Archer snickers. "Of him. He knows as well as you and me, Scar, that you're mine. Always have been, always will be."

"So arrogant and self-assured. Be careful Savage. One day, someone will throw you a curveball and knock that smug expression right off your pretty face."

"Glad you think so," he replies dryly as we pull away from the lodge.

"I bet I could knock the wind out from under you right now," I tell him, my anger getting the better of me.

He doesn't rise to it; he simply offers me a lazy smile. "Go on then."

It's on the tip of my tongue to tell him I'm carrying his child, but I reign in my emotions. I give him the finger before I turn my attention to the dark night outside my window.

I don't speak for the rest of the journey. Rafe calls Vee and lets her know we all won't be at school for the next two days and I hear him tell her I'm with them. He sighs at whatever she is saying to him down the phone. "Yeah, yeah, I know. We'll look after her. Of course. She's one of us now, whether she likes it or not."

I smirk at him through the rear-view mirror. One of them. I'll never be one of them. They'll never truly let me in.

"Where are we flying to?" I ask, no longer able to curb my curiosity.

"London," Archer replies.

"And what's in London?" I ask, seeing as he appears to suddenly be in a sharing mood.

"Trouble, Scar. That's what's in London. This weekend I need you to do exactly as I say, okay?"

As he looks at me, I study him. I can see that he's unsettled about me going on this mission and that has my anxiety levels up. "I'll be on my best behaviour."

His lips quirk up at the corner. "That was a little too easy."

The private jet flies us into London and I'm honestly exhausted by the time our driver drops us at the apartment block. Of course, the Aces have housing in London and, of course, it's the penthouse suite of an apartment block that gives you a superb view of London.

No one prepared me for how tiring early pregnancy is. I have been sleeping a lot and when I haven't been sleeping, I've been tired and constantly yawning.

"This is extravagant," I comment as I stand in the middle of the open plan living space and take in the floor to ceiling glass windows that show off London at night. The place looks like something you'd see on the cover of a magazine or the type of place I've imagined a movie star staying in.

"Only the best is good enough," Seb says, throwing himself down on a very large and comfortable looking leather sofa. Across from it is a media wall like no other with a gorgeous wrap around fireplace.

"So, what's the plan?" I ask as I watch Archer walk over to what looks to be like a control panel and start tapping lots of buttons.

"We party tonight, Little Red. We can't come to London and not enjoy the nightlife."

I shake my head, yawning. "You guys can party all you like, but I need a bed and sleep."

Seb rolls his eyes and tuts at me. "When did you become such a bore?"

Since I started growing a baby inside me and it's taking all my energy, I want to say, but I just grin at him and stick my tongue out. "It's late, and it's a weeknight. You party away. I, however, am getting changed and going to sleep."

"Suit yourself. Shall we say ready in fifteen guys?"

Archer moves to the kitchen, and he grabs two cups out of the cupboard. "I'm with Scar on this one. But you guys go ahead."

Seb snickers as he walks past Archer and pats him on the shoulder. "Aw, mum and dad want the place to themselves. I get it. I fucked a girl up against that very window the last time I was here. There's something so fucking hot about being so exposed but knowing that no one can actually see you. Plus, I got to admire the sights of London whilst nutting her."

I scrunch my face up. "You're disgusting and I now cannot look at that window and enjoy the view without that image in my head." I point a finger at him. "And stop calling us mum and dad. We're not together and there will be no sex."

Seb sighs and shakes his head in disappointment. "Still in denial, I see. We all know you're addicted to our boy here. It's nothing to be ashamed of. I mean, we all know what he's packing down there and, well, if I was a girl, I'd be the same."

Archer grabs him and pulls him into a headlock, and I watch as the two of them goof around like two kids. "Quit talking about my dick."

"I'm just pointing out what she's missing." He laughs as he wrangles himself out of Archer's hold. "Time for me to shower and get ready for the ladies of London."

I shake my head as I watch him leave the room. How he has so much energy at this time of night is beyond me. "You can go out. I don't need a babysitter."

He doesn't answer me as he moves around the kitchen. My

brows arch in surprise when he comes my way and offers me a warm drink. "Hot chocolate, with caramel syrup."

"Uh, thanks," I say in confusion as I take it from him. My nausea has settled down over this last week and I think I'm finally over the worse of it.

"I'm going to go shower. Our room is the second one on the right."

"Our room?" I ask pointedly.

"There are three bedrooms. So, you're with me unless you'd rather share with Seb and whatever girl he brings back here tonight."

"You can sleep on the sofa out here and I'll take the bedroom. That would be the gentlemanly thing to do."

He smirks as he walks off towards the bedrooms. "We both know I'm no gentleman, Scar. You're sleeping next to me, so don't fight me on this."

I throw a cushion toward where he has just gone, and it lands on the floor with a thud. "Arsehole," I mumble to myself, leaning my head on the back of the sofa. I pull out my phone to see if Damon has read my text. I text him earlier when we were in the air to say I wouldn't be home tonight and that I'd explain later. It's one thirty in the morning, so I'm not sure if I should call. I debate for a few minutes. He answers on the fourth ring, and I can tell from his voice that I've woken him up.

"Princess, do you know what time it is?"

"I'm sorry," I say, wincing. "I just didn't want you worrying. I'm in London. Going to be here until at least late tomorrow night."

He's silent for a beat. "What's in London?"

I chuckle. "No idea. The Elders have sent us here on some job. That's all I know."

"They're making you go on a job. What kind of job? You're pregnant for fuck's sake!" his voice rises in tone.

"Look, I'll be fine. I'm sure I probably just have to put a dress on and look pretty."

"And what if it's not that? What if this job puts you in danger or you have to do something physically dangerous?"

I look towards the door before I answer to make sure no one is there. "I'm pregnant, Damon, not dying."

"I don't like this. Maybe you should tell Savage. He'd be able to pull you out."

"No," I tell him firmly. "I'm not telling him, and it will be fine. Stop worrying. Look, I'll call you as soon as I know more, okay?"

I jump when my phone is wrenched from my hand, and Archer puts it to his ear. "I'll make this clear. She isn't yours to worry about. She's safe with me. Nothing will happen to her." He cuts off the call and throws my phone down on the sofa. I gulp when his gaze fixes on me, and he strides and closes the small distance between us. He wraps a hand around my waist and pulls my body flush with his.

"What aren't you going to tell me?"

"Nothing," I say, plastering a smile on my face. "Nothing, really."

"You're lying," he states, studying me with suspicion. "You blink more when you're not being truthful."

"I do not," I protest. "Look. I've just not been sleeping well with everything that has happened. Damon's just worried that I'm exhausted."

He smirks. "That's because I'm not there, Scar. We both know I keep the nightmares away." His expression turns serious. "I'll call our doctor tomorrow and ask him to write you a prescription."

"I don't want tablets," I say, shaking my head. "I just need a couple of decent night's sleep."

He looks down at me, holding my eyes prisoner with his. "I miss you in my bed, Scar." He looks like he's going to say more, but then he pulls back and offers me his hand. "Come on. Don't fight me. You're tired, you need sleep, and I can keep the nightmares away. Just for tonight, don't fight this."

I look at his outstretched hand and then up at him. He looks tired too and I wonder what is keeping him up at night. He releases a sigh when I place my hand in his and he guides us to our bedroom.

On the bed are a pair of pyjama shorts and a vest top. I go to ask but then I think why bother. They are always prepared in every situation. I pick up my night clothes and head to the bathroom and I hear him snicker as I walk away. He no doubt thinks I'm ridiculous getting changed in the bathroom, but clear boundaries need to be set. He doesn't get to see me naked anymore.

When I come back into the bedroom, he's already in bed and he's staring out at the view of the London skyline. The bed is huge but warm and inviting and I sigh in pleasure when I sink down into the extremely comfortable mattress. "Oh wow, is this thing made from magic because it is beyond comfy?"

He doesn't answer me, but I'm not surprised when he moves closer behind me and spoons me, placing a possessive hand over my waist. He nuzzles into my neck, and I try not to sigh at how good it feels to have him so close.

"Sleep, Scar. I'll chase the nightmares away tonight."

CHAPTER ELEVEN

ELIZA

I wake the next morning and moan in pleasure. Something has woken me and whatever it is it feels good. I smile in my sleep as a wave of need passes through me.

"You're soaking wet for me, Scar," says a voice in my ear before a warm tongue licks up my neck.

That's when I fully wake up and realise why I'm feeling so good. Archer has his hands in my underwear and is playing with my clit.

"Archer," I protest weakly. "We can't do this."

He sucks the skin on my neck into his mouth. "We can. Just let go and feel, Scar. I just want to give you pleasure. Don't tell me you don't miss this. I know you do." He grinds his hips into my behind and I groan when I feel his rock-hard cock against me. His fingers don't stop in their mission to wreck me, and I moan aloud when he sinks a finger inside of me.

"That's it, baby, fuck my fingers. Does that feel good?" His voice is all husky and laced with desire. It makes my body pulse with need.

"We're not together anymore," I whisper as I try to shake some sense into my brain.

He slips a second finger inside of me and I rock my hips, chasing what I need. "You like that don't you?"

"No," I half moan. With all the willpower in the world, I place my hand on his and stop his attempt to seduce me. "You don't deserve me fucker."

He's silent for a beat, and then with a deep sigh, he removes his fingers. I expect him to be angry and to call me a tease. But he surprises me when he softly kisses my cheek, gently squeezes my waist and says, "Then I'll spend however long it takes to prove to you I deserve your forgiveness."

I lie there staring after him as he leaves the bed and strides into the ensuite, closing the door behind him. Two second later the sound of running water tells me he is in the shower. I roll over and shove my head into my pillow, bashing my fists into the duvet. It's hard to say no, when your whole body is begging for him. I can deny it all I want, but I still want him. I thirst for him. I wonder if he's in there pleasuring himself seeing as I won't give him what he needs. Biting my lip I let my hand drift down into my bed shorts, I can't help it, he got me all wound up. I circle my clit and sigh in pleasure. I prefer his hand on me, but a girl's got to do what a girl's got to do. I'm so lost in chasing the orgasm he failed to give me I scream out when a hand grabs my wrist.

"What do you think you're doing, Scarlet?"

I open my eyes to find him leaning over me, drops of water, run down his chiselled chest. "You started it," I hiss in defiance.

"I did. And if I don't get to finish it, then you don't get to have an orgasm. You want to come, then it will be by my hands or my tongue." He pulls my hand that he has in his grip, and I watch open-mouthed as he lifts it to his lips and sucks my fingers into his mouth. His tongue swirls around them and his eyes roll back in his head. "I've missed your taste, Scar."

My core pulses with need and I'm a second away from saying fuck it to staying strong and begging him to eat me out when his phone rings on the bedside table.

Smirking at me, he takes one last lick of my fingers before he reaches over and grabs his phone.

"What?" he barks down the phone. "Okay, got it. We'll be there." He places the phone back on the bedside table and then his dark eyes are back on me. "Let's get something cleared up, shall we? Tonight, after this job is done, we are coming back to this hotel, and I am going to fuck you senseless. You can hate me; you can go back to pretending that you don't need me, but tonight we put it all aside and just be two people taking what they need."

I sit up, bringing my face just an inch from his. God, he's so annoyingly perfect. "We'll see about that." I pat his cheek patronisingly with my hand and drop a chaste kiss on his lips. "Sex is sex, Archer. I'm human I have needs. It's just cock in general I'm lusting for. It doesn't need to be yours."

He growls and grabs me by the waist, pulling me flush against him. "You're mine, Scar. No one will ever touch you again but me, and anyone who tries, I'll kill them. I'll beat them to a pulp and then I'll slit their throat. You get me?" He leans in and takes my bottom lip between his teeth and gently pulls. "I haven't been with anyone else since you, and no matter how much you fight this and deny me, I won't seek it elsewhere. One day soon, you'll wear my ring, and you'll take my last name and you'll be the only pussy I seek. No one else compares to you."

I take a deep swallow, my emotions getting the better of me. I hate it when he's like this. When he takes my breath away with his words and makes me feel things I don't want to feel. An angry, demanding Archer I can cope with, but this one here, now, who tells me I'm all he needs, he undoes me.

"I'm going to kiss you," I tell him. "But it means nothing."

A tiny smile touches his lips. "Sure, it doesn't."

"You're a smug, arrogant bastard," I hiss before I grasp him by the back of his neck and place my lips on his. It's like coming home. We meld together so perfectly. His tongue delves into my mouth and dances with my own. I kiss him like I may never get to kiss him again. When I pull back, we're both panting for breath and the air is thick with lust and need.

"Until tonight," he promises before he strolls out of the room, whistling to himself like he hasn't a care in the world.

"Fucker!" I shout after him and my answer is his throaty chuckle from down the hallway.

I grab my mobile and press call on a number I haven't used in a while.

"Eliza, hi!"

"Just to be clear, Vee, I haven't forgiven you, but I need you to talk some sense into me. Tell me not to have sex with Archer. Tell me he's a bastard and that I shouldn't ever let him back in."

Her answer is to giggle down. "Sorry girl, but as much as he is all those things, he's also like a brother to me and yes, I know what he did, what we all did was wrong. He is sorry. Don't you get it?" She sighs. "You can have him eating out the palm of your hand with a click of your fingers. He's never looked at any girl the way he looks at you. He looks at you like...like he'd burn down worlds to give you whatever you wanted."

"Bah, I knew I shouldn't have called you," I say sulkily.

"Just use him for sex, honey. Take it and enjoy it."

I laugh along with her before we both fall silent. "I miss you," she says. "I'm sorry I didn't tell you. It was wrong of me, and I swear it's you before my boys from now on."

"I miss you too," I admit with another sigh. I scrunch my nose up in intrigue when I hear the loud noise of an engine in the background. "Where are you?"

"Oh, didn't Archer tell you? I'm on my way to join you guys. Archer is bringing me in on a job."

"He is?"

"Yep, he said something about you not being ready for what's required."

"Oh, he did, did he?" I say, arching a brow. "Well, I'll guess I'll see you soon."

"So, are we talking again?" she asks me. I can hear the hope in her voice.

"We're talking, but you have a lot of grovelling to do and if you ever keep secrets from me again, we're done."

"Never again. I cross my heart and hope to die."

I chuckle. God, I have missed her. “No dying, please. I’ve had enough death in my life.”

“Okay, I’ll see you soon.”

I place my phone on the bedside table and ponder what Vee has just told me. I shower and change into clothes from the suitcase. How a suitcase full of my clothes was ready and waiting for me on the private jet is still a mystery. Once I’m dressed, I head into the main part of the penthouse to quiz Archer.

I find him sitting at the breakfast bar, a coffee in one hand and his phone in the other. Rafe is over by the cooker cooking eggs.

“Rafe has done you bacon and eggs,” Archer tells me, not lifting his head from his phone to address me.

“I’m not hungry,” I reply, taking a seat beside him. “A milky coffee will do, please.”

Rafe rolls his eyes. “What did your last slave die of?” he asks me as he grabs a cup and makes my drink for me.

“I had him murdered after he and his friends betrayed me,” I snipe with a sarcastic smile aimed his way.

“Don’t be like that Little Red. You know you love us really.” I jump at Sebs’ voice in my ear when he wraps his arms around my neck from behind and kisses my cheek.

“Jesus, you stink of alcohol,” I grimace, fighting the roll of nausea that I feel. “Seriously, Seb, some distance please.”

Laughing, he drops another kiss on my cheek before he pulls away and heads over to the fridge. I’m about to ask him what time he rolled in when two women enter the room from the direction of the bedrooms. Both women are dressed in tight, short dresses and heels.

Archer looks up when they giggle, and a deep frown mars his perfect face. “Leave. Now.”

Seb tuts and he saunters over to the two women, throwing his arms around the shoulders of them both. “Sorry about my friend, ladies. He’s such a grump in the morning. It’s probably because his fiancée's not putting out and he's feeling somewhat frustrated."

"I can help him out with that," one of the girl's purrs, giving Archer the eye.

"I'm standing right here," I bark, pulling the girl's attention to me.

Archer cocks a brow and stares my way.

"What?"

"So, you're mine when it suits."

My answer is to give him the finger, which has Seb chuckling again. "Ladies, let me escort you to the lift. I have a driver waiting in the foyer to take you home. Thank you for a truly memorable evening."

The brunette looks over her shoulder as they leave. "Call me anytime," she says, her eyes focused on Archer. Archer's answer is to smirk and shake his head before returning his attention to his phone.

I glare after her. Who does she think she is, propositioning him when she's just been told his fiancée is in the room? Classy girl!

"Earth to Eliza," Rafe says, waving his hand in front of my face.

I blink and give him daggers as I take my coffee from him. He's grinning at me like he knows that I'm pissed off at that girl. "You'll get used to that. He gets it all the time."

"I bet," I say dryly. I can deny it all I want, but Archer is a gorgeous guy. He commands a room when he walks in it. Of course, he has women falling at his feet. I cup my coffee between my hands and turn my attention to the man himself. "Why did you tell Vee I wasn't up for this job?"

Archer slowly looks up from his phone and looks at me. "Because you're not doing it."

I place the cup down on the island and I fold my arms across my chest. "Why aren't I doing the job?"

He sighs, as if he doesn't want to discuss this. "Because I don't want you doing the job."

"Do the Elders know you are bringing Vee in to do what they ordered of me?"

He places his phone down and gives me his full attention, his dark eyes capturing mine. "They won't find out. As far as they will ever know, you did the job, and you passed your first test of loyalty."

"What's the job?"

"Like I said, it doesn't matter, as you're not doing it. You can stay here tonight and enjoy some take away and Netflix."

I scoff. "Yeah, not happening, mate."

Shaking his head, he gets to his feet and goes to make himself another coffee. Determined not to let up, I follow behind him and when he turns, I'm practically standing toe to toe with him.

"What's the job?" I ask him, placing my hands on my hips and placing a hand on his chest to keep him where he is.

"This conversation is over," he growls, glaring down at me.

Seb strolls back into the room, so I use the opportunity. "Seb, what was my role in tonight's job?"

"Titty dancer, Little Red. The Elders needed you to be a lap dancer for a certain politician."

Archer tuts and I turn to see him glaring across the room at Seb. Seb shrugs his shoulders at him, then winks at me. "Archer didn't want you getting your girls out in front of strange men, Little Red. He wants your awesome tits all to himself."

"I'm doing the job," I say firmly. "We don't need Vee. I'm more than capable."

Archer half-smirks. "Have you ever given anyone a lap dance before, Scar? You need to look like you know what you're doing."

"Oh, and Vee knows what she's doing, does she?"

Rafe grins, staring off out of the window. "She sure does."

"Stop with your lurid thoughts of my sister," Seb orders him, throwing a tea towel at Rafe.

"Vee is professionally dance trained. You're not. She's a better fit for this job," Archer insists.

"Bullshit," I hiss, jabbing my forefinger in his chest. "You're just a possessive arsehole who doesn't want another man seeing my tits. They're just boobs, Archer. It's no big deal."

His face remains unwavering. "You're not doing it and that is that." He places his hands on my forearms and lifts me off my feet and to the side so he can get past me.

"I can do the fucking job!" I insist, chasing after him. I'm hopping mad. He thinks he can decide what I do and don't do. Do I really want to get my tits out and lap dance for some perverted old politician, no, of course not, but he's pissed me off and now I'm determined to do it. "I bet I can give just as good a lap dance as Vee."

Archer breathes through his nose and swearing under his breath, he strides over to the glass dining table and picks up a chair. I watch him as he walks into the middle of the lounge area and places the chair down in the centre and sits himself on it. "Show me what you got, Scar."

He cocks a brow, challenging me. Daring me to prove my point. "Seb, put some music on. Let's see what she can do."

I glance from Archer to Rafe and Seb, who are now both leaning side by side against the kitchen island waiting for me to take up the challenge. Seb grins wide as he presses a few buttons on his phone and a second later, sultry music plays through the room.

Archer leans back in his seat smirking, and points to his lap. He thinks I'll back down. Well, he's wrong. I reach for the bottom of my t-shirt and lift it over my head to reveal a black lace bra and I sway my hips as I stroll down to where he's waiting for me. I pull my hair from its messy bun and run my hands through my unruly waves, keeping my eyes on him. I stop a few feet from him, and I bite my lip and give him a sultry look. I run my hands seductively slowly up my thighs and around over my breasts. I give him my back and bend over slowly, trailing my fingers from my ankles up to my thighs. My hips sway seductively as I lift my hands above my head. I turn to face him and drop down onto my knees with my legs spread apart. Licking my fingers, I run them sexily down the valley between my breasts and stop just at the top of my panties. Biting my lip and winking at him in my best innocent face, I lean forward and slowly crawl towards him, making sure my hips are moving side-to-side. When I reach his chair, I run my hands up his legs, stopping just above his knees and I raise to my feet. I walk around his chair, coming to a stop behind him, and I throw one leg over his shoulder. Grabbing his hair, I tip his head back so he's looking up at me and I run my tongue over my lips. I shove his head forward and let go of his hair, releasing my leg and walking round to the front to face him. I drop onto his lap, my legs straddling him on either side of the chair. Holding on to the back of the chair, I lean back, arching my spine and I move my hips back and forth to the beat of the music. I sit up in his lap and smirking at him; I stand to my feet and give him my back. I bend over, ensuring that my arse is right there in his view, and I twerk like my life depends on it and smack myself on the bottom. Turning back around to face him, I place one bare foot on his shoulder, placing my intimate parts right near his face. Touching my breasts, I dance to the sultry beat of the music. I lift my leg down and drop myself back into his lap slowly so that my breasts touch every inch of his chest as I seat myself. Arching my spine again, I lean backwards, wrapping my feet around the legs of the chair to anchor me. I run my hand down the centre of my chest and along my spread legs before I slowly pull myself up and wrap my arms around his neck. Just as the song ends, I drop a soft kiss on his cheek.

"Is that good enough for you?" I whisper in his ear with a knowing smile as I feel his hard cock under me.

"Good, but not good enough," he replies gruffly, clearing his throat.

I rock my hips against him and chuckle in his ear. "You sure about that?"

He grasps my thighs to stop me from moving. "It was amateur. He'll spot that you're not a professional from the out." He reaches out and takes the white gold playing card charm I'm wearing around my neck. "You still wear this even though you say you hate me."

I snatch it from his hands into my own. "Don't make out this gift was special. You said yourself all females get one. I wear it because I'm expected to, as an Ace. Not because you gave it to me."

"Bullshit," he replies, a knowing and self-assured smile on his smug face. He grasps the back of my neck with his hands. "Did you ever read the engraving on the back?"

I hesitate with the snarky reply I had been ready to give. I didn't know there was anything engraved on the back. Keeping my eyes on him, I turn the silver playing card pendant over.

My queen. Always.

I gulp. He had that engraved on there for me. My heart thumps in my chest.

"Leave," he barks out into the room, and I remember that Rafe and Seb are both in the room. As I watch them leave, Seb mouths 'forgive him' to me.

"Don't' you get it, Scar. You're my queen. I knew it the moment you gave me sass that first night. I knew that night that gypsy or not, I had to have you. Can you blame me for not wanting another guy to see you like that? To have you on his lap turning him crazy with wanting you. I'm a possessive fucker. I want you all to myself. I want to be the only guy you ever do that for and the only guy that you ever give that come fuck me look to ever again."

"I hate you," I tell him. "I hate that I let you in and you hurt me, and I hate that I still fucking want you."

He sighs, placing his forehead against mine. "I know you do. I've said I'm sorry and in case you didn't notice, I don't say that to many people. Scar, I need you. I need to feel your skin against mine and I need to hear the way you moan my name when you come. Please let me have you."

My heart thumps in my chest as I war between my head and my heart. My head tells me to climb off his lap right now, to move as far away from him as possible, and tell him it's never going to happen. But my heart, my fucking traitorous heart, is begging me to give in to what we both know I need and want.

I rock my hips against him. "Okay."

He doesn't need telling twice. He pulls me to him and devours my lips with his. His kisses bring me to life again. They breathe much needed air into my lungs that I didn't know I needed. I run my hands through his hair and tug on the strands as I push my hips into his, wanting to get as close as possible to him. He reaches behind me and pushes my leggings down over my bottom and I lift my hips to assist him, my lips not leaving his. My underwear follows with them, and he discards them on the floor beside us.

"Gods, how I need you, scar," he groans in my ear as he nibbles on my earlobe.

"Please," I beg him. "No foreplay, just take me."

He growls in response, and I feel him reach between us and pull out his hard cock. I look down at his length and, impatient to feel him inside of me, I lift my hips and sink myself down onto him.

"Fuck," he hisses, leaning his neck back, his eyes rolling with lust. "Fuck, you feel perfect."

I don't move straightaway. I just savour the feel of him inside me. This is what I need. It's stupid and weak of me, but I need him. I place my hands on his shoulder and move my hips. He grabs the back of my neck with one hand, forcing me to look at him.

"Eyes on me the whole time. I want to savour it all."

With his other hand, he grasps my right hip and he pistons

up into me, meeting my hips as they create a steady, increasing rhythm.

"My queen," he says, his eyes never leaving mine.

I feel it in his gaze and his words. He makes me feel like the centre of his world. He looks at me like he would die for me if I asked him to. In this position, it feels so intimate. Our bodies are flush, our faces inches from each other as he fucks me like he never wants to let me go.

"Archer," I moan, arching my back and increasing the movement of my hips to chase the wave I feel building.

"It's okay, baby. I know what you need," he tells me as he presses his forehead against mine and rocks his hips harder, hitting that sweet spot. "Eyes on me as you come, Scar."

I nod my head, willing to agree to give him anything right now, so long as he makes me come. I cry out his name as I find my release, and he watches me enraptured. A few seconds later, he picks up his pace and moans into my ear as he spills his release deep inside of me.

We sit there for a second, just basking in post-coital bliss. Both of us are not ready to face the reality of our world. I'm a fool for letting this happen. There's no way he'll back off now. If anything, it's given him the drive to keep trying to win me over. He places a finger under my chin and forces me to look at him.

"I can hear the cogs turning in your head. Stop overthinking."

"That shouldn't have happened," I tell him, shaking my head.

He cups my face with his hand and looks at me with such tenderness it's hard to believe he's the same person who he presents out to the world. "Yes, it should, because we are meant to be, Scar. But not because someone decided us getting married would help their business, or because of some fucked up shit that happened with our parents." He takes my hand, and he places it on his chest. I can feel his heart thumping. "Because we're just meant for each other."

My heart aches at his words. Why can't I just forgive him and move forward? Because I'm scared. I'm scared that if I let him in again, he'll break me once more and the next time I won't survive. I cannot allow myself to love Archer Savage, because one way or another, loving him will destroy me.

"I'm doing the job," I tell him as I lift myself up off him and collect my leggings and knickers from off the floor.

"I don't want some pervert politician touching you," he grunts, grabbing my hand and pulling me back to him. "Besides, Vee is already on her way here." He nuzzles at my ear, sending shivers down my spine.

I place my hands on his chest and gently push him away. "Well then, she can keep you guy's company while I do what I need to do."

Archer shakes his head as he pulls up his trousers. He runs a hand through his unruly hair. "I won't be able to stop myself from ripping his head off, Scar, and that will piss the Elders off no end if I murder him."

I chuckle as I look at my reflection in the floor-length mirror. I have that just ravished look about me. My hair is all trussed up. Archer comes up behind me and wraps his arms around my waist, leaning his head on my shoulder.

"Look at how well we fit, Scar. You and me against the world."

I avert my eyes from our reflection and turn in his arms to face him. "What just happened doesn't change things, Archer. We're not together again."

The bastard scoffs. "You keep telling yourself that, Scar. Soon you'll be starting and ending your days in my bed, beside me."

Shaking my head, I take a step away from him to create some distance between us. "You're an arrogant sod, you know. It's not attractive."

He laughs and boy if it doesn't make my stomach flip. "Liar," he challenges, cocking a brow. "I should probably let the boys know the coast is clear."

I wince. Were we loud? "Do you think they heard us?"

Archer smiles at the same time he shrugs his shoulders. "With the noise you were making, calling out for god when you came, I'd say they definitely heard us."

I gawp at him in horror and slap his arm. "I wasn't that loud."

He fights a smile as he walks backwards away from me. His eyes do a slow peruse of my body from my feet to my head, and he bites his lip and fights a smile. "You were, Scar, and it was hot as sin. I love it when you moan my name."

The way he's looking at me as he retreats from the room has my core pulsing with need. Once more will never be enough with him. I'll always want more. When he's out of sight, I can't help but stray to thoughts of the baby growing in my belly. Our baby. I'm eight weeks now and time is running out. I think of how hurt he would be if I had an abortion and he found out. In some ways, it would serve him right for his deceit, but I'm not the type of person to use something like this to punish someone. How would he react if he knew I was carrying his child? Maybe he'd be angry, but then he's a possessive bastard and I can see him being pleased with himself for planting his baby in my womb. The caveman in him would beat his chest and celebrate his virility.

"Glad you two are done fucking because after my marathon session with those two honeys last night, I really need sustenance," Seb comments, as he strolls back into the room and winks at me. I can't help but flush red, and I self-consciously tidy my hair. Archer and Rafe follow closely behind him, and Archer gives me a lazy smile when he sees me redden at Seb's comments. "You really should nail her more often, Arch. It puts the colour back in her cheeks."

"Shut it, fucker," Archer says, swiping his friend across the back of the head as he fights a smile.

"So, did Little Red get her way? Is she doing the job?"

I arch a brow in challenge at Archer, daring him to say I can't, but I'm surprised when he sighs and says that I'm in for the job. "She's going to need some help, though." He looks at

Seb. "Can you call Kayla and see if she can come over and work with her for a couple of hours?"

Seb nods his head as he chews on a cold piece of toast from Archer's plate. "On it."

"Whose Kayla?" I ask, curiosity getting the better of me.

Rafe chuckles. He's so silent sometimes that I forget he's even there. "Oh, Kayla's an old friend."

Why do I get the feeling, there's more to that statement than I care to know?

"Wait!" I say, halting Seb with the phone halfway to his ear. "I've never been to London before; can we go sight-seeing first and then slut practice later?"

Archer studies me from where he leans against the kitchen island, his hands in the pockets of his joggers. "You heard our queen; she wants to go play tourist."

I clap my hands together in delight and excitement. "Thank you."

"Ahh, he just emptied his load. He'll give you the fucking stars if you asked him to right now," Seb chuckles. He dives behind the sofa when I hurl a cushion his way.

"Shut it with the sexual references, Seb. It's not funny," I say, scowling.

"It is, though," he shouts from his spot behind the couch. There's never a dull moment with him around.

ARCHER SUGGESTS WE HANG ON FOR ANOTHER HOUR BEFORE heading out to allow Vee time to arrive and join us. I retreat to our bedroom to brush my teeth and as I walk back into the bedroom, my mobile phone rings, and I see it's the clinic calling.

"Miss Holton?"

"Hi, yes, it's me," I say, popping my head around the door to check no one is within hearing distance.

"It's Doctor Turner. I believe you cancelled your appointment for today. I was just calling to see if you are okay?"

"Yes, I'm fine. Something last minute came up, that's all. Actually, can you book me in for antenatal care, please? I've decided to go ahead with the pregnancy."

"Of course. I'll get you booked in now for your twelve-week scan, and we'll get all your bloods done as well."

"Thank you. If you can e-mail my scan details to the address on your system, please?" I'd given them Silver's email when I'd provided my details. Knowing Archer and the Aces, they could be monitoring my emails. I wouldn't put it past them. Archer said they like to gather intel on all their members as collateral.

I breathe a sigh of relief when I put the phone down. Now I've made my decision, I feel I can breathe again, at least for a short while. I pull up Damon's number and type out a text to him.

Keeping the baby. Twelve-week scan date will be in your inbox shortly.

CHAPTER TWELVE

ELIZA

We arrive back at the penthouse around three in the afternoon. I can't deny I have enjoyed being with them all. Even Rafe had a joke with me at one point. Am I weak? They are worming their way back into my good graces and I'm going down without a fight. The truth is, for the first time in my life; I feel like I fit with these four. Archer because his dark depravity and icy demeanour calls to me. Seb because his humour and affection always puts a smile on my face, and Vee, because she gives me it straight, just what a girl needs in a best friend. Even Rafe has grown on me, he's quiet most of the time but I've learned that I value his opinion. He always has something meaningful to say, and he sees things that others miss. They tell me I'm one of them now, but am I? When the cards are dealt, will they stand by my side? Because I still fully intend to get leverage on Wilbur and use it to my advantage and there is no way in hell that my brother is joining the Aces.

"You're quiet," Archer comments, as he watches me change into leggings and a sports bra. Apparently, the mysterious Kayla is a professional dancer, and she is coming over here shortly to help me perfect my lap dancing skills for our mission tonight.

"Just thinking," I reply with a frown. I hate how perceptive he is of my moods.

I jump when Archer's hand appears in front of me. There's a little black box in his palm. "I bought this for you when we were out."

I take the box from his hand and turn around to face him. He rubs at the back of his neck, a sign that he's uncomfortable. I open the box and inside are two small four-leaf clover silver stud earrings.

"These are the ones I saw in that shop," I observe. "When did you go back and get them?"

He chuckles. "When you and Vee were busy admiring those engagement rings."

I grin. He's sneaky. I didn't even notice him buy anything while we were in there. My heart aches in my chest. He's doing it again, unsettling me with his attentiveness and thoughtful gestures. Can I really trust him again? This is the guy that blames my father for his mother's death and had transferred that blame to me. Could he ever move past that and want me for who I am and not resent me for something that happened all those years ago?

"Gifts won't fix things, Archer," I tell him with a weary sigh. My emotions are all over the place right now thanks to the pregnancy.

He reaches for my hand, and I allow him to take it. "I know that. I just wanted you to have them." He drops a kiss on my forehead. "Kayla should be here soon."

"How do you know her?" I ask, trying not to sound so interested.

I see him fight a smirk. "Kayla's an old friend."

"In other words, you've slept with her." I groan, rolling my eyes and snatching my hand from his. "Jesus, Arch, is there anyone you haven't slept with?"

"Many women, actually. I can be quite picky," he offers.

"Well, thank small mercies for that."

I try to fight him when he pulls me into his arms, circling them around my waist, and he looks down at me with those knowing dark eyes. "There's no need to be jealous, Scar. It was just sex, nothing more."

I arch a brow in response, snickering. "And does she know

that, heartbreaker?"

He scoffs at me, smiling. "I could always put that ring on your finger to make sure she gets the message."

I shove him playfully in the chest. "Not funny."

"Who says I'm joking," he says as he releases me and leaves me standing staring after him.

"Fuck!" I exclaim, clenching my fists. I'm a weak-arsed idiot. Why can't I just stay away? Having sex with him earlier was a stupid move. I need to make him work for it, to make him pay for how he deceived me and planned to use me for revenge. I straighten my spine and hold my head up high. No more pushover Eliza!

I hear him shout my name and, with my new resolve firmly in place; I walk into the main room. My steps falter when I see Kayla. Holy hell, she is gorgeous. Like Hollywood beautiful. She's about five-seven, with long willowy legs that go on forever without a stretch mark in sight. Her hair is black, long and shiny. She has one of those heart shaped faces with a perfect ski-slope nose and high cheekbones with glowing olive skin tone. She has to be a model. My insecurities rush to the surface. I know I'm slim, but my body is marked with scars, and I have some cellulite at the top of my legs. Not much, but I know it's there. At least she has tiny boobs. Archer likes tits and I know he loves mine. I watch the two of them talking away like old friends and he smiles at her in a way that makes my blood boil.

"You must be Kayla," I say, walking into the room with a confident smile plastered on my face.

"Hi, yes, that's me and you must be Eliza? Wow, I love your hair!" Her smile is warm and friendly, and it throws me off as she seems genuine. I don't know why, but I expected her to be a complete bitch who is up her own arse.

"Thanks. So, you're a dancer?"

"Was," she says with a nod. "I got signed up by a modelling agency a year back." She nudges Archer playfully. "This one put in a good word for me, and the rest is history."

Archer grins, shaking his head. "That was all you Kayla. Kayla recently did a shoot for Versace."

"Wow," I reply, smiling. My self-esteem just died a little more.

"And it was hot!" Seb whistles as he walks into the room and wraps an arm around Kayla's neck, dropping a kiss on her head. "I bet the sales of their lingerie went through the roof."

An underwear shoot, even better!

"Kayla!" Vee greets her warmly when she walks into the room. She's showered and changed into a cute little playsuit. The two girls hug each other like old friends. "Oh, you smell divine."

"It's the new Chanel fragrance," Kayla informs her.

Of course, it is.

I feel Archer's eyes on me and when I meet his, he's watching me with a smirk on his face. He walks over to me and slips an arm around my waist and guides me closer to where the girls stand. "Scarlet is helping us with a job tonight. I need you to make her look like the best lap dancer there is so that our target chooses her for a private dance." Archer kisses the top of my head and I see Kayla's look of surprise.

"Okay, now I need the gossip. Have you finally caught feelings for someone, Archer?" She waggles her finger between the two of us and grins in excitement.

I step slightly away from him and shake my head. "We're just friends," I insist, and I glare over at Seb when he snickers and murmurs 'bullshit' under his breath.

"Well," Kayla smiles at me, "any friend of Archers is a friend of mine. Shall we make a start? I was thinking over by the windows is enough space for us to practice."

Nodding my head, I follow her over to the floor to ceiling windows and I watch her as she puts down her bag and pulls out her phone. "I'll give you a demo of the routine I want you to master." She looks over at the boys. "Seb, do you want to be my assistant?"

Seb's eyes light up like all his Christmases have come at once. "Hell, yes!" He swings over the sofa and jogs over to where we are, picking up a dining chair as he passes. He places the chair down and sits himself on it. Winking at me, he leans back and cups the back of his head with his hands.

I chuckle at his eagerness and share a smile with Kayla. Okay, I admit it, the girl, despite being annoyingly perfect, is nice as well. Kayla fiddles with her phone and sultry music with a hypnotic beat plays out into the room. We all watch her enraptured and even I can't deny that Kayla can dance and it's hot! I fight a laugh when I turn to see Vee, whose eyes are practically popping out of her head. Rafe wraps an arm around her waist from behind her and he whispers something in her ear that has her grinning wider. I don't even want to know. Those two and their open relationship agreement is something I still can't wrap my head around.

"Think you can master that in the next two hours?" she asks me when she finishes her routine.

I nod my head, chewing on my lip, and jump slightly when I feel Archer's hand at my hip. "Scar has a natural rhythm, so I'm sure she'll pick it up, no problem."

Kayla nods and she looks expectantly at the three boys. "Well, go on. You can all find somewhere else to be. She won't be able to relax properly and let go with you three watching."

Seb groans as he stands from the dining chair, and he readjusts himself in his pants. No guesses needed what effect that lap dance has had on him. Archer bobs his head side-to-side. "I think I should stay. I need to know that she's ready and that she can handle this."

Kayla folds her arm over her chest and shakes her head at him. "No, she'll be distracted. I mean it. All of you out and don't come back until at least four thirty."

I hold my hands out and shrug as if to say, 'you heard her.' Sighing, Archer grabs his car keys and gestures for the other two to follow him and at last it's just us girls.

"Okay, Vee, you can be our sleazy politician. Take a seat," Kayla tells her, gesturing towards the empty chair.

Vee squeals excitedly and throws herself into the seat. "Ooh, I've never had a lap dance before. Better make it one to remember Eliza," she jokes as she gives me a 'come hither' with her hands.

"Honey, I'm going to be the best you ever had," I reply with a wink as Kayla starts the music.

❧

IT'S A COUPLE OF HOURS LATER AND I'VE JUST GONE THROUGH the routine one last time. Kayla's confident I can nail it and she agrees with Archer that I have a natural rhythm. The boys arrive back just as we're enjoying a coffee on the sofas.

"All done? Is Little Red ready to get our target all hot and bothered?"

Kayla nods her head, grinning. "She'll do great. Oh, that reminds me, you need your outfit," she says, wagging a finger as she stands and reaches into her bag. She pulls out a pair of tiny white pleather shorts and then hands me two red glittery nipple tassels.

"That's it?" I gawp.

"Yes," she replies, waiting for me to take them out of her hands. "I didn't bring heels, as I assumed you'd have some with you."

"I've covered the heels," Archer announces, holding up a black shopping bag.

I shake my head. "How do you even know my size?"

He shrugs his shoulders as he hands me the bag. "I know all your measurements, Scar. Made it my business to know."

I look in bewilderment at Vee, who just smiles back at me, like his behaviour is completely normal. "I'm thinking you are my stalker, after all."

He frowns at my mention of the elusive stalker. "Talking of our problem. Have there been any more parcels or messages?"

"Nothing," I confirm as I stick my head into the bag and see a pair of silver, sequined heels. The heel height alone must be five inches! God help me trying to dance sexy in these things.

"Interesting," mumbles Rafe from where he sits scrolling on his phone. He looks up when he realises everyone's attention is on him. "I just find it fascinating that since you left the Alderman mansion, there have been no more threats. It's as if he or she has got what they wanted."

Archer furrows his brows as he considers what Rafe has suggested. "Which would suggest that their aim was to get Scarlet to leave the family home."

"So could it be someone who thinks she'll be disinherited, maybe?" Vee asks.

"Like Chester and his mum, perhaps?" Seb suggests from where he sits sucking on a lollypop.

"Or," says Rafe, turning his attention back to his phone, "someone who knew about the engagement deal and doesn't want the two families joining and becoming closer allies."

"Like, Georgie," I state and give an 'I told you so' look to Archer. He opens his mouth and I inwardly groan. If he's going to defend her again, I'm going to kick him in the balls.

Rafe shakes his head and rubs at his chin. "No, I don't know. I think we're missing something here. I guess when Little Red moves back home we'll know if the threats start back up again."

I shudder and rub my arms with my hands. "I hope not. I don't want any more creepy gifts."

"Have you informed the police?" Kayla asks, looking shocked and concerned about the news of my stalker.

"Yes, they know and are investigating, but so far they've got nothing," Archer tells her, and I can tell from his tone of voice that he isn't at all impressed with the police investigations so far.

"I have to go," Kayla announces. She leans over and kisses me on the cheek and then Vee. "This afternoon was fun. Next time you're in the city, call me and we'll have a girl's night on the town."

"I'd like that," I reply, smiling. Okay, I was wrong about her, and I shouldn't have jumped to conclusions. The girl is actually so genuine and lovely. However, it will be a good while before I'll be going for a night on the town again. I'll be busy with nappy changes and bottle feeds.

Kayla picks up her bag, and she hugs Seb, squeezes Rafe's arm as she passes him, and then pulls Archer in for a hug. "And you, look after this one," she says, looking over at me. "She's a keeper."

"I'm trying," Archer admits with a sigh as he hugs her back. "Come on, I'll walk you to the lift."

CHAPTER THIRTEEN

ARCHER

Seb double checks the feed from the camera is working from inside the car. Scar looks the part in her blonde bobbed wig and coloured blue contacts that hide those big chocolate brown eyes of hers. He'll definitely go for her tonight. She looks perfect. The tiny booty shorts hug her pert little arse, and the killer heels make it look like her legs go on forever, even though she is only five foot four.

"Okay, so you sure you're up for this?" I ask her. I want her to know it's not too late to back out now.

She dips her head and gives me a pointed glare. "We've been over this. I am doing the job. I will be fine. Just trust me."

I flick a strand of her ash blonde wig. "I do trust you, Scar. It's those perverted fuckers in there I don't trust. One look at you and they'll be salivating."

Scar rolls her eyes at me. "If you say so."

It annoys me sometimes that she doesn't know how gorgeous she is. "I prefer the red hair," I tell her with a grin. She rocks the blonde wig, but red is her colour. It makes those big expressive eyes stand out, and it highlights her flawless ivory skin. Fuck! It's going to be hard to sit back and watch her do this. I was tough on her earlier when she showed me she could do a lap dance. Truth is, she killed it. I was practically salivating and panting when the song finished, and she dropped that barely there kiss on my cheek. She was seductive and innocent, and that is a deadly combination. One that most men would find hard to resist.

As far as the club knew, they had a new girl starting tonight named Lara. Their regulars would love that there was a new girl, and our target wouldn't be able to resist her. The slimy fucker better keep his hands to himself, though. If not, then he'd feel the force of my fist. I hate that she's doing this. I tried to stop it from happening. Vee was more than willing to take her place, but Scar, being Scar, wouldn't back down.

"So, remember the USB drive will be in his inner right jacket pocket. It won't be easy to take, but just make sure that he is so mesmerised by you he's well and truly distracted," Rafe explains to her.

That USB has vital information that will help the Aces secure some land in the city. That was our target tonight, to take the USB that Ron Griffin always carried on him. A paranoid MP of sixty, he carried it with him all the time. That would be his big mistake tonight.

Vee is faffing about with her lipstick, holding a small compact mirror in her hands. She wasn't supposed to be a part of the job tonight, but I didn't want Scarlet going in there alone. Vee will stand in for a bar worker that we have paid off handsomely to hand her notice in at the last minute. Conveniently, just thirty minutes before Vee rang them to see if they had any bar jobs going.

"Okay, time to go girls," Rafe announces, checking his watch and ensuring we are keeping to schedule. The three of us will be holed up in here in a car park around the corner. One that we have made sure isn't visible from any CCTV. Vee and Scar climb out of the car, and I want to grab her hand and tell her she isn't doing the job, but I know Scar, and telling her I don't want her doing it, will only make her more determined to prove that she can. I climb out of the car behind her and grab her hand, tugging her towards me.

"If anything goes wrong, we'll be straight inside, I promise," I assure her. I want her to know that we're here for them both.

She nods her head. "I know that."

I wrap my hand around the back of her neck and tug her face closer. "I hate that he gets to see you like this."

She smiles up at me, "But you got to have me dance for you first. And besides, he can look, but he can't touch. That's the club rules, right?"

I bob my head. "He may try to ask if he can see you outside the club. Just politely say no thank you and exit to the changing rooms as quick as you can, okay?"

"Trust me, I know how to make a quick exit," she replies, grinning at me and giving me a sexy little wink. "Now stop being a possessive arsehole and let me do my job." She pushes her shoulders back and stands taller. It's as if she's slipping into character mode.

I stand there, arms folded, watching as she and Vee walk away from us and round the corner, out of sight. It is taking everything in me not to go after her, fling her over my shoulder and get her out of here.

"They'll be fine," Seb says, stepping up beside me and placing a hand on my shoulder. "You know she's got this."

I nod my head, still staring after where they left. "If he so much as touches her, I'll kill him." That's a promise too, not a threat. Scar is mine. No one else gets to touch her.

Reluctantly, I climb back into the blacked-out vehicle and the three of us gather around the laptop to watch the camera feed. Both girls have cameras on them so that we can see what is happening from Vee's view over at the bar. This is going to be a long agonising evening.

As it's Scars first night at the club, she will do an introductory dance on stage for the whole clientele and then the punters will bid for a private dance with her. Ron would win. Our research shows that he has spent a small fortune in this club having lap dances from girls young enough to be his granddaughter. Griffin is a filthy fucking pervert.

We watch silently as they both enter the club and are met first by the bar manager and then by Big Mick, the owner. Vee is taken off to the bar area and big Mick takes Scar through to the back, towards the dressing rooms. Through the hidden camera on Scar, we can see as he leads her into a room where several young girls are dressing and doing their make-up. Big Mick introduces her to everyone and announces that her stage name will be Luscious Lara. The girls all greet her, some warmer than others, as they eye up the potential competition. From Vee's camera we see our target arrive. He's alone tonight. Some nights he brings along fellow MP Eric Dawson. The two have a penchant for young girls and we know they both have some involvements in sex trafficking. The aces have evidence that could take them both down, but instead they'll use it as blackmail at some time in the future. For now, the Elders' focus is on that memory stick and the vital information it holds that will further the society's power and weight.

The time comes for Scar to do her showcase dance. She's wearing a sexy pink satin bodice that displays those perfect tits of hers. Fuck, she looks edible right now. She takes the stage, and we watch her from Vee's hidden camera. All the punters go quiet when she is introduced, all of them sitting up in their seats, eager for fresh young meat. I swallow in apprehension. What if she freezes? What if she loses her confidence? The music starts, and I watch enraptured as my girl absolutely owns that stage. She's a fucking goddess up there. From Vee's camera footage, I watch the reaction of the punters. They're lapping her up. Practically salivating at the mouth for her. Ron devours her with his eyes and a predatory smirk graces his face. Oh, yes, he wants her, not that there was ever any doubt he would. I mean, look at her!

Her dance ends, and she's met with deafening applause. We sit back and wait as she exits back into the dressing room and the bidding begins for the private lap dance from Luscious Lara.

The bidding is fierce. Every punter in that room makes a bid for her. Ron remains silent, biding his time until he's ready to strike and win the auction.

"Five grand," Seb whistles, as Ron places the winning bid, outbidding his competitors by a whole two thousand pounds.

Hook, line and sinker, our target has fallen for the allure of my queen.

Now comes the tricky part.

Scar has to secure that USB stick without him noticing.

Eliza is escorted to one of the private rooms where dirty old Ron is waiting for her. He's practically drooling when she walks in. His greedy eyes drink her in from head to toe and I clench my fists in anger. How dare he look at her like that! She is mine, not his.

He asks her how old she is, and Scar lies and says she's eighteen. Like he cares how old she is. This dirty old man likes them young. The music comes on and Scar dances, perfecting the routine she practiced with Kayla. She's sinfully good and dear old Ron looks like he may have a heart attack any second. I can see the bulge in his pants, and it makes me want to vomit that she's doing this on the orders of the Elders. Once she is my fiancée, if they think they can put her on jobs like this, they can think again. Scar is our queen, and a queen shouldn't have to do shit like this to prove her loyalty. As she sits on his lap, we get an up-close and personal view of Ron's sweaty face and body. With any luck, he will have a heart attack and die and then this can end now, and I can get my girl out of that club.

"Bingo!" Seb says, clapping his hands together. "She did it."

I've been so busy watching Scar; I haven't been thinking about the whole reasons she is going through this. "You sure?"

Seb nods, grinning. "Didn't you see her pop it in the tiny pocket in the back of her shorts?"

"I'm distracted," I say gruffly.

"Our girl did good," Seb states and I wither my gaze at him.

"Our girl?"

Seb shrugs his shoulders, grinning. “What? We’re a family, aren’t we, the five of us?”

He’s right, we are a family. I will always put the four of them before everyone else. Blood isn’t always thicker than water. These were my brothers, and Vee and Scar were our girls. I’d die for both of them without question. That is what we do. We protect each other, no matter what.

I watch as Scar goes to exit the room, but sleazy Ron grabs her hand and stops her from leaving. He looks up at the camera they have in the corner of each room. The one that ensures no one breeches the clubs ‘no touch’ policy. The fucker offers her ten grand if she’ll meet him at a hotel later tonight. Scar handles it well. She tells him she is flattered, but that she has her sick mother to get back to. Ron, gets desperate, and tells her he’ll make sure she’d never have to work again and put her up in a fancy apartment if she’ll agree to be his mistress. Ron’s desperate for her. Scar thanks him for his offer but tells him she can’t, and she pulls her hand from his and leaves the room. The body camera clocks Vee at the bar, who looks Scar’s way and nods her head. Not long now, until both our girls will be back with us, where they belong. By the time poor Ron realises his precious USB is missing, we’ll be long gone and there’ll be no trace of a girl named Lara.

Never again will she do another job like this. The Elders think they have all the control, but me and my brothers have been secretly gaining the upper hand for the last three years. We were almost there. Almost.

CHAPTER FOURTEEN

ELIZA

I throw myself down on the back seat and let out the sigh I have been holding in. Archer starts the engine, and we head off into the night, back to the penthouse.

"You did really good, Little Red. It will impress the Elders," Seb says, nudging my shoulder from where he sits beside me in the car.

"Too good," Archer growls from the front. He catches my eye from his rear-view mirror, and I can see the worry there. "Now they'll just want her involved for more jobs."

"Isn't that what's kind of expected of me?" I ask him with a bob of my shoulders. Archer, after all, was the one who initiated me into this stupid society.

"It is, but maybe I just want to protect you from the shit they have forced us to deal with most of our lives, Scar."

"You should have thought about that before you went along with your Elders' orders and had me take the challenges. I assume no one leaves unless you're thrown out or you die."

Rafe scoffs from where he sits in the front passenger seat. "You got that right."

"Do we really have to head back to the penthouse?" Vee pouts, "I'm kind of in the mood to dance and party a little."

"I second that," Seb says, nodding his head in agreement and looking thrilled at the idea of extending our night further.

"Scar's tired," Archer tells him. "It's been a long day for her. I'm happy to drop the three of you off somewhere, though."

Vee gives me that face, the one that says, please say yes and come party with me. “I’m dressed like a hooker,” I say, pointing down at the skimpy shorts that are peaking out under Archer’s hoodie.

“Ah, I kind of came prepared,” she replies and grinning, she reaches over into the back of the car and pulls out an overnight bag. I watch her pull out a small pale blue strapless dress and she holds it out to me. “Keep the heels on, they’re fine.”

I am tired. Archer is right, but it’s hard to say no to Vee when she’s like this. “One hour,” I say with a sigh. “One hour and then I’m leaving and going to bed.”

“Yes!” Vee exclaims delightedly. “You can change in the car once we get there.”

FIFTEEN MINUTES LATER WE WALK INTO A SWANKY LOOKING club in London’s Soho area. The places oozes money and prestige. We walk straight to the entrance, avoiding the long queue to get in and the bouncers, of course, know the boys and let us straight in. A waitress leads us through the club and to the VIP area upstairs where you can look down over the whole of the club. As we walk past one of the other VIP tables, I nearly trip over my own feet when I see a well-known actress at the table. Was this place a celebrity hang out?

The waitress asks what we’d like to drink, and Vee orders a bottle of champagne. Archer asks for his usual Jack Daniels and coke. Vee looks at me like I have grown another head when I ask for water.

“Eliza! Water, seriously?”

“Alcohol will just make me sleepier,” I explain, batting her objections away with my hand.

Archer sends the waitress away with our order and leans into me, placing a hand on my thigh. “Are you sure you want to stay?”

I offer him a reassuring smile. "Yes, it's fine, and it keeps Vee happy."

Vee pulls my attention from Archer when she grabs my hand. "Come on, we are dancing."

I roll my eyes, but I know how persistent she can be, so I let her pull me up and we head downstairs to the main dancefloor. We have to push our way through the crowded space to find a spot to dance. Halsey plays over the speakers and Vee grabs my hips and we dance together.

"I've missed this," she tells me. "I've never had a real friend before you."

My heart pangs in my chest. "I've missed you to Vee, but if I'm going to let you back in, I need to know that you'll always have my back and that I come before any of this Aces shit and even before the boys."

She nods her head enthusiastically. "I swear. So, do I have my bestie back?"

Smiling, I tell her yes and she grabs me and pulls me into a hug. "I'll never let you down again." She pulls away, and she looks up at the VIP area. I follow her gaze and I find Archer leaning on the glass barrier, a drink in his hands. He's watching us with a smile on his face. "He won't let you down again either, you know."

Frowning, I pull my eyes from the hypnotic pull of my dark boy and give her my attention again. "Don't go there," I protest.

"Hear me out," she argues as we both dance to the beat of the new track the DJ is playing. "Archer doesn't say much, and he's not good at feelings, but he knows he fucked up." She sighs and puts her hand over her heart. "I know that guy. I see what others miss. I see the way he looks at you and I'm telling you, Eliza, he'd kill for you if you asked him."

I scoff. "That kind of commitment comes with loving someone, and Archer Savage doesn't love. He's told me as much."

Vee cocks a brow at me, as if to say, *really?* "He's capable of love. Archer just tries to shut himself off to all emotions because that's how he was brought up, to believe that to care is to show weakness. He might never say it, but sometimes actions speak louder than words."

I shake my head. I still have my doubts that his intentions are genuine. There was no ignoring that fact that he had to marry me and have a baby in order to inherit his legacy. That's some pretty powerful motivation to make anyone pretend they care for someone.

I jerk slightly when a hand comes around my waist from behind me. "Hey beautiful, I've been watching you from over by the bar."

I look up behind me to find a blond guy with a confident smile on his face. "That's nice, but I'm dancing with my friend right now," I politely tell him, hoping he'll get the hint and leave me alone.

"Ah, come on gorgeous, just one dance and a drink with me."

"Thanks, but I'm good." I try to step away from him, but his hand around my waist tightens, and he pulls me flush against his body and sways his hips into me.

"I think you want to, really. I promise I can show you a good time, baby."

I attempt to remove his hand from around my waist, but he's strong and he just laughs in my ear. What part of no does this fucker not get? I'm about to lose my shit and elbow the bastard and tell him to get his hands off me when he's dragged backwards by the scruff of his neck. I look behind him to see a blood thirsty Archer steaming with rage.

"What part of no did you not get?" he growls into the guy's ear, his teeth bared.

"Come on, man. She wants me," the idiot argues, not knowing when to give up and walk away.

"Here's what's going to happen. You're going to walk off this dancefloor, leave the lady alone and not even glance her way again tonight. If you don't do as you're instructed, I'll personally beat you to a pulp and break as many bones as I can. Am I clear?"

The fool snickers and points at me, and says drunkenly, "She's no lady. I bet she offers it out on the weekly."

Uh-oh. I see the moment he snaps. Archer still has him by the neck, and he spins him around so he's facing him. I hear the crack of bones as he pulls back his fist and punches him with force in his face.

"Fuck, man!" the guy protests as he sways on his feet. He places a hand over his now bloody and broken nose. But Archer is far from done. He punches the guy in the gut, and he staggers, groaning at the impact. He falls to the floor and Archer looms over him, bubbling with rage.

"Apologise to the lady," he insists, gripping the guy by his shirt again. "No one speaks to her like that. No one touches her like that without her permission, and no one ever suggests that my fiancée is a slut," he growls.

I can't help it. My stupid heart flips in my chest. I secretly love that he wants to protect and defend me. Not that I'll ever admit that to him.

The guy holds his hands up in front of him in defeat. "Okay, I didn't know she is yours. There's no ring on her finger." He looks at me as blood drips down his face onto his shirt. "I'm sorry lady, I'm really sorry."

Archer's lip curls up as he leans right into the guy's face. "Leave this club now before I fucking kill you." He releases him so quickly that the guy falls backwards onto his behind, and he scuttles away before he even gets to his feet. He rushes away like his arse is on fire.

Archer turns his attention to me, and I can see he's still in a deep rage, with his fists clenched.

"I'm okay," I tell him, placing a reassuring hand on his chest. "Relax, I'm okay."

He cups my face with his hands. "You sure you're, okay?" His jaw is tight with tension.

I nod my head and place my hands over his. "I'm fine."

Rafe appears behind Vee, and he embraces her from behind and nuzzles into her neck. Smiling, she reaches up and places one hand behind her to cup the back of his neck.

Rafe looks at Archer and nods.

"We're leaving," Archer announces, taking my hand in his. The feminist in me wants to tell him I'll decide when I'm ready to leave, but in all honesty, I'm shattered, and I just want my bed. This baby growing in my belly is taking all my energy right now.

"Go," Vee tells me with a wink. "Get him calm. He needs you right now."

I nod my head at her and Rafe as I allow Archer to lead me away from them and off the dancefloor. He heads for the exit and out across the road to where he parked the car. I yelp when he grabs me and spins me, pressing my back against the car.

"I want to find that fucker and kill him for touching you," he says gruffly, grinding his teeth.

I've never seen him this angry before. He is one scary fucker when he's caught in a rage like this. Even my heart thumps quicker in my chest.

"Look at me, Arch," I insist, grabbing his shirt in my fist. "I'm fine."

"You're mine," he growls. "You're mine, and he thought he could lay his hands on you. No one touches what is mine and lives to tell the tale."

I bob my head from side to side. "We'll discuss the fact that no one owns me another time, but it's done with. You taught him a lesson. He left and I'm perfectly fine. Now, can we please go back to the penthouse? I'm beat and I really need my bed."

He looks down at me, his dark eyes burning into mine as he places his lips on mine. I should tell him no, but I know he needs this right now, so I let it happen and kiss him back. "You are mine," he tells me quietly before he moves me away from the car and opens the car door, holding it open for me. He slams the door shut, making me jump. Okay. Perhaps some of that rage is still burning inside of him.

We set off for the penthouse, and he's driving like a maniac. I clutch a hold of my seat, as he takes a corner at crazy speed.

"Archer, will you please slow down?"

He ignores me. He's so lost in his anger, it's like he's not in the car with me.

"Archer! Stop this fucking car now!" I yell as my anxiety climbs. "You'll kill the both of us!"

My words have their desired effect because he pulls off the road and onto the hard shoulder under the coverage of some trees. I lean back in my seat and drag in some deep breaths. I look over at him and he's grasping the steering wheel so tightly I'm worried he's going to break it. He needs a distraction.

Knowing this is stupid, I unbuckle my seat belt and climb over the centre of the car. He lifts his hands from the steering wheel to accommodate me and looks at me in surprise and confusion. I place my hand on the lever at the side of the seat and crank the seat down until he's almost lying flat.

"Scar, what are you doing?" he asks me, his voice laced with warning.

"Shush," I tell him, placing my finger over his lips as I unzip his trousers. "I'm helping you relax." I pull him free of his boxers and wrapping my fingers around his cock, I lean down and suck him into my mouth. He hisses and swears under his breath, placing his hand on the back of my head and gripping at my hair. I tease him with my tongue, licking him up and down and swirling my tongue around the head of his now erect dick. I feel all the anger leave his body as he pistons his hips, pushing himself deeper into the back of my throat.

"Fuck, Scar. You're killing me, baby," he moans as I find my rhythm and help him find the release that he needs. His hands tighten in my hair, and he roars I'm a fucking goddess as he spills his seed down the back of my throat. I swallow it all and give his dick one last lick before I sit up to meet his eyes.

"Better?" I ask him as I tuck him back into his boxers and zip up his fly.

"Hell yes," he replies, his breathing still erratic. He shakes his head, running his thumb softly over my cheek. "How are you so perfect? It's like you were fucking made for me."

I scoff, my eyes looking heavenward. "Ah, don't tell me you believe in that soul mate shit, Archer Savage?"

He cups the back of my neck with his hands, tilting my head and staring at me like I'm some kind of enigma. "I'm never letting you go. I'll hunt you to the ends of the earth and handcuff you to my bed if you ever try to leave me."

"Where am I going to go?" I ask him. He knows as well as I do Wilbur has me over a barrel. There is no freedom of choice for me. I have to do as Wilbur orders, or I risk my brother losing everything and my own future going down the toilet. I silently climb back over to my seat and buckle my belt. Archer remains unmoving for a few seconds before he fastens his seatbelt, and we continue our journey at a more acceptable speed.

As soon as we enter the penthouse, I head straight for our bedroom, and strip down to my thong and climb under the covers. I'm beyond exhausted and my emotions are all over the place, warring with the need to keep my carefully constructed armour in place and my need to be with him. The sooner we get back to Hawk Bay, the better. I can put some distance between the two of us and these feelings that are scaring the ever-loving shit out of me.

Archer enters the bedroom a couple of minutes later. I don't open my eyes, but I hear his feet pad across the room and back again. We were silent all the way back here after our pit stop by the roadside. Both of us lost in our own thoughts as we processed all the things unsaid between us. Because you can say what you like, but there was no getting around the fact that

Wilbur is blackmailing me into marrying Archer. We both know it. We both know he will do nothing to stop it because, for one, he had to marry me to get his inheritance, and two, because he'd decided despite our parents' history that he wants me for himself.

The bed dips as he climbs inside. He pulls his side of the covers back and lifts them back over himself. I wait with bated breath, expecting him to wrap his arm around my waist and pull me against his chest, but I find minutes pass by, and he hasn't made one move to pull me closer. Part of me is relieved, but the other half of me is confused.

❦

When I wake in the morning, the other side of the bed is already empty. Despite him not holding me in his arms, I still slept like a log from just knowing he was nearby. I dress in a pair of jeans and a band T-shirt and make my way into the living area where I find Vee and Rafe cooking breakfast together. I lean on the doorframe for a minute and take my opportunity to just observe them. Watching how they work around each other and chat easily together.

Vee's head looks up, and she beams when she sees me standing here. "Hey girl. I hope you are hungry because Rafe and I are cooking up a mother of a breakfast."

"So, I see," I say with a bob of my head as I take in all the food on the hob. "Where's Archer?"

Vee shrugs. "He said he needed to nip out. I'm sure he'll be back soon."

I nod my head in response, chewing on my lip.

"Is everything okay with you two?" Vee asks me and I pull myself from my thoughts and offer a noncommittal bob of my shoulders.

"When has anything ever been okay where him and I are concerned?" I reply with a tired sigh, before taking a seat at the island. I contemplate everything that has happened in these last forty-eight hours. My mind, of course, heads straight for the hot sex that we had in this very room while his friends were in the next room. The great sex between us just makes the whole situation ten-times harder because, like it or not, my body responds to his like a drug user responds to the sight of their favourite drug. Being with him gives me a euphoria that is akin to stealing cars or fighting in the ring. It is a complete and utter adrenaline rush that makes me feel alive.

"We'll be leaving at nine," Rafe says, handing me a plate of food.

"Back to reality, huh," I comment as I stare at the overfull plate before me.

"We don't have to go back to reality just yet if you'd rather not, Little Red," he says, offering me a cup of coffee, which I gratefully snatch from his hands. "I'm sure Archer could swing us a couple more days here."

I shake my head. "I've already missed enough school as it is. At this rate I'll never pass my A-levels."

This brings a snicker from Vee, and I look up at her with a quizzical look. "What?"

She shakes her head at me and shares a smile with Rafe. "I forget she's not grown up in this world sometimes," she says to him, before she turns her gaze back on me. "Girl, you'll come away with A's. That is a dead cert. Do you know how much money our parents plough into that academy? Wilbur funded that new football pitch. Do you honestly think they'd dare to give you shitty grades?"

I look at her, dumbfounded. "Are you telling me I could totally flunk my exams and I'll still come out with straight A's?"

Vee nods her head at me. "That's exactly what I'm saying."

I sigh, placing down my coffee cup in disbelief. "Unbelievable."

The lift pings, pulling me from my shock. The doors open and Archer strides into the suite. He strolls past me without so much as a hello and my eyes follow him, trying to judge what is going on in that head of his.

He chugs down a glass of orange juice before he heads towards our room. “We leave at nine,” he says simply without a backward glance.

“What have you done?” Vee asks me. She’s also watching Archer’s exit with a perplexed look on her face.

I shake my head, still staring in the direction he went. “I have no idea.” I really don’t know either. Something shifted with him last night after we’d arrived back here, and I’m not sure what.

CHAPTER FIFTEEN

ARCHER

I feel her eyes on me as I leave the room. My natural instinct was to walk over to her and kiss her head, but I fought it. I'd lain awake for hours last night, replaying the events in the car and the words that we left unspoken after she asked me where she was going to go. A silent reminder that any ring I put on her finger will be there because she is being blackmailed into this engagement. Wilbur had leverage and without that, there would be no way she'd agree to be mine. Okay, yes, part of me feels like a shit for knowing the situation she's in and not doing a damn thing about it, but I'm a selfish bastard. Somehow Scarlet has buried deep under my skin and now I'm not willing to let her go. I will marry her knowing full well she's being forced into this, and I'll do it because I can. Truth is, as much as Wilbur needs this wedding to happen, I need it too if I'm to get my hands on my family's fortune and my inheritance. My grandfather is as insistent about this marriage as Wilbur is. Why, though, I'm not so sure. It's not like he needs the investment. He isn't the one whose empire is on the verge of crumbling because of poor business decisions. No, his reason is because he has some daft idea that it will repair the past. That it will erase the fact that Wilbur stole his rightful bride from under his nose and it will repair the damage from our parents' tragic pairing. But what if we are cursed? No marriage between the two families had occurred now for three generations. Both arrangements had ended in deceit and betrayal.

I watched her sleep last night. I just lay beside her and watched her, blown away by how fucking beautiful she is. Scarlet makes me feel things that are foreign to me. She makes me question myself and how what I do appears to her. I wanted to kill that guy last night with my bare hands for touching her. I'd never been the jealous type, despite many girls trying to make me jealous, thinking that if I saw them with someone else, I'd realise what I was missing and barge in there and take them back. But I wasn't that guy, because I didn't do feelings and I didn't get attached, ever. She's changing me and it scares me to no end. Scar's a wild card and she's thrown my carefully constructed world off kilter. She deserves better than me. Scar deserves a good guy. Not someone as twisted and fucked up as me. I know that, but that still doesn't mean I will not make her mine. She knows it and I know it and she'll likely spend the rest of her life hating me for it.

I strip my clothes off and walk into the shower, feeling the warm water run over my head and down my body. My mind strays to thoughts of what happened in the car. Her impromptu blow job had thrown me by surprise but fuck if I hadn't been able to stop thinking about it this morning. Scarlet is magic with those lips of hers and she had me writhing under her complete control last night. I wrap my hands around my now hard cock and close my eyes, remembering the way she looked as she gave me head and rocked my fucking world. Fuck, I'm going to blow my load again. I can't resist her, no matter how I try. I went out this morning and paid a visit to an old fuck buddy. Emily was surprised but pleased to see me after no contact for the last nine months. She'd invited me in and pulled me along to her bedroom, discarding her underwear as she went and laying herself out on the bed for me. I'd felt nothing. My dick didn't even twitch in my pants. The loyal fucker was still daydreaming about our girl lying fast asleep in my bed. I'd left Emily's apartment five minutes later, even more annoyed and frustrated than when I'd arrived. I knew there was only one girl able to give me what I need. Her.

I climb out the shower and towel dry myself. I reach for my joggers and pull out the small black box from the pocket. I pop the lid open and stare down at the white gold and ruby ring. I'm not sure how I ended up at the jewellery store this morning, but I hadn't forgotten how she'd quietly admired this ring yesterday. Her eyes had lingered over it for a few seconds longer than the others. I always knew she wouldn't be a diamond girl; my girl likes to be different in everything she does.

I'd told my dad the whole crazy revenge plot was over and done with yesterday. To my surprise, he hadn't got violent or angry. He'd simply taken a drink of whisky and after a few silent seconds, he'd said. "So be it, son."

"That's it?" I'd asked him, the shock clear in my tone of voice.

"Like you say, the past is the past," he'd agreed, before he picked up his mobile and left the room, leaving me standing there in shock at how well he'd taken it. This revenge plot had been all he'd talked about for the last six months since he'd known that there was an Alderman heiress. He's talked about nothing other than how I must break her by being a cruel and unfaithful husband.

My phone rings, pulling me from my thoughts over my conversation with my dad. I frown when I see Wilbur's name on my screen.

"Wilbur," I greet flatly.

"Archer, son," he replies.

"What is it?"

"I believe my granddaughter did a grand job last night. I always knew she'd be an asset to our society."

"Is that all?" I bark, my impatience running thin.

"No. As you know, Eliza has been told to return home by this Friday. I've spoken with Edward, and we've agreed that we'll announce the engagement two weeks from now. We'll throw an engagement party for you here at my home."

"Why so soon?" I ask him, frowning. "I thought you'd both said we needed to date first and be seen together. The engagement is supposed to be announced after her eighteenth birthday."

"Yes, well, things change," he replies haughtily.

"In other words, you don't have the time financially to wait," I observe. Things must be worse than I realised for dear old Wilbur.

"Remember who you are talking to, boy. I am your elder and you'll give me the respect I demand. I am giving you a beautiful bride. At least fucking her for the next fifty to sixty years won't be a chore."

My hand squeezes tighter around the phone. She is nothing but a piece of meat to him. A transaction to ensure he survives. I can understand why she wants to bring him down and once I have my inheritance and I have secured my place in charge of the Savage legacy, I will enjoy breaking him down for her.

I walk back into the kitchen in an even worse mood than when I left thanks to Wilbur and his manipulative poison.

"We need to talk," I tell Scarlet leaning on the island across from her. I'd promised her no more secrets. She studies me for a minute before she agrees with me, and she follows me out onto the large roof terrace that looks out over London. All our friends are in the kitchen, so I walk further around the terrace away from prying eyes.

She folds her arms around her chest, shivering slightly. "What's going on Archer? You've been in a strange mood since last night in the car."

I rest my arms on the glass panels that line the edge of the rooftop and look out over London. "I told you I'd be honest with you from now on, so this is me doing that. Wilbur and Edward plan to bring the engagement forward. They will announce it two weeks from now."

She's silent. I'm reluctant to turn and see her reaction. I'm expecting her to go postal and start shouting and calling her grandfather every foul name under the sun.

"Okay," is her reply.

This reaction has me turning around. "Okay?" I repeat, unsure I've heard her right.

She comes to stand beside me, and looking out over London, she exhales. "Yeah, okay. That's all I've got. It's not like I have any control over this situation. I'm just a puppet and Wilbur pulls the strings."

I reach for her hand and pull her to me. "That won't always be the case. Once you have my surname, he'll have no power over you."

She offers me a smile that doesn't reach her eyes. "No, you're right, he won't, but then you'll be the one controlling me."

"No," I assure her, placing a finger under her chin and forcing her to look at me. "You'll be my wife, Scar. My partner in life, you can have whatever career makes you happy. Of course, I'll be a demanding and obnoxious bastard who will want your full attention, but you'll be in control of what you do with your life."

"So, if I want to work as a lap dancer?" she asks me, grinning.

I growl and pull her against me. "Funny."

She smiles and looks out at the view. "Two weeks, huh?"

I can't gauge her thoughts and I've got pretty good at reading her. This is not the reaction I am expecting, and it has thrown me slightly.

"You're not going to scream and shout?"

"What's the point?" she scoffs. "It's not like it will change the situation. My destiny was set in motion the minute Wilbur discovered I existed."

I don't enjoy seeing her like this. I want her fire and her anger. She meets my eyes when I cup her head. "I know I'm a bastard. You have every right to hate me, Scar. We both know it, but I think you and I, we'll be good together."

“Well, I guess we’ll find out.” She places her hands on my chest. “Can you promise me one thing?”

“Name it,” I tell her without hesitation. I’ll give her the fucking moon if she wants it. This tiny little scarlet-haired beauty has me wrapped around her finger.

“That you won’t keep me away from Damon.”

I swallow. That fucker has wormed his way into my girl’s heart. I know she doesn’t feel for him that way, but it still stings like a fucker to know that she needs him in her life.

“You’re asking a lot there, Scar,” I admit with a sigh. “How about I promise to try?”

She smiles at me, and it makes my dead heart stutter in my chest. “I’ll take that. It’s a start.”

CHAPTER SIXTEEN

ELIZA

"You sure about this?" Silver asks me as we both sit in his car, staring up at the four gated houses at the top of the cliff.

"No, but it doesn't change that I have to go back there," I say with a weary sigh.

He reaches over the centre of the car and wraps his hand over mine. "It'll be okay, princess. You ever need me, I'm just a call away. I don't care who this fucker thinks he is."

I smile at my friend's loyalty. "I don't deserve you."

"You do," he insists. "You pull people in, princess, and they become addicted to your fire and your big heart."

"Don't," I protest, shaking my head. "You'll make me cry and I am done with crying." I squeeze his hand. "Thank you for everything."

"Anytime, princess," he replies with a lazy smile. "Now, walk in there with your head held high."

Nodding, I take a steadying breath and open the car door and climb out. I stride forward with more confidence than I feel. Before I can reach for the door handle, it swings open, and Kit stands before me with a beaming smile on his face.

"Welcome home, sis," he greets, beckoning me inside.

This place is not my home, but I plaster on a smile and, with one brief look at Silver, I step into the Alderman mansion. As Kit closes the door to the outside world, I feel my freedom slip further away. I wish my dad was here to tell me what to do.

"Ah, lass, it's lovely to see you." Edith comes bustling into the hallway and pulls me into a warm hug. Her rosewood scent surrounds me and eases my worries. She steps back and cups my cheek with her palm. "We've missed you, haven't we Kit?"

"Like a hole in the head," Kit jokes, ducking when I reach to clip him round the ear.

"You're not too big for me to pull you down a peg or two little brother."

He chuckles and winks at me as he throws an affectionate arm around me. "I think it's you that's the little one now."

Wilbur's study door opens, and the merriment quickly evaporates. I stiffen under Kit's arm.

"Wilbur," I say with a bob of my head.

"Grandfather, please," he insists, offering me a tight smile that doesn't reach his eyes. "It is good to have you home again."

I nod my head, chewing on the inside of my lip. I want to tell him he can shove his home far up his arse, but I don't, of course. I store all the rage inside me, boxing it away for the day when I will bring this man down.

"We have guests for dinner this evening, so I expect you to change into suitable attire," he advises me, glancing briefly down my body at the ripped jeans and cropped band t-shirt I'm wearing.

"Let me guess," I say dryly, "the Savages."

Wilbur nods his head, confirming my suspicions.

"Not wasting any time, are you?"

Edith reaches for my hand. "Come on now, let's go through to the kitchen. I've made your favourite cookies."

"You spoil them," Wilbur chastises from behind us, as she guides me away from my jailor.

"That's what housekeepers are for," she informs him cheerily, and I breathe a sigh of relief when I hear his study door close.

"Wait until you see what grandfather bought me, Eliza. He got me the coolest bike."

"Wow, did he now," I reply, taking a seat at the island and

giving Edith a roll of my eyes. "One thing you can guarantee about Wilbur is he will always be there with his wallet."

Kit's smile falls. "Can you not, for like five minutes," he mumbles. "I get you don't like him or trust him, but I'm happy here, sis. Don't spoil it for me like you always did."

I jerk from the emotional slap his words deliver and I mimic me zipping up my lips and throwing away the key. Hearing him blame me for our previous foster moves reminds me of what a shit sister I have been to him in the past.

"So, I hear you went to London this week with Archer and the others. What did you get to see?" Edith asks me as she places a plate of cookies in front of me. I love how Edith always tries to distract and bring warmth back into a room.

"We did, and yes, we went sight-seeing. I got to see Big Ben, and we went on the London eye. It was fun."

I look at the cookies on the plate in front of me and usually I'd devour them without a second thought, but today they just don't appeal to me.

"Do we have any custard?" I ask her and she looks at me in surprise.

"Of course we do. Would you like some? Do you want carrot cake or chocolate cake with it, my dear?"

I shake my head. "No cake please, just a big bowl of warm custard. It's my new sweet fix," I tell her, and she nods her head and sets to work on warming up some homemade custard.

"So, the black sheep of the family has returned," a deep voice I instantly recognise speaks. I turn with a frown to find Chester leaning against the doorway into the hall, shades on, observing us.

"Chester. Can't say I've missed you," I tell him with a deadpan smile on my face. His answer is to smirk and give me the finger.

"I won't be here for dinner, Edith. I'm off into the city with a few friends," he announces, turning his attention from me.

"Friends," I comment. "You found people crazy enough to agree to be your friend?"

He scoffs, giving me a dry look. "As strange as it may seem to you, there are those who enjoy my intellect and intelligent conversation."

"Well please," I gesture towards the front door, "don't let us keep you."

Smiling sarcastically at me, he winks at Kit before he turns on his heels and leaves.

"He's still not been expelled, then?" I ask, not able to hide the disappointment in my tone.

Kit shrugs, looking at me from under his mop of dark curls. "Chester's okay once you get to know him a bit better. Maybe you need to give your family more of a chance. You might be surprised," he says, giving me a pointed look before he grabs a cookie and walks out of the room.

I stare after him, opened-mouthed. Did my baby brother just chastise me?

Edith clears her throat as she hands me the warm bowl of custard. "He's growing up."

"Too quickly," I reply, staring after my brother. "It scares me that he won't need me one day."

Edith pats my shoulder as she passes me to grab some cups. "He'll always need you, Eliza. My Calvin is in his thirties, and he still needs me."

I finish my custard, chatting with Edith as I eat. She is one of the few good things about this house. I wonder if she would come and work for me when I eventually move into the Savage mansion?

I head up to my old room to find it exactly how I left it. The smell of freshly laundered sheets and my favourite plum and rhubarb candle fill the room. Edith has done what she can to make my space feel warm and inviting, and I love her for it.

I throw myself down on my bed and muster up the energy to

get some homework done before I have to change and get ready for tonight's charade.

I heard the doorbell go around five minutes ago, so I know the Savages have arrived. I slip on my kitten heels and give my reflection a once over in the mirror. There's a brief rap on my door and it opens to reveal Archer. He's dressed in a navy-blue suit. Blue is his colour. Whenever he wears anything dark blue, it has my stupid heart doing somersaults.

"I thought I'd come find you and escort you down to dinner," he explains as he walks into my room. He comes up behind me and slides his arms around my waist. "You look good enough to eat," he says, nuzzling into my neck.

"What are you doing?" I ask him, moving my neck away from his lips. "Stop behaving like we're already together."

He snickers against my skin. "We are though. Or have you forgotten that just two days ago you were bouncing on my dick like it was the holy grail?"

I spin around to face him, ready to tell him to fuck right off, but I find myself grabbing him by his shirt and pulling him to me. "I still hate you, just so you know, but I need you to help me wind down before I go down there and face those bastards." I reach up on my tiptoes and place my lips on his. He doesn't hesitate to respond, kissing me back like he is starving for me.

"You need me to get you off, baby?" He asks me as he grips me by the hips and rolls his into mine, showing me just how ready he is to deliver.

I place a hand on his chest. "We're not having sex, but you can get down on your knees and put that tongue of yours to good use."

He arches a brow at me. Archer's not used to being bossed around and I half expect him to throw me down on the bed and take what he wants, anyway. He surprises me, though, when he drops to his knees. He runs a hand up my leg under my dress and his nostrils flare when he realises I'm not wearing any underwear.

"Bad girl, Scar. Were you coming to dinner with no knickers on?" He asks me as he bunches my dress in his hands, giving him access to my core.

"Well, you know, I figure anyway I can rebel I'll take," I tell him, moaning on the last words as his tongue licks up my centre.

"You taste like heaven, as always," he groans as he gets to work, teasing me, licking me, eating my pussy like he was born to.

"Fuck, Archer, yes, like that, don't stop," I encourage, placing my hand on the back of his head, holding him against my aching core. I lean my head back and moan loudly when his tongue slides inside my pussy and he pumps his tongue in and out whilst his fingers tease my clit. "I want my cum dripping down your chin," I tell him. "I want you to use those fingers that have been inside me to shake his hand."

"My rebellious little witch," he mumbles against my flesh as he continues to provide me with pure bliss. He pinches at my clit, and it's enough to send me hurtling over the edge. I come hard and fast, moaning his name like he's my everything. He kisses my pussy before he stands to his feet, and I watch in fascination. I'm still breathless and coming down from my high when he pulls me flush against his body. "How about a quick fuck and you can go downstairs with my cum dripping down those perfect thighs of yours?"

I grin, but before I can open my mouth to tell him hell yes, there's a knock on my bedroom door. "Dinners ready," I hear Kit's voice announce from outside my room.

"Be down in a minute," I shout to him.

Archer groans in frustration and leans his forehead against mine. "Come home with me tonight? Sleep in my bed."

My heart squeezes in my chest. "I was in your bed two days ago. You missing me already?"

He sucks my bottom lip into his mouth seductively, making me want to forget all about dinner and tell him to take me on every surface in this room. "I've told you, Scar. I want you in my bed every night."

Sighing, I straighten his tie and run my hand through his hair. I messed it up when I was in the grips of my orgasm. "It's my first night home. Besides, if Wilbur has his way, you'll get your wish sooner than you think."

Archer places my arm through his, and we descend the stairs together. It might seem strange, but I feel stronger having him at my side, like I can take on anyone or anything. I still hate him, but there's a part of me that needs him.

"Ah, there you are. I thought we were going to have to send a search party," Wilbur says with an irritated tone and a false smile on his face when we walk into the dining room.

"Apologies," I say, smiling sweetly. "Archer was just eating me out before dinner." I add in a lower tone so that only Phil, who is standing to my right and Archer, can hear me. Phil coughs and splutters, spilling his drink out of his mouth, and Alexis looks over at him with a frown.

"Ah youngsters. Leave them be, Wilbur," Edward chuckles. He winks at us both like he knows exactly where and what we've just been up to. He leans in and kisses my cheek. "Me and my late wife were the same. Never could get enough of each other." He gives Archer a shoulder squeeze. "It looks like Wilbur's wish to speed things up will not meet much resistance after all."

I smile back at Edward. Despite his role in all of this, I actually like the man. What you see is what you get. Unlike Wilbur, who is a snake in the grass.

"How about we sit down to eat?" suggests Alexis, coming up beside Edward. "Eliza, it's lovely to have you home again. Come, everyone, let's eat."

Dinner is a polite affair. Edward asks me how I enjoyed London, and everyone makes small talk. It's the epitome of a polite dinner.

"Now that we have enjoyed our food. Perhaps we should talk about the engagement," Wilbur announces, dabbing his mouth with his napkin. "I've spoken with Edward, and we plan to announce it two weeks today. The media will want photos, of course, so we'll arrange for the local press to attend a celebratory ball."

Archer nods his head and I feel him squeeze my thigh under the table. "Eliza and I have spoken about the plans, and we're fine with it. However, we have one thing we'd like to discuss. Well. Actually, it's not up for discussion," he says, smiling confidently across the room at the men who think they wield all the power. "Once we are officially engaged, I shall want Eliza to live with me at the Savage mansion."

Wilbur blanches and clears his throat. "I hardly think that is proper."

Archer smiles his assassin smile that I have now seen on more than a few occasions. It's the one that says you don't want to fuck with me, mister.

"Wilbur, this is not the sixties," Archer tells him. "Most engaged couples live together before they get married. If you want us to play the loving couple at this ball, then I suggest you understand that I'm not asking. Eliza will move in with me."

Wilbur adjusts his tie, sizing up Archer before he turns to Edward. "And what do you think about this?"

Edwards bobs his head from side to side casually. "I think it's a marvellous idea. It will give them time to get to know each other and iron out any differences."

"I see," Wilbur says, clearing his throat. "Then I guess she's moving in with you, but I expect you both here for dinner at least twice a week."

"Done," Archer replies, holding up his drink. "Shall we toast to our agreement?"

Wilbur sucks in his lips like he has a foul taste in his mouth as he raises his glass. "To the engagement."

"To Eliza and me," Archer says after him, his eyes not leaving Wilbur's as he takes a sip of his drink.

Everyone retires to the formal lounge for drinks, and I take my chance to escape and get some much-needed fresh air. I feel stifled. I lean against the back of the house and close my eyes. It looks like I'm moving in with Archer.

I place a hand over my belly. I'm nine weeks pregnant now. My scan is in three weeks. I still can't quite believe there is a baby in there. One that Archer and I made. It's crazy when you think about it. I smile to myself when I picture Wilbur's face, when he finds out I'm pregnant before we're even married. He will not be too pleased about that one. It will be my big 'fuck you' moment to savour until I can get dirt on him and destroy him.

"I thought I'd find you out here," Archer says, and I open my eyes to find him standing in front of me, his hands in his trouser pockets. "Are you okay?"

I scoff. "They have just brokered me like a company asset. Why wouldn't I be fine?"

He frowns and steps closer into my space. "That's not what you are to me, Scar. I know you don't want to be here in this house, so this was my way of helping you escape."

I laugh and undo the two top buttons on his shirt. "I think it's more to do with you seeing an opportunity to take what you want as soon as you can."

"Can't it be both?" he asks me, looking down and watching me as I run my hands down his chest.

I smile. "Two birds, one stone and all that. I guess so." I step forward, closing the distance between us. "I'm still not past what you did," I remind him, as I wrap my arms around his neck. "But as much as I hate you, I hate him more and to not have to live in the same house as him is a relief."

"Come home with me tonight," he says again.

"Not tonight," I tell him, wetting my lips. "You could choose to stay here, of course."

He cocks a brow. "And if I choose to stay, what's in it for me?"

"Why, Netflix and snacks, of course." I tease him.

He frowns. "You're really going to hold out on me, aren't you?" he states rather than asks.

"It's only right," I tell him as I softly run my lips along his jawline. "You need to earn the right to have me, Archer. Prove that I'm your priority now."

"You are," he growls, gripping my hair in his hands and tilting my head so that he can stare into my eyes. "You are, Scar."

"Time will tell, I guess," I reply before I remove my arms from around him and take a step back. "I'm tired and done with playing nice for tonight. Are you coming?" I ask, stopping and looking back at him. I hold out my hand.

He doesn't hesitate. He slips his hand into mine and I guide us through the house, up the back staircase to my room.

I SLOWLY SLIP BACK INTO THE ROUTINE OF THE ALDERMAN residence. I'm back under my grandfather's control, for now. Despite all my promises that I would never forgive them and let them back in again, I'm spending most of my time with Vee and the three Aces. Some might call me weak. Others might argue that I'm making the best of a bad situation.

"I have a surprise for you after college," Archer announces as he pulls into his personal parking space at the academy.

"You're not kidnapping me again, are you?" I ask him with an arched brow.

He half smiles. "Not today. I think you'll like this surprise," he says self-assuredly.

"Is it illegal?" I ask, waggling my brows at him, and this earns me a husky chuckle.

He leans over the car and places his forefinger under my chin. "I'm afraid not, but if you want, we can head to the ring on Friday. I could get you on the line-up."

"Ah, I'm not really in a fighting mood lately," I say, quickly thinking of an excuse why I can't fight this weekend.

Archer looks at me, puzzled. "You love fighting, Scar, almost as much as I do."

I shrug my shoulders, trying to look nonchalant, but it's hard when he's so close and he's studying me. "Well, maybe I'm ready for some peace in my life."

"Nah, you thrive on danger and excitement. What's going on with you?"

"Nothing," I protest, plastering on a fake smile. "Now, watching you fighting on the other hand, I could get on board with," I tell him, waggling my brows and running a finger down this shirt.

"You could, huh?" He smirks. "Does it turn you on watching me fight, baby girl?"

I lean closer to him, biting my lips. Him calling me baby girl does all sorts of things to my body. "It gets me so horny."

His eyes are hooded, and they skate between my mouth and my eyes. "No arguments. You're sleeping in my bed tonight."

"We'll see," I say in a noncommittal tone. "Now let's go, the future Mrs Savage needs to get a good education." I go to pull away from him, but he wraps his hand around the back of my neck and pulls me back to face him.

"Say that again," he demands, his eyes burning with possession.

Oh, I see.

"What?" I smile. "You like when I say the future Mrs Savage?"

"Like it," he repeats. "I fucking love it." He dives in and kisses me deep and I hear a long moan come from me as I kiss him back. Say what you like about our fucked-up situation, but my dark boy is addictive.

We pull apart when my passenger door opens and Seb leans in, grinning. "Good morning, mum and dad. Probably best not to have sex in the school carpark. I'm thinking of your excellent reputations, of course."

Laughing, I reluctantly pull away from Archer and grab my

bag from the floor. As I climb out, Seb slings his arm over my shoulder. "Are you ready for it?" he asks me, pointing with his finger over to where Georgie and her cronies all hang outside the school entrance. "Someone is going to be fuming to see you back with my boy."

I scoff. "Like I care what she thinks."

"Good," Archer says as he comes up on my other side and he gently pulls me from Seb's embrace. He possessively swings his arm over my shoulder. "Because I intend for everyone to know that you're mine, Scar." He drops a kiss on the top of my head and steers us towards the path that leads to school. I don't miss the open stares and whispers as we pass our fellow students.

"I thought she was with Silver now." I hear one girl comment to her friends, and I glare at her as we pass, making her wither under my scrutiny. Archer's jaw tightens at the mention of Silver and me.

"Seriously?" Georgie steps into our path, arms folded, glaring at me. "You're back with the trash."

"Move," Archer orders her and I tilt my head in surprise when she doesn't immediately obey him.

"Why?" she asks him, looking at Archer in complete bewilderment. "What does she have that I don't?"

Archer studies her for a beat, his expression devoid of any emotion. I know that look. It's the one that tells me he's about to cut her down right here. "She has a personality, for a start." He moves us a step forward until we're right in front of her and she has to look up at him. "Now move, before I strip you here and now of your club status."

She swallows, straightening her back and moving to the side to let us pass. I can tell it nearly kills her to do so.

"Thanks, George," I tell her with a sarcastic smile, winking at her. I chance a glance at her from over my shoulder to see her practically breathing fire as she glares after us.

"Got to say, she really hates you, Little Red. You stole her prize," Seb chuckles as he falls back into step beside us.

"What the fuck does he want?" Archer growls, and I follow his scowl to where my friend is leaning near my locker.

"Be nice," I warn him, playfully hitting his chest with the back of my hand. "He's my friend, and you're going to have to get used to that." I duck from under his arm. Grinning at my friend, I throw myself around his neck and hug him.

"Hey, you." Silver grins at me and squeezes my waist before taking a step back from me. His eyes fall on Archer, who's looking at him like he wants to knock him out.

"Thought you might be missing this," he says, holding out my favourite Ramones t-shirt.

"Ah, I wondered where this had got to." I grin, taking it from him and shoving it into my bag.

"Emma wants to know if you're free for tea one Thursday?" he asks me.

"Who the fuck's Emma?" Archer barks, coming up behind me and placing a possessive hand on my hip.

I place my hand over his and pat it. "Emma is Damon's sister and also my friend."

"Are we friends with the whole family now?" he asks me dryly, and I can't help but smile at his jealousy. It's kind of sexy.

"Yes, tell her I'd love to do tea," I inform Damon.

"Great, we can go straight from school," Damon suggests, but before I have a chance to agree, Archer speaks for me.

"I'll drop you off. He can meet you there."

I roll my eyes at Damon, and he fights a smile. "Looks like I'm meeting you there."

"Sure thing," Damon replies with a wink. "Catch you later, princess." He turns on his heels and heads off towards the cafeteria.

"Princess," Archer scoffs.

Shaking my head, I turn to face the pissed off man at my back. I wrap my hands around his neck. "You don't think I'm a princess?"

Archer pulls me flush against him, looking down at me with

that fiery expression that turns my thoughts to mush. "You're no princess, Scar, You're a queen. My queen."

"He's my friend Archer and you are going to have to accept that because I'm not giving him up just because you're a possessive arsehole."

"We'll see," he answers gruffly, glaring over my head in the direction Damon left.

CHAPTER SEVENTEEN

ELIZA

I survive a day of whispers, stares, and glares. Some girls look at me like they wish they were me; others look at me like they'd like to stab me in the back. The girls that look wistfully at me with Archer have no idea what my life is like. I doubt they'll have to marry at seventeen.

When I walk out of school my stupid heart flips in my chest when my eyes find Archer Savage resting on the bonnet of his sports car, His shirt sleeves are rolled up to reveal those sexy tattoos. He's wearing his shades, chewing on gum and his full attention is on me, with his signature smirk on his face.

"This surprise isn't another trip to the woods, is it? Are you planning to leave me in the middle of nowhere and test me?"

He chuckles under his breath. "Not today, Scar. Today is a nice surprise. Or at least I hope it will be. Let's say this is part of me showing you that you're my priority now."

"Okay," I reply with a bob of my shoulders. "Can we get milkshakes on the way? I've been thinking about a banana shake all afternoon."

He reaches out and grabs me as I go to get in the car, pulling me between his legs on the bonnet. "Whatever my queen wants, she gets," he assures me as he nuzzles into my neck. "Hmm, you smell good."

"I always smell good," I agree, as I allow this display of affection. He's slowly worming his way back in and my stupid heart loves it.

"Come on, let's go before I decide to kidnap you and take you somewhere secluded to devour you."

Sigh, my over-excited libido likes that idea greatly.

As I climb into the passenger seat, I spot Chester leaning on the wall, a Vape in his hand, watching us. I arch a brow in confusion when he salutes Archer.

"What is that all about?" I ask, frowning at Chester.

"Let's just say the slimy fucker has his uses for now," Archer growls as he pulls off onto the path and we head away from college. We drive into the next village, and I sit up and take notice as this is where my mum grew up. The marina is full of fishing boats, and I take it all in wondering if once upon a time my mum's dad would have been down at there in a boat after a day's fishing.

"We're not going on a boat, are we?"

He side-glances at me and shakes his head. "If we were going out to sea, it would be on Libby, my grandfather's yacht."

I shake my head and snicker. Of course he's got a yacht.

We pull up in front of the marina and I look around us, puzzled at where we could be going. I'm dying to know what we're doing here. Archer holds out his hand to me and I slip mine in his, allowing him to guide me across the road to the row of quaint seafront shops.

"Wow, you're treating me to a chippy tea!" I exclaim when we come to a stop outside a chippy aptly named 'The Marina Chippy.' "This is my kind of treat."

He chuckles to himself as he pushes open the door. "We're not actually here for the food, but we can have chippy tea if you want, Scar."

We walk inside and the place is relatively busy with tables filled with families enjoying tea out and tourists enjoying a spot of food after a boat trip.

Archer walks up to the counter and I trail behind him, looking hungrily at the large plate of fish and chips a waiter brings out from the kitchen.

"Hey, I'm looking for Rebecca?"

The guy behind the counter smiles warmly at us. "She's out back. I'll grab her for you."

A minute later, the large man walks back out with a petite dark-haired woman walking behind him. She's wiping her hands on her apron and she approaches us, smiling.

"Hi, what can I do for you? I'm Rebecca, the owner."

"Could we take a seat with you for a second?" Archer asks her. He gestures at the empty table to our right.

Rebecca looks intrigued, and she agrees and directs us to take a seat. I look at Archer, puzzled. What on earth is this all about?

"You're Martha and Donald's daughter?"

"I am," she replies, looking as puzzled as I am right now.

"This is Eliza. She's Stephanie's daughter. Your second cousin."

My mouth drops open at the same time as Rebecca's does. When I take a moment to study her, I can see it now, the family resemblance to my mother.

"Stephanie's daughter?" she asks, as if she is uncertain of what she has just heard.

"Yes. This is Stephanie and Andrew's daughter. She's living in the bay now with Wilbur," Archer informs her.

At the mention of Wilbur's name, her expression turns sour. She turns her attention to me, studying me in shock. "I can see you're the double of your dad. Although you have your mum's nose."

"You're my mum's cousin," I reply, still reeling in shock. "Did you know about me? About us?"

She swallows and nods her head. "Your mum wrote to me only once, with no forwarding address. It was when you were born. Eliza Rose."

"I didn't think we had any living family until recently," I explain, and she nods her head.

"I'm sorry you lost them both. They were wonderful people. So in love."

I smile. My parents were the epitome of love. "They really were," I agree, swallowing and trying to fight the threatening tears.

"How did you know they had passed if you weren't in contact? They changed their names." I asked her, confused how she knew they were no longer here.

Rebecca looks down at her hands and sighs. "I found out when Wilbur Alderman paid me a visit about five years ago. He walked in here one day and sat at that table over there and he told me they'd both died in a car accident and left two orphaned children."

"What did he want?" I ask, a chill running through my body, knowing I'm not going to like what she tells me next.

Rebecca physically grimaces. "Wilbur told me about the two of you. He knew the chippy had been struggling. The landlord kept putting the rent on the shop up to levels we were struggling to afford, and this place had been my parents' lives. They'd worked so hard all of their lives to build up this small business. Wilbur offered us the golden ticket. He gave us the money to buy the property from the landlord, but there was a condition."

I lean my elbows on the table, eager to hear more. "Go on," I encourage her.

"There's no easy way to tell you this, but he said the money was ours if we didn't come forward to claim you."

My stomach sinks. The conniving bastard had bribed my family to leave us in foster care.

"We were on the verge of losing everything," she offers, her expression twisted in anxiety. "He knew we couldn't say no. So, we took the money and agreed to keep quiet."

"He left us in foster care for five years," I tell her, trying to make her understand the brevity of their decision.

"I know," she tells me with a nod of her head, avoiding my

eyes. "It's torn me up for years knowing that you were both out there and that we could've done something about it."

I shrug my shoulders. "That's Wilbur for you. He is always one step ahead." That bastard had it all planned out. All this time we had a family that might have been able to take us in.

"To be honest, I doubt social services would have placed you with us if it's any consolation. We didn't have a spare bedroom," Rebecca explains.

"Wilbur wouldn't have allowed that anyway. He'd have made sure of that."

Rebecca nods. "Everyone in this village knows the Aces and the power and pull they have. Gods, they own half the property here as well. He gave us a choice, but it wasn't really a choice."

I nod my head. She is right. Had they not taken his deal, he'd have made sure their business failed and seen them out on the streets.

"Tell me about her," I beg, eager to hear more about my mum as a girl my age.

"Can you hang around for a while until my evening staff arrive?"

I look at Archer and he nods his head. "We'll go get milkshakes and come back in an hour."

"That's perfect," she beams. "I have lots of family photo albums to share with you."

"That would be amazing," I tell her, my eyes brimming with tears.

Archer gets to his feet and offers me his hand. "Come on, let's get you that milkshake. We'll see you in a bit, Rebecca."

I'm shocked when she stands up and pulls me into a hug. Stepping back, she looks me over, her own eyes fighting back tears. "I'm so glad you're here. We have lots to catch up on."

I'M QUIET AS WE SIT OUTSIDE THE SMALL ICE CREAM SHOP, sipping on our drinks. It is a lot to process. We have more family here. We have gone from having no one to this.

"What's going on in your head, Scar?"

I pull my gaze from the marina to look at him. He's studying me with uncertainty.

"I'm okay," I reassure him. "I mean, I'm not okay, but it's no surprise." I run my hand over my face. "Actually, I'm raging. I'm so angry. I want to destroy him, Archer."

He nods his head in response. "Leave it with me, Scar. To bring Wilbur down will be a dangerous game. He has a lot of people in power on his side."

I sigh in frustration. I know he is right. Part of me just wants to storm into the house and confront him, but I need to take a step back and think this through. Strategize just like he does.

"I don't care what it takes. I want to see him finished. I want to destroy this legacy because it's one built on lies and deceit. I don't want a penny of his dirty money."

I scoff to myself. He has the nerve to call the Silver's money dirty, but he's no better. He just thinks because he was born in a mansion surrounded by old money that it makes him somehow better than them. The Aces society has built what they have by holding information and secrets on people so they can blackmail them to do as they say.

"Are you ready to head back to Rebecca's?" Archer asks me, and I nod my head firmly. I was ready to learn more about my parents.

WE SPEND THE NEXT TWO HOURS IN THE FAMILY FLAT ABOVE the chippy. Rebecca pulls out all the family albums and I'm thrilled to see she has a couple of photos of my mum and dad together. She tells me they met when my mum was covering a shift in the chippy for one of the girls. My dad had called in for some supper on his way home and then he'd kept coming back and asking for her. Rebecca laughed, and she said that my mum had played hard to get at first. She made him work for that first date, but that it had been inevitable. You could see the attraction between them. She shared that she knew they were planning to run away together. She'd let them store their bags with her and she'd met them at the train station the morning they left together. Rebecca was able to give me some more insight into my dad's relationship with Wilbur. She said there had been little love there, just expectation and duty to the family. When Rebecca shared that my dad had never wanted to marry Archer's mum, but he'd been pushed towards her by both their families, I felt Archer stiffen beside me. Neither of us has explained to Rebecca who Archer was.

Hearing my mum and dad's love story was precious. Listening to Rebecca say how they fell in love, two people from very different worlds and how they fought to be together, walking away from everything. I can't even imagine how hard it must have been for my mum to leave behind her family and never see them again. Rebecca sadly informs me that my grandparents, Stephanie's mum and dad have sadly both passed away. Her mum, Susan, passed away when my mum was only fifteen and her dad, Geoff, passed away ten years ago from a heart attack. I had been hopeful they would still be alive, so I'm sad that I'll never get to meet them, but Rebecca gives me some photos of them for me to keep.

"It's getting late. We should go," Archer suggests, and I nod my head in agreement.

"Thank you so much for spending this time with me," I say to Rebecca as I get to my feet.

Rebecca reaches out and snags my hand in hers. "Anytime, we're family. I wasn't there for you back then," she swallows, regret crosses her face, "but I'm here now."

"It's okay. I know what Wilbur can be like. Trust me," I tell her, squeezing her hand in reassurance. This isn't her fault, it's his.

"Regardless. I'm truly sorry." She pulls me in for another hug. "Come for tea next week."

"That would be nice, thanks."

Rebecca waves us off at the door, with her husband Lee behind her, as we walk back over to the car. Archer clicks his keys, and the doors open, but before he can walk to his side, I reach for his hand and stop him.

"Thank you," I tell him softly. "You have no idea what tonight meant to me."

Archer looks down at our joined hands. "I told you, Scar. I'm in your corner from now on."

I stand on my tiptoes and press my lips to his and he hesitates, allowing me to set the pace and take the lead. "Maybe there is a heart in there after all."

He offers me a half-smile. "I'm not sure about that."

"Oh, I am. Come on, take me home. I'm shattered."

"My home or yours?" he asks me as our eyes meet across the top of the car.

"I don't really have a home," I admit, because it's truly how I feel. I haven't felt at home anywhere since our parents died and they sold our family home.

"You have a home, Scarlet. It is with me," he says, offering me a soft wink before climbing inside.

I think my heart just melts a little. Only a little.

❧

I WAKE IN THE MORNING, IN ARCHER'S BED. I'M SURROUNDED by his signature scent and his warm arms wrapped around my waist. His face snuggled into my neck. Who knew Archer Savage was a snuggler. I don't think that will go down well with his ruthless reputation.

We had sex last night. I know, I know. I am weak. I said I'd make him work for it and make him wait, but last night it felt right. It felt right to end such a perfect evening in his arms with his mouth on my body. I threw caution to the wind and just let myself be present in the moment. To forget all the bullshit and manipulation around us and just be a girl who needed a boy to help her feel again.

"Morning," he mumbles sleepily into my hair, and I can't fight the shit-eating cheesy grin that appears on my face at the sound of his voice.

"Morning, Savage," I reply in a teasing tone.

"Oh, so it's Savage, huh?" he asks me. I yelp in surprise when he grabs tighter at my waist and rolls us until I end up under him. I giggle as he tickles at my sides, but we both jump when there is a sharp rap at the door, and it opens to reveal his father.

"Do you mind?" Archer growls at him, ensuring the duvet is covering my nudity.

Phil looks me over once, before dismissing me as if I'm not there. "I'm flying to New York this morning; Edward would like to speak with you before you leave for school."

"Business or pleasure?" Archer asks him dryly, running a hand through his bed hair.

"Both, actually." He looks at me then. "So, this engagement is going ahead then? We're going to play happy families?"

"We are," Archer tells him firmly. "The past needs to stay in the past, where it belongs."

Phil scoffs. "I wonder if your mother would feel the same way. Careful, Archer, we know how persuasive these Alderman's can be." He pivots on his heel and leaves as quickly as he arrived, sadly leaving his oppressive presence behind.

"Wow, he really hates my family, doesn't he?" I say, shaking my head, and lying back flat on the bed.

"Don't worry about him. He's just a bitter old man," Archer assures, leaning over me. "Shower with me?" he asks me, smiling.

I wish I could freeze this moment and other moments when he's like this. When he doesn't feel a need to put on this persona that's expected from him by his family and the Elders. I wish he and I weren't at their beck and call and that we could just be free.

"Lead the way," I reply, grinning. I scream in surprise when he throws me over his shoulder and strides into the en-suite.

❧

I SHOULD HAVE KNOWN THAT THE PLEASANT MOOD WE WERE in couldn't last for long. This place, with its history and darkness, would be here to remind me I don't belong. When we pull up at the Alderman mansion, the place is a hive of activity. The security company workers are everywhere. As we climb out of the car, one guy with a sniffer dog passes us, talking gravely into his walky-talky.

"What on earth's going on?" I ask Archer in bewilderment. "Do you think there's been a break in?"

Archer frowns, shaking his head. "No idea. Let's head inside and find out."

Archer escorts me into the house with his hand at my back. We walk through to the kitchen to find detective Boyd standing there speaking with Edith and Rory.

"Oh, here she is," Edith says, touching at her heart and getting to her feet. "There's been an incident during the night."

My blood runs cold as I take in their sombre faces.

"Is it Kit? Oh my god is he okay?"

Rory holds his hand up to stop me. "Kit's fine. He's in the shower getting ready for school."

My heart relaxes in my chest. Thank God. "What is it then?"

Detective Boyd clears his throat and gestures to the vacant seats opposite him at the kitchen island. "Why don't you both take a seat?"

This can't be good. Silently, we walk over and sit down opposite Boyd.

"What's going on, Boyd? Just get to it, no nonsense," Archer orders him with a frown.

"There was in intruder on the grounds last night. They left a sinister message for Eliza."

"What kind of message?" Archer asks, his tone darkening. Out of the corner of my eye, I see his jaw tighten.

"Well. Someone dug an open grave on the grounds and left a shop mannequin in a coffin. The figure was dressed as you Miss Alderman."

"It's Holton," I remind him as my brain processes his words. "I want to see it."

Detective Boyd holds up his hand in protest. "I'm not sure that is a good idea."

"I want to see it," I insist, jumping to my feet and heading for the back door. I hear Archer chasing after me and Boyd's suggestions that I don't go out there. I soon find what he's talking about when I catch sight of Calvin and a cluster of our security men gathered around an area to the west of the garden.

I stride over and push past them, then gasp when I see the freshly dug grave. But it's what is inside the grave that is beyond creepy. The coffin is open and inside is a mannequin with burgundy coloured hair. What's even more disturbing is the dummy is wearing one of my actual t-shirts. I hadn't even noticed it was missing. Around her neck is a line of blood, as if her throat's been slashed. Her hands are secured together with cable ties. Whoever has done this has really gone to town though, because there's even a gravestone. A real-life gravestone. They carved my name into it with a date two weeks from now as my date of death. Underneath the date it says, 'Leave or die.'

"Fuck!" I exclaim, taking a step back into Archer's chest. He grips both my arms to steady me against him. I hear his intake of breath as he takes in the grisly scene before us. "Someone around here really doesn't like me, do they?" I say in a shaky voice.

"This isn't funny, Scar," Archer says. "Will someone please

tell me how this maniac got on the grounds undetected and had time to do this with all this security in place?" he barks. I can feel the anger coming from him.

Calvin shakes his head, looking perplexed. "We don't know. We have hourly patrols in place and motion detecting cameras, everything."

"We think it must have been more than one person," Detective Boyd says, still wheezing for breath, from running outside after me.

"It's a fucking shambles is what it is," Archer growls. "And clearly, hourly patrols are not enough." He turns to Boyd and points a finger his way. "You better put all your resources on this. This is a threat to kill." Archer turns his attention back to me. "Scar, come here. You're shaking."

I look down bewildered and realise he's right. I walk to him, and he cocoons me into his arms. "I'm shaking with anger," I reassure him. I'm not weak, but things are different now. I don't have just myself to think about. There is a tiny human growing inside of me who needs protection.

"Where the fuck is Wilbur?" Archer demands of everyone standing here.

"He's in London," Calvin informs us. "Business."

"Fuck business," Archer exclaims, swearing under his breath. "He should be here showing some concern for his granddaughter."

"I don't feel so good," I murmur, suddenly feeling lightheaded.

Archer looks down at me and he mustn't like what he sees because the next thing I know I'm lifted off my feet and he's striding back to the house with me in his arms. Edith and Detective Boyd scurry behind us to keep up. When we enter the kitchen, he deposits me down on the kitchen worktop and steps in between my legs, cupping my face in his hands.

"Are you okay? Do you need a doctor?"

I'm struck speechless by the genuine concern I see expressed in his eyes as he looks me over.

"I'm okay. It is just a shock seeing that," I tell him, offering him a reassuring smile.

"You're pale," he replies.

"I'm always pale. I'm an English rose, remember," I jest, and his upper lift quirks at the corner.

"Edith, tea might help," he suggests.

"Actually, can I get a diet coke?" I ask Edith. She nods her head and rushes off to the fridge, bringing me back an ice-cold glass of cola.

"That's it. I'm done with this situation," Archer announces, looking determined. "Send one of the staff up to pack up her belongings. She's not spending another night in this house."

"No," I protest firmly. "If you think for one minute, I'm leaving my brother here where there is some nutter getting in, you've another thing coming Archer."

"Maybe he's safer without you here," Boyd chirps in and Archer swivels his frosty glare on him as if to say, did you seriously just say that?

"I'm just thinking that it's clearly Eliza this person is after, so maybe he'll be safer with her not here."

I shudder, feeling like someone has walked over my grave, which is such a poor description given I have an actual grave outside in the garden. "God, he's right. Me being here is putting him at risk." I feel sick that I could be responsible, once again, for putting my brother's wellbeing at risk.

"Look, I'll get Wilbur to increase the security here. We can even have a guy outside Kit's room if it makes you feel better, but it's not him I'm worried about, Scar. It's you. The Savage Mansion has the best security in place that money can buy. Edward is a paranoid old man. I'm not taking no for an answer. You're coming to live with me where I can keep you safe."

"Okay," I say, nodding my head. He's right. It's me they want, so they'll go where I am, which means Kit will be safe.

"Okay?" Archer repeats questioningly, his brow arched.

"Yes, no arguments from me this time," I tell him, rolling my eyes. He's in shock that I'm agreeing with him without a fight.

"Okay then. You heard her Edith. Get the girls to pack her things up. Calvin, could you have them delivered to my house this afternoon?"

"Of course. Not a problem," Calvin smiles at me in concern.

Edith clucks around me, asking me if I want some breakfast, but if I'm honest, the thought of food makes me want to vomit.

"Do you want to stay off today?" Archer asks me, as he dismisses everyone and gives me his full attention.

"No," I say, running my fingers through his hair. "Thank you, but I need to go to college. I have A-levels to pass."

"Fuck A-levels," he replies with a wave of his hands. "We're rich, we don't need A-levels."

I can't help but smile at his flippancy. "You might not need them, but I do."

He cups my neck with his hands. "You're going to be my wife, Scar. You'll want for nothing. I promise."

"Still. I want to pass my A-levels because I studied and because I deserve to pass them. So, we're going to school." I straighten my back. "It's going to take more than some sicko and some pathetic fake grave to keep me down."

Archer smirks down at me. "That's my girl."

"I'm not yours," I say half-heartedly in argument.

"We'll agree to disagree today," he says as he drops a soft barely there kiss on my lips as if he's scared he'll break me. I remind him I'm not that breakable by pulling him closer by his tie and deepening the kiss.

"Come on then, let's go get this precious education you're so concerned about," he orders, pulling away from me and lifting me off the counter onto my feet.

Going home to Archer's house after school feels strange. We head straight to his room, and he tugs me towards his walk-in wardrobe.

"Jenny unpacked all your clothes," he says, kissing me on the forehead before he undresses out of his uniform. He takes his trousers off and sits down on the large pouf. He looks at me for a beat with a tortured look on his face. "I need to know who is doing this to you, and when I find them, I'm going to kill them slowly."

I place a hand over my heart, smiling. "Good to know that you'd kill for me," I joke.

He doesn't smile along with me. "I would kill for you, Scar. You're my family now."

My stupid heart thunders in my chest at his words. He sits here with his beautiful tattoos on display, with his perfectly chiselled body, and those dark eyes burning into mine with so much fire. I always thought I didn't need anyone to fight for me but having him at my side telling me he'll kill anyone who hurts me makes me feel things I've never felt for a boy before. It's right on the tip of my tongue to tell him I'm pregnant, but I hesitate. I walk over to him and step between his legs. He looks up at me as I run my fingers through his dark mop of hair.

"When we find who's doing this, we'll kill them together," I say. "After all, they're my stalker."

Archer shakes his head and looks at me with wonder. "I love it when you talk violence, baby. It makes me want to fuck you into next week."

I tip my head back and laugh. Only Archer and I could find talking about killing someone a turn on. I guess we're the epitome of fucked up.

"I have Aces business to attend to tonight. I want you to promise me you won't leave this house."

I roll my eyes as his possessive and protective alpha male rears its head. "Vee and I were going to go to the cinema tonight," I tell him, pouting my lips.

"Watch a movie here," he replies. I can tell from the firmness of his tone that it's not a suggestion. It's an order.

"We can't watch it here. It's only out in the cinemas."

"No."

"Don't tell me no," I say gruffly.

"No, Scar. Someone dug a fucking grave for you last night. Now, if I have to chain you to my bed to make you stay in, I will."

I arch a brow at him as I grasp the hair at the back of his neck, making him tilt his head higher to look at me.

"Don't tell me what to do, Arch," I say with a sigh. Deep down, I know he's right, but I don't take kindly to being ordered around. "I'll stay in, but not because you're telling me to, but because I don't want to put my friend at risk. Oh, and you can pay for our takeaway."

He smirks as his hands move up my thighs under my skirt. "It's a deal. Now get undressed. We're taking a shower."

He's ordering me around again, but when it's the type of order where he wants me naked, I'm not going to argue.

❧

WE'RE EATING DINNER WITH HIS GRANDFATHER IN THE kitchen when his dad walks into the room. He loosens his tie and stops at the table. I don't miss the frown that crosses his face when he spots me.

"Eliza," he greets. "I didn't know you were joining us for dinner tonight," he says with a tight smile as he takes a seat opposite his son.

"She'll be joining us every night from now on," Archer tells him, glancing up from his plate. "I moved her in here today."

Phil cocks a brow. "Ah, yes, the stalker. I heard about the latest threat. You must regret the day you ever moved here?"

I scoff. "Well, since I had little choice about coming to live here in the bay, regret would be a useless emotion to be feeling."

Phil nods his head, continuing to study me. "Still, it must concern you that someone wants you gone so badly that they're making threats to your life. Maybe your past is catching up with you."

I frown. "What would you know of my past?"

He shrugs his shoulders. "Well, you are your father's daughter."

"Enough," Archer barks, glaring across the table at his dad. "You need to stop living in the past."

"Exactly," Edward adds in. "Our two families will finally be united again. Forging that bond and keeping our strength as the founding families. It's what built this bay and its surrounding villages and what led us to be a global powerhouse economically. Past grudges need to be buried." Edward smiles at me. "We'll show this stalker that they can't touch us. We'll carry on as normal. The party to announce your engagement will show that we're a united front. In the meantime, we have our best private investigators working to identify who this bastard is."

"That reminds me," Archer interrupts. "The engagement party needs to move here. I don't feel Wilbur has tight enough security."

Edward nods his head, wiping his mouth with a serviette. "Agreed." He smiles at me. "It's been a long time since we've had a party here, my dear. Why, I think the last time we held a social event here was when Phil and Libby announce their engagement." Edward picks up his drink. "In fact, shall we retire to the lounge and discuss plans for the party?"

Archer smiles briefly at his grandad. "Why don't you and Eliza go through? I just need a quick word with dad."

I don't miss the half smirk that Phil gives him. Edward pulls my chair out and ushers me with him out of the room. I glance over my shoulder to find the two Savage men glaring across the table at each other.

CHAPTER EIGHTEEN

ARCHER

I stare across the table at my father. All my life I've had him drum into me that the Alderman's needed to pay for what they did to my mother. All my life he's been set on making sure someone paid for the fact that his wife was in love with another man. His visceral need for revenge consumed me. It became my life's mission, but everything has changed now.

"You need to let this go," I tell him.

He scoffs, leaning back in his seat. "Is her pussy that magical that you'll forget that her family is the reason you no longer have a mother?"

I slam my fist on the table. At one time, I was too small to fight back when he became aggressive, but those days were long gone. I'm his equal now in strength, perhaps even slightly stronger.

"Don't talk about her like that," I hiss in warning.

My father laughs, tipping his head back. "Oh, son, have I taught you nothing? You've let a woman hypnotise you with sex. I don't doubt she's a little vixen in bed, but don't let that blind you into thinking she won't betray you. They're all the same, women. All out for what they can get and how they can manipulate us into their own agendas."

"You're wrong," I reply, swirling the wine around in my glass. "You brought me up with this poisoned view of women, but they're not all like that. She isn't like that."

He looks at me with such disappointment. "Love is a weakness, son. You'll see it soon and I'll be there to remind you I told you so when she betrays you."

I shake my head at him. Finally, seeing him for what he is, a bitter man stuck in the past. "Let it go, dad. Go fuck one of your little whores and gamble some more money away. Isn't that what you do best?"

Phil slams his fist on the table, jumping to his feet. "You little fucker! Remember who you're speaking to!"

I slowly get to my feet, showing him he no longer scares me or controls me. "I know exactly who I'm speaking to. A man who has tried to twist and shape me into a bitter kid who you could use to enact your revenge. I'm done being your puppet." I walk away from the table and leave him there, silently seething.

I pause when I get to the lounge, hearing laughter. It's something this house has heard little of in the last two decades. Grandad and Eliza are dancing together, both smiling and chatting as he teaches her the steps to some ballroom classic.

"What's going on in here?" I say, stepping into the room.

Scar lifts her gaze my way, smiling at me in that way that makes me want to stop the world and rebuild it for her. My heart squeezes in my chest with a foreign emotion.

"Edward is teaching me the foxtrot. I'm not very good though," she admits.

"Nonsense," my grandfather protests. "You just need practice. Come dance with your fiancée and let this old man have a rest."

"Old man," Eliza scoffs, shaking her head. "You're not old Edward."

"He's an old crock," I joke as I stride into the room and take her from him.

"Watch it," Edwards warns me, grinning. "You're not too old for a clip around the ear, my boy."

"Sit down and enjoy your whisky, while I show Scar my moves."

She fits in my arms like she's made to be there. Scar looks up at me with that smile that floors me each time I see it. She is the embodiment of beauty. I don't deserve her, but I'm taking her and keeping her for my own.

"Where did you learn to dance like this?" she asks me as we move around the room.

"Lessons and my mum. She loved to dance."

"She was never happier than when she was dancing," Edward says, his eyes glazing over as he loses himself in a memory. "When you were a toddler, she'd rest you on her hip and sing and dance around the room with you. She came alive when she danced."

"Looks like someone inherited her natural talent," Scar says, winking at me as I spin her out and back to me. She laughs, and it makes my blackened heart warm. Scar is changing me, and I quite like the 'me' that is emerging.

"What?" she asks me, tilting her head at me and studying my expression.

"You're fucking beautiful. You know that, right?"

She side-glances to where Edward sits. "You know we're not alone, right?"

I nod my head, my eyes not leaving hers. "I don't give a shit who's in the room. You are perfection, Scar, and I'm never letting you go."

"I'm not a possession for a collection, Archer. And I'm far from perfect," she replies, her fire shining through her eyes.

"I don't see you as a possession. You are your own person. I know that. I can't help that I'm a crazy bastard who wants all your attention, your smiles, and your laughter. It breathes life into my bitter soul."

Scar places a hand on my chest. "Maybe there's hope for you after all. Maybe I can thaw the ice and make you half-way human again."

I smile down at her, drinking her in. "Stranger things have happened, Scar."

I pull her flush against me and rest my head on top of hers as we sway to the music. Edward catches my eye. He sits there quietly watching us dance, and winks at me, a smile gracing his weathered and wrinkled face. Maybe my old grandfather is onto something in bringing our engagement forward. The sooner Scar has my ring on her finger and my surname, the better.

CHAPTER NINETEEN

ELIZA

I chew on my lip as I walk alongside Vee, who is chatting away about the latest episode of Love Island. I need to ask her to cover for me today after school. I just hope that I can trust her.

"Are you listening to a word I just said?" She waves her hand in front of my face. "Girl, is Archer dicking you all night and not letting you get any sleep?"

"Hardy-har," I deadpan, pulling my tongue out at her. "He's not dicking me all night, maybe just two or three times." And that's not a lie. Living with Archer has meant we have a lot of time together, which more often than not results in sex because we seem to be insatiable for each other right now.

"Uh, that glorious period of new love where you hump like bunnies on heat," she says wistfully staring off into the distance.

"Lust, not love," I tell her with a snicker, and she cocks a finely groomed brow at me.

"You two are head over heels for each other. You're both just too scared and too proud to admit it." She winks at me. "Anyway, tell me what has you so distracted if it isn't being dickmatised by Archer."

"Dickmatised?" I repeat, smiling. "That's not even a word."

"It is," she insists. "It's when a girl gets dick so good that it's all she can think about." She pops a bonbon into her mouth and offers me one.

I take the sweet from her and look around us to make sure

no nosey students can hear me. "I need a favour from you," I explain. "I need you to cover for me after school. I need Archer to think I'm with you."

Vee studies me as she chews. "And where will you be going when you're pretending to be with me?"

I bite my lip and grimace. "I can't say." I place my hand on her arm when I see her face fall. "It's not that I don't trust you. I'll tell you soon, I promise. I just can't tell you yet."

"Okay," she says softly. "I told you I'd have your back, and I meant it. Girl's code. I'll cover for you. So, what will Arch think we're doing?"

"I was thinking we tell him we're having a pamper session at yours. I can get him to drop me off at your house. He has rugby practice tonight, so he'll head off to rugby and then I can do what I need to and be back at yours before he picks me up."

"Okay, fake pamper evening, it is."

I pull her in for a hug, and she freezes up for a second, as if shocked I'm hugging her but then she softens and wraps her arms around me and hugs me back. "What are besties for if not for covering your back?"

"Thank you," I tell her gratefully as we pull apart and continue to class. I pull out my phone and tap a quick message to Damon to tell him it's sorted and that he can pick me up from Vee's.

"Talking of the dickmatiser," Vee says, grinning and gesturing with her head. I follow her gaze to find Archer waiting outside my English class.

I tilt my head at him in question.

"What are you doing here?"

He leans up off the door frame and gestures inside the room. "I swapped all our schedules around so that one of us is with you all the time."

I groan as he follows Vee and I into the classroom. Freddy, a guy who sits next to me in English, looks up in fright when Archer drops his bag down on his desk. "Move," he commands.

Freddy swallows and jumps from his seat like his arse is on fire. "Seats all yours," he says shakily before he scuttles off to an empty desk at the front of the class.

"You're an arsehole," I comment, with a roll of my eyes at Archer, as I take my seat next to him. "Oh, can you drop me at Vee's after school? We're having a pamper session at her house. Some girly time."

"Sure," he nods.

That was easy. I was worried for a minute that he'd insist one of them stay with us.

❧

ARCHER DROPS ME AT VEE'S AFTER SCHOOL. VEE OFFERED TO take me home with her, but he insisted on driving me there, saying it was safer.

"I'll see you later," I tell him as I undo my seatbelt.

He leans over the centre console and pulls me in for a kiss. "Be good."

"Aren't I always?" I reply with a grin as I climb from the car. My stomach lurches in discomfort at my deceit. I wave him off and when I'm sure he's gone, I head inside Vee's house and up to her room.

"Hey," I greet as I drop on the bed beside her. She's sitting watching television. "You're obsessed with this show," I tease, seeing she's watching Love Island again.

"I wanted to watch it again. It was so good when Connor confronted her last night."

My phone rings and I pull it out of my pocket.

"I'm outside," Damon says when I answer.

"I'll be five mins, I just need to change," I tell him. I climb off the bed and pull out a change of clothes. I could not risk turning up to the private clinic in my uniform.

Vee pauses her programme, and she nods her head, chewing on her lip. "Damon?"

"Yep," I admit, tugging my t-shirt over my head. "Nothing's going on between us, before you ask."

Vee holds her hands up. "Hey, I wasn't going to ask. Hoes before bros and all that. Whatever it is, I know you'll tell me when you're ready to."

"I will, I promise," I agree as I lean down and wrap my arm around her neck and hug her. "I'll be back in about an hour and a bit."

"Sure thing."

❧

I DASH OUTSIDE TO FIND DAMON WAITING IN HIS convertible, looking every inch the bad boy, with his shades on and Digga D pumping from the car.

"Ready princess?"

"As ready as I'll ever be," I say, as I climb into the passenger seat and buckle in.

Damon looks over at me and then back at the Collings' mansion. "Are you sure you can trust her?"

I nod my head firmly. "Yep. She won't breathe a word."

Damon puts the car into first and pulls away and we head to the clinic. We don't have long to wait when we arrive, and we're ushered into a room where the sonographer is waiting for us.

"Everything looks good," she tells me as she moves the probe over my belly. She swivels the screen around so we can see. "I'd say you are about thirteen weeks along."

My breath pauses in my throat when I see the image on the monitor. There is an actual baby. You can see its head and little arms and legs. The tiny beat of its heart flashes in and out on the screen.

"Woah," Damon says, leaning in closer to examine the little person on the screen. "How did you make a person, princess?"

The sonographer chuckles, "Well, I think you may have had something to do with it, Mr Silver."

Damon clears his throat and looks awkwardly at her. "I guess I did."

"Everything is fine. We'll get your bloods done and then get you booked in for your next scan. Would you like a video of the scan?"

"We can get that?" I ask her in surprise, struggling to tear my eyes away from the screen.

"You can. We can e-mail it over to you, so you have a digital copy."

"Yes, please," I reply keenly, and she smiles at my excitement.

We leave the clinic twenty minutes later. I have the scan photos tucked in an envelope in my bag. When we get to the car, I tug on Damon's jacket sleeve.

"Hey, can you keep these safe for me?" I hold out the envelope. "I can't risk taking them home?"

"Home?" Damon replies with a cocked brow.

I glare at him. "You know what I mean. I can't take these back to Archer's house."

Sighing, he takes them off me. "I'll keep them in my safe. You know, if you told him, there wouldn't need to be all this secrecy."

"I'm not ready," I reply sharply, shaking my head. "I just need some more time."

Damon leans his back against his car. "More time for what, princess? What is it you're waiting for? He's marrying you. You're living in his house and fucking him every night. The baby news won't change anything."

I hug my arms around my middle, feeling uncomfortable under his scrutiny. I kick at the dirt with my trainers. "I know that, but I'm still processing all this. Plus, I have a stalker out there. The last thing I need is them knowing I'm pregnant and that the likelihood of me leaving the bay is even less now."

Damon surprises me when he snags his arm out and pulls me

in for a hug. "Come here." He rubs my back, before pulling back and looking down at me. "Which is exactly why you should tell Savage. There isn't just you that needs protecting now."

"I know," I sigh. "Just let me get the engagement announcement and party out of the way, and then I'll tell him. I promise."

"Whatever you say, princess." He kisses the top of my head and peels away from me and he climbs into the car. I pause and rub my hand across my belly. I'm having a real-life baby. Shit just got a whole lot real.

CHAPTER TWENTY

ELIZA

The next week passes in a blur. Wilbur has assigned me my own personal bodyguard, Tony, who follows me everywhere I go. He's a six-foot three wall of muscle with a stern face. The type of person who, if you met them in an alley on a dark night, you'd shit yourself. I did protest about having Tony, but Archer, Edward and Wilbur, all insisted it was necessary. If I'm honest, I sometimes forget he's there. He's so stealthy and silent and blends into the background. It is reassuring to know he's there and that he's there to protect me and keep me safe when Archer and the boys aren't around.

Alexis' designer calls by the mansion and brings a tonne of dresses for me to try on in preparation for the engagement party. I choose a purple silk dress—simple but elegant. Plans are well underway for the party. Wilbur's PA, Jackie, has everything in hand and the local press are being invited so that they can take photos and share the news in the local paper.

I've been lost in my own thoughts this week. Damon emailed me across the scan video. I've watched it a few times now, on those rare times I'm alone, which isn't often because Archer or Rafe and Seb are with me everywhere I go. Archer has asked me a few times if I'm okay and I've plastered on a smile and told him I'm fine.

I'm a million miles away in my own head when we're driving home from school on Friday, so I don't notice straight away that we're not heading toward home.

"Where are we going?" I ask him, perplexed.

"Ah, you finally noticed we aren't going home huh?" he says, studying me from across the car. "Talk to me, Scar. What's bothering you?"

I falter under his scrutiny. *Just tell him.*

"I guess the whole engagement party and everything is just freaking me out a bit," I lie.

He nods his head. "I thought as much, which is why we're doing this part on our own terms."

I furrow my brow at him. "What does that mean?"

He smiles and shakes his head. "Wait and see."

We drive for another thirty minutes and I'm becoming more intrigued about where we are going. I have no clue where we are. He eventually indicates off the main road, and we drive down a winding country lane. The road opens up to reveal a house on a hill overlooking the sea. It's a beautiful house with glass everywhere so that you can enjoy the view from wherever you are.

"Let me guess," I say, climbing out of the car and admiring the property, "another Savage house."

"Mine, actually," Archer says as he comes around my side of the car and takes my hand in his. "Come on."

I shake my head in disbelief. In what world does a guy who's not even eighteen own a house like this?

He leads us to the front door and unlocks the place, then tugs me inside. I'm surprised when we enter, as I can hear music playing upstairs.

"Is someone here?" I ask him, but he ignores me and gently guides me up the glass staircase. My mouth hangs open when we reach the top and I see the view. The floor to ceiling glass walls gives an amazing view of the harsh sea crashing against the rocks.

"Wow, this is stunning." I find myself drawn across the room to the view. I jump slightly when Archer's hands land on my shoulders.

"Gorgeous, isn't it?"

I nod my head. "It's perfect."

"Come on, there's more," he tells me, as he guides me away from that captivating view. He pulls back one of the glass panels to reveal a decked balcony area which sits to the side of the house. The decked area is covered in fairy lights and candles and a hot tub bubbles away over in the corner.

"Get naked," he tells me, his stubble tickling my ear as he moves away from me and peels off his t-shirt.

Okay, now things are getting interesting. I take a moment to just ogle him before I bend down and slip off my shoes. A minute later, I'm sinking into the warm water and settling myself in his lap.

"What is this all about?" I ask him as he hands me a glass of champagne. "It's not my birthday for another four months."

He clinks his glass against mine and smirks as he takes a drink. "This is about us taking back some control, Scar."

He reaches over the side of the hot tub, putting his glass down and reaching for something in his trouser pocket. My heart stops dead in my chest when he holds a small black velvet box in his palm.

"Savage, what are you doing?"

He flips up the lid of the box and a beautiful ruby ring surrounded by diamonds stares back at me. I gulp when he takes the ring out of the box and captures my left hand in his.

"Eliza Holton, will you do me the honour of being mine?"

I swallow deeply as I look down at the ring and back up at him. "Wilbur is going to kill you. He had the proposal scene all planned out."

Archer shrugs his shoulders like he couldn't give a shit. "Like I said. I'm making sure this moment is about us and not about some PR stunt. So, what's your answer, Scar?"

I look back down at the ring. He knows my answer; he knows that I have no choice in this matter thanks to Wilbur. My heart flips in my chest at how he has made this moment so damn perfect.

"Yes, I'll be your wife," I tell him, and I watch as he slips the ring on my finger. It fits perfectly but then I should have known he'd know my ring size.

"It's beautiful," I say, wiggling my finger and staring at the expensive ring. "Oh gosh, this is the ring I saw in the jewellers in London!" I gasp, eyes wide.

"It is," he admits, rubbing his finger over the ruby. "I saw you linger on it, and I went back and bought it that morning."

I press my lips against his, silencing him. I wrap my arms around his neck and press my chest flush to his. He grips the back of my head and kisses me like I'm the air he needs to breathe. The kiss becomes heated, and it's not long before I'm lifting my hips and sinking myself down on him. I rock my hips slowly and we're silent as we kiss and touch each other. I know in this moment that despite everything that's happened, I'm totally and utterly in love with Archer Savage, but the words stick in my throat, stopping me from saying them out loud.

"Let go, Scar," he whispers as he cups my face in his hands. "Give me everything."

I come seconds later, crying out his name and clutching him tightly and shortly after he moans, his release spilling inside of me.

"Thank you," I tell him. "Thank you for giving me this."

He pushes a stray hair behind my ear. "I told you, Scar. I'd do whatever it takes to prove that you're my priority now."

Call me a fool if you wish, but I believe him.

"YOU DID WHAT?" WILBUR SHOUTS, STANDING UP AND glowering at us from across the dining table.

"Sit down, Wilbur," Archer says dryly, gesturing to his empty seat. "The proposal's done. The ring's already on her finger."

"We had everything set up, you knew this," he seethes as he sits back down and takes a large drink of his wine.

"Yes, well, I decided I didn't want to do it with an audience. Besides, you've all got what you wanted. We're engaged. She's wearing my ring." Archer squeezes my thigh gently under the table.

"You've ruined the whole PR opportunity," Wilbur protests. "Don't you have anything to say?" he barks out at Edward, who has remained quiet this whole time.

Edwards shrugs his shoulders. "It's done now. Let them be, Wilbur."

I sigh, putting my napkin down. "We're engaged. What more do you want, Wilbur? We're playing the dutiful grandchildren and cementing the Aces legacy. I'll spread my legs and pop out an heir, and everyone will get what they want."

"Let's toast," Alexis says, clearing her throat, she gets to her feet, holding up her glass. "To Eliza and Archer and the future of the founding families."

"Sit down, woman," Wilbur grumbles as he stands. "I'll propose a toast. To the continuation of our legacy. The four families, the society, and our duty to one another."

"To us," I say, refusing to toast to his words. I allow myself a small sip of the champagne.

"It can work in our favour," Alexis tells Wilbur. "The press will drink up the romantic proposal and how he whisked her away somewhere remote to do it."

"True," he bristles, looking over at Archer and me with a frown.

"Okay, girl! Show me the ring," Vee gushes from across the table, holding out her hand.

Smiling, I stretch out my arm and she takes my hand and examines the rock on my finger. "Wow. Wait a minute, that's the ring from the jewellers in London." She looks up from the ring with a wide grin on her face. "Well done, Arch. Who knew you could be smooth and romantic under that harsh exterior?"

Archer smirks. "Everything I do is perfect, Vee. You should know that by now."

Vee looks at Rafe, who is sitting next to her at the dinner table. "I hope you know what precedence he's set now. Think you can best that?"

Rafe scoffs as he sips his drink. "Baby, I'll knock that proposal to the dust when it's our turn." He winks at her and leans in, whispering something in her ear that has her giving him her full attention.

"Let's all take our drinks through to the conservatory," Alexis suggests, and everyone files out through the house. "Eliza," she calls after me and I hang back to see what she wants.

"May I see the ring?" She holds out her hand and I nod my head, slipping my hand into hers. "It's stunning. I'm glad you came to your senses and played along. I'm sure having Archer for a husband won't be that much of a chore for you."

I fight the snicker I'm about to give her and smile. "Well, it wasn't like I had much choice, was it?"

She smiles tightly back at me, dropping my hand. "Well, plan B was already in place in case you didn't come to heel."

"What does that mean? What plan B?" I ask her, an icy shiver running down my spine.

She shrugs, casually. "Let's just say I swapped out your contraceptive pill as a safety measure. You might want to get a pregnancy test and check out it's not too late."

My heart stutters in my chest as I take in her words. Before I can stop myself, my palm strikes her across her face.

"How dare you!" I hiss, seething. "My life is not yours to play with. How dare you try to take away my free will."

She glowers at me as she rubs at her red cheek. "Wilbur needs this merger; without it, it could ruin him. I haven't spent my time bouncing on his flaccid cock to lose everything because of some sullen teenager who couldn't be grateful and do what her family needed her to."

I jolt backwards at the viciousness of her words. "Wow!" I exclaim. "Good to know your feelings for my grandfather are genuine. I would hate for him to be tied with a soulless money grabbing whore."

"We all do what we can to survive," she snipes. "You're no different. You'll do what's asked of you for your brother, and I'll do what I can to give my son and I the life we deserve." She looks at me and a look of realisation crosses her face. "You haven't been drinking all night. You're pregnant, aren't you?"

"Keep your mouth shut," I warn, stepping into her space and looking behind me to check no one is in earshot.

"And why would I do that?"

"You'll do it because if you want me, the heiress, to ensure you're looked after when old Wilbur pops his clogs, then you'll keep that zipped."

"What's going on?" Archer's hand cups my hip from behind. "Is there a problem?"

Alexis smiles at him and shakes her head. "No problem at all. I was just admiring that beautiful ring." She gives me one last look before she walks past us and out of the room.

"Everything okay, Scar?" he asks me as he spins me to face him.

"Fine," I tell him, plastering on a smile of reassurance. "Come on, let's go through."

Inside, I'm shaking with anger. How dare she swap out my birth control and manipulate me like this! Now everything makes perfect sense. I knew damn well I'd taken my pill religiously. She had used me to ensure she gets what she wants. Every fucker here is trying to use me for their own end, and I'm tired of being their puppet.

❧

WE ARRIVE HOME A COUPLE OF HOURS LATER AND I'M STILL bubbling with rage inside. Edward excuses himself straight off to bed and Archer move towards the stairs to our room.

"Hey, I think I'm going to make a hot chocolate. I'll be up soon," I tell him.

"I'll make it for you," he offers, stepping down off the first step to the first floor.

I place my hand on his chest. "Honestly, I'll do it. You go up. I won't be long." I need some alone time to stew over what Alexis has done.

He studies me for a beat before he nods his head. He drops a kiss on my head and carries on up to bed. I head into the kitchen and turn on the light. Grabbing a cup, I put it under the coffee machine and pop in a hot chocolate pod.

"Argh,"

I jump when I hear someone call out in pain. It sounds like the noise is coming from outside. I open the glass doors that lead on to the patio and I hear a grunt to my left and head in that direction. I falter in my steps and cover my mouth with my hand at what I see. The moonlight exposes them against the darkness. There, against one of the old oak trees, is Georgie's mum with her naked legs wrapped around Phil as he pounds into her. The noise I heard wasn't a cry of pain, but a cry of pleasure. My eyes can never unsee this. I take a tentative step back, praying to God they don't hear me, because yeah, that would be a level of embarrassment I don't want to even think about. I reach the patio doors and step back inside, closing them quietly.

"There you are,"

"Fuckballs!" I jump a mile at the sound of Archer's voice. "You scared me. Come on, let's go up to bed."

"Argh," Georgie's mum screams and I flinch, knowing that Archer had to have heard that. He moves to go past me and open the door and I reach out my hand, placing it on his. "Don't. Trust me, if you don't want to be scarred for life. Don't go out there."

Archer frowns at me. "Whose out there?"

I sigh, running a hand through my hair. Fuck. Why did it have to be me who found them? "Your dad's out there. With

Georgie's mum and trust me when I say you don't want to see what they're doing."

Archer Scoffs. "He's been fucking her for years, Scar. I was more worried that it could have been your stalker out there."

I blink, shaking my head. "Wait a minute, you know they are having an affair?"

He shrugs his shoulders nonchalantly. "I wouldn't call it an affair, more like fuck buddies. Dad's been pounding her for years, Scar. First time I saw them together, I was eleven. I heard noises coming from my father's office. I sneaked outside and looked through his window, only to see her bent over his desk and them going at it."

"It doesn't bother you?"

Archer snickers. "Why should it? If Felicity wants to be unfaithful to her husband, that's her business. As for my dad, he's single and likes nothing better than shagging and gambling in his spare time. She won't be the first and she certainly won't be the last."

"Do you think her husband knows?"

Archer shrugs his shoulders again. "No idea. Although I have heard rumours that Caleb has been giving it to his secretary for years, so who knows."

I shake my head. "Wow, this world you live in is fucked up." What with finding out Alexis swapped out my contraceptive pill to Archer's blasé reaction to the fact his dad is boning Georgie's mum. It's all just another day in this crazy bay.

He steps away from the door and comes to stand in front of me. "Welcome to my world, Scar," he says with a weary sigh. "Let's go to bed."

CHAPTER TWENTY-ONE

ELIZA

Another week passes by with no more messages from my stalker. I start to wonder if they've backed off now that I've moved in with Archer. The engagement ball is tonight, not that any of those outside the four families know that's what the occasion is all about. They all just think Edward Savage is throwing a ball and showing everyone how much money he has. Wilbur's enthusiasm for this engagement is sickening. His assistant, Jackie, has constantly been on the phone, giving us both orders. I'm so over it all. I just can't wait to get tonight over with and have it out there. Then the people can all gossip about whether we're in love or whether it's a marriage of family convenience. Just wait until the pregnancy news gets out, that's when the gossips of this bay will twitter. No doubt they will say Archer had to propose to me because I was pregnant with his baby.

"You are awfully quiet tonight, girl," Vee comments as she puts on her heels. Vee always looks effortlessly beautiful. Her blonde hair is curled around her face, and she is wearing a beautiful pale pink gown that compliments her complexion perfectly.

"I just want the whole damn thing over. Fuck!" I exclaim when I fail to fasten the clasp on the Ruby necklace for a third time. Wilbur has insisted I wear it tonight as it will go perfectly with the engagement ring. He has given me strict instructions to only put the ring on just before he and Edward take the stage and announce the news. They have even coordinated Archer's tie to match my dress. He has every little detail planned. All part of his plan to secure the families together and help keep his failing business afloat.

"Come here," Vee says sympathetically. She walks over to me and takes the necklace from my hands. "Let me do it. Look, fuck all of them, okay? Yes, this engagement has been forced on you, but once you're married to him and you have the Savage name, you'll hold all the power. And once you put a baby in that belly, they'll be falling over themselves to praise you."

"I'm pregnant," I blurt out from nowhere.

For a minute Vee carries on trying to fasten the necklace.

"Wait, what did you just say?"

"I'm pregnant. I'm fourteen weeks," I repeat. I feel a weight lift when I tell her.

"Fuck off! You're not?" She exclaims, looking at me open-mouthed.

"I am. I've got the scan pictures and everything. It's very real."

"It's Archers?" she asks me, as she positions my necklace, so it falls centre on my chest.

I arch my brow. "Well, of course. Who else's could it be?"

She holds her hands up. "I didn't mean that to sound how it did. It's just, you know, you and Damon seemed pretty close for a time."

I place my hands on my hips, frowning at her. "You honestly thought something happened between us? He's my friend, nothing more."

Vee steps back, like she's waiting for me to pounce on her. "I know, girl. But you were hurting, and I've seen the way that guy looks at you, like he wants what he can't have. The forbidden fruit."

My brows furrow deeper. "He doesn't look at me like that," I protest.

It's Vee's turn to put her hand on her hips and give me the *'oh really'* look. "Trust me, as an outsider looking in, he would without doubt be with you if you wanted it, and that's why Archer can't stand him around you."

"Well, he's just a friend. The only guy I've slept with since I arrived here is Archer."

Vee snickers. "Of course he is. I mean, once you've sampled those goods, why would you want anyone else?"

"Something you want to tell me?" I ask, tilting my head at her.

She blinks at me. "Gods no! He's like my brother, but I've heard all the rumours and the girl's talking in the PE changing rooms. Of course, he's going to be mind-blowing at sex. He excels in everything he does, that's just Archer." Vee hands me my shoes. "I take it you're both keeping it quiet until after the engagements announced? That makes sense."

I take my shoes from her and chew on my lip at her words. She thinks he knows. "Not quite. More like I'm keeping it quiet for now."

Vee stops what she is doing and stares at me. "Hold up a minute." She holds her hand out and looks at me with wide eyes. "Girl, you haven't told him?"

I falter under her stare and suddenly find my glamorous silver sparkly heels very interesting to look at. "Not yet, no, and before you lecture me, I am going to tell him soon."

"Soon?" she pushes, her brow arching higher.

"Yes." I sit down on the sofa and concentrate on putting my heels on. I can't cope with her scrutiny.

"Who else knows besides me?"

I grimace. This isn't going to go down well. "Damon knows. He's been coming to my appointments with me, and, well, Alexis knows." I hold my hand up. "And don't even ask me how she knows."

Vee swears under her breath as she kneels down in front of me and fastens the strap on my heels I'm struggling with. "So, the guy who your fiancé hates knows before him and he's been taking you to your appointments. Eliza!" she exclaims. "I know

Archer was a bastard for keeping the planned engagement from you, but seriously. If anyone should be at those appointments with you, holding your hand, it should be Archer, the actual baby-daddy."

"I know," I admit. "But I was so freaked out, Vee. It came out of nowhere and at a time I was at my lowest. I needed time to get my head around things and decide what I wanted to do. And well, if truth be told, I fear how he'll react."

"Why?" she asks me, shaking her head like I'm crazy. "You think he would walk away and not support you? Archer is many things, but he'd never walk away from his responsibilities."

"Exactly," I say. "I don't want to be somebody's responsibility. I want him to be with me because despite our families forcing us together, he actually wants me for me, Vee."

"Oh honey," Vee takes my hands from where she is kneeling on the floor in front of me. "He wants you. He wants you so much. I think it terrifies him how much, but he'd want to be there for the bubba growing in your belly." Vee reaches out tentatively and places her hand on my tummy. "Have you felt he or she move yet?"

I shake my head. "Not yet. It's a little early."

Vee stares at where her hand rests on my stomach. "You and Archer made a person, girl. That's like so freaking beautiful and amazing. God, he or she will be stunning with both your genes."

I smile. "Despite it being terrifying, yes, it is pretty amazing, isn't it?" It's the first time I've really admitted to myself that we've created something beautiful together. "I'm terrified, Vee. I'm not even eighteen yet. I'm not sure I'm ready to be a mum."

Vee nods her head. "I get it, but then, is anyone ever truly ready? You'll be a great mum. I just know it, and of course baby will have kick-arse, cool auntie Vee to get up to mischief with."

There's a knock on the bedroom door and Vee quickly withdraws her hand from my stomach. "Tell him. Soon," she urges me before she stands up and opens the door. "Talk of the devil. Our sexy escorts are here to take us down to the ball, Cinders."

My heart pounds in my chest when I see Archer in his tux. Gods, if I wasn't already up the duff, my ovaries would beg me to have his babies.

"Scar, wow," he says, blowing out a breath as he walks in and drinks me in from head-to-toe. "Why don't you guys go down ahead of us," he suggests as he stalks into the room.

Vee places a hand on his chest, stopping him in his strides. "Uh-huh. You're not undoing the perfection because you want to stick your dick in her. You can do that later, after the party."

Archer bites on his bottom lip. "I can be quick." He smirks, and my vagina pulses in excitement.

"Nope. Rafe, grab a hold of Casanova and let's get them downstairs," Vee orders, and Rafe and Seb both step forward.

Archer dodges them and grabs me by the waist and nuzzles his face into my neck. "Scar, you look stunning tonight. I can't wait for them all to know you're mine."

"Enough now," Vee orders, tapping him on his back. "Put your tongue back in your mouth."

I chuckle and I feel his smile against my neck as he drops a barely there kiss on my skin. "Come on, you heard her."

With a sigh, he pulls away, drinking me in one last time before he shakes his head and offers me his arm. "Ready for this, Scar?"

"As I'll ever be," I tell him, slipping my arm through his.

"Looking good tonight, Little Red," Seb tells me as he comes up on my other side and kisses my hand. "You look like my favourite quality street in that purple silk dress. You know, the one with all that soft caramel inside that I like to lick out with my tongue." He winks at me, just as Vee digs her elbow in his side.

"Lick someone else's caramel," Archer barks at him, which has Seb chuckling aloud as we make our way down to the ball.

THE PLACE IS ALREADY BURSTING AT THE SEAMS WITH THE wealthy residents of Hawk Bay. All the wealthy elite in their finery and jewels. You can almost smell the money in the air tonight. Wilbur takes great joy in showing us off and taking us both round to greet all the guests. When we stop in front of Georgie and her family, I squeeze Archer's arm tighter. I can't undo the image in my head of Felicity and Phil and the noises she was making. Ugh.

"Eliza, Archer. It's lovely to see you both. I was just saying to Georgiana what a stunning couple you both make, wasn't I, dear?" She elbows her scowling daughter in the side and Georgie flashes that fake smile our way.

"Yes, you were. Although the rumours around school were that you two had split up and you were dating the Silver boy," Georgie comments, still smiling at us, like her face might crack any minute.

I laugh, "Ridiculous rumours." I look up at Archer in over-the-top awe. "It's always been him."

Georgie mutters something under her breath and her mother shoves a drink in her hand, smiling at us. "Well, of course not, and we know how much your families like to keep that tight-knit bond, so I'm sure everyone is thrilled."

"We couldn't be more delighted that Archer and Eliza found each other," Wilbur gushes. "Now if you'll excuse us." With his hand under my elbow, he guides us away.

"Dance together," he orders. "Make sure you're seen together."

Rolling his eyes, Archer escorts me to the dancefloor. Everyone watches us as we take to the floor. "

"Why is everyone so morbidly interested in us?"

Archer snickers. "Because, Scar. Together, we are a power that scares them. Plus, everyone with a daughter or son our age or similar was hoping they could match with us and marry into the families."

I shake my head. I can't believe that a part of the world still exists where families vie to make marriages of alliance to gain them greater power and affluence. We dance for two songs and then I announce I need the bathroom. Archer insists on escorting me to the toilet. I've noticed tonight that Edward has beefed up the security. There are burly looking men in black clothes with earpieces at every doorway.

I'm touching up my lipstick when the toilet door opens and Archer steps into the room and closes it behind him.

"What are you doing in here?" I ask him, my eyes meeting his through the mirror.

He stalks up behind me and wraps his arm around my waist, dipping his nose and inhaling my perfume. His hands move to the back of my dress, and he lifts it until his hands can explore underneath, his fingertips trailing up my inner thighs.

"Archer, stop," I say half-heartedly as his touch sends shivers down my body. "People will notice we're missing."

"Let them," he says as he sucks my earlobe into his mouth. "We're newly engaged. It's only natural that we can't keep our hands off each other." He bunches my dress up at the base of my back and intakes a breath when he realises I'm not wearing any underwear. "You're a bad girl, Scar."

"Am I?" I meet his gaze in the mirror. "And if I am, what are you going to do about it?"

I hear the zipper on his trousers and in the next second, he's lining himself up at my entrance and entering me. "Grip the counter, Scar. I'm not going to be gentle."

I brace both my hands on the sink countertop and push my hips back as he thrusts back inside me. "Fuck, Scar, you're perfect," he moans, his eyes holding mine prisoner through our reflection in the mirror. "Look at us, baby. Watch me fuck you."

I do as he says, moaning loudly when he pistons his hips so that it feels deeper. "More, Archer," I demand. "Harder."

He grabs my hips and pounds into me harder and faster. It's heaven on earth. No one has ever made me feel this good. He licks up my neck and I lean my head on his shoulder as I fall over that crescendo and call out his name. "Fuuuccck," he growls out as he spills his seed inside me.

He pulls out from me and tucks himself back in his pants. He grabs some tissue and turns me to face him, and he bends on one knee to clean me up, I push my dress back down and straighten my hair in the mirror. The door handle rattles and we both chuckle like mischievous children as he takes my hand and pulls it open.

Seb is leaning on the door frame, grinning at us. "They have sent me to fetch you two. By the way, I could hear you both halfway down the hallway. Disgraceful," he tells us, winking.

"You need to get laid," Archer tells him flatly.

"Oh, I plan to. There's a girl here serving tonight that has the prettiest eyes. Talk of the devil," he gestures with his head to a girl who comes from the kitchens holding a tray of drinks. I blink twice when I realise who it is.

"Milly?"

She looks over and smiles when she realises it's me. "Oh, hi, Eliza. Great party by the way."

"What are you doing here?" I ask her, surprised.

"I'm Seb," he tells her, standing in front of me, cutting me off and taking the hand that isn't holding the tray of drinks to his lips. "Do you have a boyfriend?"

"Whether I have a boyfriend is none of your business, rich boy," she hisses at him, putting him right in his place.

"Seb, this is Damon's sister," I tell him, and I watch his brow quirk at that information.

"You're a Silver, huh?" He grimaces. "That's a shame." He steps back from her and winks.

"And what's that supposed to mean?" she asks him. If looks could kill, Seb would be six feet under by now.

He holds up his hand sin defence and gives her that lazy smile of his. "Nothing, gorgeous. You run along now and do your job."

She cocks a brow at him, and I can see in my head the tray of drinks ending up all over him in about two seconds. I shove Seb out of the way. "Just ignore him. We all do." I grab Seb by his jacket and pull him away. "Come on you, before you cause any more trouble." As I drag him away, he looks over his shoulder. Milly glares at him and gives him the finger, making Seb chuckle.

"Behave yourself, Seb. And don't be mean to her, she's lovely," I warn him, as we step back into the party.

"She is lovely, for a Silver," he agrees, grinning as he pivots on his heels and disappears back the way we just came. I move to go after him, but Archer steers me by the elbow back into the room.

"Leave him be, Scar. She won't give him the time of day anyway," Archer says, and I realise he's right. I like Milly and I don't want someone like Seb corrupting her with his charm and his smiles and those sexy eyes of his.

The sounds of Edward's voice coming over the music pulls my attention and I realise it's time as I spot Edward and Wilbur on the stage.

"You ready for this?" Archer asks into my ear, as he places an arm around my waist.

"As I'll ever be." I reach into my bag and slip the ring on my finger.

"We have rather a special announcement to make to you all tonight. Tonight, is not just a social gathering for us all to come together. Tonight, we are here to celebrate the wonderful news that my grandson, Archer has asked Eliza to marry him, and she has accepted." Edward gestures with his hand to where we are standing at the back of the room, and everyone turns to look at us. "Will the happy couple come and join us up here?"

Smiling as everyone applauds us, we make our way through the parted crowd and take up our place in-between our grandfathers.

"We are delighted that they will be joining our two families together. We would like you all to join us in a toast to the happy couple. To Archer and Eliza," Wilbur says, raising his glass.

Everyone raises their glasses and they all toast to us. Archer and I join the toast and he leans down and catches my lips in a kiss and everyone applauds again. It's a fairy tale engagement announcement and the press from the local paper demand we stand and pose for photos. Archer takes my hand with the ring and holds it out so that they can get a good picture. Jackie stands by the reporters and talks animatedly to them, ushering them into a side room where they can speak with us and get the inside story. Wilbur and Edward both kiss my cheeks and shake Archer's hand and then we're escorted off the stage into the room with the waiting press.

"How did he propose?"

"Was it love at first sight?"

"Did you choose the ring together?"

Archer holds up his hand to silence them as he guides me over to the sofa and takes a seat beside me. He takes my hand and holds it in his, resting our joined hands on his lap.

"Kay, you go first," he tells the blonde reporter. He breezes through this like it's an everyday occurrence.

"Talk us through your relationship. When did the two of you start dating?"

Archer takes the lead, and he tells of how we met on my first day of school. He shares how he was bowled over by my beauty and intellect and how he pursued me from there on in. What he doesn't share is that on my first night he made me jump off a cliff, that I nearly drowned and then hypothermia nearly claimed me. Or that he had the entire school bully me, that he drugged me. Kidnapped me. Nor did he share that our families had already arranged our engagement long before I ever stepped foot in the bay. No, the press gets the fairy-tale and they gush as he speaks of how much he can't wait for our future together. I sit in silence listening to him and a part of me wishes deeply that this was the real story of us.

"Eliza, when did you realise you were in love with Archer?"

The excited reporter asks me, holding out her phone that is recording everything.

"Ah, that's an easy one. It was the weekend he whisked me away to a secluded cabin in Scotland and cooked me a romantic meal." I smile at him. "The entire weekend was a complete surprise for me."

Archer clears his throat, knowing full well what I mean by a complete surprise.

"That's so romantic," the reporter gushes. "You're both still very young. Why the rush to get married?"

Archer shrugs his shoulders. "We are young, Kay, you're right, but when you know, you know, and I know Eliza is it for me." He leans in and kisses my forehead and all the women in the room sigh at his romantic words.

We pose for photos and then Jackie ushers the reporters out of the room, telling them we need to get back to our party and mingle with our guests. Archer asks her to give us a minute, and she closes the door behind her, leaving us alone.

"Are you okay?" he asks me, approaching me like I'm a wild deer that might bolt.

"I'm fine," I say, smoothing out my dress. "I'm just not used to all of that. Not like you."

He nods his head in understanding, brushing a lock of my hair from my face. "You get used to it; I promise."

We re-join the party and spend the rest of the night receiving words of congratulations from all the guests. People ask us when the wedding will be, and Archer just tells them we haven't decided on a date yet. If Wilbur has his way, he'll probably have a church booked for next weekend.

The guests finally leave around midnight, and I'm exhausted by the time we get to our room from smiling and making polite conversation all evening. I yawn as I'm unbuckling my heels and Archer kneels and helps me out of them.

"Well, we survived the night, Scar."

"By some miracle," I sigh. "Hey, I was thinking earlier, why don't we elope?"

Archer takes his cuff links and places them in his drawers. "Elope?"

I walk over to him and sit facing him on the edge of the unit. "Yes, elope. You know, just bugger off and get married."

Archer smirks down at me as he loosens his ties and throws it in the laundry basket. "Is this another ploy to piss off Wilbur?"

I bob my head side-to-side. "Partly, yes, but it's also about us having control over our own wedding. No doubt Wilbur has some grand, expensive event planned with half of the bay in attendance."

I'm feeling so out of control over my own life right now and it's unsettling. Eloping and getting married without Wilbur's agreement would be a big 'fuck you' to him, but it would also mean that I took back some modicum of control. We could do our wedding the way we want to, not the way Wilbur insists upon.

CHAPTER TWENTY-TWO

ELIZA

I'm eating custard for breakfast when Archer comes downstairs, looking edible in a pair of gym shorts and a grey vest.

"What on earth are you eating for breakfast?" he asks me, scrunching his face as he looks at the bowl in front of me.

"Custard," I tell him with a shrug of my shoulders. "You should try it sometime. It's the breakfast of champions."

"I'll pass, thanks," he says grimacing as he fills up his water bottle. "Anyway, put that down because I have a surprise for you. Come on." He's smiling at me, holding his hand out for me to take.

Intrigued, I hop off the bar stool and place my hand in his. He leads us through the house and out of the front door. He gestures with his hand to the driveway and my mouth falls open.

"Why is there a car with a giant ribbon on the drive?"

"It's yours, Scar," he explains, and pulls out a set of keys from his pocket, dangling them in front of me. "I hope you like it. Kit assured me you have a thing for these cars."

"I do," I agree as I walk around the gleaming cherry red Mercedes. "I can't accept this. It's too much," I protest, holding out the keys to him.

Archer tilts his head at me. "You're a strange girl. Few women would react the way you do when being given their dream car."

I nod my head. "That's because I know how much these cost brand new. Trust me, I have a picture of one on my vision board."

Archer tugs me into his space and wraps an arm around my waist. "I need to know that if I'm not around, you can get about safely."

"I don't have my licence," I argue back. I admire the car, dying to sit behind the wheel and turn the engine over and see how she feels.

"You have your provisional. You can drive if one of us is with you. Maybe now's the time to think about some professional lessons. You could take the accelerated course and pass in no time."

Curiosity gets the better of me and I click the keys and open the driver's door. I slide onto the cool, leather seats. "She's a beauty," I exclaim as I run my hands over the steering wheel and take in the leather upholstery.

"You want to take her round the bay?" Archer holds up two L-Plates.

"Hell, yes," I reply, and turn on the engine as Archer sticks the plates on the car. He jogs round to the passenger side to climb in.

"Take her for her first spin, Scar."

She drives like a dream. She's super quiet, being electric, and steers like a boss. I drive us down to the beach and then back up to the cliff tops into the grounds of the Savage mansion. When I turn the engine off, I look over to find Archer grinning at me with a whimsical smile on his face.

"What?"

"Only you would react to a car like this. You're looking at this car like it's the hottest thing you've ever seen."

"It is the hottest thing I've ever seen," I reply with a wink, stroking my hands over the leather interior.

Archer's response is to snigger. "We both know that isn't true."

So vain.

"You know what else gorgeous cars do to me?" I ask him, leaning back in my seat and eating him up with my eyes.

"Do tell," he says, cocking a brow and licking his lower lip.

"They make me horny. Racing, fighting, nice cars, all drive me wild."

Archer nods his head in response. The heat in this car is on fire as we study each other. "Maybe we should do something about that."

"Maybe we should," I reply as I unbuckle my belt and clamber over the gear stick onto his lap. "Let's christen my new wheels."

Archer grips at my hips and he tugs playfully at my lower lip with his teeth. "Not out here, Scar. Security team, remember?"

I roll my hips into his. "Let them see. I don't care."

He gives me a look that says, 'not a chance.'

"They don't get to see what is for my eyes only," he tells me as he nuzzles into my neck. "Come on, I need to get you naked and in my bed right now."

"Yes, sir," I jest, saluting him as he opens the passenger door and I lift my leg over him to exit.

❧

NEEDLESS TO SAY, WE GET NAKED IN HIS ROOM, AND END UP being late leaving for school. I'm thrilled when he agrees to let me drive us there in my new baby. When we pull into the car park at school, all heads turn to take in my car.

"Talk about sending the gossip girls crazy. An engagement announcement and a sexy as sin new car."

Archer grins as he climbs out. I meet him at the front of the car, and he reaches for my hand and drops a kiss on the shiny rock on my finger. "I love every fucker here knowing you're mine and they can never have you."

"Ring or no ring, they could never have me regardless," I

inform him as we walk towards the main entrance. My smile drops into a frown when I see Georgie and Chester standing with a group of their clingers by the arches. Georgie is resting against his back and Chester has a casual arm over her shoulder, resting on her chest.

"They're like a foul smell that just won't go away." I groan as our steps take us closer to them.

Archer doesn't reply, he just grins and pulls out his phone.

"Congrats, step-sis," Chester says as we level with them.

"Step-sis?" I repeat with a snicker.

"I have to say I'm disappointed. I thought you had more defiance in you, but no, you just roll over and agree to an arranged marriage like a good little sheep."

I release Archer's hand and take a step closer to the ass-wipe. "Don't try to understand a situation you know nothing about. Maybe we're getting married because we want forever."

Georgie scoffs and her eyes glare coldly at me. "You're not fooling anyone," she says, loud enough for everyone in earshot to hear her. "Everyone knows Archer has to marry you if he's to inherit and get his trust fund at eighteen."

Emilia, her trusty sidekick, giggles and nods her head in agreement. "Like he'd marry her if he had a choice."

Her cocky smile withers when Archer steps in front of me, a snarl etched across his face. "Be careful Emilia. I can destroy you and your family with just one call. You think it's all about my legacy? It's not. She's everything. None of you could ever come close to her. I'd choose her every fucking day over any of you vultures. Am I clear?"

Emilia swallows and looks down at the floor, before nodding her head. "Crystal."

Archer offers her an insincere smile. "Glad we cleared that up." He reaches behind him and my hand slips in his and we move on past the now silent crowd.

THE REST OF THE DAY RUNS WITHOUT A HITCH. I CATCH MANY of the girls stretching their necks as I walk past, trying to get a glimpse of the ring. I'm not oblivious to the fact that near enough every girl in this place wishes it was them. It just shows how fucked up this bay is, when seventeen-year-old girls aspire to get hitched to the richest boy in the school.

"We're having a party down by the beach tonight," Seb announces, taking a seat beside me on the bonnet of my baby.

"Watch the paintwork," I hiss, stroking her tenderly.

Seb shakes his head at me. "I think you like this car more than you like Archers..."

I cover his mouth with my hand. "Don't say it," I warn him, and I feel his lips widen into a smile under my hand. "It's a Monday. Why are you planning a party on a Monday?"

"Duh," he says, his eyes bugging out of his head. "We have an engagement to celebrate, and that lame get together on Saturday was a poor excuse for a celebration."

"I'm partied out," I groan as Archer, Rafe, and Vee reach us. "Tell him Arch, no party tonight."

Archer grins at Seb. He stands in between my legs and tugs me forward by my waist. "Hey you," he says to me, smiling down at me in a way that makes my toes curl and my heartbeat ten times faster.

"Hey." I wrap my arms around his neck, and he leans down and kisses me like he's been craving me.

"Quit it," Seb groans, batting Archer's arm. "No one wants to see the two of you making babies in the school car park."

Archer scoffs like that is an absurd idea. I glance over at Vee, who arches a brow and chews at her lip. If only Seb knew that ship had already sailed.

"It might be nice to let loose for a night," Archer suggests, tucking my hair behind my ear. "Let's drink, dance and get fucked up tonight."

I'm still getting used to a laid-back Archer. He's normally always so controlled and in check. "Sure thing."

"Come on!" Seb grins. He cups his hands over his mouth and shouts across the crowded car park. "Beach party tonight people. Be there or be square!"

"How are you even related to him?" I ask Vee and she shakes her head, looking in exasperation at her brother.

"I have no idea how we shared the same womb for nine months."

WE HEAD HOME TO THE SAVAGE MANSION. THE SECURITY wave us through. Just as we pull up, Edward comes to the front door. He's dressed in a tailored grey suit, hands in his pocket.

"Everything okay?" Archer asks him as we exit the car.

"A meeting has been called. You and the boys will need to be there for six."

Archer doesn't argue, he just nods his head. "Not a problem."

"Is the meeting for all Aces?" I ask Edward, noticing that he didn't look my way when he said about the meeting.

"It's nothing for you to concern yourself with Eliza. You let Archer worry about Aces business." He smiles at me and turns on his heels and heads back inside, basically dismissing us.

"In other words, be the good little woman and keep your nose out of men's affairs, Eliza," I mime pulling my face. "God, women really are just a womb and arm candy in their world, aren't we?"

Archer pulls me to his side and kisses my head. "Don't let it get to you, Scar. We'll have to meet you and Vee at the beach."

"That's fine." I grin, looking up at him. "I can drive us there in my new baby."

"You don't want to have a drink?" he asks as we head upstairs to his room and dispose of our bags and shoes. "Nope, it's a school night. I'm being sensible."

This brings a snicker from him, and I look at him in mock offence. "I can be sensible."

"I like you wild and dangerous," he says, leaning down into my space and dropping a kiss on my lips. "I'm going to get a workout in."

"Okay. I'm going to run a bath and then it's Netflix time."

He leaves me and I sit for a minute and look around the bedroom that is now 'ours'. It feels so surreal to be seventeen and living in a mansion with my fiancé. Like who the fuck am I and what twilight zone have I slipped in to?

I run myself a bath, and soak in the tub for a good thirty minutes; I run the sponge over my belly and pause. How long will it be before I'm showing? In two weeks' time, I'll be 16 weeks gone. I know I need to tell him, and I'm not sure what is holding me back. Whether it's that I'm scared that he'll resent me or whether it's that I don't want to admit to myself that this is really happening.

My phone rings and I reach over and grab it with soapy fingers.

"Hey girl," Vee sings down the phone. "So, I hear you and I are making our own way to the beach tonight?"

"Seems that way."

"Well, listen, I need to call at a boutique down at the Marina in Haven before it closes at five. I'm thinking we get ready early, go pick up my order, enjoy some nice food out and then hit the beach."

"I like that plan, but do you really need more shoes?"

"Eliza, I am speechless," Vee gasps. "How can you even ask? A woman can never have enough shoes, and these are Chanel, darling."

"Oh well, pardon me," I say in a mock posh accent.

"So, you should be. Now go get ready. I'll pick you up in twenty."

"Wait. I want to drive my baby tonight, so you drive here and then we'll take my car."

Vee chuckles down the phone. "You can be my baby-driver! Do you get it?"

I roll my eyes even though she can't see me. "Yes, I get it. Hardy-har. Goodbye."

"Bye!" She laughs down the phone before hanging up.

CHAPTER TWENTY-THREE

ELIZA

Thirty minutes later we've parked up behind the high street and we pick Vee's new shoes up from the boutique. I must admit they are lovely, but my feet nearly went from under me when I heard the girl cash them through! Who pays that kind of money for something you put on your feet?

"Where shall we eat?" Vee asks, as she links her arm through mine as we walk towards the marina. "There's a cute little Italian just a minute down the road, or we could head back to the bay and go to the steak place?"

"How about we slum it and do fish and chips? My Aunties chippy is just a bit further up," I suggest. I haven't seen Rebecca since we first met, but we had been exchanging texts and it would be nice to see her again.

"Ooh, yes! I would love to meet the new auntie," Vee says in excitement. "Lead the way."

We're giggling and gossiping as we near the chippy and I look up to tell her we're here. Then I stop in my tracks.

"What's happened?"

Rebecca is outside the chip shop sweeping up shards of glass. The chip shop window is completely shattered.

"Rebecca, what's going on?"

She turns at the sound of my voice and when she realises it's me; she leans the brush against the shop front and strides over and engulfs me in a warm hug. "Eliza, this is a lovely surprise. I was actually about to call you." She pulls away from me and her cheerfulness dissipates.

"Did someone put the window through? Have you had a break in?"

Rebecca sighs and looks back at the shop. "We were just opening and the next thing, a brick comes hurtling through the window. It nearly gave poor Lee a heart attack."

"That's awful," Vee chips in and I realise I haven't introduced her to my aunt.

"This is Vee, my best friend. Vee, this is my auntie."

Vee smiles warmly at Rebecca and they both say hello.

"That's why I was about to call you," Rebecca says with a grimace. "You should probably come inside." She ushers us in the door and through to the kitchen.

Lee is in the back on the phone to the police. Rebecca walks over to the counter-top and reaches for a crumpled piece of paper. "You should probably read this," she says, holding the paper out for me.

I look at her, puzzled, but I take the paper from her and read the note. A chill runs down my spine. On the crumpled paper written in black ink is the message 'Tell your niece if she doesn't leave others will suffer.'

Rebecca folds her arms around herself and studies my reaction. "I only have one niece, so I assume they are talking about you. Are you in some kind of trouble?"

I shake my head, studying the note. "If you call some weird stalker trouble, then yes." I sigh; I am so tired of this fucker messing with my head. "Ever since I arrived in the bay, I've been getting warnings to leave. Some unknown person has been sending me parcels with dead birds and they even wrote a warning on my bedroom wall in pig's blood."

Rebecca gasps and reaches out to stroke my arm. "That is awful. Are you okay? Are the police investigating?"

I nod my head and attempt to give her a reassuring smile. I

don't want her worrying about me. "They are, but so far, no leads. I'm so sorry my situation has brought trouble to your door. I'll speak to Wilbur and arrange for the shop front to be repaired."

Rebecca shakes her head. "You will do no such thing. This isn't your fault and I'm not taking a penny of that ratbag's money. Our insurance will cover it." She takes the note from me and places it back on the side. "Besides, I'm more worried about you and your safety."

"I'm fine. Please don't worry about me. The police are on the case, and I've moved in with Archer, because Edward has better security. Trust me, Archer ensures I'm never left alone." I gesture across the street to where Tony is crossing the road towards us. "I even have my own personal bodyguard now."

"Wilbur needs to ensure your safety," Rebecca growls, her face scrunching in a frown as Wilbur's name leaves her lips. "Aside from the note, I was worried about you. I saw the announcement in the local paper yesterday of your engagement." She steps forward and takes my hand in hers, nothing but love and care in her expression. "Is Wilbur threatening you into an arranged marriage? Because I don't care who that man is. If he is, I will take him on."

My heart warms with her words. It's so nice to have a blood relative who actually gives a genuine shit about me. "You know, Wilbur, he always has a plan up his sleeve." I pat her arm when I see the angst in her eyes. "He has backed me into a corner, but truthfully, Archer and I are like two sides of the same coin. If I'm going to marry anyone, there isn't really anyone better suited for me."

"But marriage, Eliza." She sighs. "You're so young and you have your whole life ahead of you."

"I'm fine, honestly," I insist, smiling. "Neither you nor I have the power to take on Wilbur, and my brother's future means more to me than anything. If getting married secures it for him, then I'll do it in a heartbeat."

Rebecca cups my cheek. "I just hate the thought that he is forcing you into a situation just like he did with your father."

"I promise I'm okay."

Rebecca nods her head, but she doesn't look a hundred percent convinced.

"Archer is good for me. We didn't have the best start, but he's trying to do better. He really is."

"Show me the rock, then," she says resigned, and I hold out my hand and wiggle the finger adorned by the ring.

Rebecca stares open-mouthed at my ring. "Wow, that is a beauty. I don't even want to know how much that has cost."

"A lot," Vee tells her with wide eyes. "I could buy a lot of Chanel with the money that rock cost."

"She has a shoe obsession," I explain to my Auntie, who is looking at Vee with a strange smile.

"Anyway, putting the drama over the window aside, were you ladies coming for some dinner?"

"We were planning on a chippy tea," I say, "but we should probably leave you to sort this out."

My auntie bats my comment away. "Nonsense, take a seat in the staff room and I'll bring you both through a plate each."

Lee pops his head into the room to tell Rebecca that the police should be here within the next hour. I offer to stick around to speak to them, but she tells me not to worry. She assures me she will explain to them about how it relates to me and tell them that Detective Boyd is working the case. I pull out my phone and call Tony. He needs to know that this incident is a result of my stalker. He arrives seconds later and asks Lee for the note and frowns as he reads it. He places his phone to his ear and strides from the chippy. He's no doubt making a call to Wilbur.

By the time we've cleared our plates, I'm stuffed full. Vee has also polished off everything on her plate. We both sit there in a food coma for five minutes.

"That was hands down the best chippy tea I've had in a long

time," Vee says, undoing the button on her jeans. "Ugh, look at how bloated my belly looks for going to the party."

I scoff. What belly? "There isn't any belly there. Whereas me," I say, rubbing my tummy.

"You can't hide it from him forever, you know. You need to tell him, Eliza." She gives me the type of look a mum would give her daughter when she's trying to talk some sense into her.

"I will. When I'm ready. In my own time," I assure her and turn my gaze away from her knowing eyes.

"I hope it's a girl and then I can buy her cute designer baby dresses. She'll be the best dressed baby in the Bay thanks to her Auntie Vee." She leans her face on her hands and concentrates all her attention on me. "Have you thought about whether you'd like a girl or a boy?"

I glance at the door to make sure my auntie's not in earshot. "Not really, no. I'm still processing the fact there's a baby in here."

She sighs. "I think Archer will make a great dad; I really do. If it's a little girl, he'll be fiercely protective of her, and if it's a boy, he'll have a great bond with the kid." Vee looks at her watch. "We should go, it's gone six."

I nod my head in agreement and we both pick up our belongings and head through to the front of the chip shop where Rebecca and Lee are busy serving customers.

"Rebecca, that fish was the best ever," Vee tells her, making Rebecca beam with happiness.

"Glad you enjoyed it, and please come back anytime," she tells Vee, before turning her attention to me. She places her hands on my shoulders. "You take care. I'm here if you need me, anytime. If it all gets too much in Lala land, there's room for you here."

My heart squeezes in my chest at her care and concern, and it reminds me of how much I miss my mum and her mothering. "I know where to come," I say thankfully, smiling.

"I'll text you later once the police have been."

We head outside on to the marina and make our way back to the car. Now we've left Rebecca's, I ruminate over my stalker's new tactic of intimidating my family. "I hate that this creep's hatred for me is affecting others."

Vee places her arm around my shoulder. "I know. It's awful. It's like they're upping the ante. I worry for you and that little baba in your belly, girl."

I shiver, looking behind us. "How did they know about Rebecca? It makes me think that whoever it is, they're following me around, or having someone else do it for them.'"

Vee also looks behind her and huddles closer to me. "It makes me shudder just thinking about it. Maybe we should stick to outings with the boys from now on."

"No," I reply firmly, straightening my posture. "I won't let some spineless bully who hides behind threats control my life."

I wish I knew who the stalker was. It's the not knowing that is doing my head in. Everywhere I go, I look at people and think, is it you? Are you my stalker? And now they're targeting my family. They are crossing a line and when I find out who they are, I will use the full benefits of being an Ace to make them pay.

❧

When we arrive at the beach, there's already a large crowd from our sixth form and some kids from year eleven here, as well. I don't see the boys, so I assume they're still held up with Aces business. Business that I'm to have no knowledge of. The crowd of Hawk Bay kids are drinking, smoking weed, and dancing around a bonfire. I spot Damon over by the fire and grin when I see his sister Milly Beside him.

"Come on," I urge Vee, taking her hand and dragging her along the beach to where they are.

Damon spots me over his sister's shoulder, and grinning, raises his bottle in greeting.

"Princess. We were wondering if any of the royalty would

show tonight," he jests, winking at me, his hazel eyes twinkling with humour.

"Funny," I reply, sticking my tongue out at him. "Milly, I almost didn't recognise you with the hair," I say to his sister, taking a strand of her now pink hair in my fingers.

"Hey, you inspired me to go for something different," she informs me with a shrug of her shoulders. "Dad's not too thrilled about it."

"That's an understatement," Damon chuckles into his bottle. "I think his words were, 'what the fuck have you done to your beautiful hair?'"

"Well, I like it," I reassure her. Vee says that she thinks it really suits her too.

Milly looks behind us as if she is looking for someone. "Where are your three bodyguards?"

"Tony is over there," Vee replies, gesturing over her shoulder to where my burly minder has taken up position leaning against the fencing by the car park.

"Wait! You have a literal bodyguard?" Milly's eyes bug out in amazement. "I meant your three guys, as in the Aces."

I give her a nonchalant bob of my shoulders. It is so embarrassing having an actual bodyguard following me around. It makes me look like I think I'm someone special. "Yeah, thanks to my stalker, I now have Tony following me everywhere. The Elders insisted."

Vee snorts. "More like Archer insisted."

"Well, him as well," I admit. It was probably more to do with Archer than the Elders to be honest.

Damon leans down and pulls a beer out of his bag and offers it to Vee. Milly notices he doesn't offer me one and she frowns at him. "You not offering Eliza one?"

"Oh, it's fine," I say, holding my hand out in front of me. "I'm the designated driver tonight."

Damon winks at me, reassuring me that my secret is safe with him.

"So, has Damon told you the news?" Milly says, grinning like the cat that got the mouse.

I shake my head, not having a clue what she is talking about. She whacks her brother playfully in the ribs. "I can't believe you didn't tell her. I'm enrolling at the academy."

"You are?" I'm surprised by this news. Damon had told me he'd convinced his dad that Milly would find it hard to adjust to the culture there and she would likely be a target because of her family.

"After the school holidays." She bobs on her heels, filled with excitement. "I can't wait to start and to wear that uniform."

"You can't?" I am surprised by her enthusiasm. "I'd love to go to your school and not have to wear that stifling blazer every day."

"I talked my dad around. I told him, if I'm going to be a vet one day, then I need the best education." She grins and nudges her brother. "Plus, it means I get to bug Damon during the day and at home."

Damon casts his eyes heavenward and shakes his head in dread. "Just don't let me see you with any guys and we're good. I do not want to get expelled when I've made it this far."

We all laugh. Damon and his brother are fiercely protective of their little sister. I imagine trying to date boys is no easy task with the two of them breathing down her neck.

"Ugh, looks like that is our cue to go," Milly grumbles, her eyes concentrated behind me. I look over my shoulder and see the boys walking our way. The three of them are all in step with each other with Archer in the middle. All three of them command attention and everyone notices their arrival. I see Tony shout to Archer and gesture him over. Great! He's no doubt filling him in on the latest stalker incident.

"There's no need to leave," I say, placing my hand on her arm. "Archer and Damon have agreed to be civil towards each other."

Milly grimaces, continuing to glare their way. I follow her line of sight and realise her hostility is fixed on Seb.

"I am not hanging around to deal with that dickhead," she growls. She looks briefly at Vee and winces. "Oops, sorry. I know he's your twin, but he's so annoying."

Vee holds her hands up and chuckles. "Call him that all you like, girl. My brother is an arse when it comes to girls."

"Come on Day," Milly urges, "let's go mingle."

Damon offers me an apologetic shrug and allows his sister to tug him away from us just as the boys arrive.

"Queens," Seb greets us, grinning and coming in between us to throw an arm over both our shoulders. "Missed us?"

Vee grins wickedly at him. "We missed Archer and Rafe. You, not so much."

Seb pouts at her, and clutches at his chest, staggering back as if he's been shot. "I'm wounded, little sis."

"We're twins," she reminds him, glowering at him in annoyance.

Seb sighs and points a finger at her. "I was born first though, so you are still my little sis." Seb's eyes move to where Damon and Milly are standing with a small group over by the beer stash. "What's she doing here?"

I double blink, surprised at the coldness in his voice. "Who, Milly? She's here with her brother. I thought you liked her."

Seb glowers across the bonfire at her and I watch as the two of them briefly stare at each other. An unspoken conversation seeming to take place.

"Like is a strong word," Seb grunts.

"Oh, no. tell me you haven't?" I groan. I put my hands together in a praying symbol. "Please tell me you listened to me, and you didn't go there."

Seb snorts as if my idea is ridiculous. It was only last week he was drooling over her like a dog does a bone.

"I didn't go there," he replies dryly. "Relax. She's no longer on my radar. I have new pussy to chase." His signature grin returns, and he waggles his eyebrows.

I jump when I feel a hand on my back and a glance over my shoulder tells me it's Archer. "Hey."

He crowds into my back, wrapping his arms around my waist. "Hey, Scar. You, okay? Tony just filled me in on everything. You should have phoned me straight away."

I place my hands over his and at the feel of uneven skin; I look down and gasp. Archers' knuckles are all bloodied and split open. "What happened to your hands? Have you been fighting?"

"Stop trying to change the subject," he says into my ear. "We just had to give someone a little message."

"We're both fine," I reassure him. "And I don't need to ring you every time something happens. That's why I have Tony in the first place. I'm mainly just pissed off that they're targeting the people I care about now."

Archer kisses the top of my head, squeezing my waist affectionately. "I'll give Boyd a call in the morning. They better have some leads, or I am going to go above his head and demand that they assign a new detective to the case."

"You can do that?" I ask him and his answer is to snicker.

"We're the Aces, Scar. There's nothing we can't do."

CHAPTER TWENTY-FOUR

ELIZA

The next day, Boyd calls in to see us. There are no new leads. Whoever the stalker is, they are good at remaining invisible. I'm constantly on edge. I rang Kit this morning to check he was okay, and I called Rebecca to make sure nothing else happened since the broken window. Archer has arranged for a top-notch security system by Georgie's dads' company to be fitted at the chip shop. He's also insisting on footing the bill for the shop window, despite Rebecca's protestations.

We head to school after we've finished with Boyd and I'm glad to have something to take my mind off everything for a few hours. Seb and Vee are eighteen in two weeks' time, and they have an entire week of celebrations planned, ending with us all having a weekend in Ibiza. Seb's family has a party planned, but Seb insists he wants to 'real' party and not a black-tie event like his parents are planning. Surprisingly, Archer agrees he can have it at the Savage Mansion, and I laugh with him when he tells me that if it's at our house, we can sneak off to bed whenever we've had enough.

"I'm thinking I want two strippers and one of those sexy fire eaters that dances and does cool shit with fire," Seb explains, as we all congregate by my locker. The bell rings and I realise I need a quick wee before class starts. Rafe is in my next class, so he assures Archer he'll wait by the ladies for me and accompany me to class.

I leave Rafe outside and head into the toilets, but I stop still when I hear sobbing coming from a cubicle that is occupied. Whoever is in there is sobbing their heart out.

"Hello," I say softly, walking up to the cubicle door and tapping lightly on it. "Are you okay in there?"

"Go away!" a broken voice shouts at me from the other side of the door.

"I can't do that, I'm afraid, because it sounds like you're upset, and I need to check that you're okay," I insist. Whoever is in there, they aren't in a good place and I'm not leaving them alone in the girl's bathroom until I know they're okay and they're not going to do anything stupid.

"Come on, open up. I'll stand here all day if I have to. A problem shared is a problem halved and I promise I'm a good listener."

I wait for a response, and none comes. Sighing, I contemplate my next move when I hear the latch of the door lock lift and I take a step back. The cubicle door opens, and I stare in shock at a red eyed Georgie.

"Happy now?" she snaps, storming past me. She bends over the sink and splashes water on her face.

"Georgie, is everything okay?" I ask her tentatively. I'm worried as I've never seen her looked so bedraggled and unhinged.

"Oh, I'm just fucking great," she snickers. "Why do you have it all? Why are you so fucking perfect?"

I scoff and shake my head at her. "I'm far from perfect. Trust me, I don't have it all, believe me. I have no parents and a grandfather who's only interest in me is how he can use me to benefit himself."

"Everything I thought I knew about my life is a lie," she says, looking at her own reflection in the mirror with glazed eyes. "Nothing is real."

"Did you and Chester have a fight or something?" I ask her, completely befuddled about what is going on here.

"Chester," she snorts. "Chester is just a distraction, nothing more. You think I'd cry over someone like him?"

When she puts it like that, no, I can't imagine Georgie crying over him. I can't imagine anyone crying over him.

She turns from the mirrors, hugging her arms around her waist. Her face is devoid of any makeup. She really doesn't need all that makeup. She's genuinely pretty without it.

"Look, Georgie, I know we haven't exactly got on well, but this is the girls loo's," I say, gesturing around me. "What is said in here stays in here."

Georgie scoffs. "Talking about it won't make it any less true. Talking won't take it back and let me carry on living the lie," she says becoming more high pitch and hysterical. "Talking won't change the truth."

"Little red what's taking you so...Oh, Georgie's here too. Are you two kicking off in here?" Rafe interrupts, stopping in his stride at the doorway when he realises Georgie is in here with me.

"Oh, look, your little bodyguard's here," Georgie says, pushing her shoulders back and attempting, but failing, to look composed. "Go to hell, the both of you," she snaps. She shoulder checks Rafe as she storms out into the corridor.

Both Rafe and I stare after her, feeling the aftereffects of hurricane Georgie. Rafe turns back to me and blinks. "What on earth crawled up her arse?"

I shake my head. "I don't know, but I've never seen Georgie so undone before."

Rafe snickers and holds the door open. "Chester's probably been shagging her best friend."

I smile and nod my head. "Probably." I shouldn't care. After all, she's been nothing but horrible to me, but I recognise the look she had in her eyes. I remember it well. It's the one you get when you feel so lost and alone.

Lunch time rolls round and as I listen to Vee chatter away about our plans for Ibiza, I spot Chester sitting at the table where the Jacks and their girls sit. I grab a bottle of water and tell Vee I'll meet her at our table and make my way over there.

"Eliza. To what do we owe the pleasure?" Chester asks me, as he leans back in his chair and looks me over slowly.

"My eyes are up here, Chester. I need a word." I gesture with my head for him to follow me.

With a slow eye roll he stands and joins me where I hope no one can hear us. "Do you need me to break into Wilbur's office again?"

I glare at him, and he chuckles in response. "Well, spit it out."

I double check that no one is listening before I lean into his ear. "Is Georgie, okay? It's just I saw her this morning in the girls' toilets, and she seemed really upset."

Chester shrugs his shoulders. "How the fuck would I know? Her daddy probably refused to buy her a new pony. Do I look like I spend my time talking to her when I'm with her?"

"Probably not, no," I say with a defeated sigh. I should have known I'm wasting my time talking to Chester. "Forget it."

I head over to our table and sit down beside Archer. I could feel him watching me talking to Chester. "Do I need to hurt him for anything?"

I look up at him in confusion and follow his eyes to where Chester is lording it over his table. "Oh no, I was just asking him if Georgie is okay."

"You were asking about Georgie's welfare?" he asks me, his tone oozing with surprise.

I offer him a deadpan look. "Yes, I might not like the girl, but she was in the loo's this morning in absolute bits. She was full on sobbing like a baby."

Archer frowns for a beat then shrugs. "I'm sure it will be some drama over nothing."

"Yeah, you're probably right," I agree. I spot Georgie enter the cafeteria and take a seat beside Chester, who throws his arm over her without even a hello. She just sits there and stares off into space as if her thoughts are a million miles away from where she is right now.

My last class of the day ends ten minutes early as we have a test, and we can leave once we're finished. I head to my locker and swap over the books I'll need for my homework tonight. I decide to head out and wait by Archer's car for him. I have my head down, lost in my own thoughts, as I round the corner to the side car park. I'm not looking where I'm going, and I walk smack straight into a hard body.

I look up, ready to apologise, but blink in surprise when I find Archer's dad. He has his hand gripped around Georgie's arm like he's trying to get her to go with him. I look from Phil to Georgie and back again.

"Everything okay here?" I ask, pointing my question particularly at Georgie.

"Eliza. What a pleasant surprise," Phil says, releasing his firm grip on Georgie's elbow and adjusting his tie, trying to make the move look casual.

"Phil, what are you doing here?" I question him, making it clear I am concerned about Georgie.

"I'm meeting Callum up at the clubhouse, and he asked me to pick Georgie up on the way. Isn't that right?" he adds, his dark eyes fixed on Georgie.

"Yes, that's right." Georgie swallows and she gestures towards her silver Mercedes up on the car park. "Dad must have forgotten I'd driven here today, so I'll head over there now."

"Great," Phil says, his eye studying Georgie. He blinks as if remembering he has an audience. "How are you enjoying being engaged to my son?"

"It's just fine," I reply, finding his question strange.

"I bet it is," he says, but I'm not sure if he's talking to me or himself here. "Well, I should go meet Callum. I don't want to keep him waiting." He gives Georgie one last look before turning on his heels and striding over to his car.

Both Georgie and I remain quiet as we watch him climb in

and drive away. When I turn back to look at Georgie, she's staring after Phil's car with tears in her eyes.

"Georgie, is everything okay? Was Phil hurting you?"

Georgie snaps out of her trance and scowls at me coldly. "Why don't you mind your own and stay out of other people's business?" She taps the end of her nose with her finger before she turns her back on me and heads over to her car. I stay where I am and watch her as she climbs inside. She briefly rests her head on the steering wheel before she starts the engine and pulls out of school.

What on earth was that all about?

I wait on the bonnet of Archer's car and scroll through my social media accounts. Archer comes out some ten minutes later with Rafe and Seb on either side of him. Vee has drama club tonight, so she's staying behind.

Archer looks up, and when he spots me waiting for him, he breaks out into a smirk. That smirk that undoes me every time. It blindsides me and makes me feel all these emotions that I'm too scared to read into.

"Hey, Scar." He strides up to me and steps between my legs, wrapping his arms around my waist. He nuzzles into my neck. His day-old stubble prickling against my skin. "Hmm, you smell good enough to eat," he whispers quietly into my ear, and I giggle like some love-struck fool.

"Can you drop me off at Wilbur's place? I promised Edith I'd call and see her, and I thought I'd hang with Kit for an hour."

"I can, but I'll ring Tony and have him meet you there."

I roll my eyes; I know it's because he cares, but seriously, what harm is going to come to me sitting eating cookies with Edith and Kit in the Alderman kitchen?

"No arguments, Scar," Archer adds, obviously knowing I'm about to protest. "I need to know you're safe."

"Fine," I grumble, giving up without a fight. The sexy fucker knows how to play me.

ARCHER DRIVES ME TO WILBUR'S HOUSE. BEFORE HE DRIVES away, he pulls me in for a quick kiss and tells me to ring him when I'm done, and he'll come and get me. I gesture to the left of me and point out that we live next door, and that Tony will either walk or drive me back around.

"Edith," I shout as I enter quietly via the front door. "Are you here?"

"In the kitchen, my dear, come through," she shouts in reply from the direction of the kitchen.

I walk in to find her in her trusty pinny with a mixing bowl in her hand. "Eliza," she beams, "it's lovely to see you. Take a seat. I promised Kit some blueberry muffins, so I'm just making some now."

"You spoil him," I say with an arch of my brow, and she chuckles.

"That boy deserves to be spoiled, as do you." She places down the mixing bowl and takes a plate from the fridge. She places a pile of cookies in front of me. "Raspberry and white chocolate."

I moan as I pick one up, it's still warm and gooey inside. "Edith, you are a saint! Any chance before I go you can mix me up some of your custard to take back with me. Jenny doesn't make it as good as you do."

Edith blossoms at my words and bats my comment away. "That's because she doesn't know the secret ingredient to add." She winks at me and returns to her mixing bowl. "So, how are things over at the Savage household?"

I nod my head, chewing on a mouthful of cookie. "They're okay. Edward is lovely. Phil, we don't really see that much. It's a strange house. I don't know, it just feels like it's keeping secrets. Does that sound crazy?"

Edith stops her mixing and gives me her full attention. "No, it doesn't. That house has never been the same since Libby passed away."

I pause, wondering if I should ask my next question, but I've nothing to lose. "Do you believe she killed herself?"

"Honestly, I don't know dear," she replies, shaking her head and looking off into the grounds of the estate. "She wasn't herself; I often wonder if...well, I shouldn't be saying all this."

"Please," I beg her, placing my hand on her arm, "say whatever it is you were about to."

Edith picks up her cup of tea, then takes the seat beside me at the island. "Libby had been really unhappy after your father left, but she got better. When she was pregnant with Archer, she was beaming and really excited about the baby. And for years she seemed to be back to her old self. So, you see all this talk about her killing herself because she hadn't got over your father doesn't wash with me. Something must've happened though, as after years of seeming her old self, she went downhill again." Edith sighs and shrugs her shoulders. "I don't know. Maybe she just had depression and had her ups and downs. Calvin and she seemed to develop a good friendship towards the end. He found it hard when she died." She pats my hand and returns to her baking, splitting the mixture into muffin cups. I sit and watch her, and I contemplate what she just told me. I can't help this feeling in my gut that there was more to the whole story.

I hear the front door go and footsteps in the hallway and I shake my head of my thoughts as Kit jogs into the room.

"Sis, you're here!" Kit grins, coming over and wrapping his arms over my shoulders and giving me a back hug. "Are you staying for tea?"

I grimace, about to say that I'm not.

"Wilbur and Lexi are in London," Edith chirps in, winking at me.

"Okay, I'll stay for tea. Could we eat in here, though, and eat with Rory and Calvin?"

"Of course." Edith smiles delightedly at my suggestion. "They would love that."

I smile back at her, feeling guilty that the reason I asked is so that I can quiz Calvin about Archer's mum. Kit and I catch up over muffins. He has a match this weekend, and he makes me promise to come and watch him. It's so lovely to see him looking so happy and relaxed. When we were in foster care, I always felt like he was never truly relaxed in any of the placements we were in. At the back of his mind, he was always wondering when we'd have to move again. Getting married at eighteen would at least secure his home and keep that smile on his face. I'd truly do anything for him.

Calvin and Rory come in for tea at six and we all sit together around the little table in the kitchen and it's just perfect. This is what a real family feels like. This is what I want to build for myself one day. Could I have this with Archer, though? With the Aces Elders always in the background dictating what we do and who we mix with. I think about the baby in my belly. I don't want him or her having to marry someone because it is what's 'expected' of them. I want them to be free to choose, be free to go off and live life and not be at the beck and call of some ancient society.

Once we have eaten, Edith gets out a deck of cards and we all play queenie. Kit enjoys teaching me, as I've never played it before. I feel more settled now about Kit being here without me because I know he has these three wonderful people who are giving him the love and care of a family. I get my opportunity to speak with Calvin when he insists on washing up and I offer to dry. Edith is old school. She doesn't like dishwashers.

"So, how is school going?" Calvin asks me as he passes me a plate.

"Good. I can't quite believe that I'll be thinking about university soon." I internally grimace. Is uni even an option for me anymore now that I am pregnant?

"Make sure you get out there and experience life, Eliza. Don't let this Bay hold you here," he says, his pale blue eyes holding sympathy.

"I intend to, Calvin," I assure him. "I was chatting with your mum before and, well, she mentioned you and Libby became good friends."

Calvin's smile drops. Clearing his throat, he nods his head as he concentrates all his attention on the plate he's cleaning. "We did."

"It's just, I don't know. This whole suicide verdict doesn't sit right with me. I think there was maybe more to it than that. Your mum said she'd been happy again, like her old self."

"She was," Calvin blurts out, and he looks over his shoulder to check that the others can't hear us. "Just be careful in that house, Eliza. Libby was happy. She adored Archer, he was her life. Yes, she had depressive episodes, but she wasn't always like that. They came and went. The night before they found her, she came to see me. I found her at my cottage door, soaked to the bone in just her pyjamas. She was hysterical, saying she'd had enough, that she wasn't taking anymore."

"Not taking any more of what?"

Calvin shakes his head. "She wouldn't say, but that night she asked me to help her leave. She asked me to leave the Bay with her and Archer."

I almost drop the glass in my hands at this news. "So, she was planning to leave and the next day she's found dead?"

Calvin looks at me with solemn eyes and nods his head. "Like I said, be careful in that house."

I study him and nod my head in agreement at his warning. "Were you in love with her?"

Calvin pauses with his hands in the soapy water, and he looks off into the darkness through the window. "I think I'd always secretly loved her, since being a young boy, but I was younger than her and back then, she only had eyes for your father. But towards the end we became friends, and I think she started to see me differently. I became her confidant and I think that yes, if we'd have left together, our relationship would have evolved into a romantic one."

I place my hand on his arm, and he looks down at my hand and then at me. "I'm sorry you lost her, Calvin."

He smiles sadly, the pain of her loss reflected in his eyes. "Me too."

CHAPTER TWENTY-FIVE

ELIZA

The next morning when I wake for school, I lie there for a while just running over last night's conversations in my head. I no longer believe Libby killed herself, but then that means that if she didn't, there's a murderer in our midst. Could Libby's murderer and my stalker be one and the same?

I'm quiet on the car ride to school. If Archer picks up on it, he says nothing. We meet the boys and Vee in the car park, and we all walk into school together. I decided when I was lying there thinking about Libby that this coming weekend, I'd tell Archer about the baby. There being a chance that whoever hurt Libby could be the one stalking me has made me realise I need to protect my unborn child and to do that I had to tell Archer. Am I scared about how he will react? Yes. I'm terrified, but I know Archer and his honourable sense of duty, and he'll love and protect this child.

We split up from the boys in the corridor as they head to their lockers over on the left side of the hallway, Vee's and mine are on the opposite side.

"Are you excited about the party?" I ask her as I turn the combination to my locker.

Vee grins. "Girl, wait until you see my dress. It's Versace and pure silk," she gushes over said dress, and I can tell she's picturing herself wearing it right now.

"I don't even want to know what obscene amount of money that has cost you."

She bats away my comment. "I'm only eighteen once, so I deserve a spectacular dress."

As I open my locker, my attention is concentrated on Vee. As I reach my hand inside, an expression of horror crosses Vee's face as she lets out a blood-curdling scream.

"Snake!" She grabs my hand and yanks it back, and we both stumble backwards and land on our arses. I look up at my locker to see a pissed off snake inside. It's coiled, ready to attack. I don't have time to process anything as Archer jumps over us. He slams the locker door closed with a loud bang just as the snake looks ready to attack. I jerk back when I hear it hit the inside of the door.

"What the actual fuck?" I look from Archer to Vee in complete shock.

"Rafe, get the headteacher and call Boyd," Archer orders, as he checks the locker is securely closed.

"Why Boyd? It's just a snake, Archer. Probably some dumb prank," I tell him, I don't understand why he's so worked up about this.

Archer's furrowed brow tells me he isn't taking this as a prank. He crouches down in front of me and Vee. "Are you both okay?" I nod my head and take his hand when he offers to help me up.

"We're fine. It's just a stupid school prank," I insist, not sure what all the fuss is about.

Archer pulls me into his arms and kisses the top of my head. His heart is beating ten to the dozen and I can tell he's struggling to keep calm.

"Hey, I'm okay," I reassure him, standing on my tiptoes to place a kiss on his lips. He pulls me in, deepening the kiss.

"Scar, that snake was a venomous snake. If that thing had bitten you, you would have had minutes before the venom would have killed you."

I pale at his words, letting them sink in. "So, someone just tried to kill me?"

Archer cups my face in his hands, and he pauses before he nods his head. "Whoever put that thing in your locker wasn't playing a prank, Scar. They want you gone."

My bodyguard, Tony, strides into the school. He scans the area as he walks towards us, assessing for any dangers. "Is she okay?" he asks Archer.

"I'm fine," I insist. Inside, though, I'm shaking like a leaf. My stalker has upped their game. They weren't sending warnings anymore. No, now they are trying to take me out.

"Come on, we need to get her home. It isn't safe here until we've done a full sweep of the school," Tony tells Archer. Archer picks up my schoolbag and ushers me towards the exit. Vee and Seb follow behind us and the entire school watches, phones out, recording the incident and whispering as we pass them.

Archer bundles me into the car. Vee and Seb climb in the back, and we take off at speed, with Tony and another security guy travelling behind us in their four-by-four. Rafe has stayed behind at school to wait for the police. Archer is gripping the steering wheel so tightly that I'm worried he might actually break the thing, so I place my hand on his leg and draw his attention.

"I'm okay," I assure him. "Now try to relax because you're going to break your car."

Archer removes one hand from the wheel and grips mine in his, keeping our joined hands resting on his leg. We pull up outside the mansion in no time, and Tony opens our doors and escorts us into the house. All the while, talking to someone on his mobile about upping the security detail.

We all congregate in the informal lounge. No one talks. We are all still in shock. Vee answers a call from her parents, who have heard from Rafe about the incident and are checking that she is okay. She reassures them she is fine, that it was just a shock.

Archer sits down on the sofa and pulls me onto his lap. He searches my face and tucks a strand of unruly hair behind my ear. He cups my face and leans in to kiss me, and I pour every ounce of reassurance I can into the kiss.

"Fuck, Scar," he exclaims. "I could have lost you."

I smile, placing my hands over his. "But you didn't. I'm right here and I'm fine."

He shakes his head and leans his forehead against mine. "I can't lose you. You've become my fucking everything. I can't live in a world where you're not in it, Scar."

I gulp. "What are you saying, Archer?"

He swallows deeply, our heads still pressed against each other's. "I'm saying I love you. I love you more than fucking anything, Scar."

I think my heart stops beating in my chest. He loves me! Archer Savage, the cold unfeeling brute of our school, is in love with me.

"You do?" I ask him, my voice coming out all shaky.

"You're my everything, Scar, and I vow to you now, I'll find out who is doing this. When I find them, I'll make them feel a world of hurt before I end their life."

My dark and disturbed heart swoons at his promise to end my stalker's life. This should horrify me, right? It doesn't though, it just makes me want to rip his clothes off right here and now and show him how much I like it when he threatens death to anyone who would try to hurt me.

"Later," he whispers in my ear with a smirk, clearly picking up on the lustful pheromones I'm giving off right now.

"Archer, there's something I need to tell you," I say with a sigh. Its time I tell him about the baby.

"Boyd's here," Seb announces, making me remember we're not alone in the room.

At the news Boyd is here, Archer places me on the sofa beside him and grips my hand in his. I actually don't give a flying shit that Boyd is here. I'm still processing the fact that Archer just told me he loves me. I catch Vee's eye and she smiles at me. She places her hands over her heart and mouths 'wow' to me. It's safe to say Seb and Vee both heard his proclamation of love.

"Mr Savage, Miss Alderman," Boyd greets as he strides into the room with his sidekick coming in close behind him. "The snake has been secured, and you were right, Mr Savage. It is indeed an Adder snake. Highly venomous and deadly."

"This was an attempted murder, Boyd. Do you understand that?" Archer growls. "If you weren't throwing everything at this case, then you had better do."

Boyd nods his head. "I can assure you this case has been getting the undivided attention of my department and it will continue to do so."

"You can't pick up a snake like that from nowhere," Seb states from where he is standing, leaning against the fireplace. "There has to be a purchase trail."

Archer nods his head in agreement. "You have to have a licence to hold a venomous snake."

"We're on it," Boyd assures him. "I have got half my team looking at every registered snake breeder and exotic pet shop within a seventy-mile radius. We'll search further afield if we need to."

"You do need to," Archer insists firmly. "I mean it Boyd, no stone left unturned. My fiancée could have died today."

It still sounds so odd when I'm referred to as his fiancée but I'm not going to lie and say I don't like it. Because I kind of do like it, a lot. I look down at the ring on my left hand and I rub my finger across the ruby. I have a fiancé and he loves me. I can't help the smile that breaks out on my face. This earns me an odd look from Boyd, who probably wonders what the hell I have to smile about when someone has just made an attempt on my life.

Edward and Wilbur both arrive ten minutes later and usher Boyd into Edward's office to discuss the threat further. I hear Archer insist that I have more security with me at all times and I inwardly groan at the thought of having more people following my every move.

My phone rings and I pull it out of my pocket to see it's Damon calling me.

"Hey."

"I just heard. Are you fucking okay, princess?" I can hear the worry in his voice.

"I'm fine. I promise. It will take more than a venomous snake to take me down," I jest, trying to make light of the situation.

"It's not funny, princess. Someone tried to end you. I hope Savage is taking this seriously?"

I scoff. That is an understatement! "If you mean, am I going to be tailed by a team of elite bodyguards everywhere I go, then that would be a yes."

"Good," he says firmly. "Princess, have you told him yet?"

"Not yet. I was going to this morning."

"Tell him. Soon. He needs to know that he has two of you to protect now," Damon urges me.

I know he's right. I'll tell him when he's less angry and he's not wanting to go out and burn down the world to find who did this to me. I'll tell him after the twins' eighteenth party this weekend.

"This weekend, I promise. Oh, and by the way, this is your invite to the pre-party, party."

Damon chuckles down the phone. "There's a pre-party party?"

"Yep, Seb likes to milk the excuse to party for as long as he can, so Friday night there's a pre-party at Archer's house."

There's a pause of quiet before he answers. "I don't think I'll be welcome, princess. You know that."

"You are welcome because you are my guest," I insist. "I've told Seb you're coming and that there's no discussion about it. You can bring Milly."

"I'll think about it, princess. Actually, I was planning to ring you today, anyway. My sister invited you for tea on Friday night, but I guess if you have a party, you won't be able to make it."

"I can come," I say. "The party doesn't start until eight. That gives me time to come for tea. I'll pick you up in my new ride."

"Oh yes, the engagement present. Fancy!" His teasing tone doesn't go unnoticed.

I blush even though he can't see me. "I know, I know it's ridiculously extravagant."

Damon chuckles in reply. "I'll let her know you can make it. You take it easy tonight, okay?"

"I will," I assure him. I put the phone down to find Vee watching me with a pointed expression.

"What?"

"You know what!" she replies, looking out towards the corridor to check no one can hear us. "Tell him. Tonight."

I shake my head. "I'm not telling him tonight. He's too fired up and angry. Can you imagine how he'll be if he finds out I wasn't the only one put in danger today? No. I'll tell him at the weekend when he's had time to calm down."

I can tell by the look on her face she doesn't agree with me, but I know if I tell him now, he'll explode. He'll likely lock me in his room and not let me leave until I give birth. It's better to wait and tell him after the party when he's had a chance to wind down and have some fun. I rest my head against the back of the couch and close my eyes. I'm exhausted. Growing a baby and having someone make an attempt on your life is a tiresome experience.

❧

I OPEN MY EYES AND STARE STRAIGHT INTO THE EYES OF MY dark boy. I realise I'm in our bed and he must have carried me up after I fell asleep.

"Hey."

He smiles softly, leaning on one elbow beside me. "Hey, sleeping beauty. How are you feeling?"

"I'm fine," I say, leaning up to press my lips against his. He kisses me gently as if I might break, and I pull back and meet his eyes. "I'm fine, Arch. Now undress me because all that talk of un-a-living someone for me earlier has me horny as hell."

Archer smirks down at me. "Talking about killing someone is a turn on?"

"It is when you say it," I admit, climbing into his lap. I take his hand and place it on my right breast. "Love me, Archer. I need you."

My words seem to have the desired effect because he grasps me by the back of my neck and pulls me in for a soul deep kiss that sets me on fire. He unbuttons my school shirt, his lips never leaving mine, as he tugs it off, throwing it over his head. Archers' hands find my nipples and he runs his fingers over them, making me shiver in delight. He reaches behind me and unclasps my bra.

"Tell me what you need, Scar," he commands, pinching roughly at my nipples, making me gasp with pleasure.

"I need you. I want it rough and dirty," I confess. Tonight, I don't want a gentle, loving Archer. Tonight, I want the dark and deadly Archer that fills my dark desires and doesn't hold back. He grips my hair in a fist at the back of my neck and yanks my head back to look him in the eyes.

"What my queen wants, she gets," he promises, and my heart pounds in my chest in excitement. He holds my hair with one hand as his other pulls roughly at the zipper of my skirt. I lift up slightly on my knees and he pulls it down, and it lands across the other side of the room. He rips my knickers at the seam, and they fall away from me. For a second he leans back, and drinks in my naked body with lust-filled eyes. "Go to the end of the bed and bend over. I want your pretty arse in the air." He slaps my bottom hard, making me yelp in surprise. Breathless, I climb off his lap and do as he says. I walk around to the bottom of the bed, purposely giving my hips extra sway and I grab a hold of the wooden bed post and bend over. He watches me like a lazy lion watching over his pride. He's still lying on the bed, his head resting on one bent arm. He unzips his trousers and pulls out his cock. Watching me he strokes himself, never taking his eyes off me. As I study him, I bite my lip in anticipation. I want his cock buried deep inside of me; I want him to fuck me until I can't walk without knowing he's been inside of me.

"You want this, Scar?" he asks me, his dark eyes burning into mine, hungry with lust and desire.

"Please," I beg him, squirming with need.

"Touch yourself. Show me how wet you are for me, baby," he commands as he continues to pleasure himself.

There's something so debase and lustful about watching him pleasure himself while I do the same. I run my finger down between my legs and I'm already soaking for him.

"Rub your wetness on those pert nipples for me, Scar."

I pull my wet fingers from my sex and keeping my eyes on him; I circle my nipples with them, coating them in my own juices.

"Finger fuck yourself for me, beautiful," he demands, as he grips his cock tighter and pumps up and down. I lick my lips, wanting to taste him. I need him closer to me. I want his skin against mine. I want his lips against mine. I wanted to feel him everywhere.

I do as he asks of me, and I slip two fingers inside of myself. I moan with pleasure as I pump my fingers in and out, my hips grinding against my hand, needing it deeper.

"Is that good, Scar? How does it feel?"

"Good," I moan in response, holding his eyes with mine. "But I need more Archer. I need you inside me."

He smirks, letting go of his erection and he stands from the bed. He shrugs off his trousers and his boxers completely and pulls his T-shirt over his head. He's standing here before me in all his naked gloriousness. I want to kiss and lick every single inch of his body. He slowly walks around the bed and comes to stand behind me. I wait with bated breath to see what he is going to do next. He grabs my hips firmly and in one hard thrust, he pushes deep inside me, making me cry out in both shock and pleasure. There is no build-up. He just gives me what he knows I need. A good, hard, fucking. I grasp tightly to the bedpost as he thrusts in and out in hard and fast movements. I cry out when he angles his hips and hits that sweet spot inside of me. He slaps my bottom hard, and it rings out around the room. I groan in pleasure.

"You like this, baby? You like me fucking you like a dirty whore," he states rather than asks me. I'm too lost in my lust to form words so I just moan, loudly. "I'm going to fuck you until you're sore. I'm going to fuck you until you beg me to stop, Scar."

"Don't stop. Never stop," I breathlessly tell him.

"Touch yourself, Scar. I want to feel your come dripping down my cock. I want your juices all over me as I fuck you, baby. Come for me," he orders as he pistons his hips and somehow takes me even harder and deeper. I detonate into a thousand pieces. Screaming his name as I come. I think I see stars as I come, and I come. Wave after wave of pleasure roars through my body and he moans my name loudly as I fall apart. "I'm going to fucking explode, Scar. I'm going to come so deep in you, you'll have my come dripping down those perfect thighs for days." He grips my hips tighter. I'm going to have bruises tomorrow, but I don't care. He is relentless in his pace, chasing his euphoria. When he comes, he roars my name over and over and slumps over me as he basks in the comedown from his release. He kisses my back as he leans up and pulls himself out. My inner thighs spasm from the intensity of our fucking. I lean up and spin to face him, draping my arms over his neck.

"Well, that was mind-blowing," I say with a chuckle. He picks me up by the back of my knees and I wrap my legs around his waist as he walks us into the ensuite. He doesn't put me down. He steps under the showerhead and turns on the water. I tip my head back and allow the water to rain down my body and cover my face and chest.

"You're like a drug I crave constantly," he tells me, staring into my eyes and sending my heart into a gallop. "You're the only one who can give me what I need, Scar."

Sometime later, we fall asleep in each other's arms. Archer holds me tightly, as if he's worried if he lets go something bad will happen to me. I place my hand over my belly. A part of him is growing inside of me, a product of our coming together. It still blows my mind that we made a person together. One that will grow and change and become a fully functioning part of this world.

THE REST OF THE WEEK PASSES WITH NO FURTHER ATTEMPTS on my life. I now have three big burly bodyguards with me wherever I go. They sweep the school every morning before I go in, much to the head teacher's ire. They escort us to and from school every day. Kit also now has a security guy following him everywhere he goes. It was something I'd insisted on. I needed to know he was safe.

I try to put the worries of my stalker behind me for now. This weekend is all about the twins and celebrating their eighteenth. It will also be the weekend that Archer finds out he's going to be a dad. Everything is going to change once I tell him.

I'm at my locker putting some books away at the end of the school day on Thursday when someone clears their throat behind me. I arch a brow in surprise when I find Georgie hovering.

"Georgie."

"I heard about the snake. Do they know who did it?" she mumbles, scuffing her shoes and looking very uncertain and uncomfortable.

"No. The police are investigating, but they haven't come up

with any leads." I close my locker, and clutching my iPad to my chest, I face her. "Are you okay?"

Georgie nods her head and clears her throat; this conversation is all kinds of awkward. "Anyway, I just wanted to say, I'm sorry you went through that," she blurts out before hurrying off down the corridor.

"What did she want?" Vee asks as she comes up beside me, glaring down the corridor at Georgie's retreating figure.

I shake my head, also watching her leave. "I'm not really sure."

"Odd," says Vee with her shrug of her shoulders. "Anyway, on to important matters. The weekend. The pre-party Friday. Will you pick me up on your way back from Damon's sisters? I'm not heading over at the same time as Seb. I need some pamper time to make myself look extra delicious."

I laugh. "Vee, you're beautiful without even trying, but yes I'll pick you up." up."

"I could get used to having my own personal chauffeur", she grins. "Come on, let's go eat and find the boys."

CHAPTER TWENTY-SIX

ELIZA

Damon and I leave school and head straight for his sister's house. I'm excited to see Emma again, and the twins. Emma has kept in touch with me via text. When I'd messaged her to say I had decided to keep the baby she said she'd go through the twin's old baby things and keep them to one side for me. I think the baby is a girl. I don't know why, it's just a gut feeling I have but Emma said the twins wore a lot of neutrals as newborns, so she'd still have some clothes for me.

"So, you're telling him tomorrow?" Damon asks me as he changes over the radio station in the car.

"Not tomorrow, Sunday. Ooh I love this song, leave it on," I tell him as Swift's new song starts to play. "How are you feeling about Milly enrolling at the academy?"

Damon arches a brow at me and sniggers. "I know what you are doing. Changing the subject, but I'll allow it for now."

I give him my best *'what?'* look. "So, Milly?"

Damon sighs and bobs his shoulders. "Honestly, I'd rather she stayed at the state school, but in other ways I get what she means about the academy opening doors for her. But you and I both know how unwelcome outsiders are made to feel."

"But she'll have us there. No one will dare give her hassle."

Damon bobs his head in agreement. "True, but we'll only be there for another six months. After that she'll be on her own."

He had a point, but even after we move on, the school

would still have Clubs and senior Aces and I'd be able to make sure they looked out for her. We pull up outside Damon's sisters house and don't get the opportunity to discuss Milly any further as Noah and Ollie come bounding out of the house to greet us. Emma appears at the door and waves to us as the boys come running up to us cheering in excitement that we are here.

"Noah, let go of Eliza's leg." Emma chuckles as Noah wraps his arms around my lower leg and clings to me. Damon already has Ollie in one arm, so he saves me, swooping Noah up with his other arm.

"What have you two monsters been up to, huh?"

"We made a den in the playroom," Ollie tells us as we walk to the house. "It's a pirate den."

"Wow," Damon exclaims. "Can I come in your den?"

"You can be our prisoners," Noah suggests excitedly.

"Uh-oh, you hear that, Eliza? They want to lock us up in their den. We have a birthday party to get to later Ollie, so will you promise to let us out."

Ollie ponders the question. "Is their cake and games at the party?"

Damon and I share a look and fight back a laugh. "No, I don't think there's a cake."

Noah crinkles his nose up. "That's a rubbish party then."

We reach the door and Emma steps back and holds it open for us. "They are full of energy today," she says with a tired smile. "Damon, please tire them out for me for a bit and then they'll sleep early tonight?" She holds her hands together in a begging motion.

"Want to play hide and seek boys?" Damon suggests and both boys jump up and down and shout yes. "Come on then, let's start in the playroom." He looks back at us as the boys drag him through the house. "You owe me, sis."

"I'm feeding you, aren't I?" She grins, hand on her hip. We both laugh and Emma ushers me into the kitchen.

"Have a seat. Do you want coffee or tea?" she asks me as she heads over to the kettle.

"Tea, please. Coffee tastes odd." I grimace; just the thought of coffee makes me shiver.

Emma laughs. "For me it was milk. I suddenly hated the taste, all through my pregnancy. Have you had any cravings?"

I nod my head. "Oh yeah. Custard and diet coke. I even had custard for breakfast the other day."

Emma makes our drinks and comes and sits with me at the island. I cup my hand around my cup and blow on the hot drink.

"How have you been?"

I sigh. Where do I start? "Considering everything that is going on right now, I'm good. I've moved in with Archer and we're engaged," I tell her, waggling my engagement ring at her.

Emma reaches out and takes a hold of my hand in hers so she can admire the ring. "Wow, that is beautiful. Is it a family heirloom?" she asks me as she stares at the sparkling ruby stone.

"No, I actually saw it at a jewellery store in London and Archer went back and bought it. My wedding band, though, will be Archer's grandmother's ring."

Emma grins at me and puts her hand over her heart. "That's quite sweet. I thought this Archer guy was a bad-ass brooding guy?"

"Oh, he is," I say, nodding my head firmly and smiling. "He's all those things but he can also be really thoughtful and caring at times."

She is watching me with a knowing look on her face and I blush under her scrutiny. "What?"

"You love him," Emma states.

"I like him. A lot," I reply. Why am I still denying it? Emma nods her head but looks at me like she knows full well I'm not being entirely honest with her.

"Anyway," she says standing and picking up a bag over on the dining table. "I picked out any neutrals for you. There are some plain baby grow's, vests, socks, and scratch mittens."

I take the bag from her and take a peek inside. I pull out a tiny pair of white scratch mittens and hold them in my palm. "It's still not sunk in properly. Maybe it won't until he or she is here." I bite my lip. "I'm terrified, Emma. I really wish my mum was here."

Emma reaches for my hand. "You'll be fine. You have me and Day and your bad-boy fiancé. I'll be there for advice and with a supply of coffee and chocolate when you've had a sleepless night."

I surprise her when I reach out and pull her into a hug. "Thank you," I whisper. "I don't have many females around me who I can call on, so it means a lot to me that you're being supportive."

"You're welcome, Eliza," she assures me. "Now, I hope you're hungry because I have made a lot of food. Day tells me Carbonara is one of your favourites. I hope he is right?"

I smile. "It is, but you really didn't need to go out of your way to make something I like. I will eat anything you put in front of me." I grimace. "Well, maybe not anything, but I'm a fairly easy feeder."

TWENTY MINUTES LATER WE ALL SIT DOWN TO EAT. NICK arrives home just in time for tea and the boys are full of beans wanting to tell him all about their day. I can't stop smiling as I sit and observe their little family unit. Could I possibly have this one day? After losing my parents I never thought I'd find it again. Day catches my eye and tilts his head and winks at me, checking if I'm okay. I silently nod my head at him. After the Carbonara, Emma serves up fudge cake with custard. She laughs at me when my eyes light up at the sight of the jug of custard. She makes sure to fill my bowl first before everybody else gets some.

After we have eaten, we all move into the front room and the boys get to choose a movie before bed. They argue at first as Noah wants Toy Story and Ollie wants Minions but they both eventually agree on Toy Story. Both boys want to sit with me and Damon, so we take the larger sofa and they both sit in-between us. Ollie starts yawning and he leans his little head against my arm. When it's time for bed they both protest but then when Day offers to read them their bedtime story they cheer and get very excited.

While they're having their bedtime story, I call Tony and tell him we'll be leaving in fifteen minutes. He tells us he'll set off and meet us at the bottom of the drive. Whilst Damon reads the boys bedtime story Emma gets her baby albums out and shows me photos of the boys when they were born and of her throughout her pregnancy. She tells me how she was sure she would be a terrible mum but how it all just came naturally, and she assures me that I'll be the same. When we leave, I feel lighter. Emma has given me the confidence boost that I needed. I can do this. I can be a mum at eighteen.

"Are you okay?" Damon asks me, as we buckle in and I start the engine. I wave at Tony who has pulled up on the lane ready to follow behind us.

I nod my head firmly and half smile. "Yes, I am. I think it'll be okay."

"It will," he agrees. "Now, are you sure about me coming to this party?"

I roll my eyes at him. How many times did we need to have this conversation? I had invited him, and the boys had agreed to him coming.

"Yes," I say. "They know you're coming and are fine with it."

Damon chuckles and his right brow lifts. "I think 'fine' might be a generous description of how they feel about it."

As we pull out onto the road I frown. The car makes a funny noise at the front. "Do you hear that?" I ask Damon who is busy fiddling with the radio station again.

"What?" he shouts as he turns up the music and starts singing.

"Nothing," I say shaking my head. I pick up speed. The roads are quiet around here so you can generally drive at fifty without worry. I hear it again, that clunking noise from the front of the car. "I think there's something wrong with the car."

Damon pauses and listens, and I hear the noise again. "Tell me you heard that?"

He nods his head frowning. "I heard something, yeah. Might be worth getting this car into a garage tomorrow princess. It doesn't sound healthy."

We climb the winding road that climbs the cliff front and I hear a loud clunk. "Damon!"

"I think we should pull..."

There's another loud clunk and the right front wheel bounces off in front of us causing the car to veer and lose control.

"Shit!" Damon exclaims. "Let me take the wheel, princess. We're going to crash. Hold on tight and I'll try to veer us into the trees."

The wheel chooses to come off just as we hit dangerous corner, a sharp bend in the road that is notorious around here. I've only been here nine months and even I've heard about it. As we round the corner at speed, Damon steers the car and hit the brakes and we slide sideways towards the embankment.

It's like I am back there again—with my parents. You feel like everything happens so quickly but in slow motion at the same time. I scream, my eyes wide with fear as we hit a large tree with a bang.

CHAPTER TWENTY-SEVEN

ARCHER

The party is in full swing. Seb has been missing for the last half an hour, no doubt off somewhere with a girl. I can't believe I let him talk us into another party, buts it's his eighteenth birthday and I love my brother. My phone chimes and I pull it out of my jeans pocket. It's Scar, letting me know she is setting off now and bringing Damon with her. I hate she is off spending time with him and his family. I wonder if the reason she is because she can't get that with me – a normal family, who look out for each other and love each other. It's hard to trust anyone when you have grown up in the world I have, with a father that has taught you to trust no one. Scar does trust me though, despite the fact that I lied to her when we first met and kept things from her, including my plan of revenge. None of that matters now, though. I'm free of the past, much to my father's abhorrence. Scar has made me want a different future. One that I'm finding I want more and more as each day passes and I wake to her in my arms. I look over at Rafe, who is sitting in the armchair beside me, a bourbon in one hand and his phone in the other. He's about as interested in tonight's party as I am.

"Scar's on her way. She's going to pick up Vee en-route."

Rafe nods his head. "Archer, I've just had an interesting email from our private investigator we hired to look into the stalker. He says he may have a lead. He's going to look further into it and get back to us."

I nod my head. It's about time someone gave us something to

go off. This sick fucker has been toying with us and it's driving me insane not knowing who he is and why he wants Eliza gone.

"Uh-oh, eleven o'clock," Rafe says, looking across the room. I follow his line of sight and groan when I see Georgie heading our way. And what is she wearing? She's in some ratty old hoody that's too big for her and leggings. Her make-up is smeared with panda eyes from where her mascara has run. "Look what the cat dragged in." Rafe snickers, looking as puzzled by Georgie's appearance as I am.

Georgie spots me over the heads of the crowd, and she makes a beeline our way. I groan internally. When will she get the message that I'm not interested?

"Archer, we need to talk. Now!" she demands as she comes to a stop in front of me, panting for breath and looking slightly more manic than usual.

"Not now Georgie. I'm trying to relax. Go find Chester, get him to give you a good time," I suggest to her, but she shakes her head.

"It's important. There isn't much time. We need to talk," she insists, and she looks around the room as if she's checking if there's anyone listening. "It concerns Eliza."

Okay, now she has my attention. "What about Eliza?"

"We need to have this conversation somewhere private," she insists. "And hurry."

Frowning at her, I look at Rafe and he bobs his shoulders, looking as perplexed as I feel. Sighing, I stand to my feet and gesture to the door behind me that leads through to the library. I glance Rafe's way and gesture with my head for him to come with us. I don't trust that Georgie won't do something drastic to pull Scar and me apart.

We all exit through the door into the library. I shut us inside and I turn to find Georgie pacing up and down the room. She winds her hair tightly around her fist and she twists it until it almost looks painful.

"They've been planning this all along, for years Archer," she mumbles as she paces, not looking at me. It's like she's lost in her own head.

"Georgie, let's cut to the chase. You said something involving Eliza."

Georgie's eyes snap to mine at the mention of Scar's name. "Is she here? She's in danger Archer. They want her out of the way. The threats haven't worked, so they mean to take her out permanently."

A cold chill travels through my body at lightning speed. "Who wants to hurt her, Georgie?"

She releases what seems a mix of a half-sob and a half-laugh. "Our father. He's going to kill her."

I stride over to Georgie and grip her by her wrists, forcing her to look at me. "Snap out of it and start talking sense. What do you mean, our father? You mean yours?"

Georgie looks at me with wide eyes and shakes her head. "We slept together as well, and they knew, and they let us. They make me feel sick. All this time, they've been together, plotting how to unite the families and form their own dynasty."

"What are you talking about? You're not talking sense!" I shake her slightly, trying to pull her out of this trance she seems stuck in.

"We have the same dad!" she wails. "My mum and your dad, they've been having an affair for years. Your dad is my dad, Archer."

I drop her wrists like they have electrocuted me. "You're fucking crazy!"

She shakes her head and moves towards me, and I take a step back. "I know it sounds crazy. I came home early one night, and I could hear voices in the pool house. Your dad and my mum were arguing when I snuck in. Sorry, our dad," she scoffs in disgust. "I heard Phil say that he wouldn't fail their daughter. And I was standing there listening and thinking, what daughter? He doesn't have a daughter. Then my world collapsed at his next words. 'Georgie and Archer are my children. We will secure their legacy."

"My mum stepped up to him and spoke about how she has spent years married to a man she despises and that he's told her to bide their time but that she is tired of waiting. Georgie needs you, her father, to step up and secure her future." She clutches at her face. "Phil is my dad, Archer. Not Callum."

I laugh. This was utter bullshit, right? Georgie has finally had a mental breakdown. That could be the only rational explanation, surely.

"You're lying," I say coldly. I am done with her crazy story.

She grabs at my hands and clutches at them. "I swear to you, I'm telling the truth. Why would I make this up? You and I are siblings, Archer, and our dad, and my mum have been plotting to remove Eliza so that they could suggest we get engaged. They want us to marry and secure the family's future. Ensure a loyal and committed bloodline to rival the Aces."

"You're talking fucking incest, Georgie. You expect me to believe that my dad and your mum conceived you and they hid it and spent all these years plotting to marry you off to me, your supposed brother? Do you realise how insane that sounds?" I growl out the last part, getting frustrated with her.

"Hold up," Rafe chirps in, studying Georgie. "We always said that the stalker seemed to have inside information and was always one step ahead. Your dad would have the means. Georgie's mum would have access to all the ways to get around the security system."

"It's been a few weeks since I overheard that conversation and I've been a mess, Archer. I mean, you and I we had sex and you're my...you're my brother. And they encouraged it. They took great joy in knowing we had sex. My mum encouraged me to seduce you. She said that a match was on the cards, that I'd be the next Savage wife." Running out of energy, she sits down on the sofa and holds her head in her hands. "I started watching them closely. I was desperate to find out more, and that's when I overheard their plans tonight." She looks up at me, her skin ashen and her eyes bloodshot. "They've tampered with her car, Archer. They plan to make it look like a car accident."

"You're saying my dad and your mum are Eliza's stalkers?" I ask her in total disbelief. This has to be Georgie playing a game here, right?

"I'm saying that my mum and OUR dad are the stalkers. Eliza, coming back, ruined their plans. Edward and the other Elders were coming round to the idea of a match between you and me and then she shows up and suddenly the agreement that Edward and Wilbur reached years ago was back on the table. The plan was always to unite the two families again."

"If my dad is your father, that would mean they were carrying on when my mum was alive." That cold realisation washes over me like ice.

"They were together before my mum married my dad. I don't think our dad ever loved your mum." Georgie shakes her head. "This isn't important right now. Eliza's in danger Archer. I heard them. They were going to mess with her car. Phil had heard you and her talking about how she was going to Damon's sisters for tea. Phil said he'd tamper with the car when everyone was eating. That way, it would happen on the way back here. They want her gone Archer and they're prepared to do whatever it takes now."

"Fuck," Rafe exclaims. "Call her now, Arch. She may not have set off yet."

With shaking hands, I pull out my phone and dial her number. It rings out and my heart pounds in my chest as I hit redial. "Nothing. We need to go, now!" I tell Rafe, and all three of us rush through the busy party and out the front door.

"My cars blocked in." I swear, looking at the drive that is packed with cars. There's no way we can get out of here without getting everyone to move.

"My car is down by the main gates," Georgie tells us, pointing down the drive. I tell her to pass me her keys and we all run to the car and climb in. My hearts pounding in my chest. Fuck! I can't lose her. The thought of her not being here makes my chest tight and I struggle to breathe.

"I'll keep trying her number," I tell Rafe as we speed through the dark country lanes. I press the call button on my steering wheel, but her number just rings out and goes to voicemail again. Damon's sister lives in a neighbouring village. Would we get there in time?

My phone rings and I breathe a sigh of relief. "Tony! Tell me that Eliza's with you and she's safe."

There's silence for a second. "Archer, there's been an accident. We're trying to get them out of the car now."

"Where are you?" I bark. I need to get to her, fast.

"We're on dangerous corner. The car's hit a tree on the embankment. They lost a front wheel."

"Fucker must have loosened the wheel nuts! I'm on my way," I growl, as I press down on the accelerator and speed up. I can't breathe.

⁂

We turn around a corner, and I brake at speed, causing the car to slide slightly. My heart drops into my stomach as I take in Eliza's car smashed into a tree with smoke wafting into the cold dark night.

"Holy fuck!" Rafe exclaims as we both jump out of the car and rush over to the wreckage.

Tony and his men have a crowbar out and are attempting to pry open her door.

I rush over to the driver's window. It's smashed in and she's unconscious, with blood dripping from her head down onto her face.

"It looks like the passenger side took the brunt of the crash.

We need to get them out pronto. This car's going to blow," Rafe warns us all.

"Get another crowbar from my boot," Tony orders, throwing Rafe his keys.

"Scar, baby, can you hear me?" I say softly, stroking her cheek and wiping the deep red blood from her pale face. Fuck! I can't lose her. I need her. I need her like I need fucking air to breathe. I knew I cared for her, but that's not true. That doesn't describe the depths of what I feel for her. She has my whole fucking twisted heart in her hands.

"Here," Rafe says, shoving the crowbar into my hand. We get both the bars in place and Tony and I pull on the crowbars as hard as we can. Rafe holds the top of the door and pulls with me. It resists at first, but then it opens with a groan. I throw the bar to the floor. My only focus is her. I unbuckle her belt. We shouldn't move her really in case she has a spinal injury, but Rafe's right there's leaking fuel and the smoke is getting stronger. I lean into the mangled car, and with my hands around her waist, I half drag her out. Rafe grabs her legs and together we move her away from the wreckage, laying her gently on the floor. I lift her head and place the blanket that Rafe hands me under her head. I check her pulse. Thank God, it's strong and steady. Rafe is on the phone to the ambulance service. Headlights come to a stop behind us and Vee and Seb rush from their car and over to us, both of them in shock at what they are seeing.

"Can you watch her?" I ask Vee, my eyes reaching hers and I see the same anguish I feel reflected in hers.

"With my life," she assures me, taking Scar's hand and holding it in hers. I race back to the car and aid Tony and his men in the attempts to free Damon. His side of the car has taken the worst of the hit. The front is crumpled up around his legs. Flames ignite from the bonnet, and we all share a concerned look, knowing we are on borrowed time.

"He's stuck," Tony states as he attempts to lift Damon's leg from the mangled metal. Flames lick up at where Damon's feet are, and we know are all out of time.

"Okay, you two grab him and slide his upper body out. I think if we can angle him, I might be able to get his feet out." Seb reaches in under Damon's mangled legs and curses as the flames catch at his hand.

By some miracle we get him free and carry him quickly to lay him beside where my whole fucking world is, pale and unconscious.

Boom!

Two seconds later the car bursts into flames and we all stare in shock knowing how close things got back there. In the distance I hear sirens and I thank the big man upstairs that help is on its way.

Tony is busy checking Damon over. I grab some water for Seb and he pours it over his burning hand, wincing in pain as the cold water meets his skin.

"Eliza," Damon mumbles, his eyes open and he looks around in panic as he tries to get his bearings.

"She's okay, man," Rafe tells him, gesturing with his head to where my girl lays.

"The baby," he mumbles, turning his head and looking at Scarlet.

"Baby? What the fuck are you talking about, man?" Rafe asks him, looking up at me with a confused frown. I shrug my shoulders.

"The baby. She's pregnant," Damon says. His eyes roll backwards, and he groans in pain. "The baby, she's sixteen weeks gone."

I look from Silver to my girl as his words sink in and I see red. I shove Rafe out of the way and, injured or not, I grab Silver by the scruff of his neck. He cries out in agony, but I'm not concerned about his pain right now.

"What the fuck are you saying? Is it yours, fucker?"

Damon coughs, and blood pools on his lips. "Baby, save them

both. Promise me." He grasps his hand around mine, where I hold his jacket in a firm grip.

"Okay, sir, can you step away from the patient please and let us check him over? He needs urgent care."

I've been so lost in my emotions I haven't even noticed the two ambulances arrive. Rising to my feet, I take a step back and let them crowd around Damon and start their observations. Two paramedics are by Scarlet, checking her over and providing her with emergency care. I stumble towards them, lost in a haze of shock.

"She's pregnant," I tell them. "Sixteen weeks."

Rafe grips my shoulder in support from behind me as we all stand back and watch helplessly as they do their job.

I turn to Vee, "Did you know?"

Vee swallows and nods her head. "I've known since the engagement party." Vee steps into my space and looks up at me. "She was planning to tell you. I swear, I think she just wanted some time to get used to the idea herself first."

"Is it his?" I ask her, devoid of any emotion. Was my dad right all along and the Alderman's were nothing but manipulators, playing on people's emotions?

"No," Vee says, shaking her head and frowning. "Gods, no, Archer. It's not like that between them. The baby's yours."

I stumble slightly as her words hit me. "We made a baby?"

"You did," Vee says, smiling sadly at me, her eyes welling up with tears.

I watch as the ambulance crew and some of the fire crew roll her and get her onto a board and onto the stretcher. A guy who arrived in an ambulance car and seems to be in charge of the whole situation comes our way.

"Are you their friends?"

"She's my fiancée," I tell him, and he nods his head.

"We're airlifting her to Meadow Hill trauma centre. She's stable, but she has several injuries and we're worried about internal bleeding."

"And the baby?" I ask him, now realising that I have two people to think about.

"Time will tell. It's too early to say. Right now, Eliza is our priority. Have you got someone who can drive you over to the hospital?"

I nod my head. Vee rubs at my back as we watch the heli-med crew disappear into the night with my girl. I feel so fucking helpless. It's my job to protect her. Fuck, it's my job to protect them both.

"Excuse me," a police officer walks over to us, clearing his throat. "Did anyone witness the accident and know what happened here?"

I remember then that Georgie is with us. She stands by my car shivering and her eyes stained with tears, and suddenly I remember everything that led us to being here. "I'm Archer Savage and that girl they have just airlifted out of here is my fiancée. I don't think I need to tell you I want every resource on this. I need Boyd to meet me up at the hospital now! He's investigating my fiancée's stalker, and this is all linked. She's a key witness," I inform him, pointing over to Georgie.

"I'll call him," the officer agrees. "I'll take the girl to the station, and I'll have my other two colleagues escort you up to the hospital, Mr. Savage."

The police know who's in charge in this Bay and they don't question what we tell them.

"Arch, what's going on?" Vee asks, watching as the police officer helps Georgie into his car.

I sigh, running a hand over my face. I'm strung out with everything that's happened. "It's a long story. Rafe will fill you in when we get to the hospital. You and Seb follow us there." Vee nods her head and Seb surprises me when he pulls me into his arms and claps me on my back.

"She'll be okay," he assures me. "Our queen is made of strong stuff."

I nod my head and smile at him. We all climb into our vehicles. Rafe and I get in with Tony in his car. I'm in no fit state of mind to drive. One perk of being a Savage is that the police escort puts on its blues and gets us over to the hospital in no time. I need to be with my girl and know that both she and our baby are going to be okay.

CHAPTER TWENTY-EIGHT

ARCHER

On the way to the hospital, I call Wilbur, who's in London, and I let him know about the accident. I don't mention the baby. Fucker doesn't need to know right now. Next, I call Edith, getting her out of bed and I ask her to get Calvin to bring Kit up to the hospital. Edith assures me that all of them are coming. My last call is to my grandfather. That conversation is not an easy one as I relay to him what Georgie divulged to me. He doesn't believe me, saying Georgie has made the whole thing up. I get it; it sounds so far-fetched. He checks my father's room and tells me he isn't there. No doubt the fucker is holed up somewhere with Georgie's whore of a mother. I shake my head as I come to terms with the fact that my own flesh and blood has done this to us. My father has tried to end the life of the one person in this world that means everything to me. His own selfish greed and ambition led him to a crazed plan to marry me off to my half-sister and ensure his bloodline and legacy.

When we arrive at the hospital, we're ushered into a family room. The nurse tries to tell our friends that they'll have to wait in the main hospital reception. I coldly remind her that my grandfather funds a large amount of this hospitals research facilities and she soon backs down and leaves us all to file into the family room.

Seb has the burns on his hands treated and bandaged; then we all sit and wait for news. It's agony. I need to know they're both okay. Rafe fills Vee and Seb in as I quietly sit with my own thoughts and process everything. "I'm going to kill him," I announce coldly. This causes all three of them to stop mid-conversation and look my way. I look at my two brothers. "I want you to find him before the police do, and then I want you to take him where no one will find him until I'm ready to deal with him."

Both my brothers nod their heads. They don't question my orders because that's what brothers do. We have each other's backs always. I'll make sure that fucker rues the day he ever tried to take my girl and my unborn child away from me.

"Did she know if it was a girl or a boy?" I ask Vee, as my thoughts flit to the baby my fiancée is carrying inside of her.

Vee smiles softly and shakes her head. "No, she said that you could find out at the next scan, but she'd already decided she wanted it to be a surprise. She's convinced it's a girl, though."

I smile. A girl. A mix of me and Scarlet. A product of our love. Hell knows I don't feel ready to be a dad, but I want our baby to make it. I want to hold him or her in my arms and watch them grow and develop. I want to see Scarlet ripe and round with my child inside her and watch her blossom into a devoted mother. I want it all. I want my forever with her. I want to build a family and have a life of happy memories.

I haven't noticed Vee take a seat beside me, too lost in my own thoughts. She takes my hand and holds it in hers. "They're both going to make it, Archer. I know it."

I nod my head. They have to, because I can't exist in a world where they aren't a part of it.

CHAPTER TWENTY-NINE

ELIZA

My head feels sore. I attempt to open my eyelids, but they feel fused together. I feel so tired. I try to swallow and groan. My throat feels so dry. I need water.

"Water," I mumble. It comes out as barely a whisper.

"Eliza!"

I recognise that voice. It's Kit.

"Eliza, can you open your eyes?" I hear him urge me. He sounds so close, but so far away at the same time.

"Tired," I reply, feeling sleep trying to claim me again. I attempt to open my eyes again and this time I manage to open them just a sliver. Bright lights assault my senses and I wince.

"Turn the lights down," I hear another voice command, but I can't place who it belongs to.

I try to open them again, and this time I open them fully. As my sight adjusts to the room, I take in the surroundings. I try to sit up, but someone gently stops me.

"Stay still, just relax."

"Where am I?" I ask, confused. Why are all these people here? "Rebecca," I say when I realise my aunt is here.

"Hey, flower," she says, leaning over me and stroking my hair away from my forehead. "You had us all worried there for a while."

"Sis," I feel someone squeeze my other hand and I turn to

find my brother leaning over the other side of my bed. He looks pale, and he looks like he hasn't slept in days.

"Hey, kidder," I say, smiling warmly at him, my dry lips crack as I smile. "Am I in the hospital?"

Kit nods his head. "You don't remember?"

I shake my head, feeling so confused.

"You were in a car accident," he tells me, rubbing his thumb over my palm. "I think you and cars should stay far apart from now on." He grins down at me. I can tell he's putting on a brave face.

"A car accident?" I repeat, searching through my brain, trying to remember, but everything feels fuzzy. I feel like something bad happened, but I can't think what.

"Hey there, little lady," a nurse greets me with a smile as she comes up to my bedside and Rebecca moves away to allow her room. "I need to check you over, okay? You've had a lot of people worried."

"Can I get some water?"

She pats my hand. "Soon, I promise. I'm just going to do a few checks and then we'll get that water for you."

I remain quiet as she does her job, then sip graciously at the water when she holds the paper cup to my mouth. She tells me she is going to inform Doctor Simon that I'm awake and that he'll likely want to pop in and check me over as well. I tell her that my mind feels fuzzy, and she tells me not to worry, that my brain just needs some time to catch up.

The door to my room opens and my blonde-haired friend pops her head in. "Can we come in? We hear she's awake."

"Vee," I say, smiling. "Were you outside this whole time?"

She nods her head as she comes into the room, closing the door behind her. She takes Rebecca's place beside my bed and leans down, dropping a kiss on my cheek. "We had to take it in turns in your room. We kept getting told off by the nurses for too many of us being in here." She rolls her eyes like the nurses are the bane of her existence.

Archer. His name springs into my mind, and my heart flips in my chest. "Archer! Is he here?"

Vee shakes her head and grimaces. "No. And he'll kick himself that he wasn't here when you woke up. Honestly, that boy hasn't left your side. He literally only left about a half hour ago to sort a few things and get a change of clothes."

Sighing, my heart settles, knowing he has been here with me this whole time. "How long was I out?"

"Three days, girl. We named you sleeping beauty," she tells me, chuckling. "Everyone's been up here, taking turns to sit with you, Archer and the boys, Edith, Rory and Calvin, and even Damon's sister has been to visit."

I scrunch my face up. Damon's sister? "With Damon?" I ask her, assuming that if she has visited, then she likely came with her brother. Vee's face falters, and she looks over at my brother and Rebecca, and that's when I know something is wrong.

"What's wrong, is it Damon?"

Vee strokes my hand and smiles down at me. "Damon was in the car with you, Eliza. He's here in the hospital. He was hurt in the accident."

I frown. Why can't I remember what happened? I don't remember being in a car with Damon. I wrack my brains, but there's nothing, just a hazy fog. "Is he okay?"

Vee bobs her head side-to-side. "He will be."

My heart settles with this news. I've already lost my parents. I don't want to lose anyone else. "I'm tired," I tell her.

"Then sleep, girl. We'll be here when you wake up again. You're safe and you're going to be okay, I promise."

I nod my head, feeling reassured that they'll stay with me. I don't know why I feel so unsettled. I know something is off, but I can't put my finger on it. What am I not remembering? My eyes fight the exhaustion, but it's no good and sleep claims me again.

CHAPTER THIRTY

ARCHER

I wipe the blood from my hands before I answer my phone. It's Vee. My anxiety rises. Is Scar, okay?

"Is she okay?" I ask her on answering. I stalk out of the dark room, closing the door behind me, and taking the stairs to the ground floor.

"Eliza woke up. She's fine," Vee adds in quickly. "She was a bit confused, and she doesn't seem to remember anything from the accident, but Doctor Simon says that's not uncommon, that the brain often blocks out the trauma of the event until it's healed enough to deal with it."

"And they're sure she's over the worst?"

"She is," Vee assures me. "She doesn't remember Damon being with her, and she didn't ask about the baby. I don't think she remembers."

I nod my head, my other hand clenching into a fist. Our baby didn't survive the trauma of the accident. We'd lost our baby boy.

"How am I going to tell her, Vee?" I ask. How do I tell her that the baby she'd carried inside her was no longer there?

"You're just going to have to be honest with her Arch. I know you want to protect her from the pain, but she'll be okay. She has all of us to love her and get her through this."

"I know," I reply, nodding my head. My girl has so many people who love and care for her, that's for sure.

"How are you doing?" Vee asks me softly. "Everyone keeps asking about Eliza, but you lost him too, Arch."

I gulp, swallowing back the anger and regret I feel that I'll never get to hold our son in my arms. "I'm dealing, Vee. When she's ready, we'll hold a memorial, and we'll all say goodbye to him properly."

"We will," she replies, and I can hear in her voice that she's fighting back the tears. "She's sleeping right now, but I've assured her you'll be here by the time she wakes up again."

"I'm on my way. I just need to clean up." I look down at my blood-stained chest. My father's blood adorns my skin.

"I hope you're making him pay." Her voice is cold and devoid of emotion as she references the man who I no longer call my father.

"Let's just say I'm enjoying making him scream and beg for his life."

"Good," she says firmly. "It's nothing more than he deserves. Anyway, go get cleaned up and get your arse down here."

I assure her I'll be there as soon as I can and end the call. I return to the basement to tell my brothers the good news that Scar is finally awake and talking. Both Seb and Rafe are relieved to hear she's awake. My girl has become a part of our tight little family. She's one of us now. The side door opens and Chester strolls into the room with his vape in his hand.

"Eliza's awake," I tell him. I gesture over to my bloodied and unconscious father. "We're all heading up to the hospital. Can I trust you to watch him?"

Chester grins. It's the type of grin that would cause you to shudder. Me and my brothers are messed up, but Chester is a whole other level. I've never seen someone get so excited by blood and screams.

"Oh, dear Phillip will be just fine. We'll carry on getting to know each other," he tells me with a wink as he reaches for the knuckle dusters. He lifts them up to his mouth with a wicked gleam in his eyes. "Go. Leave me to my fun."

Seb arches a brow in silent conversation with me. My brothers are also shocked at how much Chester has a craving for violence. We'll need to keep a leash on him in the future to keep that violence under control.

The police are still out looking for my father. The story in the papers is he's on the run. Boyd came straight out and asked me if I had him stashed somewhere and I denied any knowledge of knowing where he was. The police will get him when I've finished with him, and not before. I need to see him suffer first. I need to make him pay for what he's done to Scar, and for the death of our baby.

CHAPTER THIRTY-ONE

ELIZA

When I open my eyes, it's to meet those dark eyes of the guy who my world orbits around. He's here. When I went to sleep earlier, I was worried he wouldn't be here when I woke up. His dark hair is dishevelled, and he looks tired.

"You look awful," I tell him, reaching my hand out and stretching to run my hand through his hair and tidy it up.

"Hey, Scar. It's good to see you awake." He leans in and kisses me on the lips, and my heart skips a beat. It looks like my body isn't completely knackered from the accident, after all.

"I don't remember what happened," I tell him. This brain fog is so frustrating. It is like I know it's there somewhere in my mind, but it's evading me.

He takes my hand in his and squeezes it gently. "It'll come back. Don't put yourself under too much pressure to remember, Scar. Just concentrate on healing and getting stronger."

I nod my head. I know he's right, but there's something niggling at me. It's as if there's something important I should remember, but I can't. I know it will come, eventually. Doctor Simon explained how the brain often deals with traumatic events, but this didn't happen when I lost my parents. As soon as I woke up from the accident, I remembered everything, all at once. Maybe it's better this way though, may be this way I'll process it in stages when I'm ready.

"I can see the cogs turning in there. Just relax, Scar," Archer says with a soft smile as he gently strokes my check. He hasn't stopped touching me since I woke up. It's as if he needs to touch me to know I'm here and okay.

Nodding my head, I pull my eyes from him and notice Seb and Rafe sitting at the back of the room. "Hey, guys. I didn't realise you two were here, too."

Seb snickers and smiling. He winks at me. "It's okay. We know when Arch is in the room, you see no one else but him."

I roll my eyes. "I do not."

"You do," Rafe says, smiling at me. "Good to see you awake, Little Red. You gave us all quite a scare."

I nod my head. "You know me, I like to cause drama."

Seb leaves his seat and comes and sits beside me on my bed. "You? Drama? Never. How are you feeling?"

"Sore and tired and I feel like I've been in a car crash," I jest, and he laughs along with me.

"Scar, talking about your stalker. There's something you need to know," Archer announces, pulling my attention back to him. His sombre expression tells me it's not good news.

"We'll go get coffee. Do you want anything Little Red?" Seb asks, letting go of my hand and standing to his feet.

"Ooh, I'd kill for a caramel Frappuccino." I tell him. It feels like so long since I enjoyed one.

"Okay, I don't think they do those here, but no worries. We'll hop in the car to the nearest drive through."

"You're an angel," I tell him, and he winks at me.

"I'm no angel darling, but it's a pleasure."

When they leave and close the door behind them, I look to Archer to tell me whatever news there is about my stalker. My heart hammers in my chest. Have they caught them?

"Scar, we know who the stalker is," Archer tells me, taking both of my hands in his. He moves from the chair beside my bed to sit beside me on my bed. "This is going to be a shock and, well, I'm still processing it all myself, if I'm honest."

"Go on," I urge him. I just want him to spit it out and rip off the plaster.

"The stalker was two people, not one. Scar, it was my dad and Georgie's mum."

I blink. He's joking, right? "You're not serious?"

"I am," he tells me, his face remaining serious and strained. "It turns out Phil and Felicity have been together for a lot longer than we thought. They were together before he even married my mum. They wanted you out of the way so that I would marry Georgie."

With my brow scrunched, I nod my head, letting him know I'm processing this. "So, all this just because they wanted to wed you to Georgie."

Archer shakes his head. "It's far more twisted than that, Scar. Georgie isn't Callum's biological child, she's my dad's kid."

My eyes widen at this news. "But that would mean...and you two have..."

Archer sighs, his shoulders sagging like he has the weight of the world on his shoulders. "Don't remind me."

I shake my head, grimacing. "But I don't get it. If you two are half-siblings, then why on earth would they want you to marry each other? That's incest. It's also illegal."

"I know," he agrees. He grips at my hands, and I can feel his anxiety. "Phil became obsessed with our family, not joining with yours. He also became obsessed with creating his own legacy and thought that by having both his kids marry, he'd be ensuring the bloodline. It's completely messed up. When you came back to town, you ruined their plans, and they needed you out of the way."

I sigh. This is a lot to digest. It's crazy and messed up and you don't expect things like this to happen in the real world.

"Are you okay? You're very quiet," he says, chewing on his lip, watching my reactions and trying to gauge them.

"It's just a lot," I confess. "The car accident!" I sit up in bed as a memory hits me, of Damon and me crashing the car. My chest tightens and I struggle to breathe.

"It's okay, Scar. Just take a deep breath. Breathe baby," he reassures me, cupping my face in his hands. "In and out, that's it."

I copy him and take steadying breaths. "Tell me," I beg him. "I need to know."

Archer looks uncertain about whether he should continue. "Phil tampered with your car. They wanted to remove you from the equation once and for all."

"They wanted to kill me?" I gasp, realising what he is saying to me.

"You might find it hard to believe, but if it wasn't for Georgie, you may not be here today. She overheard them discussing what they had done, and she came to warn me. She found out a week or so ago about us sharing a father."

"So that's why she was crying in the bathroom," I mutter to myself, remembering that day the other week in the girl's bathroom at sixth form. "Is she okay?"

I bob my shoulders. "I guess. It's messed up, and I think we'll both struggle with all this moving forward."

I can only imagine how they are both feeling. Especially Georgie, she's been obsessed with Archer for so long, so to find out the guy you've obsessed over for years and have slept with in the past, is your brother is so disturbing.

"Does everyone know?"

Archer shakes his head. "Edward locked it down. The story is that they were just obsessed with the two families joining together because they were in love. No one knows that we're actually half-siblings, thank God."

I squeeze his hand to reassure him it's okay. "So, the police have caught them both. They're in jail?"

Archer grimaces. "Not quite. Felicity is missing, and Phil is being dealt with. I'll hand him over to the police when I'm done with him. I'd rather bury the fucker six feet under and make sure he never takes another breath again for what he's done to you."

I cup his cheek, wanting to take the pain he's feeling away from him. "And for what he's done to you and Georgie." He must be hurting just as much as I am. "So, it's not all over because she's still out there somewhere," I comment, a cold shiver running down my spine. Archer leans in and kisses me.

"I promise you, you're safe. She's out there somewhere hiding, trying to save her own skin. My dad was the driving force behind the whole sinister plan. I think she just got caught up in it because she was in love with him."

"So, all that about him loving your mum was bullshit?"

Archer nods his head. "I don't think he ever loved her, and it makes me question everything he's ever told me about her and why she took her own life."

I nod my head in agreement. I think there's more to that story than we may ever know. There's a knock on the door and Seb sticks his head in.

"Is it safe to come in? We come bearing a caramel Frappuccino!"

"Bring me the goodness!" I tell him, beckoning him in and eyeing the cup in his hands. My mouth waters at the thought of some flavour, having only had water so far. Seb hands me the drink and I take a sip and groan. "That is heaven!"

"Custard," I blurt out. "I miss custard."

Archer grins at me. "You had a bit of a thing for custard recently, didn't you?"

My expression drops and my heart plummets to my chest. My other hand flies to my stomach and I look down. That's what was niggling at me since I'd woken up!

"Oh my god, the baby. Archer, I should have told you, I'm pregnant." I pause, and my mind moves at a hundred miles an hour. "The accident. Archer, is the baby okay?"

Archer, Seb and Rafe all have a private conversation with

their eyes and the two boys say they'll leave us alone and make a quick exit.

"Scar," Archers says as he takes my drink from my hand and places it down on the bedside cupboard. He cups my face with his hands. "I'm so sorry, but the baby didn't survive the accident."

I shake my head. He is lying. "No. No, don't say that to me."

I watch the pain on Archer's face, and I know what I'm seeing. Grief and loss. "Why? Why has he taken someone else from me?"

Archer pulls me into his arms, and we sit on the bed and cling to each other. "This is my fault," I mumble as the tears fall down my face. "I hid this baby from everyone, and now this is my punishment."

"No, Scar. Don't do this to yourself. If it's anyone's fault, it's mine. You didn't feel you could tell me because of the way I treated you and lied to you. This isn't your fault."

I pull slightly away from him so that I can look into his eyes. "It's not your fault either, Archer. I wanted to tell you, I swear, I was just so scared and unprepared, and it just took some time to sink in. I wanted the baby. I wanted our baby."

His eyes hold mine and I see the pain and regret reflected there. "I know you did, Scar. And just so you know, I wanted him to. I would have loved him and been a good dad."

"Him?" I say, my voice breaking. "Our baby was a boy."

He nods his head and my heart breaks as I watch a tear fall down my dark boy's face. Seeing that tear brings me a mix of pain and relief. Archer doesn't cry. He hasn't cried since he lost his mother, just like me. But these tears show he's not bottling his emotions up and that is a good thing.

We sit there in each other's arms and comfort each other, and despite the pain I feel at losing our baby boy; I know this will bring us closer.

It takes a full day of harassing the nurses and all my visitors before they finally relent and help me into a wheelchair to take me to see my friend. Archer insists he'll take me, even though I pleaded for Vee, because well, Archer and the Silver in one room doesn't seem like a smart idea.

We take the lift to the next floor and Archer wheels me down the long corridor. At the far end, I can see a group of people sitting together and I realise it's Silver's family—his sister Emma, his older brother and his little sister Milly.

"Eliza!" Milly says, spotting me first and jumping to her feet. This grabs the attention of the other two. Emma smiles and waves at me whilst Luca remains in his seat, his arms folded, and glares my way as Archer wheels me closer.

"It's so good to see you up and about," Milly says as she leans down and hugs me gently. "How are you feeling?"

I bob my shoulders. "Like I've been in a car accident," I jest.

Emma hovers behind her and leans down next and drops a kiss on my cheek. "How are you?"

I sigh and pick at a fingernail. "A bit broken and bruised, but I'll live."

"But everything's okay?" she asks me, her eyes looking briefly down to my stomach. I feel Archer's hand tighten on my shoulder from where he's standing behind me, so it's clear he didn't miss her hidden question.

"We lost the baby," I tell her, my voice threatening to break on the last word.

Emma's face pales and she crouches down so she can look me straight in the eye. Her warm hazel eyes are full of sympathy. "Oh, Eliza. I'm so sorry. I'm here if ever you want to talk."

"Thank you. That means a lot." I offer her a reassuring smile. "How is he?" My eyes focusing on the closed door to my left.

Emma sighs and brushes her blonde hair off her shoulder. "He's getting there. They placed him in an induced coma because of the extent of his injuries. He's stable now."

I swallow deeply. It's my fault he's in here. It's my fault that he very nearly could have died. Everything is my fault.

"And his legs? Archer told me the car caught fire and burned his legs," I ask Emma, scared of what her answer may be.

"He's had surgery on his left leg. It was pretty smashed up. He's had to have a lot of metal pins in place. The burns will heal." Emma's attention turns to Archer. "I understand we have you and your friends to thank for getting my brother out of that car."

"It was nothing," Archer insists from behind me, and I place my hand over the one that rests on my shoulder. "We did what anyone else would have done in that situation."

Emma shakes her head at him. "No, you and your friends knew the car could blow at any second, and you made sure he was safe. No words can express how grateful we are."

Luca has been sitting quietly, his expression unreadable. He stands to his feet, and I think we all hold our breaths as we wait to see what he'll say. He looks at me and then offers his hand to Archer.

"Thank you for getting my brother out and saving his life."

There's a second where Archer stares down at his open palm before he reaches for it, and they shake hands. I release the breath I've been holding and Emma smiles at me wide-eyed, her relief clear.

"I hear you know which fucker did this to them?" Luca growls, rubbing his hand in his fist.

"We do," Archer confirms. "And trust me, they'll both pay for what they have done."

Luca Silver nods his head, the anger burning in his eyes. "We'll talk later."

"Sure thing. Now can I take her in and then she'll stop pestering everyone and get back to her own bed?"

Emma chuckles and gestures to the door. "Go for it. We will all grab a brew and some food at the cafeteria while you're both here."

"Yes, go and take a break," I assure her, and smiling at me Emma grabs her bag then they all head for the lift.

Archer opens the door and wheels me through. I gasp when I see my friend lying there, bruised and battered. He has a large cut on his cheek and stitches across his forehead.

"Let me take the wheel, princess," he orders. Reaching over me, he takes control of the car. "We're going to crash, Eliza. There's no avoiding it. When we round the next bend, I'm going to veer us towards the trees, and I'll make sure this side of the car takes the impact."

"No! Damon! That means you'll get hurt."

Damon looks at me as he steers the car from his position in the passenger seat. "We're both going to take a hit anyway princess. I'd rather I take the brunt of it than you and that baby in your tummy."

❧

"Scar, Scar! Are you okay?"

I blink to find Archer crouched down in front of me, a deep frown wrinkling his forehead. "Should I take you back to your room?"

I reach out and squeeze his hand, my eyes filling with unshed tears. "No, honestly, I'm fine. I just had a flashback to the accident. He saved me Arch. He made sure the car hit the woodlands on his side so that I would be okay." I wipe at my eyes as a tear falls. "He made sure his side of the car took the impact."

Archer leans in and wipes another tear from my face. "Then it sounds like I owe this guy a huge debt."

"How will a thank you ever be enough for what he did for me?"

Archer shakes his head in response. "I don't know, Scar, but I know one thing: The Aces will leave his family alone from now on, or they'll have me to deal with. I'll never forget that he is the reason that you are sitting here in front of me today." He gets to his feet, and he leans in to drop a kiss on my forehead before he wheels me to the side of Damon's bed.

I reach up and take his hand in mine. "Hey Day. Thought I'd come and hold my hero's hand for a while."

"Scar, I'm going to give the two of you some time alone. I'll be right outside the door. Just shout if you need me."

I nod my head. I love how he wants to give me time alone with my friend. As the door closes, I turn my attention back to Damon. "I need you to wake up, Day. I need to know you're going to be okay, because I can't live with myself if you're not okay. This is all my fault. I'm the reason you're lying in this bed and I'm sorry for that. No apology will ever be enough." I stroke my fingers over the inside of his palm as I allow the teas to come. "I lost the baby. It's hard to explain Day, but I feel like something is missing in me now. Like I've lost a little piece of myself. It was a boy."

I swallow, trying to control my tears. Hearing myself tell him the baby has gone makes it all feel very real. "Anyway, you need to get better. I need you to wake up and be okay, Day. You have been there for me so much these last few months, and now I'm going to be there for you."

There's a light tap on the door and Milly sticks her head inside. "Hey, we're back. How are we doing in here?"

I shrug my shoulders and smile at her. "We're just catching up and I'm telling him I'm going to kick his arse if he doesn't wake up soon."

"You hear that, Damon? A girl is going to kick your arse," Milly says, grinning as she comes up beside me and looks down at her brother. "He'll be okay, Eliza. He's strong, and he's over the first hurdle."

I nod my head firmly. She's right. He's going to be okay. He has to be okay because I can't bear to think of any other outcome.

CHAPTER THIRTY-TWO

ELIZA

I smile and shake my head as we pull up in front of the Savage mansion. Vee and Kit are holding up a welcome home banner and balloons. Rafe and Seb stand beside them, too cool to hold balloons and banners. My heart warms, knowing they are all here for me.

After five days in the hospital, the doctor finally deemed me medically fit for discharge. My arm is still in a cast, but it isn't too painful. My ribs are healing nicely, too. The head hurts a little less each day but my memories of the accident and the events leading up to it are still fuzzy and full of gaps.

"I told them not to do this; that you needed quiet and rest, but they insisted," Archer grunts, frowning at my welcome party as he turns the engine off.

"It's nice," I assure him, patting his leg. "Now be a good fiancé and help me out." The boot on my right leg is a pain in the arse, but at least I'm not on crutches, and I can still hobble about. Archer comes round to my side of the car and opens the door. I wrap my arms around his neck, and he lifts me from the vehicle. He places me gently onto my feet, ensuring I'm steady before he lets go.

"You guys," I gush, pointing to the banner. "You didn't have to do this."

"Oh, we did," Seb snorts. "When Vee says we're doing something, there's no arguing with her."

"Got that right. You're finally learning, brother," she says, grinning as she elbows him in his side.

Kit passes his side of the banner to Rafe and strides towards me, enveloping me in a big hug. "Hey sis. So glad you're finally allowed home."

I close my eyes and enjoy being close to my brother. Wilbur has caused us to drift apart since moving here, and I hate it. "Thank you for being here."

He pulls away from me and looks down at me. "I nearly lost you a second time, sis. Don't ever put me through anything like that again." I can see in his eyes how much this has affected him. He's already lost his parents. "I know I've been a bit of an idiot, but you will always be my priority. I'm sorry I didn't put you first before. For my own selfish reasons, I didn't fight in your corner.

I gently pat his cheek. "You don't need to apologise. I know how long you've longed for family, for that connection. It's okay to want that."

Kit shakes his head, a deep frown still marring his face. "No, it's not okay. We've always looked out for each other, and I let you down."

Smiling at him, I pat his cheek. "Kit, stop apologising. You're here now and that's what matters. I love you little brother and I always will."

Kit loses the frown and relaxes a little. "I've brought your favourite cookies. I got Edith to make some up," he tells me, pulling a sandwich bag full of Edith's homemade cookies out of his bag and dangling them before me.

"See all is forgiven. You brought me cookies," I joke, and he wraps his arm around me grinning as we head into the house. We all pile inside and head to the den. Archer and Kit both fuss over me, ensuring that I am comfy. Seb starts up the X-box and the boys turn their interest to the game while Vee and I catch up on any school gossip.

There's a rap on the den door and Edward sticks his head in. "Hello, I just wanted to pop in and say welcome home."

I beckon him in, smiling. I like Edward. I have a bit of a soft spot for him. "Hi, come in."

Edward comes into the room and sits on the end of the sofa and checks me over. "We were all so worried about you." He looks downcast, looking down at his hands. "Eliza, I can't apologise enough for what my son-in-law did to you. I had no idea he could be so cold and calculating. I'm still coming to terms with it to be honest."

I nod my head and reach out my hand to pat his. "No one suspected him or Felicity. I think we're all shocked."

"If there's anything I can do to make it up to you, just say the word," Edward vows. I can see that he is really upset by everything and that he's blaming himself for what's happened.

"Well, you can stop feeling guilty for a start. It's no one else's fault but Phil's and Felicity's," I pause and lean up in my seat. "However, if you really mean it about helping me, then there is something you can do."

"Name it," he states, without hesitation.

"You can help me take down Wilbur and the rest of the Elders. I want Archer and I to be free to live our lives the way we want to."

Edward doesn't respond at first and I can't work out what he's thinking. Kit is busy playing Fifa against Rafe so he doesn't hear us, but the others do and they all stare waiting to see how Edward will react.

Edward sighs and nods his head. "Maybe it is time to change things. God knows my family has suffered enough." He looks me straight in the eye with a look of determination. "We'll talk more this week, but for now relax and recuperate."

When Edward leaves the room. Everyone releases the breath they have been holding. Archer looks the most shocked out of us all.

"I can't believe you just came out and asked him," he comments, looking at me in bewilderment.

I shrug my shoulders at him. "If you don't ask you don't get."

I am more determined than ever that we'll escape the power the Elders hold over us and the inhabitants of this bay. I don't care how long it takes this was now my main focus in life.

CHAPTER THIRTY-THREE

ELIZA

We arrive at the country club where Archer has booked us some of the best seats available. I'm excited to cheer Rafe and Seb on and hopefully see them win this thing. Vee is wearing a t-shirt with Rafe's face on it that says 'game, set, match' and she's eyeing up the competition.

"Who are those two?" I ask her, pointing to two guys who are stretching out by the side of the courts. They look like they are super focused and like they will bring their A-game.

Vee sneers at the two guys. "Harvey Tate and Fred Botham. They go to Alderwood prep school. They're so far up their own arses it's untrue. The rivalry between them and our boys is fierce. As much as I hate to admit it, they are good."

"Have Rafe and Seb beat them before?" asks Damon who is sitting beside me in his wheelchair. He has been out of the hospital two weeks now after spending six weeks in there recovering. I have been round at his house every day, sitting beside him on his bed and watching movies and just keeping him company.

Vee scoffs. "Of course they have. I said they were good, but that doesn't mean they're better than our boys." One of the two guys catches Vee watching and with a smirk on his face, he waves at her. Vee snickers and looking round to make sure her parents aren't watching, then she gives him the finger.

"I wouldn't be surprised if that's who they end up facing in the final," Archer adds in.

"Then it will be a good final to watch," Damon comments, rubbing his hands together in anticipation.

Damon arriving here with us caused a lot of commotion. The accident changed many things. Perhaps the best change is Archer and Damon agreeing to bury the hatchet and attempt friendship. Both of them mean the world to me, so to spend time with the two of them together is amazing. I wouldn't say they were friends yet, but they are heading that way.

The first match starts. It's Tate and Botham against two players from a neighbouring village. The two boys wipe the floor with their opponents. I think Archer is correct in his prediction that these two will end up in the final. I spot Georgie over the other side of the court with Callum and two of her friends. She catches my gaze, and she gives me an awkward but not unfriendly smile. Things still felt weird. We were all still very much processing the fact that she is Archer's half-sister. The Elders have kept the news about their shared parentage out of the media. We all knew that eventually when, or if, things went to court, everyone and the world would know. Archer couldn't tolerate being around her much. I think he's really struggling with the fact that they had slept together once. It was something he felt terrible about, even though it wasn't either his or Georgie's fault. They were both victims of Phillip and Felicity's crazed plans as much as I was. I hope that over time they will find some semblance of a sibling relationship.

Vee pats my arm excitedly. "The boys are up next!" She gestures with her head to where Rafe and Seb are standing on the side-lines by the entrance to the changing rooms waiting to come on to the court. Seb looks our way and I grin at him and give him the thumbs up. Seb's reply is to blow on his knuckles and smirk, as if to say this will be a walk in the park.

At the interval our boys are in the lead and their skill at the game is far superior to those of their opponents.

"I'm going to nip to the ladies quickly before the next set starts," I tell them. Kit grabs my hand when I stand.

"Make sure Tony goes with you."

I look down at him, and smiling, I squeeze his shoulder. "I will, I promise." Since the accident, Kit has become quite protective of me.

He's been extra anxious about my safety since the car accident and the revelation that Archer's dad and his lover are my stalkers. I know seeing me in a hospital bed unconscious and injured must have brought back terrible memories for him of the night we lost our parents.

I head towards the entrance of the clubhouse. Tony is stationed by the door, constantly surveying the area for any threats. "I'm heading to the bathroom," I tell him.

"I'll follow you in, miss, and wait for you outside."

Nodding my head, I head inside, with Tony following behind me. A few months ago, I would have moaned my head off about having someone tailing me all the time, but not anymore. Felicity is still out there somewhere. Whilst I don't doubt that Phillip was the brains behind most of the plans to take me out, we don't know what she is capable of. Or how desperate she might be now that their plans have turned to dust.

I empty my bladder and, lost in my own thoughts, I exit the cubicle. I'm not alone. A bedraggled and crazed looking Felicity stands before me. Her eyes are glazed over, like she is somewhere else. This isn't the elegant, put together woman I met at the ball months ago.

"I didn't know," she mumbles, chewing on her fingernails and shuffling from one foot to the other. "I didn't know about the baby. If I'd have known..."

I try to keep a calm demeanour, even though inside my heart is beating out of my chest with anxiety. "I could have died. My friend almost died, and he still has a long road to recovery."

Felicity sobs and pulls on her hair as she stares wide-eyed at me. It's the stare of someone who is unbalanced and clearly mentally unwell.

"I love him. I wanted us to be together as a family. The four of us," she explains to me. I'm not sure what she is hoping for here. If it is understanding and forgiveness, then she's wasting her time. I lost our baby because of her and her 'love.'

"Phil's not a bad man. He really isn't. He's just passionate about what he wants, and he wanted the Savage legacy to come to both of his children, not some outsider." She mutters something under her breath that I can't make out. "Phil didn't mean to kill Libby. He just wanted to scare her; you see."

My blood runs cold.

I replay the words she just spoke in my head to ensure I heard her correctly.

"He killed Libby?"

"Yes, but..." she takes a step towards me, and I take one back, hitting the doorframe of the toilet cubicle. "He just wanted to scare her. He had her meet him up on the roof." She shakes her head as if trying to clear her mind. "We shouldn't be telling her this. I need to explain, though, so that they'll all understand."

The woman is clearly unwell. Is she hearing voices?

"He just wanted to tell her she couldn't leave and that if she tried, he'd find her and make sure Calvin never got employment anywhere again. He just needed to make her see that she couldn't take his son away from him." Felicity's nails dig into her own face. "But Libby wouldn't listen, she said she was leaving that night and made to move past him. Phil, he just grabbed her to make her stay, but she fought him and well, he pushed her, and she lost her footing. She toppled over the side of the building. He never meant to hurt her, not physically." Felicity slaps herself across the face. "Shut up, stop talking," she mutters to herself in.

"Felicity, I think you need some help. You don't seem very well. Georgie has been worried about you. I know she misses you. Why don't you let me go get her? She's here. I can bring her to you."

"Georgie," Felicity sobs, "my baby girl. It was all for her."

I step slowly towards the door. "I'll just get her."

"No!" Felicity snaps, grabbing for me. She yanks me back by my hair and I stumble and crash into the wall. She's on me before I have a chance to recover. Felicity slams her hands into my chest and pins me to the wall. What she doesn't know is that I'm a fighter. I've taken girls twice her size on in the ring and beat them easily. I rear my head back and head butt her hard. She yelps and stumbles back, clutching her head, giving me the chance to make my escape.

I run out into the corridor, shouting for Tony. He comes bounding around the corner, gun at the ready. I open my mouth to tell him about Felicity, but before I get the chance, she grabs me from behind by my hair.

She has me again. She pulls me flush against her chest and I feel something cool at my neck. I gasp when I look down to find Felicity is holding a knife to my throat.

"Don't come any closer," she yells to Tony. "We must stop her, she'll tell the police," she mumbles to herself, shaking her head back and forth.

"Miss, put the knife down. We don't want anyone getting hurt now," Tony urges her softly, taking a tentative step forward, his gun aimed at us.

"Stay back!" she shouts, moving us back a step. "I don't want to hurt her, but I can't go to jail."

"Mum," Georgie gasps as she comes into the corridor completely unaware. "Mum, what are you doing?" She looks in horror at the knife held to my throat.

"Georgie!" Felicity homes in on her daughter. "I've missed you, baby. Daddy and I have both missed you, but we'll all be together again soon. We'll all go where no one can find us, me, you, daddy and Archer. We'll be a family."

"Mum, let Eliza go. I've missed you." Georgie shakily holds

her arms open, waiting to embrace her mum. "I need a hug, mum." Tentatively she steps past Tony, who tries to hold her back, but she looks at him from the corner of her eye and shakes her head. "Please put the knife down, mummy. You're scaring me," she begs.

Felicity whimpers, looking from her daughter to Tony, who is standing with his gun aimed at her. "He'll shoot me."

"He won't, I promise," Georgie assures her. She looks back at Tony and gestures with her hand for him to lower the gun. Tony doesn't look happy, but he does as she asks. "See. Now put the knife down and come to me. I need my mum."

Felicity nods her head and the knife clatters to the floor. I don't hesitate. I move fast, and Tony grabs me and pushes me behind him. Felicity throws herself into her daughter's arms and she sobs. "It was all for you and Archer."

"It's okay," Georgie soothes her, stroking her hair. "It's all over now, mum."

Tony pushes me back and gestures for me to get out of here. I slowly take a step backwards and then another. A hand touches my shoulder and I jump out of my skin. It's our other two security men. They move past me and quietly moving up to Georgie; they take a hold of Felicity.

"No! You can't take me away from her. I'm her mother. She needs me," she wails as they secure her arms behind her back. Tony ushers me and Georgie away and he escorts us to an empty room.

"Stay here. I mean it, Eliza. Do not leave this room until I come to collect you both." He points his finger at me in warning. The old me would have likely ignored him and left that room as soon as he was out of sight, but the new me is a little more safety conscious these days. I have had a dance with death a few times now and I have decided that sometimes I need to stop and think.

The sound of Georgie sobbing pulls my attention. I turn to

find her sitting on the floor, hugging her legs to her chest. I sit down beside her and throw my arm over her shoulder.

"Are you okay?"

Georgie shakes her head, and she leans on my shoulder. "This is all my fault. You heard her. Everything they did was for me."

"No," I tell her firmly. "This is all on them, no one else."

"Are you okay?" she asks me, silent tears falling down her face. "You're the one who's just had a knife held against their throat."

"I'm fine," I reassure her. "She's your mum and it must've been hard to see her like that?"

I offer her a tissue from my jacket pocket, and she takes it from me and blows her nose. "That wasn't my mum out there. Not the one I knew all my life, anyway."

I nod my head. "I think she's having some kind of breakdown. She needs help."

I know we have had our differences, but I really feel for her right now. Georgie's had her entire world turned upside down and I know what it feels like to have everything you've ever known taken from you.

"I've lost everything," she sobs, wiping at her eyes.

"You haven't," I tell her, squeezing her shoulder and shaking my head. "I saw Callum out there before with you. To him, you're still his little girl. He brought you up and nothing can ever change that. He loves you like a father should love his child. Plus, you have Archer now."

She scoffs at me. "He hates me."

"He doesn't hate you." I grimace. He's not exactly warm and fuzzy towards her, but he's still processing everything. "He just doesn't know how to be around you yet, Georgie. Just give it time. If there's one thing I know about him, it's that he looks after his own. He's loyal."

The door to the small office space flings open, making both Georgie and I startle.

"It's only me," Archer says softly, seeing our fear. He stands in the doorway and looks at Georgie with a frown when he sees her crying. "Are you both okay?"

"We will be," I reply with a weary smile. The adrenaline and stress have left me feeling shattered. "Georgie was great out there. She saved me."

Archer and Georgie both look at each other. "Thanks," Archer says, clearing his throat. "The police are here. They're taking her away now."

"Good," Georgie says, straightening her shoulders back and putting on a brave face. "That way, she can't hurt anyone else. Now they just have to find Phil."

Archer and I share a brief look. Everyone thinks Phil is on the run, but we know exactly where he is. Archer has him tied to a chair in a warehouse, bloodied and broken.

"Georgie!" Callum barges through the door, pushing Archer out of the way. His eyes are frantic with fear until he sees his daughter is safe.

"Daddy!" she sobs, stumbling to her feet and falling into his open arms.

"I've got you, darling. Daddy's here."

I don't miss the smirk on Archer's face on hearing him referred to as daddy, and I give him a pointed glare. Leave them alone. He shrugs his shoulders and holds his hand out to me.

"Come here. I need to hold you."

I don't hesitate. In his arms is the one place I know I'm safe. We have had our difficulties, but somewhere amongst all the lies, hidden agendas and attempts to end my life, we became each other's everything. I can't imagine my life without him in it now. Just the very fleeting thought of it causes my heart to squeeze in my chest. There's no doubt about it. I'm in love with Archer Savage. That is something I never thought I'd hear myself admit.

"I love you," I whisper softly into his neck, and he stills, pulling back so he can look into my eyes.

"Say it again," he demands, his dark eyes burning into mine with so much emotion.

"I said, I love you Archer Savage," I repeat, with a big stupid smile on my face. He cups my jaw and leans down to press his lips against mine.

"Took you long enough, Scar," he chuckles, that signature smirk of his melting my heart and my knickers all in one go.

"I had to make you work for it. It's nothing more than you deserved."

He rolls his eyes but smiles at the same time. "I was a bastard, I admit it. And I'll probably always be a bastard, but I'll be *your* bastard, Scar. I'll turn the fucking world upside down to see that smile on your face."

I'm so lost in our little bubble that I don't notice Boyd lurking in the doorway.

"Miss Alderman, we'll need your statement." He clears his throat and gives me an apologetic look.

"She'll do it later," Archer growls, his eyes narrowing at Boyd. "She's just had a mad woman hold a knife to her god-damn throat." Georgie catches his eye. "Sorry."

She shrugs in reply. "It's fine. She is mad. I've never seen her like that before. Her eyes were glazed over like she was in some kind of trance."

"I'll come down to the station shortly, but I need to talk to Archer first." I hold my hand out to him. "Let's go for a drive."

Archer looks perplexed at my suggestion coming at a time like this, but without asking, he slips his hand into mine. We exit the small office and Vee is waiting outside for us with Damon. She's chewing on her nails and gripping the handles on Damon's wheelchair tightly. She breathes a sigh of relief when she sees me.

"Girl, are you okay?" she asks me, throwing her arms around me and hugging me to death. "I'm growing tired of people trying to hurt my bestie."

"I'm good, Vee. I'm hard to kill," I joke, attempting to bring humour into this messed up situation.

"This big brute wouldn't let me in the room with him." She punches Archer in the arm, and he mock yelps and rubs his arm.

"Listen, we'll catch up later, okay? Archer and I have something we need to do," I tell her and Damon. Whatever she sees in my expression, she reads it right. She nods her head, pulls me in for a final squeeze and says she and Damon will head back out to support the boys. Luckily, somehow the tournament has carried on, ignorant to what has just gone down within the clubhouse. Although I'm sure there was some commotion when the police arrived with their sirens on. Archer and I slip out of the back exit just as Felicity is being placed inside the back of a police car. She doesn't look our way, she looks miles away, lost in her own crazy world. I'm hoping she'll get the help she needs, and that Georgie can get some semblance of her old mum back.

CHAPTER THIRTY-FOUR

ELIZA

"Are you going to tell me where we're going?" he asks me as he throws me the keys to his car. I am carless at present. Archer offered to replace my beautiful car, but I said I was happy just to drive his when we're together. After the crash, I was determined to get back behind the wheel. I didn't want to let two car accidents leave me with a crippling fear of driving. I will not lie. That first time I sat behind the wheel of Archer's golf, I had to get a grip on the anxiety threatening to climb its way to the surface, but I pushed through and dealt with it.

I'm taking us somewhere secluded to tell him the terrible news about his mum's death. Knowing my dark boy as I do, we need to be somewhere he can't go into a rage and do something he can't take back. My heart hurts at the thought of what I have to tell him. How do you tell the person you love that their own father killed their mother? How do you even start that conversation?

I take us up to the cliff point, where on my first night in the bay, dearest Georgie pushed me off the top and I plummeted down into the cold, dark ocean below. He'd saved me that night and today I will save him. I'll hold him and love him and help him get through this. We've dealt with a lot of shit these last nine months, the both of us, but together we can make it through.

We park up and take the ten-minute walk up to the cliff top.

He doesn't ask me what we're doing here until we reach the top and the breath-taking views of the sea are before us. Archer comes up behind me. He wraps his arms around my waist, hugging my back to his chest. He rests his chin on the top of my head and for a few minutes, we just enjoy the silence and the sound of the waves crashing against the rocks below us.

"Okay, Scar, I know you well enough to know you've brought me up here for a purpose. All the drive here, I could see the turmoil and angst imprinted all over that expressive face."

Sighing, I turn in his arms so that I can look into his dark brown eyes. Here goes nothing. "Archer, what I have to tell you will not be an easy listen." I'm just going to rip the plaster off and tell him. "Your mum didn't jump off the roof of your house and kill herself. Your dad pushed her. Felicity just shared the awful truth. He'd found out she was leaving and lured her up to the rooftop. They got into an altercation, and he pushed her, and she went over."

Archer doesn't respond. He just swallows and looks out at the sea. I don't like a quiet Archer. Quiet Archer unnerves me. I know what to do with a raging Archer. When he's like this, I don't know how to handle it.

"Say something," I urge him, stroking my hands up and down his arms in comfort.

"I'm going to kill him," he replies in a cold and calm voice. "I'm going to kill him, slowly and painfully."

"No, you're not," I insist. "You won't do it because you're not like him." I place my hand over his heart. "Once you cross that line, there's no coming back from it."

He looks down at me, towering over my tiny frame. "I'm no saint, Scar. Do you know the things I've done under the orders of our Elders? I've left people as good as dead. I've hurt and tortured people because I was told it was in the interests of our society. I'm more than capable of killing."

I shake my head. "I'm under no illusions. I know you've done things that I probably wouldn't like but loving someone means you take them with all their flaws and scars. Loving someone means you take the good and the bad. You love all of them without question."

He smirks at me. "You have a way with words, Scar. That was almost poetic." Archer sighs. "Phil doesn't deserve to continue breathing. He's almost taken everything I love away from me. He's taken my mum and our unborn child."

"I know. I feel it too. I hate what he has done to the both of us, but if we want to live and be free of him and his legacy, then we need to let go and move on."

"I need to hear him admit to it. I need to look him in the eye and ask him," he confides.

"Then let's go." I look at my watch. "Call the boys. They should be done by now. Have them meet us there." I place my hand over his mouth when he goes to speak. "Don't even dare suggest that I'm not coming, Archer Savage, because there's no fucking way I'm letting you do this without me by your side." I pause. "Plus, with me there, you won't kill him."

I wait for his response, and he surprises me when he leans down and kisses me. "God knows you were meant for me. You see my darkness and you meet it head-on. My fierce fiancée."

Chuckling, I return his kiss, and for a minute or two we get lost in each other. Reality awaits us though. It would be nice to stay up here and ignore that the world has gone to shit around us, but it's okay because we'll get through it together.

CHAPTER THIRTY-FIVE

ARCHER

Scar holds my hand throughout the drive to the old warehouse where we have been holding my father. She hums along to a song on the radio, and I just stare at her in awe. How did I get so lucky? I never thought I'd ever meet someone who would make me question everything. Someone who would be so perfect for me that sometimes I have to pinch myself to make sure this is real. I love this girl with every breath in my body and I'd give her my last breath if it meant she survived.

I'm excited about the future for the first time in my life. I have spent my life full of bitterness, hating a family for something they weren't responsible for. Phil had shaped and moulded me into his weapon. He didn't protect me and love me. He used me to get what he wanted. I won't kill him, but only because Scar's asked me nicely not to. Once I'm coated in his blood, I'm going to strip her naked and fuck her until she doesn't know her own name.

I turn off the engine and we silently climb out of the car. Meeting at the front, she slips her hand in mine. The boys are already here. Rafe's car is parked beside mine. We head inside and down to the underground level. It's cold and damp and with any luck, the fucker will have frozen to death.

My brothers are both waiting for us outside the door to the large open space where we're holding him.

"You, okay?" Rafe asks me. Holding out his hand, I grip his

firmly and we lean into each other.

"I'm good. He killed my mother, but I need to hear it from him."

Seb lets out a long breath. "Fuck!" he exclaims his face going pale. "What do you need from us?"

There it is. That unwavering loyalty. My brothers will always have my back. Whatever I need from them, they'll do it without question, and I know now they'd do the same for Scarlet. She's one of us now. The five of us are the dawn of a new legacy in this town. Once I'm done with the scum in the next room, we'll break away from this toxic life we've been bred into. We'll be in control. We are done being at the beck and call of the Elders. Scar doesn't know it yet, but we've been working to take power for the last few years now. We've grown tired of them being the ones to give out the orders and using us to do their dirty work while they stay clean, with no blood on their hands. We're not there yet, but we've been slowly building a loyal following of those that want to see the Elders taken down. And we will take them down, one at a time. Eliza has weaved her spell over Edward, and he is slowly coming around to the idea that changes are needed in our society. With one elder on our side it will make the battle that is to come that bit easier.

"Just stop me if I go too far. You know how I get when the darkness gets its grip on me."

They both nod. Seb squeezes my shoulder and we all file into the space where my father awaits us. He's slumped in the chair he's tied to, with his head resting on his chest. He's bruised and bloodied and looks like he's nothing left to give.

I kick the leg of his chair, making him jump awake. For a second, he looks bewildered and unsure where he is, and then his focus falls on me.

"Son," he grins, "It's been a while." He looks over my shoulder and chuckles when he sees Scar standing there. "And you brought the whore as well."

I break. I kick the chair so hard that it topples over and he cries out in pain. His arms that are tied behind him take the full brunt of the fall. Seb and Rafe step round me and they both grab my dad and put the chair back upright.

"Still can't control that temper of yours, son. Have I taught you nothing all these years?"

"I'm not your son," I growl. "Felicity's been arrested."

He doesn't react. There's not even a slither of emotion on his face. Maybe I did learn something from him after all. "She also had a lot to say while she was holding a knife to my fiancée's throat. I think she's a little loopy," I tell him, whirling my fingers around the side of my head to emphasise my point.

Phil smirks, laughing. "Shame she didn't cut that pretty throat and let her bleed out. The Alderman's," he hisses. "Always thinking they're top dog. The four founding families. Thinking they control everyone and everything. Well, they weren't quite as in control as they thought, were they? I was forging my own legacy right under their noses."

"A fallen legacy," Scar says from behind me, and I smile at her words. She's right. He has nothing now and that will be something he will have to live with as he serves time behind bars to pay for all his crimes.

I take a step towards him, and smile when he flinches and leans back in his chair. He should fear me. I'd like to peel the skin from his bones and cut him up piece by piece. "Your legacy is over and we're forging a new one. While you will rot in your little prison cell, staring at four walls, we'll be taking control. Scar and I are going to marry, have babies and live a long and happy life together. I will erase your name and existence from the family history books. No one will talk about you or remember you. No one will care who you were or what you did because you'll be a ghost."

Phil's nostrils flare. "You can't erase me. I'm a part of you, son. Remember that when you're living your perfect, insignificant life. And remember that she's an Alderman by blood and they are poison."

"My mother." I lean into him, bending down into his space so I can look him dead in the eye. "Did you kill her?"

Phil snickers. "So now we get to it. Let me guess? Felicity." He shakes his head. "That woman and her mouth." He raises his eyes and meets mine. "Yes, I'm the reason she fell from the roof. She thought she could leave and take you with her. My son. My blood. There was no way in hell I was letting her walk off into the sunset with that pathetic ginger bastard to bring up my son. If she'd have just done as she was told, she would still be alive, but no, she had to fight me." He sniggers. "Did I mean to kill her? No, but she was fighting me, and I pushed her too hard, perhaps." He shrugs, as if admitting to her death is nothing. "Am I sorry? No. She was out of the way once and for all."

"Untie him," Archer barks out, his fists clenched at his side.

Seb and Rafe do as I ask. They unbind Phil's hands, and he staggers to his feet. I see his eyes glance at the door behind us. "There's no escape. We're miles from anywhere. Now face me. Man to man."

My father's sways on his feet. The weeks of beatings and limited water taking its toll on his body. "You want me to fight you, son?" He leans his head back and laughs. "You think you can beat me when I taught you everything you know?"

My mind flicks back to the many hours as a boy when he would have me in the ring, hitting me and urging me to hit him back harder. I remember the sick satisfaction he would show when I would get frustrated that I couldn't beat him. Those days were long gone now, though. I'm the stronger one now. I hold my arms open and beckon him with my fingers. Mimicking what he used to do when he had me in the ring as a child. "Go on. Hit me. Let's see what you got, old man."

My words have the reaction I'd hoped for. Pure rage grips him and snarling he charges me, his fists clenched and ready. Adrenaline rushes through my body. I channel all the hate and anger I feel for this man before me, into my fists, but I'm not out of control. I'm calm and calculated. I'm going to enjoy this.

CHAPTER THIRTY-SIX

ELIZA

Archer ducks his dad's attack easily. He smirks at Phil, cocking a brow and Phil roars and tries to attack again. Archer side-steps him and Phil's fist hits nothing but air, causing him to stumble and almost lose his footing. I grin in satisfaction. This was going to be fun to watch. I grab a chair from the side of the room and sit on it back to front, resting my arms on the back of the chair.

"Do you want some popcorn while you watch the entertainment, Little Red?" Seb asks me as he comes to stand beside me. Rafe comes up to my other side and we all watch as Archer drives his fist into his father's jaw and something cracks. Never have I enjoyed the sound of bones breaking more than I am tonight. I realise I've missed being in the ring, and the thrill of the fight. I think I'll ask Archer to get me on the line-up for Friday night. I'm in the mood to get bloody.

Phil manages to get a punch in to Archer's face and Archer just laughs and asks him if that is all he's got. Phil loses control, and that is the last thing you should do in the ring. You need to keep your composure. You need to be in charge. Watching your opponent's moves and calculating what they might do next. It's like a game of chess—moves and countermoves.

"This is fun." Seb chuckles. "Shall we place bets on how many broken bones Phil leaves here with tonight?"

"Ten," I say. "Twenty quid, says ten."

Rafe scoffs. "Fifteen."

"I'm going to go with twelve," Seb announces. "Fifty quid says he breaks twelve."

Seb shakes my hand first and then Rafe's, and we return our attention to the fight before us. I get a high watching my man take down the man who was supposed to love and protect him. The man who manipulated him and used him and planned to marry him to his own sibling. Blood coats Archer's skin, but it isn't his, it's Phil's. The next blow he lands knocks Phil out cold, and he hits the floor with a hard thud. His head cracks against the concrete floor.

"Fractured skull, I reckon," Seb chuckles, winking at me.

Archer looks down at his father, wiping the sweat from his brow. "Take him and drop him somewhere they can find him. But don't let them find him too soon, let him feel the cold and the rain for an hour or two." He grins, the thrill of the fight still running through his veins, and he looks at me with a hunger that has me gulping for air. He strides towards me, and I yelp in surprise when he picks me up and throws me over his shoulder.

Seb wiggles his brow at me as we move away from them, and I wave at him and smile back. I am about to get fucked hard, and I'm brimming with delight. He climbs the metals stairs up two floors and we enter a room that looks much more inviting than anywhere else in this building. There's a desk over to the right of the door and a small kitchenette over by the far end of the room. In the middle of the room, against the wall, is a black four poster bed. He drops me on the bed forcefully and I bounce on the mattress. He looks at me like he wants to devour me, like he wants to feast on my bones.

I'm still dressed in my nice clothes from the tournament at the clubhouse. A little green skater dress and my converse. He lifts one of my legs and slowly unties my shoelace and takes my shoe off, followed by the other. Standing at the foot of the bed, he undoes his jeans, and he's commando underneath. His hard cock springs out of his pants, standing to attention, and I swallow in excitement.

"Come here," he orders, beckoning me with his finger.

Grinning, I get on my knees and shuffle down the bed until I'm kneeling before him. He cups the back of my neck with his hands and kisses me. He kisses me like he might never kiss me again, and I'm breathless and burning with need. His tongue dances with mine and I edge nearer to him, needing to get as close as I can. I want to wrap myself around him and weld myself to him. His two hands grip on the neckline of my dress and he pulls, tearing it straight down the middle. It's a good job we're rich, as I think over the years he's going to destroy a lot of my wardrobe. I'm kneeling before him in my black lace bra and knickers and his eyes lazily peruse my body.

"Like what you see?" I ask him with a throaty chuckle.

His dark eyes snap up to mine, filled with lust. "I'm going to spread that pretty pussy and I'm going to eat you out until you don't know your own name, Scar. You are going to be exhausted from orgasm after orgasm. I'm going to fuck you for hours and leave you sore."

Archer doesn't ask. He takes what he wants.

He pushes me back and I land on my elbows, and he pulls off my knickers and spreads me wide. I'm open and exposed, and he licks his lips as he drinks me in. Archer sinks to his knees at the foot of the bed and places his nose against my sex and takes a deep inhale.

"You smell like the fucking nectar of the gods, Scar. Let's see if you taste as good." His tongue licks up my folds and I buck my hips, the sensation sending shivers through my body. I'd die happy right now, with his mouth between my thighs. If there is a heaven, then this is it. He licks and sucks and teases me until I'm panting and begging him for what I need. I come hard. The waves of my orgasm ripping through me, making me scream his name in pleasure. Just as my breathing steadies itself, he starts again and I'm a whimpering and incoherent mess. By my third orgasm, I'm almost in tears. I'm spent, and I need him inside of me. To feel that connection that forges us together as one. He smirks at me as he leans down to feast on me again. I think I may die tonight, but if I do, it had better be with him buried deep inside of me or I will come back and haunt this tease for the rest of his life. I come for a fourth time, barely able to make a sound as the waves crash through me and leave me boneless and blissful.

"Are you ready for me, Scar?"

I moan, breathlessly. "Give me it all, Archer. Give me everything you've got. I'll take it all."

Smirking down at me, he grabs my legs under my knees and pulls me towards him. Lining himself up at my entrance. Keeping his eyes on mine, he slowly enters me, each delicious inch filling me and completing me. I lift my hips to try to seat him fully inside of me, but he pauses as shakes his head. "I'm in control, baby girl. You play by the rules that I make." He pushes ever so slowly further in, and I moan long and loudly when he's seated inside of me. I want to bottle this feeling and drink it every day. Still holding my legs under my knees, he pulls out and pushes back in and from this angle, it hits the spot and has me moaning and writhing beneath him. He fucks me slow and hard and it's delicious fucking torture. He never takes his eyes off me and I stare back at him, enraptured. As his need builds, he picks up the pace, fucking me harder and faster and I take it all, begging him for more. I beg him to be as rough as he can. I splinter apart, my cum milking his cock and his eyes roll in his head as I moan his name and tell him I love him. It doesn't take long for him to follow me. He comes inside of me, telling me I'm his queen and moaning my name. Breathless, he leans over me and kisses me deeply. "I can't wait to put another baby in your belly, Scar. I want to see you round and ripe with my child growing inside of you. I'm going to knock you up again and again."

I gulp. My ovaries swooning at his words. "Do I get any say in this?" I chuckle, reaching up and stroking his cheek with my palm.

"No." He grins. "But I think I'll just enjoy having you to myself for a few years first."

"I think I'd have to agree. I'm selfish. I want you all to myself. I want to be the only thing you need or want, Archer."

He presses his forehead against mine. "Scar, you're already the only thing I need and want. You're my fucking world. I never knew you could love someone like this. It's all consuming."

"It is. It's like an obsession. A dark and dangerous obsession." I crave him like a drug. His body, his lips, his attention, his love. I will never get enough of him.

"Marry me," he says.

"Erm, I think you already asked me, and I said yes, remember," I tell him, laughing as he runs the pad of his thumb softly across my lower lip.

"I'm asking you again, with no knife at your back. If you don't want to. I'll deal with Wilbur. He won't use Kit or anything else against you. If you want to walk away now, I'll let you go."

I look up at him and shake my head. "I want this. I want us forever. I can never walk away. So, yes, I'll marry you."

"We'll do it our way. Just us, the boys, Vee and Kit and hell, even your buddy, Damon. Fuck them and their expectations. We're done bending to the will and desires of our families."

"Really?"

"Truly," he replies, leaning down to press his lips against mine. The world could crash and burn right now, and I wouldn't care. Here and now, all I want is this guy. To cocoon myself in a bubble with him and forget about everything beyond this room. I have a family now. This guy and our friends are all I need. I belong with them and for the first time in years, I feel like I'm home.

EPILOGUE

TWO YEARS LATER

ELIZA

I never thought this day would come. I've dreamt about it for so long. The day we are free from the control of the Elders. The day we get to create and forge our own destinies free from their manipulation and veiled threats.

The five of us climb out of the blacked-out car and place our masks over our faces. Archer holds out his hand and I slip mine in his.

"You ready for this, Scar?"

I nod my head firmly. My scarlet curls bobbing with the movement. "I'm so ready for this moment."

Archer lifts my hand to his mouth and kisses the wedding band on my finger. "Then let's rip out the foundations and rebuild this society."

Seb releases a sigh, a satisfied smile adorning his face. Like us, he has something to fight for now. He has fallen for a girl the Elders told him he couldn't have, and he isn't prepared to give her up. I never thought I'd see the day when Seb was loved up, but when you see them together, it's clear they were meant for each other.

We all have our reasons for wanting this. Mine was Kit. Vee and Rafe wanted to be free to live with the third person in their relationship, Ruby. They'd both fallen hard for her, and they didn't want to be bound by the traditional conventions of our society. And why should they? Seb wasn't willing to marry the girl our society had chosen for him. Archer just wanted to give us the freedom we all craved. He wanted any children we had in the future to be free from the clutches of the society. Free to choose their own partners and their own future careers.

The door opens and we head inside. The five of us have become a formidable force. We're tight knit. No one gets between us. We are a family, and we have each other's back's no matter what.

We head towards the chambers. Everyone has gathered tonight. Archer has called for a vote to remove the Elders. The society rules dictate that if ten plus senior members support a vote, then it must be actioned. Seniors were classed as anyone who was a diamond or a Jack or above. We had five votes between us, and we'd spent the last two years working on other members and convincing them of our cause. Callum Hamilton had been the first to offer his support. Archer's grandfather Edward surprised us by being our second. After the revelations over his daughter's death at the hands of his son-in-law, he wanted to change things for the better. Our third vote came from Georgie's elder brother. As a gay man, the society had forced him to marry a girl and to live a lie. He was tired of playing a part and not being free to be himself.

When we enter the room, the chatter dies down. My eye finds Georgie standing over by the alcove and she nods her head to me and raises her glass. Chester stands behind her. My sort of stepbrother was a crazy fucker, but he'd proved his loyalty to us over these past two years. The two were no longer whatever they had been to each other, but they were friends in some fashion.

The master of ceremonies rings the bell, and everyone falls silent and gathers around the circular ring that is carved into the stone floor beneath our feet.

"Aces. We gather here today as a motion of change has been

submitted with ten supporting votes. Would the challenger please step forward."

Archer lets go of my hand and walks to the centre of the room, turning to greet the members. "My fellow members. I, like many of you, have grown up as part of this society and its rules. I have abided by them and done the bidding of my Elders. Recent revelations have made me question the ways of our society and the path which our Elders have made for us. Our society is built upon blackmail and veiled threats. We are told who to marry, who to kill, who to do business with. I stand before you today to motion that the Elders be removed as the leaders of our society." Archer holds his hand out and I step forward and walk over to him to hand him a USB stick.

Archer holds the stick up in his hands. "On this USB is every file the society holds on each of its members. Tonight, we will erase these files and you will be free to choose to be part of a new society or to leave all together. We have the only files. The originals have been deleted from every source the Elders have. This society will no longer use blackmail to make its members bend to its will. The society will return to one that's soul focus is to better the lives and businesses of the Bay's inhabitants on both sides of the village."

"This is ludicrous," Wilbur hisses, getting to his feet and glaring across the room at Archer. "This society is what it is today because of your current serving Elders. Without us, the society's power will dwindle to nothing. The boy doesn't know what he is talking about."

"You have no power anymore, Wilbur," Archer says. "As we speak, the shareholders of Ace conglomerates are calling for a vote of no confidence in its senior board members. Trust me, the numbers calling for the motion are significant."

Wilbur smirks. "You stupid boy. The other Elders and I hold the majority shares."

"I'm afraid that isn't true, Wilbur," Edward says, stepping forward and removing his mask. "As of midnight, the majority of my shares have been sold to an independent member. The Elders now only own forty percent of the company shares and, therefore, no longer have the majority vote."

"You stupid old fool," Wilbur growls, glaring across the room at Edward. "You'll regret this."

Edward shakes his head. "I don't think I will. My family has suffered terribly at the hands of this society. It's time to return to the values of our founding fathers." Edward turns his back on Wilbur and addresses the master of ceremony. "You have your ten votes for the motion. It's time for the society members to take a vote."

The master of ceremony swallows and nods his head, not daring to glance over at the other three remaining Elders. "As bound by our society rules. All those in favour of the removal of the Elders from the society please cast their cards in the stone font on my right. All those against the motion, please cast your cards in the font to my left."

At first no one moves, cautious of being the first one to vote, but then Vee and Seb's mum steps forward and places her card in the supporting font and this leads to a raft of members following suit. We watch with bated breath as the cards stack up in favour of our motion. Out of all the members gathered here tonight, only three place their cards in support of the Elders. The master of ceremony waits until everyone has voted. Even though its' obvious the motion has passed he counts the cards in each font.

He bangs his staff on the floor to quieten the room. "The votes have been counted and the motion to remove the current serving Elders has the majority. Elders, please remove your masks and return your keys. Spades, please escort the Elders from the lodge."

Wilbur jumps to his feet and slings his mask down. "I will not allow it! We made this society what it is today. We are in charge here!"

The master of ceremony gestures with his head to the spades, who are gathered around the edge of the room, and they tackle Wilbur, grabbing him under his armpits. They more or less carry him from the room. Wilbur is shouting and swearing that we'll regret this as he is removed. The other two Elders don't fight the spades when they reach for their masks and keys; they instead leave the room quietly. "Now that business is out of the way. Moving forward, our Elders will be selected by member vote," the master of ceremony announces. "Anyone wishing to be considered must express their intention to run by midnight this Friday. Votes will be cast a week on Friday and the new elder council announced accordingly. In the interim, the Aces will hold overall authority until the election is complete."

"Now that business is over. Let us make a toast. To the dawn of a new era in our society," Edward says as a group of servers with trays of champagne circle the room. "Blood of my blood. Kin of my Kin. Now and always."

I raise my glass and, along with my fellow members, I repeat the words of our society. We'd done it. It had been two years in the making and there had been times when we felt we were fighting a losing battle, but our hard work paid off.

Archer meets my eyes from across the room and we both move towards each other like magnets.

"Happy?" Archer asks me, as he envelopes his arms around my waist and smiles down at me.

"Blissfully," I tell him. A hand taps my shoulder, and I turn in Archer's arms to face Edward.

"Both your parents would have been proud of you tonight. I am proud of the two of you." He looks at us with such love and tenderness, I feel my eyes welling up. We couldn't have done this without his support.

"Thank you," I tell him, placing my hand on his arm. "Thank you for believing in us."

Edward bats my comment away with his hand. "Nonsense. I need to apologise to you both, though. I pushed the two of you into this marriage almost as much as Wilbur did."

Archer clears his throat. "How can we hold it against you

when it gave us this? This woman makes me the happiest man alive. I love her more than words can say."

I glance back at my husband and beam up at him. When he talks like that about what we have, it blows me away. "It's true. Yes, I was forced into this marriage by Wilbur and his blackmail, but I wouldn't change it for the world. I love your grandson, and I want nothing more than to spend my life with him."

"Then I am glad we got one thing right in all this," Edward says as he leans in to kiss my cheek and I surprise him when I step out from Archer's arms and embrace him in a hug.

"Oh, my dear. You are too kind. I have to ask, does this mean you'll be moving out and leaving this old man to rattle around in his mansion?"

Archers pulls me into his side and winks at me. "Actually, we have decided to stick around. Kit is hopefully moving his stuff in as we speak and as Jenny has decided to retire, we were hoping Edith and her family could come and work for us."

Edward's eyes light up at our news. "I think that is a splendid idea. And maybe in a few years we can open up the nursery and see it put to use?"

Archer and I both laugh. "Maybe in about five years or so, Edward. I like having your grandson all to myself right now."

"Edward. Can I steal these two for the evening?" Seb says, grinning as he throws his arm over my other shoulder. His blue eyes are sparkling with the promise of mischief and mayhem.

"Of course. Go. I'll head home and make sure young Kit is settling in okay," Edward insists.

We all head out to the car and drive away from the lodge, feeling a lot lighter than when we arrived.

"Well, my family. We did it!" Seb's cheers, clapping his hands together. "Now we party! Let's go get my girl, Ruby, and the others and let loose."

"No shots tonight," I warn him, wagging my finger. Last weekend we'd met up with Kayla and gone clubbing in London.

Seb had me on the tequila rose shots and to say I was delicate the next day would be an understatement.

My phone alerts me of a text and I smile when I see it's from Damon. His text says he'll meet us there. My eyes widen when I read the second part of the text. "Damon's bringing a girl tonight."

"Ooh, gossip," Vee says gleefully. "Who's he bringing?"

I shake my head as I type out a text to ask him who she is. "I've no idea. I'll ask him."

I groan in frustration at his reply.

Wait and see.

"Ugh, he's holding out on me. I wonder who she is?" I say, my curiosity is eating at me. He hasn't mentioned he was interested in anyone to me.

"I know who it is," Archer announces, with a smug smirk on his face and we all stare at him in shock.

"How do you know before I do?" I ask him, arching a brow. Damon and I will be having words later when I see him.

Archer shrugs and returns his stare to the window. "He wanted some man-to-man advice, so of course he came to me."

I snicker. "Relationship advice from you. Did you tell him to kidnap her and bully her?"

Archer smirks again. "Any advice I gave him is private."

I eye my husband in frustration. As the other's fall into conversation about the weekend, I place my hand on his thigh and lean into him. "Tell me who is she is, please?"

"What's it worth?" he challenges me, whispering in my ear so the others can't hear us.

I bite my lip and checking our friends aren't watching us; I run my fingers up his thigh towards his zipper. "Whatever you want?"

"Anything?" He asks me, his voice becoming gravelly as a hunger I recognise flares to life in his eyes. He chuckles and shakes his head. "Nice try, Scar. Besides, you wouldn't believe me if I told you."

"Okay, now I really need to know," I insist. I'm invested now.

Archer smiles, knowing how miffed I am that he knows before I do. He grasps the back of my neck and tilts my face towards his. "Have I told you how much I fucking adore you?"

I roll my eyes, but I can't keep the shit-eating grin from my face. "Yes. You told me this morning during shower sex, and then again when you came back from your jog and pinned me up against the fridge in front of a blushing Jenny. You have no shame, Archer Savage, but I love you, too."

"Is my Red Raven ready to win in the ring tonight?" he asks me. We were on the way to the underground ring, where we were both fighting tonight. We both still needed our vices to keep our demons at bay.

"I always win," I reply in a deadpan tone. "I don't think I can think of a more perfect evening. Ridding ourselves of the Elders, fighting, and then ending the night with drinking and dancing with our friends."

He nuzzles into my neck. "I think you'll find the perfect evening ends with me between your legs, Scar."

Archer pulls my lips to his and kisses me in that perfect way that makes my heart flip and my toes curl.

We were free now to create our own legacy together. Archer Savage is my forever, and this is our story to write.

THE END.

ARE YOU SAD THAT OUR STAY IN HAWK BAY IS OVER?
DO YOU WISH THERE WAS MORE?

WHAT IF I TOLD YOU WE'RE NOT DONE WITH THE INHABITANTS OF THE BAY?
GET READY FOR SEB AND MILLY'S STORY.
SILVER TEARS.
AVAILABLE FOR PRE-ORDER NOW.

BOOKS BY CARA E. HOLT

The Soul Mark Series

Soul Matched

Soul Bound

Soul Surrender

The Endgame Series

Endgame

Grayson's Endgame

Playing Games

The Hexborn Series

Infernal

Inescapable

Infusion (coming 2023)

The Boy I Once Loved

(Standalone)

Hawk Bay Duet

Ruthless Legacy

Fallen Legacy

Upcoming Books

Shadow Kissed
(Coming 2023)

Silver Hearts Duet.

(A Hawk Bay spin off)
Silver Tears
(Coming 2024)

ABOUT THE AUTHOR

Cara lives in the northwest of England with her two sons, her husband, and the family dog, Bella. When not writing, she can be found immersed in a good book or binge-watching her favourite Netflix series.

Connect with Cara on social media to hear about upcoming book releases, teasers and cover reveals, etc.

Facebook:
https://www.facebook.com/caraeholtofficial
Instagram:
https://www.instagram.com/caraeholt_author
TikTok:
https://www.tiktok.com/@caraeholt_author

Sign up to my newsletter to hear news and updates on my next book, teasers, and cover reveals.
https://subscribepage.io/yCXNOV

Printed in Great Britain
by Amazon

17292474R00183